SEEKING OUT
MURDER AND MAYHEM

Simon Brett's actor Charles Paris is asked to find the stalker of a theatrical grande dame in "The Haunted Actress."

Dorothy Cannell's Ellie Haskell appears as a child in this witty tale of a spunky spinster on a dangerous quest in "The January Sale Stowaway."

Carole Nelson Douglas's Irene Adler—the Irene Adler of the Sherlock Holmes stories—receives a plea for detective help from poet Oscar Wilde in "Parris Green."

The motive may be obvious in the baffling death of a young woman, but the ingenious method for murder is the real mystery in "Anna Said . . ." featuring Peter Robinson's Inspector Alan Banks.

FIRST CASES, VOLUME 2

FIRST CASES,
Volume 2

First Appearances
of Classic Amateur Sleuths

EDITED BY

Robert J. Randisi

A SIGNET BOOK

SIGNET
Published by the Penguin Group
Penguin Books USA Inc., 375 Hudson Street,
New York, New York 10014, U.S.A.
Penguin Books Ltd, 27 Wrights Lane,
London W8 5TZ, England
Penguin Books Australia Ltd, Ringwood,
Victoria, Australia
Penguin Books Canada Ltd, 10 Alcorn Avenue,
Toronto, Ontario, Canada M4V 3B2
Penguin Books (N.Z.) Ltd, 182–190 Wairau Road,
Auckland 10, New Zealand

Penguin Books Ltd, Registered Offices:
Harmondsworth, Middlesex, England

First published by Signet, an imprint of Dutton Signet,
a division of Penguin Books USA Inc.

First Printing, August, 1997
10 9 8 7 6 5 4 3 2 1

 REGISTERED TRADEMARK—MARCA REGISTRADA

Printed in the United States of America

(The following page constitutes an extension of this copyright page.)

PUBLISHER'S NOTE
These are works of fiction. Names, characters, places, and incidents either are the product of the author's imagination or are used fictitiously, and any resemblance to actual persons, living or dead, events, or locales is entirely coincidental.

CONTENTS

INTRODUCTION

On the heels of *First Cases: Classic Private Eyes* we give you this book, a collection of the first short story appearances of series, uh, amateur detectives. No, you can't call them all amateurs. Peter Robinson's Inspector Alan Banks is a policeman. Sue Dunlap's Jill Smith is a policewoman. Neither are Margaret Maron's Deborah Knott (a judge) and Sharyn McCrumb's Spencer Arrowood (a sheriff) exactly amateurs.

You might want to call this a collection of "cozies" except there's nothing particularly cozy about Larry Block's Bernie Rhodenbarr or Ed Hoch's Nick Velvet, both professional thieves.

While Joan Hess's Claire Malloy, Amanda Cross's Kate Fansler, and Simon Brett's Charles Paris *are* amateurs, we had to find some other way to describe the contents of this book. My publisher, in my contract, described the books as "One hard-boiled, and one not . . ."

So, you hold in your hands the non-hard-boiled version of *First Cases*.

This book, however, while perhaps not as "tough," is every bit as good a read as *First Cases* was—which is probably the reason why. After all, would you want to read another collection of the same kind of stories so soon? (Would you? My publisher wants to know.)

These stories are very different in tone and somewhat different in content. All the stories contain crime, but how a *non*–private detective goes about solving the crime as opposed to the professional P.I. makes for an interesting read.

In point of fact all these stories are good, albeit—in

some cases—early efforts of some authors who have since honed their crafts to near perfection. It's a pleasure to watch these authors put their creations through their paces.

—Robert J. Randisi
St. Louis, Mo., 1997

ONCE UPON A TIME
Amanda Cross

FIRST APPEARANCE: *In the Last Analysis*, 1964

Carolyn G. Heilbrun began writing Kate Fansler novels as Amanda Cross in 1963 because she couldn't find any detective fiction she enjoyed reading. Since then she's managed to produce *plenty* of detective fiction others enjoy reading. This first Kate Fansler story appeared in *Ellery Queen's Mystery Magazine* in August of 1987.

Her most recent book is *The Collected Stories,* Ballantine, 1997.

This was the only true story she had ever heard, Kate Fansler used to say, that properly began "once upon a time." Kate, who had never seen the beginning, said it was, nonetheless, as clear to her inner eye as any personal memory, sharp in all its detail, as immediate as sense itself.

The family to whom it happened was named Grant and they were in their summer home in New England. "The King was in the counting house, counting out his money; the Queen was in the parlor, eating bread and honey." That is, the father, as in this context we should call him, had gone into town for the papers; he had money invested and wanted to study the stock-market page. The mother, a college professor, was upstairs in her study, ostensibly writing an article for a conference on the uses of fantasy, in fact reading a novel by Thomas Hardy—which seemed, as she later said, sounding prophetic, to answer to her condition. The children were on the lawn playing a ragged and hilarious game of volleyball.

There were four of them, three boys and a girl, all twelve years of age. The girl and one of the boys were twins; the other two boys were school friends, come for the weekend. They, too, were twins, identical as opposed to their fraternal-twin hosts, and the badminton set had been their hostess gift. They had been invited for two weeks, as a favor to their parents, and because the resident twins were judged too self-reliant, and requiring outside stimulation. It had taken a whole day to put up the posts for the net and another day to practice with the rackets and shuttlecocks. The father had pointed out that they could play volleyball with the same net, and had, the next afternoon, provided the ball.

There the four of them were, having both learned and invented the game, playing at it furiously and with much shouting—the girl was as good at it as the boys, and taller than the visiting twins—when one of the visiting twins (they do not remain in this story long enough to be named) shouted, "Look! It's a baby!"

And, as the four of them would remember the scene and tell of it for the rest of their lives, a baby, wearing a diaper and shirt and nothing else, came toddling toward them out of the bushes that lined the property and across the lawn. The baby was about a year and a half old and appeared to have learned to walk only recently. It rocked toward them with that unsteady gait characteristic of babies and laughed, holding out its arms, probably for balance but, as it seemed, reaching toward them. And, what seemed most marvelous, it chortled in that wonderful way of babies, with little yelps of delight as it staggered toward them.

The volleyball players ran down the lawn toward the baby. An adult, even the sort of twelve-year-old girl who played house and dreamed of herself in a bridal gown, would have scooped up the baby. These children simply stood one on each side of her—which two took the baby's hands could never afterward be agreed upon, perhaps they took turns—and slowly moved, midst coos of encouragement, toward the house. The girl then ran ahead—allowing a boy to take the baby hand she held, or so she insisted—to alert their mother. "Ma!" she called. "A baby walked out of the bushes!"

The professor, reading of how Clym Yeobright's mother died, returned to the New England summer afternoon with difficulty. "What do you mean?" she is reported to have said rather crossly. (The story had been retold so often that parts of it became "authentic," as other parts continued to be debated.) She was dragged by her daughter to the window—after having returned her eyes to her book as though her daughter had merely said, "An elephant with wings has landed on the lawn"— where she witnessed the baby's progress toward the house, its hands being held by two attentive boys.

"Where did it come from?" she not unreasonably asked.

"Just out of the bushes," her daughter answered. The professor rushed downstairs and out onto the road. There was no sign of any car or person. Their house was at the end of a dirt road and any car or person on the road was clearly visible.

"Did you hear a car?" the professor asked. By this time she had reached the baby and held out her arms; the baby walked into them. The professor held and smelled a baby, and put its cheek next to hers, as she had not done for a decade—and then there had been two, which had (as she admitted only to herself and the mother of the visiting twins) doubled the work while halving those intense moments of a mother and baby alone in the entire world.

"We didn't hear anything," the children all said, jumping around her. "Of course we would have heard a car if there had been one." This was so obviously true, the professor argued no further. Someone must somehow have crept along the side of the road, set the baby toddling toward the children, and crept away.

"What did you think of when you saw the baby and heard that story?" the professor was often asked.

"I thought of Moses," she always answered. "And, of course, of Silas Marner."

This latter allusion turned out to be, on the whole, the more appropriate. The baby was a girl, as they discovered after the father, returning with his papers, had been immediately dispatched back to town for diapers and baby food. The mother, with three of the children, the fourth being left downstairs with the baby, searched the attic for a portable crib that had been retained from earlier years for the possible use of visiting young. When the father returned and they had changed and fed the baby, they all sat down at the table, the parents with a stiff drink, and discussed the matter.

"We could advertise," one of the children said. "Or put up a notice like they do with lost cats and dogs." Everyone laughed but, as the parents were quick to point out, no one had a better suggestion. And then the father looked at the professor and said: "Geraldine and Tom."

"Of course," the mother and the home twins said. "But," the children asked, "couldn't we keep her?"

"Our arms are full," the professor said happily. "Besides," she added, "if we'd wanted anyone else, we would have her by now. Our family is complete."

"Geraldine and Tom then," the home twins said, not really disagreeing with their mother. "But," the girl twin added, "she did seem to choose us."

"That's because we were playing on the lawn," her twin said. "It seems a good place where children are playing on the lawn."

"We'll have to tell that to Geraldine and Tom," the father said.

And that was where the "once upon a time" part of the story ended. The professor went away to call Geraldine and Tom, who immediately drove up from New York and looked at the baby as though she had indeed dropped from the skies. "It was *much* better than that," the children insisted. And they had to tell the story again, the first repeat of many. After that, it was courts and judges and social workers and the long, slow process of the law.

Geraldine and Tom, who might as well be known as the Rayleys, were friends of the Grants. Tom was a corporate lawyer who had made partner five years before, and was wildly successful and overworked. Geraldine ran an elegant clothing shop. Unlike those who discovered late in their thirties that they wanted a child, the Rayleys had always wanted one, but it had just never happened. Only lately, consulting doctors and learning that there was no evident reason for their failure, had they decided to adopt. Here they immediately ran into trouble; they were too old and they were of different religions, to mention only the major points emphasized by the adoption agencies. The other markets for babies they had not tried. Tom was one of those whom anything even touching upon the illegal or shady disgusted: he was a person of almost flaming rectitude and integrity, which, as the Grants used to point out to each other, was a pretty odd thing in a corporate lawyer, dearly as the Grants loved the Rayleys.

Geraldine and Tom's desire for a baby seemed to swell with the passing years—almost, the professor used to say, as a mother's body swells with the growing baby inside her. Afterward, many people were to remark how amazingly simple-minded the Grants had been. They had a baby who had toddled toward them out from the mountain laurel. They had friends who longed for a baby. What could be more logical than, pending discovery of the baby's provenance, bringing them all together? "But," people would say later, hearing the story, "the disappointment later for the Rayleys if the baby's mother had been found."

"It was all we could think to do," the professor would say when this point was made. "We all seemed to be acting as though we were in some fairy story; well, we were in a fairy story. And it did work out, so we did the right thing, Q.E.D."

For the Rayleys, after many years' experience of the law's delay, got to keep the baby. They adopted her legally, but even before that she was registered for the best school in New York, which Geraldine had attended. She spent her earliest years as a Rayley at an excellent nursery school. The baby, whom they named Caroline, remained as she had first appeared, a laughing, happy child. With adolescence she grew more serious and seemed oddly dissatisfied with her richly endowed life. Fortunately, her parents, as one might expect of a man of Tom's principles and a woman who endorsed them, were not advocates of material indulgence for children. Caroline was kept on a strict allowance and had to account for her evenings. Her parents were of a liberal persuasion, however, and despite all the horrors reported daily of adolescent extravagances, they and Caroline always got on. She went away to college and, eventually, to graduate school. In time, she became an assistant professor at a university in New York. That, of course, was where she met Kate Fansler.

* * *

It was, however, not Caroline but her father, Tom Rayley, who first talked to Kate at any length about that amazing scene on the lawn almost thirty years earlier. Caroline and Kate had become friendly, as happens now and then with full professors and much younger assistant professors. As Kate would often say, the friendship is not one of equals, nor can it pretend to be when one friend has such power, direct or indirect, over the destiny of another. All the same, they suited one another. Kate was reaching that difficult point in some lives when, growing older, one finds one's ideas and hopes more in accord with those of the young than of one's own contemporaries. Kate's peers seemed to grow more conservative and fearful as she grew more radical and daring. Not that Kate was then or ever of the stuff from which revolutionaries are made. Perhaps because of her fortunate life, her indifference—either because she had them or did not desire them—to many of the goods of life, she seemed not to barricade herself against disturbing ideas or changing ways. The same could not, surely, be said of Tom Rayley. He came to Kate in fear, though he could scarcely tell her of what. Fear came, he suggested, with his time of life.

"I've turned sixty," he said. "It humbles a man. For one thing," he added darkly, "the body starts falling apart. I've never had very much wrong with me, and all of a sudden I find I have to make a huge effort to hold onto my teeth, I've got a strange disease of which they know the name but not a cure, I've also acquired what they call degenerative arthritis, which turns out to be another term for old age, and when I got the laboratory report from my doctor, not only was my cholesterol up, but the lab had noted 'serum appears cloudy,' which didn't bother the doctor but sounded ominous to me. On top of all that, I'd rather Caroline didn't go off to live with her new-found mother or father in a community somewhere full of strange rites and a profound mistrust of life's conventions."

Kate and Tom Rayley had met when Caroline invited Kate home for dinner. Geraldine, like Tom, lived a life in which the strict control of emotion and the avoidance of untidiness, literal or psychological, were paramount. Highly intelligent, they were good conversationalists.

Geraldine in particular offering amusing and revealing accounts of the international world of fashion and the Manhattan world of real estate, with which fashion, like everything else, was so intimately connected.

Tom seemed rather the sort who takes in information while giving out as little as possible. He was pleasant but, after the dinner, Kate realized she knew little or nothing about him. Only when she had been, to her astonishment, summoned to a private interview did Kate discover that Tom Rayley was an impressive man, just the sort one would think of as a senior partner in a corporate law firm. Kate wondered if his democratic convictions came from an open mind or his Southern boyhood at a time when all Southerners were Democrats. Since Rayley had not turned Republican like so many of his sort, and had settled in New York, she gave him the benefit of the doubt: his was an open mind, fearful perhaps of aging and of loneliness, but not of those chimeras requiring for their alleviation—belief in nuclear weapons, separation of the races, and the strict domestication of women.

Kate was so astonished at his sudden frankness, helplessness, and revelations that she hardly knew what to say.

"What is this disease with a name but no cure?" she asked without really thinking.

"It's a rather personal male disease, apparently of no great significance but calculated to detonate every hideous male fear ever recorded. It's called Peyroni's disease, but whether Peyroni had it, identified it, or dismissed it is unclear. The only problem once it is named, at least in my case, is that my liver responded in a regrettable way to the drug supposed to alleviate it. I can't imagine why we're discussing this."

"Because it made you fearful of Caroline's defection. I have to say," Kate went on, "that children seem to me notably unsatisfactory when it comes to the question of their parents. Between those who fantasize other parents and those who seek biological parents, it seems that no one is satisfied. Perhaps we ought to follow Plato's suggestion and have a world where biological parentage is neither known nor significant."

"I'm perfectly aware that my anxiety is irrational and

illogical. As a lawyer, if not as a practical realist, how could I not be aware? I think that's why I wanted to talk with you. You, I surmise, deal in stories like this. Caroline admires you and will probably speak to you about her 'original appearance' more intently than she has spoken to anyone else. Also—and I hope you will not desert me totally at this honesty—I did infer that as a sister of the famous Fansler lawyers you would hardly be, shall we say, a disruptive person."

"Not disruptive, but not soothing either. I'm very unlike my brothers in every possible way; perhaps you've heard that. And if you're expressing some naive belief in genes, let me point out the inefficacy of that attitude from an adoptive and loving parent."

"Oh, dear, yes," Tom Rayley said, in no way offended. "But that's part of my fear, you see. How can I say it? That Caroline, discovering something, one hardly knows what, will fall out of our world and into some other world to me unspeakable. And you, at least so far, while in another world, are not unspeakable. I understand your language; I can even learn it."

Kate stared at him. "That is a remarkably intelligent thing to say," she said. "I'm happy to talk with you, though Caroline is my friend, and I shall certainly talk to her also. But I am bewildered: what can you possibly think I can do for you? Isn't this all between you and your wife and Caroline, isn't it all about the life you three have had together for all but a year and a half of Caroline's existence?"

"You've heard the story then, the appearance from the bushes of the laughing child?"

"Yes. I've heard it from Caroline. As she's heard it, and as it has been disputed and refined over the years. But she and I have not talked about it, not as you and I are talking now. It's an amazing story certainly. Almost mythic."

"Exactly. It's myths I fear, you see. That's the whole point. I don't mind a bereft mother or even father appearing after all these years. I fear the power of the myth. I was wondering if you could detect it: demythologize it. Isn't that what they do in literary criticism these days?"

"All I can do is talk to Caroline, which I do anyway.

And to you, if an intelligent question occurs to me. But where can this lead except around in the same circles? Caroline isn't desperate for the truth, resting her whole identity and future life on some revelation. Your fears seem excessive."

"They are. They are the fears that come with the youth of senility, as another lawyer once described it. Will you just accept my trepidation as part of your agenda, one of those 'cases' you think about?"

"I can do that, certainly," Kate said, half amused, half fearful of his intensity, inadequately masked. "What of the mother of the twins, the one who was reading Hardy? Is she still alive?"

"Oh, yes—still a professor. And she's never moved an inch from the story, nor have her children. It's legend now. It's a truth beyond truth."

Kate had intended to mention the conversation with Caroline's father the next day, when she and Caroline walked home together, as was now their custom. They lived within a few blocks of one another but never, to their amusement, met except at the university. Those few blocks separated one New York City neighborhood from another. Caroline, however, mentioned the conversation first. Her father had called her the previous night to report upon the lunch he and Kate had shared.

"The general hope, I'm to gather, is that you'll come to dinner with the parents from time to time and head off the effects of any terrible revelation, or the lack of such a revelation, upon their daughter. I hope you don't feel unduly burdened. In the beginning, my appearance from the bushes seemed a good story—I don't know why it has become so fearsome."

"Stories of that sort do," Kate said. "Like the moment after an electricity failure, when the bright lights go on and the candles are scarcely visible, superfluous. Here we are, talking now about your amazing appearance, while before we used to chat on about everything, nothing outshining the rest."

"Do you mind?" Caroline asked.

"Partly. Partly I want to shout out that it doesn't matter how you were born or miraculously shone forth. What matters is that you have a blessed life and the chance for an interesting future. But then I know that's nonsense. The question is, shall you be able eventually to forget the story, let it fade into the general history of things, or shall it keep, as they so wonderfully say in criticism today, foregrounding itself?"

"Certainly it will fade if it never changes, never gets any commentary added to it, never gets reinterpreted. Do you think you might be persuaded to go and see Henrietta Grant?"

"The mother of the twins—the one who was reading Hardy? What could I go to see her for? I could hardly request to hear the story again, as one might have asked a bard to recite the lines about Odysseus's meeting with Nausicaa. I mean, if she wants to keep telling it, why not tell it to someone who hasn't heard it before?"

"I don't think she tells it much, or likes to. Mostly others tell it now—her children, me, Mom and Dad. It's just that she's got to be the answer."

"The answer to where you came from?"

"Yes. She's the only one who could possibly know."

"Caroline, that's obviously untrue. Unless she was in two places at once, and nothing in the story allows one to believe that, the only person who can possibly know is the one who set you off toward the volleyball players from behind the bushes and then crept away. And at least with the needle in the haystack, you supposedly know what haystack you lost the needle in."

"You mean someone spotted that house, the children, the geography of the lawn, the dirt road, all of it, and just decided it was a good place to dump a baby."

"That's the likeliest explanation, surely."

"Perhaps. Except, Kate, I know I was a happy child and all that, but if someone the child knows puts her down, is she likely to go running, happily gurgling the while, toward complete strangers in a strange place? I mean, she couldn't have known the children, but mightn't she have known the place?"

"You're looking for a rational explanation, my dear. That is the great temptation with a story like this. As in the Gershwin song, where the Pharaoh's daughter is suspected of being the mother of Moses, the baby *she* found. Surely the whole point about marvelous happenings is that there isn't an explanation—anyway, not one that would satisfy a rationalist. I think that's why your father's so worried. He half hopes for a rational explanation, and half fears the lack of one: if you consider yourself miraculous, even miraculously adventurous for a baby, you become otherworldly, part of legend, not simply his child."

"Does that mean I ought to look for a mundane answer or not?"

"Myself, I'd feel tempted to accept it just as it is, be glad you landed in that place, that your parents were there to claim you when called, that you were born at a later age than most in an improbable way. It all seems to me a kind of blessing, better than fairy godmothers around your cradle. But who am I to talk, having always known exactly where I came from, and regretting it the greater part of the time? There is, you see, the danger that you will waste your energies on the past and miss the present and the future. I think that's often a danger, and one worth risking only under the most extreme conditions—total despair or anxiety, for example. What can you learn from the past before you burst upon that volleyball game that's worth knowing? That's what I'd ask myself."

"There's always plain old curiosity."

"So there is. But maybe that's more my problem than yours. After all, I've made curiosity a kind of avocation. If you give me permission, I can promise to be curious enough for both of us."

"Does that mean you might try to discover something?"

"Probably not. It means that I'll go on wondering; you go on living."

"Should your curiosity ever lead to any answers, will you promise to tell me? No, don't protest," Caroline said as Kate started to speak. "Let's make it a bargain. I'll stop thinking about the whole scene, stop even telling it to new people I meet—I'll just say I'm adopted and let it go at that. I think you're right about the past entrenching itself in the present and future. But if I give up this wonderful question, you have, in turn, to promise to tell me if there ever is an answer. Agreed?"

Kate agreed, and with relief. The story was beginning to frighten her in the hold it was getting on Caroline

and Tom Rayley. She called Tom Rayley and told him
of the bargain, urging him to forget myths and concentrate on his satisfactory daughter.

And there for a time the matter rested.

The resurrection of the myth was an outcome of
Kate's meeting with Henrietta Grant. They found themselves together on a panel, both last-minute substitutes.
Each, it later transpired, had agreed to fill in as a special
favor, Henrietta to the remaining panelist, Kate to the
man who had organized the panel in the first place. They
were introduced five minutes before the panel began,
each trying to remember where she had heard the other's name. Both thought of Caroline as the connection
during the first paper, and nodded that recognition to
one another as the man's words on the New Historicism
in the Renaissance prepared the way for Henrietta on
the New Historicism in French Writing of the Eighteenth
Century and for Kate on English Writers of the
Nineteenth.

"Shall we have a drink," Henrietta asked when they
had answered the last of the questions and watched the
audience disperse, "or do you feel duty-bound to remain
for the next panel?"

"Neither duty-bound nor so inclined," Kate answered.
"After all, we are substitutes—it's not as though we had
signed on for the whole bit. And even if I had, the truth
is I would like to have a drink with you."

They soon settled themselves in the bar of the hotel
where the conference was being held. Kate felt she deserved a martini complete with olive.

"How is Caroline?" Henrietta asked. "I understand
working with you has been a real opportunity. Not that
I've seen her lately."

"I wouldn't call it an opportunity. We're friends,
which is a good thing. The fact is," Kate added, as her
martini and Henrietta's scotch arrived, "I never expected
really to meet you, any more than I expected to come
upon two sets of twelve-year-old twins playing volleyball.
Or upon Huck and Jim on a raft, if it comes to that.
Certain scenes live only in the imagination."

"The twins are not *that* much younger than you,"
Henrietta laughed. "My twins, at least, have turned out

rather well. I've lost track of the other two, so they remain always twelve in my mind. They moved away after that summer."

"I wonder if they tell the story of Caroline's arrival."

"I'm pretty sure they do. They got used to telling it that summer. It's not the sort of story you forget."

"It's all passed into legend by now. How does it feel to be part of a legend?"

"It was an amazing moment. I feel a kind of wonder about Caroline, as though, after that birth, as amazing and as charming in its way as that of Botticelli's Venus, she was bound to be a marvel, do something that would reverberate, become, in her own way, a myth."

"The birth of the hero, as Raglan and others have it, only this time a woman hero. More Moses than Effie in *Silas Marner*. And of course the two sets of twins add a note—a kind of amazing circumstance."

"Not really," Henrietta laughed. "Think of the Bobbsey twins. Just a convenient circumstance." Henrietta looked for a moment down at her hands. "I do hope Caroline's stopped brooding about it. I worry about the Rayleys. I worry about her. Like those babies conceived *in vitro*: how can anything in life equal its first moment? I mean, can a life hold two miracles?"

"The whole point of heroic lives is that they do, isn't that so? The miraculous birth, therefore the awful and wonderful destiny. Not that I can imagine that for Caroline, who is such a sane person, which heroes rarely are."

"Male heroes," Henrietta said, and they went on to talk of other things.

But, the ice being broken, they met again from time to time, when Henrietta was in New York or Kate in Boston. And then one spring day Kate, finding herself at Williams College and remembering that Henrietta's country house, on whose lawn Caroline had appeared that long-ago afternoon, was nearby, telephoned on the chance that Henrietta might be there, might ask her to stop by.

"Your sense of geography is rather wonderful," Henrietta remarked. "I'm an hour at least away, and despite the careful directions I shall now give you you will get lost. Stop and telephone again when you realize you've made a wrong turn. And plan to spend the night if you come at all. You'll be far too late to drive anywhere today. I'm all alone, so there's plenty of room. I'll put you in the room where I was reading the day Caroline appeared."

Kate did get lost, did call again, did arrive as the day was darkening, the trees beginning to be outlined against the evening sky. Kate drove down the dirt road on which Henrietta's house stood; was shown the bushes that lined the property at its sides, and the lawn where the badminton net had been. Beyond the lawn was woods. The silence was amazing to Kate.

"Come in," Henrietta said. "We'll sit by the fire and lift a glass to Caroline."

"Has she been back here often?" Kate asked.

"Oddly not. The Rayleys visited with her once, but they wouldn't take their eyes off her. I think they feared she would wander off just as she had come, holding out her hands to someone else. It took them years to believe that Caroline was there to stay. They used to go into her room at night to be sure she hadn't vanished into thin air. Eventually Caroline became a real little girl who could be trusted out on her own. Fortunately, she was small when they got her, so she had time to grow into independence and they had time to accept it. The Rayleys are very sound people, which was a great relief."

"You knew that when you called them that day?"

"I knew them well, of course. But all I thought of that day was their longing for a child, and the child's need of a home. I felt, even though I'd just met Caroline, an urgency that she find the right home, not just be adopted by people I'd never heard of, however worthy."

Kate started to ask another question, but restrained herself. The time for questions had passed. The time for answers might come, but only Henrietta could decide that. They sat with their drinks in front of the fire and let the evening darken altogether before they turned on the lights and thought about dinner.

"I've a thick soup I made last night. It improves with age, like the best of us. Will that do? There's also homemade bread and decent wine."

"It sounds like the beginning of another fantasy," Kate said. "I don't get to the country much and rarely am offered homemade soup and bread. Mostly I subsist on nouvelle cuisine and fish, neither of which I especially like. When we're home, we eat omelettes or Chinese food, delivered by an intense young Oriental on a bicycle. This is a lovely change. Can we eat in front of the fire, looking like a scene from a made-for-television movie?"

"We are, I fear, insufficiently rustic."

But nothing else was insufficient. One of those times, Kate thought, when it is all just right and you never quite understand why, except that it was unplanned and in the highest degree unlikely ever to happen just that way again.

Dinner over, they sat sipping their coffee by the fire, dying because Henrietta hesitated to throw on another log—it would commit them to a delayed bedtime. Kate was beyond the most minor decision. It had been a long day, but she was in that odd state of fatigue past weariness. She simply sat. And Henrietta, having, it seemed, decided, threw a large log on the fire.

"I'd better tell you," she said, sitting forward and staring at the fire. "Someone, I suppose, should know. But if I tell you, it will end our friendship. I'll trust you, but I won't want to know you anymore. Which is a pity— the world is not that full of intelligent friends."

Kate couldn't argue with the truth of that. "But if I say don't tell me, shall we go on being friends? Is it my decision?"

"Probably not," Henrietta said, sighing. "In telling you there was anything to tell, I've already crossed that bridge—I've already burned it."

"It's ironic," Kate said. "Like so much else. I guessed, of course—not what you would tell, but that there was something to tell. Once you knew that, we were destined to have only this one night by the fire."

"Truncated friendships are my fate," Henrietta said. "As you shall learn. There never is any turning back." Henrietta paused only a moment.

"It began with a young woman very like Caroline now, a graduate student. We became friends, as you have with Caroline. But it was, or seemed, a more perilous friendship then. Women didn't become close to one another; their eyes were always on the men. I was an associate professor, rather long in the tooth for that, but women didn't get promoted very rapidly in those days. We talked, this graduate student and I, about, oh, everything I seemed never to have talked about. Such talk became more ordinary later, with CR groups and all the rest. It's hard now to recall the loneliness of professional women in those years, the constant tension and anxiety of doing the wrong thing, of offending.

"You have to understand what a conservative woman I was then. If I felt any criticism of the academic world I had fought my way into, I never let it rise to consciousness, let alone expressed it. I just wanted to be accepted, to teach, to write. I liked to tell myself it was simple. And my life was very full. There were the twins. There was my marriage—good then, better now, fine always; we've worked on it, examined our assumptions. But to understand this story, you have to imagine yourself back then, back before Betty Friedan described the 'problem that has no name.'

"I asked my new friend to the country, alone, just as you are here tonight. The children stayed in Boston with their father—he was good about helping me to get away now and then, and they were all involved in Red Sox games and other things I could never pretend interest in. He thought it might be good for me to talk to someone—'girl talk,' he called it. None of us had any decent language for women friends." And Henrietta stopped and began to cry, not loudly, no noise at all. The tears fell silently. "Maybe you can guess the rest," she said.

Kate nodded. "She misunderstood, or you did. She made what used to be called a pass. Today I think they would say she came on to you. Were you terrified?"

"It isn't even right to call it a pass. It was a gesture of love. I can see that now. Then, I simply went rigid with terror. And that's what I felt: sheer, paralyzing terror. I knew nothing about women loving women, except that I feared it; we had been taught to fear it. My terror was obvious."

"And she ran away?"

"No. She didn't run. We went on with the evening—we'd arrived in late afternoon—we went on with dinner, we 'made conversation.' I never really understood the agony of that phrase until then. Somewhere in her diaries Woolf talks of beating up the waves of conversation.

We did that. Nothing helped—not wine, not food. We said nothing that mattered. The next morning she was gone."

"Gone from graduate school, too?"

"Yes. I had no idea where she was or what had become of her. I tried, discreetly of course, to find out, but she seemed simply to have vanished—the way graduate students do vanish, from time to time. Sometimes they surface again, sometimes not. Once in a while—and this is what terrified me most—they kill themselves."

"But she went off and had an affair with a man."

"You seem to know the story. Is it as ordinary as all that?"

"Not a bit. One doesn't need to be a detective to guess the next step as you tell it. You've just kept it a secret so long."

"It was such a daring plot, you see. I didn't ever want to wreck the magic of that scene by telling anyone. It succeeded beyond my wildest hopes."

"You planned it."

"Of course. She was very clear about not wanting the baby, as she had been clear about having it. A rarely honest woman, for that time. She adored the child, but recognized her impatience, her lack of desire to be a mother, let alone a single mother. She had never told the father she was pregnant; she never told me who he was. I keep saying how different it all was in those days. You have to remember that.

"Caroline was a magic child—that made the plot easier. One of those children who are friendly, open, greet all the world with delight. I made excuses to visit the country house alone. It wasn't hard. I had work to do, and my husband knew the summer with the children here and guests was not an easy time for intense work. Caroline was brought here secretly, for a short time each day. I played with her. A game. I was in the house, Caroline was put down by the bushes, and she came toward the house to find me. It's simple, isn't it, when you know?"

"Did your husband know?" Kate asked.

"No. I was terribly tempted to tell him, but it was clear he would play his part better if he didn't know it was a part. His being off the scene was just chance; I didn't plan that."

Kate thought about it a while. "And your friend," she finally asked, "what became of her?"

"She died. In some freak accident. It was horrible. I heard only later, by chance. All the time she was here with the child, she never melted, never said anything meaningful beyond 'Help me' in the beginning, and, just before the end, 'Goodbye.' She crept off through the woods as Caroline moved toward the twins."

"Your plot worked more perfectly than most plots. Like magic."

"Just like magic. I didn't even know the Rayleys would be reached immediately that day or would come so soon. That afternoon's legend has always seemed to me to have some of the qualities of an Homeric hymn. But before and after the afternoon, that's the sorrow. We never made it up; she never forgave me."

Kate could find nothing to say except, "There's Caroline."

"Yes," Henrietta answered. "And she's your friend. Neither of you is my friend."

"That can always change," Kate said. "Maybe this time you'll find the words to change all that."

"Don't tell Caroline," Henrietta said. "Don't tell anyone."

"No," Kate said. "But I shall be breaking a promise to Caroline. I promised to tell her if there was ever an answer. Perhaps one day you'll let me keep that promise, or you'll keep it for me."

"Perhaps. But there are no parents for Caroline to find."

"There is a friendship between two women when that was rare enough. And there is the magic afternoon. That's more than most of us begin with."

Henrietta only shook her head. And after a time, she went to bed, leaving Kate by the fire. In the morning, before Kate left, Henrietta spoke cheerfully of other things. The sun was not yet bright on the lawn as Kate drove away.

THE THEFT OF THE CLOUDED TIGER
Edward D. Hoch

FIRST APPEARANCE: *This story*

Ed Hoch is something of a short story–writing legend, having published more than 700 of them since 1955. He's created many series characters, most of which have appeared within the pages of *Ellery Queen's Mystery Magazine.* This Nick Velvet story appeared in the September 1966 issue of *EQMM.* Velvet is a thief who steals only items of trivial value, while commanding a five-figure fee to do so.

Mr. Hoch has written five novels, three of which were science fiction, and two in the mystery genre, *The Shattered Raven,* about a murder at a Mystery Writers of America banquet, and *The Blue Movie Murders,* written as Ellery Queen.

Hoch is a past winner of the Edgar Award for his 1968 story "The Oblong Box," and a past president of MWA.

Mostly he just liked to sit on the front steps with a beer, watching the homebound workers from the electronics plant down the block, pleased that he wasn't one of them. Sometimes, after supper, Gloria would join him on the steps to see the neighborhood fathers playing ball with their boys in the lot across the street, then watch them stroll down to the corner grocery for a forgotten loaf of bread or pack of smokes. It was a peaceful, settled neighborhood—that was why he liked it. No curious neighbors, no snooping.

"Nicky?"

"Huh?" He glanced up at Gloria, perched on the porch railing, swinging her long legs in graceful rhythm. She was a great girl, but she always wanted to talk.

"Nicky, what do you do when you go away?"

"Travel, like I told you. These companies hire me to pick new plant sites. There's a lot of money in it." He sipped his beer from the punctured can, wishing she'd quiet down for once and let him breathe in the evening air.

"When will they send you out again, Nicky?"

"I don't know."

"Do you think some day we'll be able to get married and settle down?"

He'd often considered marrying Gloria. Sometimes he could even imagine himself spending the rest of his life on this little street, walking up to the corner for beer in the evening. He could imagine it, but not for too long. "Some day," he said, because that was the answer to everything.

It was later, almost ten o'clock, when the telephone rang. She brushed his hand from her thigh and rose in the darkness to answer it. "For you," she called out.

He took the telephone and heard an unfamiliar voice ask, "Is this Nick Velvet?"

"Yes."

"We'd like to talk to you about a job."

"Tonight?"

"If you can come over. Foster Hotel, Room 229."

Nick smiled at the telephone. "I don't meet people in hotel rooms. They're only for sleeping and making love."

"All right, where?"

"The park across from the hotel. By the fountain."

"In the dark?" the voice asked, uncertain.

"I do my best work in the dark. Eleven o'clock—and come alone."

"How will I know you?"

Nick smiled again. "I'll know you," he said and hung up. He always knew them. They always looked the same.

Gloria came in off the porch. "Who was it, Nicky?"

"A job. Be back around midnight."

He picked up his jacket on the way out the door. Sometimes the nights were cool.

Nick Velvet was a product of New York's Greenwich Village, in an era when the Italian-American population still dominated the section against the encroachment of the bohemians. He'd shortened his name from an original version that sounded like a cheese, and gone off to the wars with a good many other high school dropouts.

Somehow, over the years, his life's work had begun to take shape, and now—nearing 40—he was an acknowledged expert. They phoned him now, and made trips to see him, because for certain jobs he had no equal in the world.

Nick Velvet was a thief. Of a special sort.

He never stole money as such, and never stole on his own. Rather, he stole on assignment, taking the things that were too big or too dangerous or too unusual for other thieves. He'd stolen from museums, from corporations, from governments. He'd stolen a statue of the Roman god Mercury from the top of a Post Office building, and a stained glass window from a museum of medieval art. Once he'd even stolen a complete baseball team, including manager, coaches, and equipment.

It wasn't so much that he liked the work, or had planned it as a career. But when it happened he had voiced no complaints. The fees were substantial, and he worked only four or five times a year, for no more than a week or so at a time. He saw a good deal of the world, and he met some highly interesting people.

Harry Smith was not one of the most interesting.

He stood in the shadows by the fountain, looking for all the world like a gangster of the prohibition era waiting for the boat from Canada. Nick didn't like his looks, and when he said his name was Smith, Nick didn't like his name, either.

"A man in Chicago recommended you, Velvet," Smith said, clipping off the words like an electric typewriter.

"Could be. What do you want?"

"Do we have to talk here? I have a hotel room."

Nick Velvet smiled. "Hotel rooms can be bugged too easily. I don't like tape recordings of my business deals."

Harry Smith shrugged. "Hell, these days they can bug you anywhere. They could be aiming one of them long-range things at us right now."

"That's why we're standing by the fountain. It's quite effective for covering up conversations. Now get to the point."

Harry Smith stepped into the circle of light cast by a tree-shrouded lamp overhead. He was a bulky man, built

like a small gorilla, and both cheeks were pockmarked.
"We want you to steal something," he said.

"I assumed as much. My price is high."

"How high?"

"Twenty thousand and up, depending on the job."

Harry Smith took a step backward into the shadows.
"We want you to steal a tiger from a zoo."

Nick had learned long ago to control his reactions. He
simply nodded and said, "Tell me about it."

"It's in the city—the Glen Park Zoo. Something called
a 'clouded' tiger. Supposed to be rare."

"How rare?"

The man shrugged, and Nick was somehow reminded
of a gorilla again. "A Middle Eastern prince with a private zoo is willing to pay well for the beast. We can
afford your twenty thousand."

"Thirty for animals," Nick told him. "There is more
danger involved."

"I'll have to ask the others."

"Do that. You know where to reach me."

"Wait!" Harry Smith grabbed Nick's shoulder. "We
want to do this thing in three days—on Monday morning. We should decide tonight."

"I'd have to look the zoo over first."

"You'd have tomorrow and Sunday for that."

"Thirty thousand?"

The man hesitated only a moment longer. "All right.
Five in advance."

They shook hands on it, and Nick Velvet went back
to Gloria's to pack his bag. The night was hesitant with
the beginnings of an overcast, and above his head the
stars were gradually going out.

There were three of them—Harry Smith, and a tall
slim Englishman named Cormick, and a youngish blonde
girl who answered to Jeanie. The girl seemed to be with
Cormick, and it was obvious that the Englishman was
the brains of the operation. He ordered Harry Smith
around in the flat monotone so often used for servants.

"I'll need to look the place over," Nick told them
again.

Cormick shrugged his lean shoulders. "Look all you
want."

"Why does it have to be Monday morning?"

"You're not paid to ask questions, Mr. Velvet."

They'd left the hotel room and were sitting now in a little house trailer hooked on behind a new black convertible. The car and trailer, like the girl, belonged to Cormick.

"Tell me something about the tiger," Nick said, sipping a glass of warm scotch.

Cormick might have been lecturing a class in Zoology I. "Though the ordinary tiger is quite common in zoos, there are a number of rare specimens that are highly valued. The great heavy-coated Siberian tiger is an extremely rare zoo specimen, as is the albino tiger, and the blue-gray tiger known to parts of China. But the so-called 'clouded' tiger—a strangely mottled beast long thought to be legendary—is perhaps the rarest of all. This specimen was captured near the Sino-Indian border a few years ago and donated to the Glen Park Zoo. It may be the only one in captivity, and our prince will pay dearly for it."

"I'll need some equipment."

The Englishman nodded. "We have a small closed pickup truck, and Jeanie can be your driver. The job is to get the tiger out of its cage and into the truck, and then to get the truck away from the zoo."

Nick lit a cigarette. "Is the zoo guarded?"

Cormick nodded. "They've got a squad of private patrolmen, mainly to keep the teen-agers in line. I understand they had some trouble last year with the animals being annoyed."

"Protecting the animals from the people." Nick chuckled for the first time and began to relax. The old feeling of success was beginning to course through his veins. He never liked them to seem too easy. Then, as if he'd just thought of it, he said, "I'd better take Jeanie with me in the morning. A man alone at the zoo might look suspicious."

Cormick hesitated only a moment before indicating his approval with a wave of his hand. "If you wish. It might be a good idea, since she'll be with you Monday."

"Where will you two be?" Nick asked.

"Here in the trailer, waiting for you. We have a plane

waiting to fly the beast to Canada and then on to the Middle East."

"You'll have trouble getting a tiger out of the country," Nick said. "How are you planning to do it?"

Cormick merely smiled. "Do I ask you how you plan to steal him in the first place?"

Nick took out another cigarette. "I'm glad you don't. At this point I have no idea how I'm going to do it."

Saturday morning was breezy, with high white clouds that glided swiftly across the sun in irregular formation. Nick helped Jeanie from her car and guided her around a puddle left over from an early morning shower. It was a day for the zoo, and even this early the parking lot was beginning to fill.

Nick dropped two quarters in the turnstile and they passed through. "I can remember when city zoos were free," he commented.

"They still are, in smaller cities. Here they have to pay for guards." She motioned toward a uniformed man standing near the polar bears. There was a revolver on his hip, and he wore the square silver badge of a local security service.

"Do they need to carry those guns?"

Jeanie shrugged. "Probably not loaded."

"We'll assume they are. Where's this clouded tiger?"

"Down this way. Let's stop in the monkey house first, in case the guard is watching."

She was a smart girl, with brains that even showed through the blonde hair and the long-legged fullness of her body. He liked being with her, even at the zoo. Even in the monkey house.

After a time they drifted toward the big cats, while Nick carefully observed the zoo's routine—a truckful of dirt coming through a service gate in the fence, a keeper hosing down the concrete near the seals, an aging vendor inflating balloons from a tank of gas. Something back near the front gate caught Nick's eye and he asked, "What's the armored car for?"

She glanced over her shoulder. "Picking up yesterday's haul of quarters."

"Quarters are money."

"Forget it. On a good weekend they're lucky to get two or three thousand dollars. We're after big game."

He paused in front of the cage they sought. "It's big, all right."

The clouded tiger was a massive, mocking beast with mottled fur unlike anything Nick had ever seen. The animal paced its cage with a vibrant stride that seemed to shout its superiority, even over the lion and the more orthodox tiger in the adjoining cages. It was not a beast to meet on a dark night near the Sino-Indian border; it was not even a beast to meet on a sunny Saturday afternoon at the zoo.

"I don't like him." Jeanie shuddered. "He looks as if he could pounce right through those bars."

"Maybe he could. My job is to get him through, somehow."

"Cormick is crazy! Who ever heard of stealing a tiger from a zoo?"

Nick smiled. "I've stolen stranger things—ten tons of slot machines, once." But his eyes were busy. The cages all had connecting gates, but the ones on either side of the clouded tiger were heavily bolted. A door in the rear wall led into the beast's den, and the only other exit was a small gate at the front of the cage, for feeding and cleaning purposes. He studied the padlocked chain on the gate and decided it would present no problem.

"Seen enough, Nick?" she asked him finally.

"I guess so."

They strolled down by the camels and then stood for a time watching a shaggy old bison who almost seemed to realize it was one of the last. The animal depressed Nick, and he was glad to get back to the car.

Cormick was pouring drinks when they returned to the trailer. He smiled and held out a glass for Nick. "I thought you might have the tiger with you."

"I thought you wanted it on Monday."

Harry Smith settled into a chair. "That's right—Monday morning at a quarter to ten."

"Why such close timing?"

The Englishman sipped his drink. "We've made arrangements for the plane at that time. Can you get the tiger then?"

"It would be easier at night," Nick said.

"Not with those guards around. You'd never get by the front entrance. At least in the daytime you can walk right up to the cage without attracting attention."

Nick leaned against the wall, eyeing Jeanie's long legs as she settled into a chair. "Sometimes it isn't all bad, attracting attention. Now tell me your plans for after I get the tiger."

"Jeanie will be driving the pickup truck," Cormick said. "She'll follow your orders until you're away from the zoo, then she'll drive you to the meeting place. We'll pay you the rest of the money there and take over the truck. It's our job to get the animal on the plane for Canada."

"Will that truck hold the tiger?"

"Steel sheeting with a few air holes. It will hold him."

Nick Velvet nodded. "I have to pick up a few things. Be back before dark."

He borrowed Jeanie's car and drove to the city—to a laboratory supply house that happened to be open on a Saturday afternoon. There he purchased an ugly-looking pellet gun that fired tranquilizing darts. Just in case the tiger got nasty about its kidnapping.

On Sunday afternoon Nick went back to the zoo with Jeanie because he wanted to study the keepers' uniforms. And incidentally because he wanted to study Jeanie. "How did you meet Cormick?" he asked as they strolled near the reptile house.

"How do those things ever happen? I was a dancer in a little off-Broadway musical, with dreams of doing my own choreography some day. He said he'd help—invest some money."

"Did he?"

"After this job, he says. It's always after just one more job. But he's not a bad guy. He keeps Harry in his place."

"How long have the three of you been together?"

"About a year. Harry had a girl for a while, but she took off. He used to beat her, and she didn't like it."

"How did Cormick hear about me?"

She turned to smile at him. "You're famous in certain

circles, Nick Velvet. But I never thought you'd be so handsome."

Nick wasn't handsome and he knew it. He stopped looking at her legs and started to worry. "Let's go back," he suggested.

On the way out he stopped at the balloon vendor's stand and purchased two balloons, a blue one and a red one. The blue one he gave to Jeanie, but he released the red one and watched its progress as it rose with the slight breeze. He watched it for quite a long time, and then they left.

Monday dawned rainy, and Nick cursed his luck. He was about to suggest a postponement, but by eight o'clock the sky was beginning to brighten and the rain had settled into a half-hearted drizzle.

They met for a final conference in the trailer and Cormick shook his hand.

"Good luck, Nick. The rest of the money will be waiting for you."

"Can't you tell me where you'll be?"

"Jeanie knows. We'll see you this afternoon."

Nick dressed quickly in a close approximation of the work clothes worn by the keepers. Then he followed Jeanie in the truck while she parked her car at a suburban shopping center.

"All right, boss," she said, getting behind the wheel of the truck. "What are my orders?"

"The service gate will be open. We'll drive in there and then I'll leave you. From there you can see the tiger's cage, and as soon as I reach it you start driving toward it, slowly. You'll have to turn the truck around and back up to the railing outside the cage. That'll be the tricky part."

"What will the guards be doing all this time?"

He told her.

"You're quite a guy, Nick Velvet. Will it work?"

"If it doesn't, I'll have a lapful of clouded tiger."

"Should we buy another balloon, just to make sure?"

He studied the sky for a moment, watching the progress of fluffy white clouds. "No, the wind direction is about the same as yesterday." He checked the bulges in his various pockets, and decided the two of them were ready.

As Jeanie drove the truck slowly through the service gate, a uniformed zoo patrolman turned toward them curiously and started walking in their direction. Nick left the truck and hurried forward.

"You working here?" the patrolman called out.

"Cleaning the tiger cage."

"Huh?" the patrolman kept coming, looking puzzled.

"Somebody threw a bottle in there during the night. Broken glass." Nick hoped that the real keepers hadn't already found the glass and removed it. He'd had to hurl the bottle over the fence from a distance of fifty feet, but his throwing arm was still good. It had dropped into the right cage and smashed in one corner of the clouded tiger's domain.

The patrolman turned and stared at the broken glass and the pacing tiger. "Damn fool, whoever did that! I'll make out a report."

"The night man reported it."

"Huh? All right." He started to turn away as Nick jumped over the outer railing in front of the cage. Then, as an afterthought, the patrolman asked, "You got an identification card? I don't remember you."

"Wait till I finish this," Nick told him. "I need both hands." He shielded the padlock with his body and snapped the chain with a quick pressure of powerful wire cutters.

"What . . . ?"

But now the cage door was beginning to rise, and Nick hoped that Jeanie was getting the truck into position. "Stand clear, officer. We don't want an accident."

"You going to clean the cage with those wire cutters, wise guy? Who the hell are you?"

Nick brought the heavy cutters up quickly, catching the guard on the temple. He gasped and started to go down, as Nick's other hand pulled something else from his pocket.

Jeanie arrived with the truck, and was backing it into position. Somebody shouted and Nick turned to see a keeper running toward them. Far off, near the gate, another guard had turned in their direction.

Nick paused only an instant to gauge the wind direction again, then hurled two smoke bombs at the oncoming figures.

"Nick!"

"Hurry! We've only got a minute!" He pulled a plank from the truck and laid it across the railing to the cage door. Then he tossed another smoke bomb into the cage and pulled the door open all the way.

The tiger, momentarily terrified, turned toward its den, then changed its mind and bolted out of the cage, up the plank, and into the waiting truck.

"Done!" Nick yelled, yanking out the plank and slamming shut the steel door of the pickup truck. "Let's get out!"

One of the guards had made it through the smoke-screen and was pawing at his holster when they heard the shots.

"Those came from the main gate," Nick said, scrambling onto the seat next to the girl. "What's going on?"

She didn't answer, but thumped hard on the accelerator, shooting the truck forward through the service gate. He'd been prepared to smash through, but the gate was still open. Behind them a patrolman fired one wild shot and then they were away.

"This truck won't be safe for long," Jeanie said.

Nick glanced out the side window as the truck roared past the zoo entrance. The armored car was there, standing at the main gate with its door open. Two uniformed men were stretched out on the pavement near it.

"Never mind the truck," Nick growled. "What about that?"

"What?"

"You know damn well what! Your friends have played me for a prize patsy!"

She spun the steering wheel like an expert, cutting off suddenly onto a side road. It was dusty and bumpy, and almost at once the tiger started to growl.

"You're getting paid," she told him. "Stop complaining."

"Cormick didn't want the tiger at all! You didn't even care if I got it. The whole thing was just a diversion while Cormick and Smith knocked off the armored car."

"I didn't know there'd be any shooting," she said, keeping her eyes on the road.

"If the guards caught me you'd have left me there.

Did you do all this for a few thousand dollars in quarters?"

She snorted in disdain. "Use your head, Nick. The armored car stops at branch banks on its Monday morning run. With any luck we've got close to a million bucks!"

"They waited inside the zoo, jumped the armored car men, and took their keys. Both armored car men came into the zoo?"

"They always did," she told him. "They figured it was a safe stop, like a church. All we had to do was distract the zoo guards somehow. That's where you came in."

"And I also make a good fall guy for the cops to chase."

"I'm sorry, Nick." Behind them the tiger roared again.

"I'll bet you are! You just came along to keep me on schedule."

"That's about it. I'm leaving you with the truck and this damned tiger and taking my car."

"Where are you meeting them?"

"Sorry, Nick. You're not making the trip."

He reached past her leg and switched off the ignition. The truck shuddered and rolled to a stop on the narrow dirt road. "Tell me," he ordered.

Jeanie yanked open the door on her side, and began to run as soon as she hit the dirt. He sprang after her, and she turned quickly, her hand coming out of her shoulder bag.

"I can take care of myself, Nick," she said, swinging a tiny pistol toward his stomach.

"You crazy fool!" His own hand had moved almost as fast—to the pellet gun he carried in a bulky side pocket. He dropped to his knees and squeezed the trigger, putting a tranquilizer dart into the wrist of her gun hand a split second before she fired.

Nick left her sleeping in a field and drove the truck to the shopping center where she'd left the car. Already the news of the robbery was on the radio, and he listened with a kind of foggy indifference.

"Two armored car guards were slain this morning in a daring holdup at the Glen Park Zoo. The zoo's patrolmen, distracted by the theft of a tiger from its cage, were unable to assist the armored car personnel. The two masked gunmen escaped with an estimated seven hundred thousand dollars, while another man and a girl were stealing the tiger. The missing beast—a rare clouded variety—is described as being extremely dangerous."

Nick switched off the radio as he turned into the shopping center, then changed his mind and turned up some loud music. The tiger was beginning to growl again. Nick wondered if there might really be a prince willing to pay $30,000 for the animal.

He found a road map in the glove compartment of Jeanie's car, and studied it carefully. Four circles had been drawn with pencil. He frowned and thought about it. Cormick and Smith wouldn't be near the zoo, or the airport, or the last place he'd seen the trailer. That left only one logical circle, and he decided to chance it.

"Say, mister," somebody called as he went back to the truck, "you got an animal in there?"

He smiled at the man. "My dog. He's a big fellow."

"Sounds like it."

Nick was still smiling as he wheeled the truck onto the highway. He hoped he wouldn't have to use the tranquilizer gun again.

There was a trailer camp where the circle had been drawn on the map, but Cormick and Smith were not there. Nick parked the truck in some nearby woods and waited. It was almost dark before they pulled in, near the edge of the camp. Nick smiled for the first time in hours.

When it was dark he slowly backed the truck against the side of the trailer and got out. "What in hell's that growling?" he heard Harry Smith ask from inside. Nick unlocked the back of the truck.

It was Cormick who opened the trailer door, pistol in hand. "Who's there? That you, Jeanie?"

"One tiger, as ordered, Cormick."

"Velvet!"

"Hungry and mean, but in good condition." Nick opened the back door of the truck.

The tiger leaped for the lighted trailer and made it to Cormick in a single bound. Behind him, Harry Smith started to scream.

Afterward, Nick used the tranquilizer gun on the tiger and then scooped up the loot of the holdup. He pushed through a gathering crowd of frightened spectators and drove away as the first police car was coming down the road. . . .

Nick Velvet stopped at the corner grocery for a six-pack of cold beer. He walked slowly, enjoying the feel of the warm evening, until he came in sight of the house and saw Gloria waiting for him on the porch. Then he smiled and started walking faster.

"Hello, Nicky," she said. "Home to stay?"

"For a while," he answered, and opened a couple of beers.

AFTER THE TWELFTH CHAPTER
Francis M. Nevins, Jr.

FIRST APPEARANCE: *This story*

A law professor, writer, editor, and legendary collector of mysteries, Mike Nevins was invited by Fred Dannay himself—one half of Ellery Queen—to try his hand at writing a story for *Ellery Queen's Mystery Magazine.* This story appeared in *EQMM*'s "Department of Second Stories," and Mensing—a law professor himself—went on to appear in two novels, *Publish and Perish* and *Corrupt and Ensnare.*

Mr. Nevins has also written *Royal Bloodline: Ellery Queen, Author and Detective* and *Cornell Woolrich: First You Dream, Then You Die.*

This story was first published in 1972. His newest novel is *Into the Same River Twice* (Carrol & Graf, 1996).

When Loren Mensing got home it was almost 2:00 o'clock Saturday morning. He stabbed his key into the lock, slammed the apartment door behind him, threw his tie and jacket in a heap on the sofa, and began nibbling leftovers as he mixed himself a drink. He expected the worst. For twelve hours the biggies had debated how to handle next week's anti-war demonstrations. Bosley, the chief of the Tactical Force, was in the mood to break heads. Mensing's arguments about constitutional rights and the undesirability of open warfare on the city's streets won few converts. Nothing had been settled and a final conference was called for Monday morning. Mensing wished fervently that his sabbatical were over so that he could retreat to the sweet peace of his law professorship.

Sipping his second highball, he noticed the letter. It lay on the scatter rug just inside the front door. Apparently, as so often happened in these high-rise buildings, the mailman had dropped it in the wrong slot down in the lobby and the person who got it had slipped it under Mensing's door.

Picking it up, he saw that it was addressed to him at the old apartment near the law school, which was still listed in the phone book as his residence. Printed in the envelope's upper left corner were TELEFILM ENTERPRISES, INC. and a city address. He tore the envelope open and adjusted his glasses. Beneath the letterhead and his own name and former address he read:

Dear Mr. Mensing:

Last summer when you became Deputy Legal Adviser to the Police Commissioner's office and the local station interviewed you, you mentioned that as a boy back in the Forties you loved the great action and adventure movie serials, and that you wished they'd be shown on TV. I hope then that you'll recall The Thunder Men series with Jon Nordeen and Lana Marra that I produced and directed in those golden days? Of course I retired from active moviemaking long ago; all this company of mine does is sell syndicated series to TV stations. But I love the past like my own dead children, and sometimes I screen an old serial to get me through the long and lonely evenings.

Two nights ago I ran The Thunder Men vs. Satan's Legion, the last of The Thunder Men stories, which I made in 1944. You'll remember that poor Jon Nordeen was murdered in his home right after shooting was completed. That unsolved crime has haunted me ever since. But suddenly, now that I've screened the serial, I think, *I think*, I may have the key to that crime's solution. And if I'm right I don't know what to do.

I am inviting a small number of the people who were involved in making The Thunder Men serials to a private screening in my office at 1:00 P.M. this coming Sunday. I invite you, in a purely unofficial capacity, to

join us, and to favor us with your comments, and to give me some guidance on how
to proceed.

I look forward to meeting you over the
weekend.

Sincerely yours,
Spencer English

And suddenly Loren Mensing was young again, was
the fat, near-sighted, squeaky-voiced adolescent who sat
enraptured in dim cavernous movie palaces on Saturday
afternoon as the rites of fast action and derring-do ex-
ploded on the screen. Images of boyhood heroes raced
through his mind—The Three Mesquiteers, Wild Bill El-
liott, Spy Smasher, The Thunder Men.

He plucked Alan G. Barbour's *Days of Thrills and
Adventure* and Raymond William Stedman's *The Serials*
from his shelves and refreshed his recollection of The
Thunder Men and their abrupt extinction in mid-career.
The first three chapter-plays in the series were *The
Thunder Men Strike* (1941), *The Thunder Men Strike
Again* (1942), and *The Thunder Men Return* (1943). All
were produced and directed by Spencer English who,
judging by the photographs of him in Barbour's book,
was a short, frail, painfully thin and studious-looking
man rated by both Barbour and Stedman as one of the
greatest action film makers of all time.

The series starred Jon Nordeen as Lance King, who
created The Thunder Men organization to rid the Old
West of legalized oppression, and beautiful Lana Marra
as The Flame, the girl outlaw leader who fought at
King's side against the evil ones they both hated. The
storylines were merely pegs on which to hang some of
the most exhilarating action scenes ever filmed—wild
chases, desperate fights, hair's-breadth escapes, spectacular scenes of bloodless destruction. All the serials had
been scripted by Tulliver Warde and had been graced
with outrageously exuberant agitato musical scores by
Gustave Wenzel.

Barbour mentioned that rumors of an offscreen romance between Nordeen and Marra added a certain pi-
quancy to their cinematic exploits, but if Mensing had
heard such rumors in his adolescence he would have

been much annoyed, since at that time Lana Marra had been the private goddess of his fantasies and he would share her with no one, not even with Jon Nordeen.

Stedman's volume added that Nordeen had volunteered for military service after completing *The Thunder Men Return,* had been with Marine Intelligence in the Pacific, been wounded and discharged, had returned to the States to make another serial, *The Thunder Men vs. Satan's Legion,* and was mysteriously shot to death in his cliffside bachelor bungalow a few days after the filming had been completed.

The last serial was released posthumously, and hundreds of thousands of American youngsters (including, Mensing remembered with a shock, himself) had watched its fifteen- to twenty-minute segments on Saturday afternoons over the next three months in a kind of fragmented mass wake. That was the end of The Thunder Men, although a few years later the studio tried with the aid of new stars to update the series, making The Thunder Men a secret organization of good guys fighting escaped Nazi war criminals. It had been a thumping flop.

Mensing closed the books, threw off his clothes to take a hot shower, then fell into bed, dog-tired but with the prospect of an interesting weekend before he had to face the grim realities of Monday and Bosley. He slept till eleven and cooked himself a heavy brunch, and it was early afternoon before he decided to take a chance and call Spencer English at home, hoping for a sneak preview of what was in store. He got the number from the directory, dialed, and a voice he knew growled, "Hello?"

It was Lieutenant Ellsworth, Homicide Division. Mensing thought of him as "Batman" Ellsworth because of his incessant communion breakfast orations on the theme of the police as the thin blue line between order and atheistic anarchy.

"Ellsworth, what are you doing there?" Mensing demanded.

"Is that you, Mincing?" Deliberately mispronouncing the name, Mensing had decided months ago, was Ellsworth's private way of calling the Police Commissioner's Deputy Legal Adviser a Maoist faggot. "I'm here officially. Runt named Spencer English that lived here got himself strangulated with some picture wire last night between ten and midnight. What are you calling for?"

Mensing explained briefly and was half politely ordered to come out to English's house at once and bring the dead man's letter with him. Forty minutes later he braked his VW beetle behind a police car in front of the late director's fieldstone rancho. Since no other official vehicles were in sight, Mensing deduced that the body and the Departmental technicians had left. Inside, only Ellsworth, Sergeant Hough, and two uniformed men remained. Mensing and Ellsworth sat in the living room, surrounded by autographed photos of cowboy stars of the Forties.

"None of the neighbors saw anything or heard anything," Ellsworth concluded. "No prints found that don't belong. No way we can trace the picture wire. The woman that comes in to clean—same one that found the body this morning—we had her look around and she couldn't see anything missing. Victim was a widower in his middle sixties, both his children dead, no close relatives, well fixed financially, and his will leaves everything in trust for scholarships to the UCLA film department. So your letter's the best lead I've got, and I'm going to assume for now that whoever killed this Nordeen character killed English, too, probably to shut his mouth. Come on with me."

"Where?"

"Down to Telefilm Enterprises. I don't know zip about these old serials—I was busy killing Krauts in the 1940's. You call yourself an expert, and I need an expert to go through English's office with me and see who else got a letter like yours."

Telefilm Enterprises, Inc. took up a corner office on the 21st floor of a turn-of-the-century commercial building downtown. A cramped knotty-pine reception room, a work area with two secretarial desks each equipped with an electric typewriter, a tacky private office with SPENCER ENGLISH on the door, a tiny ten-seat screening room, its dirty window concealed by thick black drapes— that was all.

They found the carbons of the letters under English's desk blotter, all neatly typed on an IBM Electric, the same model as the two machines in the outer office. There were five carbons, including the one of the letter sent to Mensing. Picking up one at random Mensing read:

> Mr. Gustave Wenzel
> 206 Pryor Lane
> Coast City 90271
>
> Dear Gus:
>   I was screening The Thunder Men vs. Satan's Legion here the other night and I
> think I saw something that throws light on
> who murdered poor Jon back in '44, but
> now I don't know if I was seeing things or
> not, and I need some other opinions. I'm
> running the thing again here Sunday at 1:00
> P.M. Please make it if you can, Gus. I don't
> know what the hell to do.

It was signed "Spence." Mensing picked up another letter.

> Mrs. Bertrand Harbage
> 1471 Center Court, Apt. 12-D
> Coast City 90271
>
> Dear Lana:
>   When I was running The Thunder Men vs.
> Satan's Legion here the other night, I
> stumbled across something I think may be a
> clue to the murder of Jon Nordeen, back
> when you were young and I was, well, in mid-
> dle life anyway. This Sunday at 1:00 P.M.
> I'm going to screen the picture here again.
> Please come if you possibly can. I need to
> know if I really saw what I think I saw, or
> whether I'm going blind as well as senile.
> My love to Bertie.

It, too, was signed "Spence," as were two more letters, one addressed to Mr. Tulliver Warde, in the city, and the other to Mr. Dino Sarpi, in an oceanside suburb. Sarpi, Mensing recalled, had been one of the great movie stunt men of the Thirties and Forties, a second Yakima

Canutt. Mensing hadn't realized that Sarpi had been in The Thunder Men serials; he wondered if the man had doubled for Nordeen or Lana Marra, or both.

"You know who any of these people are?" Ellsworth grunted.

Mensing gave him a thumbnail sketch of the role each had played in The Thunder Men series. "Lana Marra was supposed to have been in love with Nordeen," he concluded. "I've always wondered what happened to her after he died; all I knew was that she'd left movies. I gather from this letter she wound up marrying someone named Bertrand Harbage, whom I've never heard of."

"We keep coming back to the damn bang-bang movies, don't we?"

"Why, don't you like the old serials?"

"Hell, no. I'm against violence," said Lieutenant Ellsworth. "But the point is that if these people who worked on the serials with English are the only ones he told about what he thought he saw, then I'm betting one of them must have strangulated him. *And* shot Nordeen too."

"Yes, but of course one of these recipients might have happened to pass the news to someone else, to the person who actually killed Nordeen, and *that* person killed English," Mensing suggested. "It's a possibility we can't dismiss."

"We'll check it out. Hey, Charlie!" Ellsworth bellowed toward the screening-room doorway. "You find the film can yet that has The Thunder Men thing in it?"

Sergeant Hough stuck his thinning carrot top through the opening. "It wasn't in the storage cabinet with all the other fillum cans, Skipper, but I just now found it." He held out three battleship-gray metal cylinders. "They were taped to the underside of the bottom shelf of the cabinet with heavy masking tape so no one could see them. And that ain't the only funny thing I found there. I—"

"You found signs that someone had been searching through the cabinet before you, right?" Mensing interrupted.

"A Perry Mason yet," Ellsworth snorted.

But Hough nodded. "You hit it, Mr. Mensing."

"Nothing spectacular," Mensing said. "I just thought

that if Nordeen's murderer would go to the trouble of killing English, he'd probably also try to get hold of the film from which English apparently derived his clue. Luckily English had the prudence to conceal the film after he'd made his discovery. It wouldn't take any special skill to break into this office, I'd guess."

"Like child's play," Hough said. "The front door could be opened with a paper clip, and the old geezers they hire for night men in these buildings are asleep half the time they're on duty."

"So we can safely assume that our man or woman paid a visit here," Mensing said. "You can have the lab men check the place for prints, Ellsworth, but I doubt it'll do you any good. Right now, though, I want you to round up the girls who work here and find out if any of them typed the five letters in this sheaf."

"The point being?" Ellsworth asked.

"You'll notice that none of the five bears the customary secretarial initials at the lower left. I conclude that English typed these himself. But I'd like verification."

"You'll get it. Charlie, find the secretaries' names and addresses in the files and get going on it. Any other ideas?"

"Several. I want your men to go around to the recipients of these letters and find out if any of them passed the information to an outsider. Don't forget to check out Mr. Bertrand Harbage along with the actual recipients. And I want you to have all of them assemble here tomorrow at 1:00 P.M. for a special screening of *The Thunder Men vs. Satan's Legion.*"

"And where will you be while I'm doing all this?" Ellsworth quizzed sarcastically. "Knocking off early today?"

"Why, I'll be right here, previewing the serial," said Mensing, almost smacking his lips, "and trying to spot what Spencer English saw."

They drafted one of the projectionists who ran training films at the Police Academy for weekend service, and within an hour Loren Mensing was sitting in the stuffy darkness of the screening room, stripped of several thousand yesterdays, his blood pounding with the ceaseless action and furious music.

The Thunder Men vs. Satan's Legion was set in an immense tract of land claimed by both the United States and Mexico but under the control of neither, legal and political power being in the hands of a megalomaniac named Colonel Cain whose policies included slave labor, torture, a private Gestapo (the Legion of the title), and a confiscatory taxation of the peasants. Early in the serial Lance King and The Flame stumbled into this domain, were arrested, then enslaved in Cain's underground mine. They escaped, began to organize a revolution, shaped the peasants into a fighting force, and, unlike most of history's rebel generals, found themselves an inch from death every time they joined battle with even the smallest enemy force, until at the spectacular climax the revolutionaries invaded and destroyed Cain City.

When the screening was over, more than four hours after the lights had first gone out, Mensing had learned nothing about the murders of Jon Nordeen and Spencer English; but he had learned a great deal about himself.

Suddenly realizing that he had not eaten since morning, he locked up the office, told the projectionist to come back at one the next day, took the elevator down, and walked east three blocks to a smorgasbord place he knew. After dinner he decided he needed to walk off the heavy meal. Half an hour later he was at Headquarters with his feet up on a chair and aching like open wounds. He read through the reports of the afternoon's interrogations, which made the creators of the serial begin to come alive for him as individuals.

Wenzel, Gustave. For the past 20 years he had been teaching music at a junior high school in the city. Like English he was a widower, but unlike English he was a grandfather. The musician and the director had maintained a slight acquaintance but Wenzel claimed he had not seen English for more than a month before receiving the invitation letter. He had phoned English at Telefilm Enterprises and said he would come. He had told no one of the letter.

Sarpi, Dino. Living on social security and a pension in a small beachfront cottage. The interviewing officer noted that he was in superb physical condition for a man in his sixties, certainly powerful enough to strangle a man with picture wire. Sarpi stated that he had seen

almost nothing of Spencer English in recent years but
that he had kept up some ties with Lillian Harbage (better known as Lana Marra), for whom he had doubled in
the Forties. When he received the letter from English
he had called Mrs. Harbage and learned that she, too,
had been invited. He had later called English and agreed
to attend the screening.

Harbage, Lillian. Screen name: Lana Marra. Married
since 1952 to Bertrand Harbage, a British national and
BOAC executive working out of the company's West
Coast office. One son, presently attending prep school
in Dorsetshire. Mrs. Harbage had left movies after the
death of Jon Nordeen and worked as a secretary for
several years until her marriage to Mr. Harbage. She
admitted to having seen Spencer English once or twice
at cocktail parties since her husband had been trans-
ferred last year from the London office, but had not seen
or heard from him for at least two months, mainly because the Harbages had just finished moving from their
fifth-floor apartment to more spacious quarters on the
twelfth floor of the same building and Mrs. Harbage had
been too busy redecorating to attend her usual round of
parties. She had shown the interviewing officer her letter
from English, had confirmed Sarpi's story of his phone
call to her, had not contacted English to say she would
or would not attend his screening. She had not mentioned English's letter to her husband, until noontime
Saturday when she heard the news of the murder on the
radio, but the letter had been lying around the apartment in plain sight and Mr. Harbage might well have
seen it. Mr. Harbage had denied all knowledge of the
matter prior to Saturday noon. The Harbages had had
separate engagements Friday evening and neither could
provide an airtight alibi for the crucial hours.

Warde, Tulliver. The officer had found no one to interview at the address on the upper left of the carbon of
English's letter to his former scriptwriter. It was an
apartment deep in the black ghetto, now stripped clean
of everything but roaches. The officer suspected that
some brand of black militance had been brewing at the
address. An APB had been put out.

Parks, Jean, and *Donahue, Diane.* The Telefilm Enterprises secretaries had stated positively to the inter-

viewing officer that they had typed no invitations to any Sunday screening.

Mensing took a cab home but slept fitfully, anticipating the next day when he would meet in the flesh the people he had begun to know a quarter of a century before.

One P.M. and there they sat, fidgeting in the light from the overheads in the screening room. Mensing stood in front of them, blocking the empty screen with his bearish bulk. He had chatted briefly with each of them as they came in, but to them he was some kind of police bureaucrat and to him they were suspects. What they had meant to him worlds ago, they would never know.

Dino Sarpi sat at the extreme left of the front row, tall, bronzed, long-limbed, his face wrinkled as a monkey's above bushy gray hair. Mensing guessed that beneath his shiny serge suit were the scars of many spills.

Next to Sarpi was Bertrand Harbage, a chubby pink-faced cherub with snow-white hair and heavy-rimmed glasses, dressed in conservative British tweeds. Every minute or so he would give a reassuring little pat to the hand of the woman on his left.

The woman. Lana Marra's hair had grayed and wrinkles radiated from the corners of her bright blue eyes, but she still moved with a dancer's grace.

On her left, obese Gustave Wenzel sweated mightily, running his sausage fingers through the moist gray ringlets of his hair when he wasn't rubbing his red-streaked eyes.

The seat at the extreme right was empty.

At 1:10 there was a flurry at the doorway. A giant strode in, breaking free of the grip of Lieutenant Ellsworth who was a step behind him. He was the largest black man Mensing had ever seen. He was gray-bearded, wore a dashiki, and sported a huge *Free Angela* button at the breast.

"You people wanted to see me, I understand?" he boomed. "My name is Mahmoud Naguib. You know me as Tulliver Warde."

Ellsworth and Hough led him to a corner and exchanged furious whispers with him, while the four seated suspects turned and craned their necks to see what was happening. After about five minutes Ellsworth motioned Naguib to the vacant seat in the front row and beckoned Mensing to the corner.

"Same story as the others," Ellsworth reported, "except that he hadn't planned to come to the screening at all till he heard about the murder on TV. He claims he didn't tell anyone else about getting the invitation. Refuses to say where he was Friday night at the time English got strangulated."

"What did he say about the vacant apartment?" Mensing asked.

"He won't say. My guess is he was doing something for the Panthers or one of those groups, heard about English getting killed, knew he'd be questioned, and shut up shop in a hurry. I'm calling the subversives squad right away to keep an eye on him. That boy's doing more than writing kiddie serials nowadays."

Mensing was tempted to comment that he hadn't just been writing a kiddie serial when he wrote *The Thunder Men vs. Satan's Legion* either, then thought better of it. If Ellsworth couldn't see the prophetic and revolutionary aspects of that serial for himself, Mensing wouldn't point them out.

Ellsworth and Hough took seats in the second row and Mensing stepped in front of the small group again, introduced himself again for Naguib's benefit, and explained that he wanted them all to watch the serial very closely and be on the alert for anything that might throw light on the murder of Jon Nordeen. He would have the film stopped at the end of each chapter and poll the audience for ideas.

Then Mensing took his own seat and signaled to the projectionist, who killed the lights, and suddenly the screen blazed with life and noise and action.

End of Chapter One: no comments.

End of Chapter Two: no comments.

After seven chapters there were several comments, all to the effect that the audience was getting hungry. Hough took their sandwich orders and handed the list to a uniformed man.

At the end of Chapter Eight they broke to eat. Over his roast-beef-on-white Bertrand Harbage asked his wife, in a tone of polite amazement, "Goodness gracious, Lillian, was that woman doing all those acrobatic tricks really you?"—and Lana Marra replied, "No, darling"— pointing to Sarpi—"it was he." Sarpi ate nothing. Mensing got into a discussion with Wenzel on how many of the classics had been converted into agitato music for Westerns and serials during the golden age of the B picture. Mahmoud Naguib, formerly Tulliver Warde, ate alone, standing in a far corner. After half an hour's munching and chatting the lights were killed again and work was resumed. Still no one saw anything helpful.

Late in Chapter Eleven, Mensing spotted the answer. Satan's Legion had captured The Flame, and Colonel Cain had sent a note to Lance King that if he did not ride alone and unarmed into Cain City at sunrise the next morning, the girl would be shot. When a close-up of the note filled the screen, Mensing saw the truth. He sighed, and settled back with detached calm to enjoy the final cliffhanger and the climactic twelfth chapter.

At THE END the overheads glared into life and they all blinked and stirred as though wakened from a long dream. Mensing pushed himself up and stood facing them again. "See anything?" he asked for the twelfth time. Noes and negative headshakes were the answers.

"Well, I did," said Loren Mensing. "I still don't know what Spencer English saw or thought he saw. But I don't need to know. Because I know now who killed English, and therefore who killed Nordeen."

Ellsworth and Hough snapped alert, took up positions at the door as though to block someone's escape route.

"That note delivered to Nordeen in Chapter Eleven," Mensing explained, "returned my mind to the notes that four of you, and I myself, had received from English, inviting us to this screening. Ellsworth, hand me your photocopies of those carbons, will you? . . . Thanks.

"I'll try to do this by the Socratic method. What was English's object in inviting all of us here for the screening? What do you think, Mr. Sarpi?"

Sarpi cleared his throat. "To get our opinions on what he saw—at least, that's what his letter to me said." The others hummed or nodded agreement.

"Doesn't it follow then that the last person in the world he would want at the screening would be the person he thought was the murderer of Jon Nordeen?"

"Why, yes, it does, doesn't it?" volunteered Bertrand Harbage. "Good point, sir."

"But where does it lead?" Gustave Wenzel growled.

"To the truth. Look—none of you told any person not here that this screening was to take place, and yet somehow the murderer of Jon Nordeen found out, strangled Spencer English, broke in here and made a futile attempt to steal the print of the serial."

"Wait, man." Tulliver Warde held up his enormous hand. "You violate the canons of your own white logic. First you say Spence didn't invite the murderer here, then you say the murderer is here."

Bertrand Harbage, as if suddenly realizing that he alone had not received a letter from English, turned pale.

"No, Mr. Naguib. I can avoid that contradiction if I can show *that one of the apparent recipients of an invitation letter from English was actually not invited by him at all.*" He held up the sheaf of photocopies. "We've established that English himself typed the letters he sent. We've been assuming that he typed *all* the letters in this sheaf. That assumption is demonstrably false. One letter is a fake, one letter was not typed by English.

"Notice the letter addressed to me, for example, and the one addressed to Mr. Wenzel. Look at the spacing at the end of each sentence. How many blank spaces do you see after each period, Mr. Sarpi?"

"One," Sarpi replied.

"Now look at *this* letter. How many spaces after each period?"

"Two."

"Ever hear of a typist who alternated between depressing the space bar once and twice? No, neither have I. By force of habit every typist will do it one way or the other, but will not skip back and forth between one and two spaces. A self-taught typist, as I gather English was, might do it either way, but a trained secretary will skip two spaces.

"The only one of these letters with two spaces between sentences is yours, Mrs. Harbage. You were a secretary before your marriage, I understand?"

Lillian Harbage sat bolt upright. "You're accusing *me*?"

"I'm sorry," said Mensing. "Your secretarial training betrayed you. You did *not* receive a letter from Spencer English. The first you heard of his plan for a screening was when Sarpi phoned and told you. You saw at once that you might be in danger, so you lied to Sarpi that you, too, had received an invitation. Then you proceeded to strangle English with picture wire.

"When you broke into this office after the murder to steal the film, you decided to use the typewriter and office stationery to fake a letter that would conceal your lie to Sarpi, support the assumption that you could not be the person English suspected, and plant a hint of English's senility in case his discovery was ever rediscovered. You slipped the copy of the fake letter-invitation into the sheaf of genuine carbons and took the original home with you. But you made the mistake of depressing the space bar once too often between sentences."

Ellsworth, his face beefsteak-red with anger, lunged toward Mensing. "What the hell kind of a gag are you trying to pull? That double-spacing stuff isn't evidence. It's *nothing!* It's blank space. If I made an arrest on that they'd have my badge. What are you trying to do, get me kicked off the force?"

Mensing looked at the lieutenant as he would at a fly that had chosen to light on his dinner. "You interrupted me. I'm not finished." He turned back to Mrs. Harbage. "You also made a second mistake. Take a look at the heading on the letter addressed to you. 'Mrs. Bertrand Harbage, 1471 Center Court, Apartment 12-D.' *The apartment you just moved into.* Since you admit you've had no contact with English for a couple of months, how could he have known that you'd changed apartments in your building?"

"Oh, God," Bertrand Harbage whispered. "Did you say a minute ago that Mr. English was strangled with picture wire?" Mensing nodded. "I hadn't known that," Harbage said. He stared at his wife as if he had never seen her before. "Last night when I was hanging the paintings in our new flat I ran out of wire. And I knew I had bought more than enough just last week—"

"Shut up!" Mrs. Harbage screamed. "Do you want me to be executed? Think of our child!"

Ellsworth stepped forward and faced the pale woman.

Her eyes were sick with fright. "Mrs. Harbage, I think we've now reached the point where the Supreme Court requires me to let you know what your rights are. I must warn you that anything you say may be taken down and used in evidence against you. You have the right to remain silent. You have the right to be represented—"

Suddenly Lana Marra moved. She kicked upward, toppling Ellsworth backward into Mensing. Both men hit the floor. Lana streaked to the windows, tore back the thick drapes, hurled herself through the glass, screaming.

This time there was no last-minute rescue. Her dancer's body slammed into the garbage cans in the alley below with an explosive clatter. Bertrand Harbage collapsed on the screening-room floor. Mensing phoned for an ambulance, then raced down in the elevator with Ellsworth and the others.

She looked like nothing human, but she was not yet dead. Mensing was sick in the alley, then crept close enough to hear her confession to Ellsworth. Nordeen had been going to leave her and take up a Gauguin life with a dusky native girl he had met in the Pacific, and Lana Marra had loved him too much to lose him. She was dead before the ambulance shrieked into the fetid alley.

As the others began to separate and leave, Mensing took Mahmoud Naguib aside for a moment. "Whatever you were doing, cool it for a while. They're going to be watching you and probably bugging you, starting now." The black man said nothing—as though it were raining and Mensing had told him it was raining. Then he nodded, without changing expression, and walked away.

Suddenly Mensing felt directionless and afraid—like a man trying to fight a forest fire he knows is out of control. It was going to be a brutal Monday.

THE HAUNTED ACTRESS
Simon Brett

FIRST APPEARANCE: *Cast, in Order of Disappearance*
(Scribner, 1976)

This story appeared in a Simon Brett collection called *A
Box of Tricks* (U.S. title *Tickled to Death*), in 1985. Mr. Brett
worked for nine years as a producer for the BBC in England. He began writing full time in 1979. His non-Paris
novel *A Shock to the System* was made into a film starring
Michael Caine.

His most recent Charles Paris novel is *A Reconstructed
Corpse*, 1995.

Mariana Lythgoe took the center of the stage as if
by right. It was a matter of habit and instinct,
helped by the natural deference of those around her.
But the dominance of her presence was never resented;
force of personality demanded a tribute that was will-
ingly given. Nor was that force of personality noticeably
diminished by the actress's seventy years. Though the
famous brown eyes were foxed with gray, they retained
their magnetism.

The stage whose center she so naturally took was, on
this occasion, a small one. It was a low wooden table,
surrounded by a cluster of plastic-upholstered armchairs,
in BBC Radio's Ariel Bar.

The audience was also small, but more theatrically dis-
criminating than many she had faced in her long career
on the stage. Every member was, to a greater or lesser
extent, "in the business." They had all just completed
recording a radio play, for which the producer, Mark
Lear, had lured Mariana Lythgoe from her much-
publicized retirement.

It was a tribute, Charles Paris thought wryly, to her
enduring magnetism that Mark was now listening to her
with such concentration. During the two days of the re-

cording the producer had been patently earmarking a young, purple-haired actress for his attentions, and the fact that he was deferring the inevitable post-production chat-up for Mariana said a lot for the old lady's power.

"But, of course, no one remembers me now," she was saying with self-deprecating charm.

"Absolute balderdash," Mark Lear protested. "The less work you do, the more you seem to be in the public eye."

She laughed in fond disagreement.

"No, really, Mariana. You should have heard the reaction I got from people who heard you were going to do this play for me. And then there's been all this recent publicity about your autobiography."

"A nine-days' wonder," she said dismissively. "Publishers spend their lives creating nine-day wonders. A month hence everyone will have forgotten about the book."

"Don't you believe it," Mark persisted. "Then there's this new production of *Roses In Winter* at the Haymarket. There hasn't been a single review of it which hasn't mentioned you."

"Oh . . ." The vowel was long with denial, but still asked for more.

"That's the way to get reviews," the producer continued, "—without even being in the show. Get all the critics saying, 'It's hard to forget Mariana Lythgoe's creation of the part of Clara in Boy Trubshawe's original production.' You ever had any notices like that, Charles?"

Charles Paris grimaced. "No. I've had one or two that wished I hadn't been in shows I was in, but none that actually praised me *in absentia*."

Mark laughed. "Well, I'm afraid the poor kid who's playing Clara in this production hasn't got a chance. What's her name?"

"Sandy Drake," Mariana supplied. "I haven't seen it, but I gather she's awfully good," she added loyally.

"The only good things I've read about her have been in comparisons with you," said Mark. Charles couldn't decide whether the producer was being more than usually sycophantic or whether this was just the effect Mariana Lythgoe had on people. From his own reactions to her, he inclined to the second opinion.

"No, but really," Mark continued, "she's only getting your reflected glory. Same with that nephew of yours."

"Oh, now, darling, I won't have you saying that. Dick's sorting out a wonderful career for himself, without any help from me."

"Hmm. Well, I read an article on him in the *Standard*, and the whole piece seemed to be about you. You needed to be a trained detective to find the one reference to Dick."

"Ah." Mariana let out a long sigh. "Wouldn't it sometimes be nice to have a trained detective on hand."

Mark pointed to Charles. "Well, there's the one you want, Mariana."

Charles Paris felt the faded brown eyes burning into him. "Are you a trained detective?"

"Far from trained," he hastened to assure her. "A dabbler. Strictly amateur. Weekends . . . oh, and of course during those brief, brief patches of 'resting.' "

This understatement of their endemic unemployment brought its predictable laughter from the other actors present, which Charles hoped was sufficient to shift the subject of conversation.

"Right," he said, standing up. "Who wants another drink?"

But, as he took the orders, and as he made his way to the bar, he could still feel the old actress's eyes on him.

"And you really think someone's out to get you?"

"Yes," Mariana Lythgoe replied firmly.

Charles looked out of the tall windows over Regent's Park. Her flat was on the top of one of the beautiful wedding-cake blocks north of the Marylebone Road. At one time its interior had been expensively decorated, but little had been spent on its upkeep since. The furnishings had a wistful air of dated elegance, like an old stage set that has done duty in a tour of many theaters.

"And when you say 'get you,' what do you mean?"

"I'm not sure." She sat regally in an upright armchair, a cut-glass goblet of gin and tonic in her freckled hand. From her bearing, she could have been on stage as Cleopatra. She spoke slowly as she defined her thoughts. "I think I mean 'to frighten me.' I think someone is trying to harass me with a view to frightening me."

"I wouldn't think you frighten easily."

She inclined her head at the compliment. "No, I don't. As a rule. I am not frightened by anything rational, anything that I can make sense of. But anyone can be frightened by a sudden shock."

Charles nodded. "Why should anyone want to frighten you, though? What might there be in it for them?"

"I don't know. It's because the whole thing's irrational that it actually *is* frightening."

Charles was silent for a moment, thinking. Then he spoke. "But there must be a reason. Unless we're dealing with someone who's mentally unbalanced, the person who is persecuting you must be doing it for a reason. That reason might be to punish you for some imagined wrong. . . . Know anyone you've offended recently?"

The splendid head was shaken slowly from side to side. "No. There's no one I've offended wittingly."

"Or they could be trying to frighten you to stop you investigating something they want kept quiet. Anything you can think of that might . . . ?"

Again the head was shaken slowly but positively.

"Or to back up a blackmail threat, to show that the people you're dealing with mean business. But that, of course, presupposes that you have had a blackmail threat . . ."

She shook her head for the third time. "There has been no mention of blackmail. The letters contained nothing that could be construed in that way."

"What letters are these?"

"Oh, I'm *sorry.* I haven't shown them to you. It's the letters that really got me worried. The phone calls were ambiguous, but the letters . . ."

As the old lady eased herself out of the armchair and moved across to a writing desk, Charles queried her mention of telephone calls.

"Oh, nothing was said, Charles. Just the telephone ringing and no one at the other end when I answered it."

"Heavy breathing?"

"Perhaps. I didn't notice it. They could have been that sort of call, of course. I gather any lady listed in the telephone directory is likely to get a few of those."

"I'm surprised you're in the directory."

Mariana smiled knowingly. "My dear, when I was *fa-*

mous, of course I kept my name out of the book. But now . . ." She shrugged. "Now my name doesn't mean a thing, so the danger of *nuisance* from my admirers is considerably lessened."

She produced three letters, held together by a paper clip, from the writing desk, and handed them over to Charles.

Their threats were not specific, but disturbing. Unsettling for an old lady. "WE'RE OUT TO GET YOU, MARIANA" was the basic message. As she had said, there was nothing that could be interpreted as blackmail.

"When did these come? Presumably not all together?"

"No. Over the last three weeks. The first one was here when I got back."

"Got back?" Charles echoed.

"Oh yes, darling. I was doing a little . . . now what did the sweet girl at the publishers call it? . . . *promotional tour,* that's right. Being driven round the country and talking to all these very young people in radio stations. Very strange. Of course, one was used to press interviews about plays, but at least then you were going to the places to *perform.*"

"A book is a kind of performance."

"Is it?" She looked at him with vague earnestness, not untinged with humor. "A very self-indulgent performance in the case of my book. Just an old lady maundering on about herself. I can't imagine why anyone's going to be interested in that."

Charles was now getting used to her method, and could recognize that this, though cast with the usual charm, was angling for contradiction and compliment. He withheld both, but Mariana did not appear discomfited. Instead, she looked at him with a new irony, possibly a new respect.

"How did these letters arrive?" he asked.

"Pushed through the letter box."

"No stamps?"

"No."

"So someone came through the main entrance of the block and up the stairs to deliver them."

"Yes. Lots of people come and go here. The security is very slack."

"No doorman?"

"Not as such. The caretaker lives in the basement of the adjacent block, but he never seems to be there. Has another job, many of the residents believe. What do they call it . . . moonshining?"

"Moonlighting."

She inclined her head wryly in acknowledgment of her error.

"Why haven't you been to the police about the letters?" asked Charles suddenly.

"The police." She articulated the word pensively, as if it were a new idea. "I'm sure the police have quite enough to think about without being worried by old ladies."

"I wouldn't say—"

"Besides . . ." Her timing of the word stopped him neatly.

"Besides what, Mariana?"

"Well . . . one wouldn't want the police involved if it turned out that the person doing this was . . ." Her voice went suddenly quiet. ". . . someone one knew."

"Does that mean you *do* have an idea of who might be responsible?"

"No. No. Of course not."

Charles let it go at that. For the time being. "You say the block's not very secure. What about the flat itself?"

"There are two locks on the front door. It would be hard for anyone to get past those." After a pause, she added, "So long as I remember to lock them."

"And do you?"

"Usually. But old ladies get absentminded."

Charles smiled. There was a teasing quality, almost a flirtatiousness, about the way she kept harping on her age.

"However," Mariana continued, "the kitchen door is less secure."

"Kitchen door?"

She led him across to the small room which had been planned and decorated in the days before the concept of kitchen units and toning work surfaces. A glass-topped door opened on to the top landing of a zigzag fire escape. It was secured by one fairly primitive lock.

"Wouldn't hurt to get another lock on this. A few bolts, too. The glass is a hazard."

"But it does make the kitchen light."

Charles nodded. "You could get it replaced with reinforced glass. At the moment it's an invitation to anyone who wants to walk in."

"Yes." For the first time in the evening, Mariana looked frail. "Yes, I suppose I had better get it done. Though it seems rather a lot of trouble to protect an old lady who'll be dead soon in the natural course of events."

Charles put a hand on the angularity of her shoulder. "Don't you believe it. You've got another twenty years in you."

"Oh, I hope not. Sometimes I think it'd be rather a relief if whoever-it-is came and got me quickly."

" 'Got you'—we're back to that. Do you think they really mean violence against you? Do you think they're really out to kill you?"

Mariana Lythgoe gave a thin smile. "They wouldn't need much violence."

"What do you mean?"

"I have a serious heart condition. All it's going to need to kill me is a sudden shock."

The pounding on the door first merged with, then detached itself from Charles's dream. He fumbled for the light switch, screwed up his eyes and looked at his watch. Quarter to three.

He opened the door of his bedsitter and was confronted by an aggrieved Swedish girl in a brushed nylon nightdress. The rest of the rooms in the house were occupied by Swedish girls, all, like this one, built on the lines of nightclub bouncers. In their dealings with Charles, they all always wore aggrieved expressions, though on this occasion the annoyance had some justification.

"It is for you the telephone," the girl snorted, and stumped upstairs, her footsteps heavy with offense.

He took up the receiver that dangled from the landing payphone. "Yes?"

"It's Mariana." The famous voice was breathless, almost gasping. "Something's happened."

"I feel terrible," she said, handing him a cup of coffee, "disturbing you in the middle of the night. I'm sorry, I overreacted. It was just such a shock."

"Don't worry about it." Charles felt better now. The taxi ride had shaken the sleep out of him. "Your reaction was quite reasonable. It must have been horrible for you."

"It was. But I feel better now. I'm sorry."

"You didn't think of ringing the police?"

"Over something like this? They'd have thought I was mad."

"I don't know. There's the trespass element, anyway. Whoever planted that thing broke into your flat to do so. Any sign of forcible entry?"

"No." She looked sheepish. "Mind you . . ."

"What?"

"I was out most of today and I'm afraid when I came back . . . I found I'd left the kitchen door unlocked."

She looked pathetically at him, fearing his reprimand, so Charles just said, "Never mind. Let's just have another look in the wardrobe."

Mariana stayed in the sitting room as he went into the bedroom. He turned off the bedside light and moved toward the wardrobe, just as she must have done a few hours previously.

She had woken, she said, at half-past two, woken with that raw knowledge that there was no chance of sleep for another couple of hours. She had read for a little, then decided to get up and make a cup of tea. It was early November, chilly when the block's central heating was off, and she had gone to the wardrobe to fetch a cardigan. She had turned off the bedside light to save going back across the room, got up and walked across to the wardrobe. Then she had opened the door and seen it.

It was a luminous skeleton, about two foot high, and it had been suspended from a hanger in front of the clothes. To eyes that expected it, the cardboard outline looked faintly ridiculous. To an old lady taken completely by surprise, it must have been horrifying.

Charles detached the figure. Its limbs were joined with paper clips. It had been manufactured by Hallmark in the United States. It looked brand new.

There was something familiar about the ornament. Charles had seen things like it somewhere before.

He concentrated and the memory came back to him.

Yes, Halloween. A couple of years previously he had gone to a Halloween party given by some expatriate American friends, and they had garlanded their house with cutouts of pumpkins, witches and skeletons.

Maybe there was an American connection with Mariana Lythgoe's persecutor.

Mariana was so ready to give him a copy of her autobiography that Charles felt remiss in not having asked for it earlier. She brushed aside his request for a loan, insisting that he should have a copy of his own and inscribing it to him with fulsome, but apparently genuine, affection.

The next day, rising late after making up the night's deficit of sleep, Charles started to read the book. It was a day for reading, cold, dull November, as usual no work to go to. He sat till the pubs opened at five-thirty, in his armchair, feeding coins into the meter for his gas fire and reliving Mariana Lythgoe's extraordinary life in the theater.

The story was extraordinary not for any particularly bizarre incidents, but for the sheer breadth of experience it demonstrated. She had known and worked with every major theatrical figure of the twentieth century. Charles knew she was famous, but the variety of justifications of her fame amazed him.

But the book was not just a catalog of dropped names. Her personality came across in every line; the story was written just as she spoke, and a reader who had never met, seen or even heard of Mariana Lythgoe could not have failed to be charmed by it.

From the point of view of the current investigation, the book offered very little. Even allowing for the fact that the writer was giving her own version of events, Mariana did not seem to be the sort of person who made enemies. She had worked with some notorious ogres of the theater, but seemed with all of them to have maintained extremely sunny relationships. Professional revenge was an unlikely motive for the persecution.

The only name of which Charles made a mental note was Boy Trubshawe, the director of the original production of *Roses In Winter*. Mariana indulged in no criticism of his professional work, but did detail some of the practical jokes for which he was famous, and in her description of these (some of which sounded rather heartless), her writing almost took on a note of censure. That, coupled with the nature of the attack that had been made, raised in Charles the mildest of suspicions of Boy Trubshawe.

But there was nothing which impugned the director's professional reputation. Of *Roses In Winter,* Mariana wrote, *"Given such a wonderful script and such a wonderful cast, there was no doubt that Boy Trubshawe was about to have his first major success. Which he duly did."*

It was of course possible that the director did not share this assessment of his contribution to the triumph of *Roses In Winter.* The theater is a profession which attracts outsize egos, and Boy Trubshawe might have found Mariana's reference to him too dismissive.

To follow up this thought, Charles went the next day to the London Library, a haven of Victorian quiet in St. James's Square, and climbed up to the Biography section. He wasn't exactly sure what he was looking for, but as soon as he saw a book entitled *Boy—The Star-maker,* he knew that he had found it.

It was a show-business autobiography of the late thirties, and it showed all the vices of the genre. Here the names dropped with the subtlety of a pile driver, an additional dullness given by the unfamiliarity of many of them, vogue names of show-business parvenus who didn't last the distance.

But Boy Trubshawe was not content only to drop names; he also felt it a duty to chronicle his own part in developing the careers of the famous. There was no humor in the "Star-maker" of the title; Boy Trubshawe appeared genuinely to believe that all of those he mentioned owed their eminence exclusively to his favor.

There was a whole chapter on Mariana Lythgoe. The director described how he had spotted her talent, how he had nurtured it, how he had sat back to watch it flower. Ostentatiously, he did not ask for praise, but the reader was left in no doubt that Mariana Lythgoe "owed it all to him."

The account, at least in its emphasis, did not tally with her own.

Charles Paris decided that Boy Trubshawe deserved a visit.

"I am a trifle *jette laggé*," announced the director, overemphasizing the unattractive franglais coining. "Just back from the States. New York. Staying with a *chum*."

He then went on to name one of the British actors who had made a recent conquest of Broadway. Habits of name-dropping died hard. What was more, the tone implied that Boy's relationship with the actor was *very, very* close. Meeting the octogenarian director in the flesh did nothing to dispel the impression his autobiography had made on Charles. Boy Trubshawe was a particularly unpleasant example of the bitchy theatrical queen. He knew everyone, but could allow no one to be mentioned without some snide aside.

The neat little Chelsea flat, all velvet chairs and fine porcelain, fitted its owner's appearance. He wore a blue blazer, gray flannels, cream silk shirt with, at the neck, a roguishly-knotted Indian print scarf.

Charles didn't feel he was going to enjoy the ensuing interview, so reckoned there was nothing to be gained by subtlety. "I've come to talk about Mariana."

"Dear Mariana," Boy Trubshawe cooed. "The *grande dame* of the English stage." Then, inevitably, he added the diminishing qualification. "In ambition, if not in deed. How sad for the poor darling that the Queen never has coughed anything up for her in the Birthday Honors. Dear Mariana *thinks* of herself as a Dame— how sad that she's been passed over."

Charles pressed on. "You know that Mariana's just written an autobiography?"

"Well, I had heard, yes. Writing books now—what will the little minx think of next?"

"Have you read the book?"

Boy Trubshawe widened his eyes coquettishly. "Now *why* should I do a thing like that? I mean, I'm delighted for Mariana that she's managed to persuade some publisher that she's *marketable*. Good for her, splendid effort . . . but what possible interest could her little book have for me?"

"You worked together a lot. I thought it might have a bit of nostalgic appeal."

"Now, my dear, just because Mariana lives in the past,

there's no need to suppose that I do too. *I* know exactly what I did for Mariana's career—I don't need books to tell me that."

"What did you do for her then?"

"Simply shaped her whole life. She had nothing before she met me. Oh, talent, yes . . . a *modicum* of talent. It was I who taught her how to *husband* that modicum. And she followed my advice so well that people even started to believe that she was *rather good.*"

He smiled ingratiatingly, apparently expecting some reaction of amusement. Presumably, in his usual circle, his sallies of bitchery were greeted with gales of laughter. But Charles knew too many people in the theater whose malice passed as wit, and determinedly withheld even a sycophantic smile.

"Were you in New York for Halloween?" he asked abruptly.

Boy Trubshawe was thrown by the change of tack. "Well, yes. Yes, I was," he stuttered.

"Shops full of seasonal decorations?"

"Yes."

"Pumpkins . . . witches . . . ?"

"Yes." He still looked bewildered.

"Skeletons . . . ?"

The old man's face colored with petulance. "What is this? What are you talking about?"

"Someone," said Charles fiercely, "is making Mariana's life misery. And I'm trying to find out who it is."

"But surely you don't suspect . . ." The blotched but manicured hands flopped on to Boy's chest in a gesture of identification. ". . . *moi?*"

If Charles could be said to have a usual method of investigation, it would have to be described as "tentative" or "indirect," but on this occasion he broke away from type. Boy Trubshawe was annoying him, and Charles saw no reason to hide the fact.

"You have a reputation as a somewhat insensitive practical joker, Mr. Trubshawe. I want to know if you've been practicing this habit on Mariana recently?"

The eyes widened in mock innocence. "And why should I do that?"

"Because in her book she didn't accord you the kind

of praise and thanks which you seem to feel to be your due."

"No, she certainly didn't!" the old man snapped, making a nonsense of his earlier denial of having read Mariana's book. Then he let out an unattractive little snigger. "So someone's been playing nasty tricks on Mariana?"

"Yes. Someone broke into her flat sometime the day before yesterday and planted a particularly nasty—"

Charles was stopped by Boy's limply upraised hand. "Don't look at me, chum. Can't say I'm sorry to hear about the old duck's discomfiture . . . but I only got back from the States in the wee small hours yesterday."

And the director smiled smugly.

"I didn't take to Boy, certainly. He's a nasty bit of work."

"Oh, I wouldn't say that, Charles."

"Come on, Mariana. He is. Bitchy and horrible. You don't owe him any loyalty."

"Well . . ." She looked pained at the idea of having to think ill of anyone.

"*But* he has got an alibi. Well, I haven't checked it, but if he says he came back on a certain flight . . ."

"Oh yes, you have to believe him."

"So we're back to trying to think of someone else with a grudge against you. Having read your book—which, incidentally, I enjoyed very much—" Mariana colored daintily at the compliment "—I can't imagine there's anyone else you've offended."

"I hope not."

Charles rubbed his chin reflectively. It was the morning after his encounter with Boy Trubshawe. A watery November sun trickled into the room where they drank coffee.

"So we have to think of people who might have some other motive . . . Hmm. What about this girl in the revival of *Roses In Winter*?"

"Sandy Drake?"

"That's the one. Must be pretty galling for her to have these constant, unflattering comparisons with you."

"Do you really think . . ."

Charles shrugged. "Possible. I mean, if she were unbalanced or . . . I haven't met her. Have you?"

Mariana shook her head.

"Well, I could ask around. I'm sure I've got friends who've worked with her at some point."

"Doesn't really sound very likely that . . ."

"No. Well, look, let's think of the obvious motive. Inheritance. Who's your heir?"

"Oh, surely that couldn't be . . . I mean, I haven't got any money. Nothing to leave."

"Do you own this flat?"

"Yes, but . . ."

"At today's prices that's worth having. Then there'll be royalties from the book and a few other things. You'd be surprised how much you're worth, Mariana."

The old lady gave a little dismissive smile. "Would you like some more coffee, Charles?"

"You haven't told me."

"What?" She turned an expression of self-conscious innocence on him.

"Who inherits."

"Oh, well, I'm sure there wouldn't be any reason to—"

"Who?"

"My nephew. Dick." She followed this admission up quickly. "But I'm sure he'd never—"

"Do you see a lot of him?"

"No. Not a great deal. But when we do meet, he's always perfectly friendly."

"Is he well off?"

"Well, he's . . . You know, it's difficult when you're making your way in the theater. At first there are a few years when . . . I'm sure he's doing fine now."

"Perhaps I ought to go and have a word with him."

"Oh, no, Charles, no." She sounded horrified. "No, there's no need for that. It would be terribly embarrassing."

"Perhaps so. I just feel I should be doing something for you. Some sort of investigation. There are so few leads to follow up and Dick at least has a kind of motive to get rid of you."

"It's all right, Charles. Don't feel you have to do anything."

"But if I don't, all we can do is sit and wait for something else to happen."

"Then perhaps that's what we'd better do." She flashed her famous smile at him. "And let's look on the bright side. It's quite possible that nothing else *will* happen."

The subject was left and they chatted for another hour about Mariana's book and some of the productions in which she had starred. Charles, even after more than thirty not very successful years in the theater, remained incorrigibly stage-struck and enjoyed the conversation. But at twelve, in spite of Mariana's offer of lunch, he felt he should go.

"I'll see you downstairs."

"Oh, don't worry."

"I have to go down just to see if there's any post. Not that there ever is much except bills these days. Most of the people who might have written to me are long dead."

"Maybe today," said Charles jovially, "will be your lucky day. Maybe today you will receive something totally unexpected."

He was right. She did.

Fortunately she opened the package down in the hall while he was still there.

The note read: "WON'T BE LONG NOW, MARIANA."

With it was an audio cassette.

"You will not escape my vengeance. I have sworn to destroy you and that oath will be fulfilled. You may try to escape, but all attempts will be in vain. As surely as if by a court of law, your death sentence has been pronounced."

A click sounded on the tape, then a slight hiss as it ran on. Charles left it for a few moments before switching off.

It was a male voice, fairly young, full, well-articulated, slightly theatrical perhaps.

He looked across at the old actress's haunted face.

"Do you recognize it, Mariana?"

"No," she whispered, with an appalled shake of her head. "No, I don't."

Charles knew she was lying, but no amount of persuasion could elicit the truth from her.

*   *   *

He rang the BBC from the payphone at the bedsitter and asked for Mark Lear's office.

"Charles. How are you? Hey, you remember that actress who was in the play we did with Mariana Lythgoe—the one with purple hair? Well, let me tell you she is the most amazing—"

"Mark, listen. I want you to identify a voice for me."

"What?"

"You know the radio scene. I've got a recording of a voice that sounds to me like someone who's done a lot of radio. I'm going to play it on the cassette down the phone and I want you to tell me if you recognize it."

"What is this?"

"Just listen, Mark. Please."

Charles held the portable cassette to the receiver and pressed the start button.

"You will not escape my vengeance. I have sworn—"

"Of course I recognize it."

Charles stopped the machine.

"Who?"

"I should recognize it. I only produced him in —"

"Who?"

"Dick Lythgoe. As I say, I was the producer on—"

But Charles wasn't in the mood for showbiz recollections.

"Thank you, Mark."

Charles got the name of Dick Lythgoe's agent through the actor's directory, *Spotlight*. As he was doing so, he looked at the actor's photograph. There was a family resemblance to Mariana, but in her nephew the sharp outlines of her famous face were blurred, the eyes were set more closely together and the mouth showed a slight droop of petulance.

The agent told Charles that his client was not currently working, thinking at that stage the inquiry came from a potential employer. But when Charles said it was a personal matter and asked for Dick Lythgoe's address, he got no further information. Though it was annoying, Charles couldn't object to this. He hoped his own agent would show similar discretion in the same circumstances (though he didn't feel total confidence that his would).

However, a few calls to friends in the business soon

elicited an address for Dick Lythgoe in Kilburn, which was within walking distance of Charles's bedsitter.

It was a house divided into flats. Blue paint had flaked off the frontage, leaving a mottled effect. There was a tangle of wires and doorbells by the front door, but none of the stained cards offered the name "Lythgoe." Charles stepped back and looked through the rusted railings to the separate basement entrance. He walked down the worn steps, picking his way over polythene bags of rubbish which had been dumped there.

Dick Lythgoe's surroundings suggested that he could certainly use an inheritance.

The fourth ring at the doorbell brought him to the door. His face looked crumpled, as if he had just woken up. It also showed that Dick Lythgoe's *Spotlight* photograph had been taken some years before. And those years had not been kind to its subject. His hairline had retreated, leaving only a couple of ineffectual tufts on top, and the skin around the eyes had pouched up. Dick Lythgoe was no longer going to impress Casting Directors as a Juvenile Lead.

"What do you want?" he asked truculently.

"I want to talk about Mariana."

A spasm of anger twisted the face. "Oh God, story of my bloody life! It's all anyone ever wants to talk about. My bloody aunt. I should have changed my name before I went into the bloody theater!"

"Then why didn't you?" asked Charles.

The lower lip trembled, then decided not to answer. The silence was quite as expressive as words. Dick Lythgoe had clung to his famous name for shrewd business reasons; without it he might have had even less success.

"Anyway, what do you want? Are you another bloody journalist? Because let me tell you before you start, I don't talk about my dear auntie for free. If you want more heart-warming insights into the private life of the First Lady of Yesterday's Theater, you're going to have to find fifty quid. At least."

"I'm not a journalist," said Charles. "I am just a friend of your aunt's."

Dick Lythgoe looked him up and down with an insolent smile. "Have to admire the old girl's resilience, don't you?"

Charles ignored the innuendo. Like Boy Trubshawe, the actor was making him uncharacteristically angry. "Someone is conducting a campaign of persecution against Mariana and I'm going to find out who it is."

"Campaign of persecution?"

"Yes. And I have some pretty strong evidence of who's doing it. I think you'd better let me come inside."

Dick Lythgoe gaped at this sudden assertiveness, but drew aside to admit the older man.

The flat inside was a tip. Dirty plates, glasses and encrusted coffee cups perched on every available surface. There was a smell of damp from the house, compounded by a human staleness. Charles wanted to throw open every window in the place.

"Sorry about the mess," Dick Lythgoe mumbled. "My girlfriend walked out a few weeks back." He slumped on top of a pile of grubby shirts draped over an armchair. "Now what is this?"

"Your aunt has received a series of threatening phone calls and anonymous letters. An unpleasant practical joke has been played on her. Today she received this tape."

Charles had the portable recorder set up in readiness and pressed the start button.

Dick Lythgoe sat in silence while the message ran through.

"Now," demanded Charles as it ended, "do you deny that that is your voice?"

"No," the actor replied, again with his insolent smile. "I don't deny it."

Charles poured another slug of Bell's whisky into Mark Lear's glass and, topping up his own, went across to sit on his bed. "And there's no doubt that's where the speech came from?"

"None at all. As Dick said, it was part of a *Saturday Night Theater* he recorded for me last year. I was about to tell you that when you rang off this morning."

"Oh, damn. When was the play broadcast?"

"January of this year."

"So somebody must have got hold of the tape and—"

"They wouldn't need to do that. Just record it off air."

"Yes. If they did, it implies a degree of long-distance planning."

"Mm. And, I would have thought, rules Dick out of your suspicions."

"I suppose so."

"Come on, he's not going to send a threat like that that's so easily identifiable. It took you less than a day to find out where it came from."

Charles nodded ruefully. "Mind you, he wasn't to know Mariana had talked to anyone about what was happening. He may have thought that she would keep it to herself, then listen to the tape when it arrived and drop dead of a heart attack on the spot . . . ?"

Mark Lear gave his friend a pitying look. "And then the body is discovered with the tape still in the tape recorder just beside it. No criminal would leave such a huge signpost pointing straight at him, would he?"

"No. So I'm really back to Square One. Trouble with this case is a dearth of suspects."

"Who else have you got?"

"No one, really. Well, I had one other, but he's ruled out by sheer logistics."

"Who was he?"

"Boy Trubshawe."

"Oh, him. Malicious old queen, isn't he?"

"You can say that again. Do you know him well?"

The producer shook his head. "No, met him for the first time this week. Sort of cocktail party at Lucinda's. He'd just come in from a trip to the States, which he was very full of."

"Yes, I know."

"Not a single reputation on Broadway was unsullied by the end of the evening."

"That's my Boy," said Charles wryly. "When was this?"

"What, Lucinda's party?"

"Uhuh."

"Monday night."

"Can't have been."

"What do you mean?"

"Monday night Boy was still in New York. I know that. I saw him Wednesday and he said he'd come back in the small hours of Tuesday morning."

Mark Lear shook his head. "Charles, I know I drink too much in the BBC Club, but I can tell the days apart. I have good reason to remember Monday night. After Lucinda's I had dinner with that actress with the purple hair and let me tell you—"

Charles cut short this sexual reminiscence. "Good God! You swear that Boy Trubshawe was here on the Monday?"

"Of course I do. What the hell should I—"

"So he lied to me! And he could easily have—"

The phone rang from the landing. Charles was silent.

"Aren't you going to answer it?"

"No. It'll be for one of the Swedish girls."

But apparently none of the Swedish girls was in. The phone rang on.

Charles picked up the receiver.

"It's Mariana."

"What's up? Has something happened?"

"Charles, I'm worried."

"Why?"

"I thought I could hear some noise from the fire escape. Outside the kitchen."

"What sort of noise?"

"Well, as if someone . . . I don't know . . . as if someone—"

There was a sudden sound of breaking glass from Mariana's end of the phone. She let out a little whimper. There was a heavy thud.

Then silence.

The caretaker was roused from his basement in the adjacent block and, responding to the urgency of Charles's demands, hurried up the stairs and unlocked the door to Mariana's flat.

She lay by the door between the sitting room and the kitchen. The phone, receiver off, was on the floor at the full extent of its cable. When she rang Charles, she must have been trying to see what was happening in the kitchen. The glass of the door to the fire escape was shattered.

Mariana herself was moaning softly. As Charles gently raised her body to cradle it, she put her hand to her forehead where a marked swelling showed already.

"She all right?"

Charles looked up into the anxious face of the elderly

caretaker. "I think so. Better get a doctor. Do you know who her doctor is?"

The old man shook his head.

Mariana's eyelids opened and the pupils swam into focus. "Charles," she whispered gratefully.

"Mariana, who is your doctor?"

She spoke slowly, as if drunk. "Oh, he doesn't make house calls. If I'm ill, I have to go there."

"I think he'll come this time. What's his name?"

She told him. "But it's not necessary. I'm all right."

Charles told the caretaker to ring the doctor, as he picked Mariana up gently and moved toward the bedroom.

"Shall I ring the police as well, guv?"

Charles looked off into the kitchen. "No, hold fire on that for the moment."

He stayed with Mariana until the doctor arrived. The latter's complaints about actually having to *visit* a patient *and* to have to do so late in the evening justified the old lady's comment on him. But at least he had arrived and Charles left him with the patient.

The actor went into the kitchen. He looked at the floor by the exit door, then turned the handle. It was not locked.

On the metal grille of the fire escape landing outside lay a brick, surrounded by a few larger pieces of glass.

"Mr. Paris."

The doctor was standing in the doorway from the sitting room.

"Yes."

"There's nothing wrong with her. Just a bruise on the forehead. I must say I resent being called out for something so minor."

"She is an old lady, Doctor."

"If I came out on a call for every old lady who fell over, I would never get home at all."

"She didn't fall over."

The doctor shrugged. "That's not really important. The fact is that she has suffered a very minor injury and I have been called away from a dinner party."

"It's not the minor injury that should worry you, Doctor."

"What on earth are you talking about, Mr. Paris?"

"I am talking about the effect a shock like that might have on Miss Lythgoe's heart."

Charles sat on the side of Mariana's bed. She smiled up at him. She looked weary, but peaceful. The soft bedside light washed years off the perfectly shaped face.

"Has the doctor gone?"

Charles nodded. "He doesn't seem too worried about you. Rest, he says, that's the answer."

She grinned. "Not a lot else one can do at my age."

"No." There was a silence before he continued. "Mariana, you asked me last week to do some detective work for you."

"Yes."

"Well, I've done it."

Her graying eyes sparkled. "You mean you know who it is who's been doing all these things?"

"Yes." The word came out like a sigh.

"Who? Charles, tell me who."

"Mariana, I've looked in the kitchen and on the fire escape. There is no glass on the kitchen floor. There is a brick and some broken glass on the fire escape."

"Yes, well, that's how he must have got in. It means—"

Charles shook his head slowly as he interrupted. "It means that the window was broken from inside the flat, Mariana."

"Oh."

"I spoke to the doctor about your health. He was very complimentary about your general condition. Your heart, in particular, he said, would do credit to a woman twenty years your junior."

"Ah." She looked up at him. Frail, vulnerable, but still in control, still with a small twinkle of humor.

Charles grinned. "Why, Mariana?"

She spread her hands in a gesture of selfishness. "What I've always suffered from, Charles—innate sense of theater. And, I suppose, the desire to be the center of attention."

"But to go to the lengths you did . . . Even to hit yourself on the forehead . . . I mean, why?"

"Sorry. Got carried away. Always like that on stage—

really got into my parts. I never could play any character unless I believed, at least for a few moments, that I *was* that character."

"Which is what made you a great actress."

"Thank you." Once again, by her usual blend of charm and cunning, Mariana had exacted her tribute of compliment.

"And what made you so convincing to me. I believed you were really frightened because, at the moment you told me all that nonsense, you believed it. You really were frightened."

She nodded with a mixture of shame and impertinence, like a schoolgirl caught smoking.

"Have you done this sort of thing before, Mariana?"

"No. I promise. Really. When I retired ten years ago, I was determined to sink gracefully into anonymity. And I managed it. I was really good about it. I had friends, I spent time with them, and, for the first time in my life, I took a back seat. And, to my surprise, I found I didn't really mind."

"What changed things?"

She smiled sadly. "My friends died. I was increasingly alone. Yes, I must use the word—increasingly *lonely.* But what really started it was the book. Writing it, thinking about all those performances . . . and then the 'promotional tour.' I'm afraid once again I was center stage—and I found I hadn't lost the taste for it."

"I'm a small audience, Mariana," said Charles gently.

"I know. I'm sorry it was you who got involved. Unfair. You didn't deserve it. It's just, when Mark said you were a bit of a detective . . . And then I got caught up in the drama of the situation—as I say, got carried away. I'm sorry. You were just the victim of another lonely old lady, craving attention."

Charles gave a little laugh. "And has my 'attention' been satisfactory?"

Mariana Lythgoe's famous smile irradiated her face. "Oh yes, Charles. Thank you."

He picked up her fine but freckled hand and kissed it. "I must go."

"Yes." A little silence hung between them. "But, Charles, you will come and see me again, won't you?"

"Oh yes, Mariana," said Charles Paris. "I will."

LIKE A THIEF IN THE NIGHT
Lawrence Block

FIRST APPEARANCE: *This story*

This is the first Bernie Rhodenbarr story, albeit an atypical one. The story is not written from Bernie's first-person point of view, as are the rest of the stories and all the books, but it is his actual first appearance. The story appeared for the first time in *Cosmopolitan,* and then in the Block collection *Sometimes They Bite* (Arbor House, 1983).

The most recent Bernie book is *The Burglar in the Library* (Dutton, 1997).

A t 11:30 the television anchorman counseled her to stay tuned for the late show, a vintage Hitchcock film starring Cary Grant. For a moment she was tempted. Then she crossed the room and switched off the set.

There was a last cup of coffee in the pot. She poured it and stood at the window with it, a tall and slender woman, attractive, dressed in the suit and silk blouse she'd worn that day at the office. A woman who could look at once efficient and elegant, and who stood now sipping black coffee from a bone-china cup and gazing south and west.

Her apartment was on the twenty-second floor of a building located at the corner of Lexington Avenue and Seventy-sixth Street, and her vista was quite spectacular. A midtown skyscraper blocked her view of the building where Tavistock Corp. did its business, but she fancied she could see right through it with x-ray vision.

The cleaning crew would be finishing up now, she knew, returning their mops and buckets to the cupboards and changing into street clothes, preparing to go off-shift at midnight. They would leave a couple of lights on in Tavistock's seventeenth-floor suite as well as elsewhere throughout the building. And the halls would remain lighted, and here and there in the building someone would be working all night, and—

She liked Hitchcock movies, especially the early ones, and she was in love with Cary Grant. But she also liked good clothes and bone-china cups and the view from her apartment and the comfortable, well-appointed apartment itself. And so she rinsed the cup in the sink and put on a coat and took the elevator to the lobby, where the florid-faced doorman made a great show of hailing her a cab.

There would be other nights, and other movies.

The taxi dropped her in front of an office building in the West Thirties. She pushed through the revolving door and her footsteps on the marble floor sounded impossibly loud to her. The security guard, seated at a small table by the bank of elevators, looked up from his magazine at her approach. She said, "Hello, Eddie," and gave him a quick smile.

"Hey, how ya doin'," he said, and she bent to sign herself in as his attention returned to his magazine. In the appropriate spaces she scribbled *Elaine Halder, Tavistock, 1704,* and, after a glance at her watch, *12:15.*

She got into a waiting elevator and the doors closed without a sound. She'd be alone up there, she thought. She'd glanced at the record sheet while signing it, and no one had signed in for Tavistock or any other office on seventeen.

Well, she wouldn't be long.

When the elevator doors opened she stepped out and stood for a moment in the corridor, getting her bearings. She took a key from her purse and stared at it for a moment as if it were an artifact from some unfamiliar civilization. Then she turned and began walking the length of the freshly mopped corridor, hearing nothing but the echo of her boisterous footsteps.

1704. An oak door, a square of frosted glass, unmarked but for the suite number and the name of the company. She took another thoughtful glance at the key before fitting it carefully into the lock.

It turned easily. She pushed the door inward and stepped inside, letting the door swing shut behind her.

And gasped.

There was a man not a dozen yards from her.

"Hello," he said.

He was standing beside a rosewood-topped desk, the center drawer of which was open, and there was a spark in his eyes and a tentative smile on his lips. He was wearing a gray suit patterned in a windowpane check. His shirt collar was buttoned down, his narrow tie neatly knotted. He was two or three years older than she, she supposed, and perhaps that many inches taller.

Her hand was pressed to her breast, as if to still a pounding heart. But her heart wasn't really pounding. She managed a smile. "You startled me," she said. "I didn't know anyone would be here."

"We're even."

"I beg your pardon?"

"I wasn't expecting company."

He had nice white even teeth, she noticed. She was apt to notice teeth. And he had an open and friendly face, which was also something she was inclined to notice, and why was she suddenly thinking of Cary Grant? The movie she hadn't seen, of course, that plus this Hollywood meet-cute opening, with the two of them encountering each other unexpectedly in this silent tomb of an office, and—

And he was wearing rubber gloves.

Her face must have registered something because he frowned, puzzled. Then he raised his hands and flexed his fingers. "Oh, these," he said. "Would it help if I spoke of an eczema brought on by exposure to the night air?"

"There's a lot of that going around."

"I knew you'd understand."

"You're a prowler."

"The word has the nastiest connotations," he objected. "One imagines a lot of lurking in shrubbery. There's no shrubbery here beyond the odd rubber plant and I wouldn't lurk in it if there were."

"A thief, then."

"A thief, yes. More specifically, a burglar. I might have stripped the gloves off when you stuck your key in the lock but I'd been so busy listening to your footsteps and hoping they'd lead to another office that I quite forgot I was wearing these things. Not that it would have made much difference. Another minute and you'd have realized that you've never set eyes on me before, and at that point you'd have wondered what I was doing here."

"What *are* you doing here?"

"My kid brother needs an operation." ·

"I thought that might be it. Surgery for his eczema."

He nodded. "Without it he'll never play the trumpet again. May I be permitted an observation?"

"I don't see why not."

"I observe that you're afraid of me."

"And here I thought I was doing such a super job of hiding it."

"You were, but I'm an incredibly perceptive human being. You're afraid I'll do something violent, that he who is capable of theft is equally capable of mayhem."

"Are you?"

"Not even in fantasy. I'm your basic pacifist. When I was a kid my favorite book was *Ferdinand the Bull.*"

"I remember him. He didn't want to fight. He just wanted to smell the flowers."

"Can you blame him?" He smiled again, and the adverb that came to her was *disarmingly.* More like Alan Alda than Cary Grant, she decided. Well, that was all right. There was nothing wrong with Alan Alda.

"*You're* afraid of *me,*" she said suddenly.

"How'd you figure that? A slight quiver in the old upper lip?"

"No. It just came to me. But why? What could I do to you?"

"You could call the, uh, cops."

"I wouldn't do that."

"And I wouldn't hurt you."

"I know you wouldn't."

"Well," he said, and sighed theatrically. "Aren't you glad we got all that out of the way?"

She was, rather. It was good to know that neither of them had anything to fear from the other. As if in recognition of this change in their relationship she took off her coat and hung it on the pipe rack, where a checked topcoat was already hanging. His, she assumed. How readily he made himself at home!

She turned to find he was making himself further at home, rummaging deliberately in the drawers of the desk. What cheek, she thought, and felt herself beginning to smile.

She asked him what he was doing.

"Foraging," he said, then drew himself up sharply. "This isn't your desk, is it?"

"No."

"Thank heaven for that."

"What were you looking for, anyway?"

He thought for a moment, then shook his head. "Nope," he said. "You'd think I could come up with a decent story but I can't. I'm looking for something to steal."

"Nothing specific?"

"I like to keep an open mind. I didn't come here to cart off the IBM Selectrics. But you'd be surprised how many people leave cash in their desks."

"And you just take what you find?"

He hung his head. "I know," he said. "It's a moral failing. You don't have to tell me."

"Do people really leave cash in an unlocked desk drawer?"

"Sometimes. And sometimes they lock the drawers, but that doesn't make them all that much harder to open."

"You can pick locks?"

"A limited and eccentric talent," he allowed, "but it's all I know."

"How did you get in here? I suppose you picked the office lock."

"Hardly a great challenge."

"But how did you get past Eddie?"

"Eddie? Oh, you must be talking about the chap in the lobby. He's not quite as formidable as the Berlin Wall, you know. I got here around eight. They tend to be less suspicious at an earlier hour. I scrawled a name on the sheet and walked on by. Then I found an empty office that they'd already finished cleaning and curled up on the couch for a nap."

"You're kidding."

"Have I ever lied to you in the past? The cleaning crew leaves at midnight. At about that time I let myself out of Mr. Higginbotham's office—that's where I've taken to napping, he's a patent attorney with the most comfortable old leather couch. And then I make my rounds."

She looked at him. "You've come to this building before."

"I stop by every little once in a while."

"You make it sound like a vending machine route."

"There are similarities, aren't there? I never looked at it that way."

"And then you make your rounds. You break into offices—"

"I never break anything. Let's say I let myself into offices."

"And you steal money from desks—"

"Also jewelry, when I run across it. Anything valuable and portable. Sometimes there's a safe. That saves a lot of looking around. You know right away that's where they keep the good stuff."

"And you can open safes?"

"Not every safe," he said modestly, "and not every single time, but"— he switched to a Cockney accent— "I has the touch, mum."

"And then what do you do? Wait until morning to leave?"

"What for? I'm well-dressed. I look respectable. Besides, security guards are posted to keep unauthorized persons out of a building, not to prevent them from leaving. It might be different if I tried rolling a Xerox machine through the lobby, but I don't steal anything that won't fit in my pockets or my attaché case. And I don't wear my rubber gloves when I saunter past the guard. That wouldn't do."

"I don't suppose it would. What do I call you?"

" 'That damned burglar,' I suppose. That's what everybody calls me. But you"—he extended a rubber-covered forefinger—"you may call me Bernie."

"Bernie the Burglar."

"And what shall I call you?"

"Elaine'll do."

"Elaine," he said. "Elaine, Elaine. Not Elaine Halder, by any chance?"

"How did you—?"

"Elaine Halder," he said. "And that explains what brings you to these offices in the middle of the night. You look startled. I can't imagine why. 'You know my methods, Watson.' What's the matter?"

"Nothing."

"Don't be frightened, for God's sake. Knowing your name doesn't give me mystical powers over your destiny. I just have a good memory and your name stuck in it." He crooked a thumb at a closed door on the far side of the room. "I've already been in the boss's office. I saw your note on his desk. I'm afraid I'll have to admit I read it. I'm a snoop. It's a serious character defect, I know."

"Like larceny."

"Something along those lines. Let's see now. Elaine Halder leaves the office, having placed on her boss's desk a letter of resignation. Elaine Halder returns in the small hours of the morning. A subtle pattern begins to emerge, my dear."

"Oh?"

"Of course. You've had second thoughts and you want to retrieve the letter before himself gets a chance to read it. Not a bad idea, given some of the choice things you had to say about him. Just let me open up for you, all right? I'm the tidy type and I locked up after I was through in there."

"Did you find anything to steal?"

"Eighty-five bucks and a pair of gold cuff links." He bent over the lock, probing its innards with a splinter of spring steel. "Nothing to write home about, but every little bit helps. I'm sure you have a key that fits this door—you had to in order to leave the resignation in the first place, didn't you? But how many chances do I get to show off? Not that a lock like this one presents much of a challenge, not to the nimble digits of Bernie the Burglar, and—ah, *there* we are!"

"Extraordinary."

"It's so seldom I have an audience."

He stood aside, held the door for her. On the threshold she was struck by the notion that there would be a dead body in the private office. George Tavistock himself, slumped over his desk with the figured hilt of a letter opener protruding from his back.

But of course there was no such thing. The office was devoid of clutter, let alone corpses, nor was there any sign that it had been lately burglarized.

A single sheet of paper lay on top of the desk blotter. She walked over, picked it up. Her eyes scanned its half dozen sentences as if she were reading them for the first time, then dropped to the elaborately styled signature, a far cry from the loose scrawl with which she'd signed the register in the lobby.

She read the note through again, then put it back where it had been.

"Not changing your mind again?"

She shook her head. "I never changed it in the first place. That's not why I came back here tonight."

"You couldn't have dropped in just for the pleasure of my company."

"I might have, if I'd known you were going to be here. No, I came back because—" She paused, drew a deliberate breath. "You might say I wanted to clean out my desk."

"Didn't you already do that? Isn't your desk right across there? The one with your name plate on it? Forward of me, I know, but I already had a peek, and the drawers bore a striking resemblance to the cupboard of one Ms. Hubbard."

"You went through my desk."

He spread his hands apologetically. "I meant nothing personal," he said. "At the time, I didn't even know you."

"That's a point."

"And searching an empty desk isn't that great a violation of privacy, is it? Nothing to be seen beyond paper clips and rubber bands and the odd felt-tipped pen. So if you've come to clean out that lot—"

"I meant it metaphorically," she explained. "There are things in this office that belong to me. Projects I worked on that I ought to have copies of to show to prospective employers."

"And won't Mr. Tavistock see to it that you get copies?"

She laughed sharply. "You don't know the man," she said.

"And thank God for that. I couldn't rob someone I knew."

"He would think I intended to divulge corporate secrets to the competition. The minute he reads my letter of resignation I'll be persona non grata in this office. I probably won't even be able to get into the building. I didn't even realize any of this until I'd gotten home tonight, and I didn't really know what to do, and then—"

"Then you decided to try a little burglary."

"Hardly that."

"Oh?"

"I have a key."

"And I have a cunning little piece of spring steel, and they both perform the signal function of admitting us where we have no right to be."

"But I work here!"

"Worked."

"My resignation hasn't been accepted yet. I'm still an employee."

"Technically. Still, you've come like a thief in the night. You may have signed in downstairs and let yourself in with a key, and you're not wearing gloves or padding around in crepe-soled shoes, but we're not all that different, you and I, are we?"

She set her jaw. "I have a right to the fruits of my labor," she said.

"And so have I, and heaven help the person whose property rights get in our way."

She walked around him to the three-drawer filing cabinet to the right of Tavistock's desk. It was locked.

She turned, but Bernie was already at her elbow. "Allow me," he said, and in no time at all he had tickled the locking mechanism and was drawing the top drawer open.

"Thank you," she said.

"Oh, don't thank me," he said. "Professional courtesy. No thanks required."

She was busy for the next thirty minutes, selecting documents from the filing cabinet and from Tavistock's desk, as well as a few items from the unlocked cabinets in the outer office. She ran everything through the Xerox copier and replaced the originals where she'd found them. While she was doing all this, her burglar friend worked his way through the office's remaining desks. He was in no evident hurry, and it struck her that he was deliberately dawdling so as not to finish before her.

Now and then she would look up from what she was doing to observe him at his work. Once she caught him looking at her, and when their eyes met he winked and smiled, and she felt her cheeks burning.

He was attractive, certainly. And unquestionably likable, and in no way intimidating. Nor did he come across like a criminal. His speech was that of an educated person, he had an eye for clothes, his manners were impeccable—

What on earth was she thinking of?

By the time she had finished she had an inch-thick sheaf of paper in a manila file folder. She slipped her coat on, tucked the folder under her arm.

"You're certainly neat," he said. "A place for everything and everything right back in its place. I like that."

"Well, you're that way yourself, aren't you? You even take the trouble to lock up after yourself."

"It's not that much trouble. And there's a point to it. If one doesn't leave a mess, sometimes it takes them weeks to realize they've been robbed. The longer it takes, the less chance anybody'll figure out whodunit."

"And here I thought you were just naturally neat."

"As it happens I am, but it's a professional asset. Of course your neatness has much the same purpose, doesn't it? They'll never know you've been here tonight, especially since you haven't actually taken anything away with you. Just copies."

"That's right."

"Speaking of which, would you care to put them in my attaché case? So that you aren't noticed leaving the building with them in hand? I'll grant you the chap downstairs wouldn't notice an earthquake if it registered less than seven-point-four on the Richter scale, but it's that seemingly pointless attention to detail that enables me to persist in my chosen occupation instead of making license plates and sewing mail sacks as a guest of the governor. Are you ready, Elaine? Or would you like to take one last look around for auld lang syne?''

"I've had my last look around. And I'm not much on auld lang syne.''

He held the door for her, switched off the overhead lights, drew the door shut. While she locked it with her key he stripped off his rubber gloves and put them in the attaché case where her papers reposed. Then, side by side, they walked the length of the corridor to the elevator. Her footsteps echoed. His, cushioned by his crepe soles, were quite soundless.

Hers stopped, too, when they reached the elevator, and they waited in silence. They had met, she thought, as thieves in the night, and now they were going to pass like ships in the night.

The elevator came, floated them down to the lobby. The lobby guard looked up at them, neither recognition nor interest showing in his eyes. She said, "Hi, Eddie. Everything going all right?''

"Hey, how ya doin','' he said.

There were only three entries below hers on the register sheet, three persons who'd arrived after her. She signed herself out, listing the time after a glance at her watch: 1:56. She'd been upstairs for better than an hour and a half.

Outside, the wind had an edge to it. She turned to him, glanced at his attaché case, suddenly remembered the first schoolboy who'd carried her books. She could surely have carried her own books, just as she could have safely carried the folder of papers past Eagle-eye Eddie.

Still, it was not unpleasant to have one's books carried.

"Well," she began, "I'd better take my papers, and—''

"Where are you headed?''

"Seventy-sixth Street.''

"East or west?''

"East. But—''

"We'll share a cab," he said. "Compliments of petty cash.'' And he was at the curb, a hand raised, and a cab appeared as if conjured up and then he was holding the door for her.

She got in.

"Seventy-sixth," he told the driver. "And what?"

"Lexington," she said.

"Lexington," he said.

Her mind raced during the taxi ride. It was all over the place and she couldn't keep up with it. She felt in turn like a schoolgirl, like a damsel in peril, like Grace Kelly in a Hitchcock film. When the cab reached her corner she indicated her building, and he leaned forward to relay the information to the driver.

"Would you like to come up for coffee?"

The line had run through her mind like a mantra in the course of the ride. Yet she couldn't believe she was actually speaking the words.

"Yes," he said. "I'd like that."

She steeled herself as they approached her doorman, but the man was discretion personified. He didn't even greet her by name, merely holding the door for her and her escort and wishing them a good night. Upstairs, she thought of demanding that Bernie open her door without the keys, but decided she didn't want any demonstrations just then of her essential vulnerability. She unlocked the several locks herself.

"I'll make coffee," she said. "Or would you just as soon have a drink?"

"Sounds good."

"Scotch? Or cognac?"

"Cognac."

While she was pouring the drinks he walked around her living room, looking at the pictures on the walls and the books on the shelves. Guests did this sort of thing all the time, but this particular guest was a criminal, after all, and so she imagined him taking a burglar's inventory of her possessions. That Chagall aquatint he was studying—she'd paid five hundred for it at auction and it was probably worth close to three times that by now.

Surely he'd have better luck foraging in her apartment than in a suite of deserted offices.

Surely he'd realize as much himself.

She handed him his brandy. "To criminal enterprise," he said, and she raised her glass in response.

"I'll give you those papers. Before I forget."

"All right."

He opened the attaché case, handed them over. She placed the folder on the LaVerne coffee table and carried her brandy across to the window. The deep carpet muffled her footsteps as effectively as if she'd been wearing crepe-soled shoes.

You have nothing to be afraid of, she told herself. *And you're not afraid, and—*

"An impressive view," he said, close behind her.

"Yes."

"You could see your office from here. If that building weren't in the way."

"I was thinking that earlier."

"Beautiful," he said, softly, and then his arms were encircling her from behind and his lips were on the nape of her neck.

" 'Elaine the fair, Elaine the lovable,' " he quoted. " 'Elaine, the lily maid of Astolat.' " His lips nuzzled her ear. "But you must hear that all the time."

She smiled. "Oh, not so often," she said. "Less often than you'd think."

The sky was just growing light when he left. She lay alone for a few minutes, then went to lock up after him.

And laughed aloud when she found that he'd locked up after himself, without a key.

It was late but she didn't think she'd ever been less tired. She put up a fresh pot of coffee, poured a cup when it was ready and sat at the kitchen table reading through the papers she'd taken from the office. She wouldn't have had half of them without Bernie's assistance, she realized. She could never have opened the file cabinet in Tavistock's office.

"Elaine the fair, Elaine the lovable. Elaine, the lily maid of Astolat."

She smiled.

A few minutes after nine, when she was sure Jennings Colliard would be at his desk, she dialed his private number.

"It's Andrea," she told him. "I succeeded beyond our wildest dreams. I've got copies of Tavistock's complete marketing plan for fall and winter, along with a couple of dozen test and survey reports and a lot of other documents you'll want a chance to analyze. And I put all the originals back where they came from, so nobody at Tavistock'll ever know what happened."

"Remarkable."

"I thought you'd approve. Having a key to their office helped, and knowing the doorman's name didn't hurt any. Oh, and I also have some news that's worth knowing. I don't know if George Tavistock is in his office yet, but if so he's reading a letter of resignation even as we speak. The Lily Maid of Astolat has had it."

"What are you talking about, Andrea?"

"Elaine Halder. She cleaned out her desk and left him a note saying bye-bye. I thought you'd like to be the first kid on your block to know that."

"And of course you're right."

"I'd come in now but I'm exhausted. Do you want to send a messenger over?"

"Right away. And you get some sleep."

"I intend to."

"You've done spectacularly well, Andrea. There will be something extra in your stocking."

"I thought there might be," she said.

She hung up the phone and stood once again at the window, looking out at the city, reviewing the night's events. It had been quite perfect, she decided, and if there was the slightest flaw it was that she'd missed the Cary Grant movie.

But it would be on again soon. They ran it frequently. People evidently liked that sort of thing.

HIT-AND-RUN
Susan Dunlap
FIRST APPEARANCE: *Karma,* 1984

Sue Dunlap is the author of three excellent series. One features P.I. Keirnan O'Shaughnessy, another meter reader V.J. Haskell. Her first series, however, featured Berkeley policewoman Jill Smith. This story first appeared in an anthology called *Great Modern Police Stories.* She also edited, with Bob Randisi, *Deadly Allies II* (Doubleday, 1994).

Her most recent novel is *High Fall* (Delacorte, 1994).

It was four-fifteen Saturday afternoon—a football Saturday at the University of California. For the moment, there was nothing in the streets leading from Memorial Stadium but rain. Sensible Berkeleyans were home, students and alumni were huddled in the stands under sheets of clear plastic, like pieces of expensive lawn furniture, as the Cal Bears and their opponents marched toward the final gun. Then the seventy-five thousand six hundred sixty-two fans would charge gleefully or trudge morosely to their cars and create a near-gridlock all over the city of Berkeley. Then only a fool, or a tourist, would consider driving across town. Then even in a black-and-white—with the pulsers on, and the siren blaring—I wouldn't be able to get to the station.

The conference beat officer Connie Pereira and I had attended—*Indications of the Pattern Behavior of the Cyclical Killer in California*—had let out at three-thirty. We'd figured we just had time to turn in the black-and-white, pick up our own cars, and get home. On the way home, I planned to stop for a pizza. That would be pushing it. But, once I got the pizza in my car, I would be going against traffic. Now, I figured, I could make good time because University Avenue would still be empty.

When the squeal came, I knew I had figured wrong.

It was a hit-and-run. I hadn't handled one of those since long before I'd been assigned to Homicide. But this part of University Avenue was Pereira's beat. I looked at her questioningly: she wasn't on beat now; she could let the squeal go. But she was already reaching for the mike.

I switched on the pulser lights and the siren, and stepped on the gas. The street was deserted. The incident was two blocks ahead, below San Pablo Avenue, on University. There wasn't a car, truck, or bicycle in sight. As I crossed the intersection, I could see a man lying on his back in the street, his herringbone suit already matted with blood. Bent over him was a blond man in a white shirt and jeans.

Leaving Pereira waiting for the dispatcher's reply, I got out of the car and ran toward the two men. The blond man was breathing heavily but regularly, rhythmically pressing on the injured man's chest and blowing into his mouth. He was getting no response. I had seen enough bodies, both dead and dying, in my four years on the force to suspect that this one was on the way out. I doubted the C.P.R. was doing any good. But, once started, it couldn't be stopped until the medics arrived. And despite the lack of reaction, the blond looked like he knew what he was doing.

From across the sidewalk, the pungent smell of brown curry floated from a small, dingy storefront called the Benares Cafe, mixing with the sharp odor of the victim's urine. I turned away, took a last breath of fresh air, and knelt down by the injured man.

The blond leaned over the victim's mouth, blew breath in, then lifted back.

"Did you see the car that hit him?" I asked.

He was pressing on the victim's chest. He waited till he forced air into his mouth again and came up. "A glimpse."

"Where were you then?"

Again he waited, timing his reply with his rising. "Walking on University, a block down." He blew into the mouth again. "He didn't stop. Barely slowed down."

"What kind of car?" I asked, timing my question to his rhythm.

"Big. Silver, with a big, shiny grill."

"What make?"

"Don't know."

"Can you describe the driver?"

"No."

"Man or woman?"

"Don't know."

"Did you see any passengers?"

"No."

"Is there anything else you can tell me about the car?"

He went through an entire cycle of breathing and pressing before he said, "No."

"Thanks."

Now I looked more closely at the victim. I could see the short, gray-streaked brown hair, and the still-dark mustache. I could see the thick eyebrows and the eyes so filled with blood that it might not have been possible to detect the eye color if I hadn't already known it. I took a long look to make sure. But there was no question. Under the blood were the dark brown eyes of Graham Latham.

Behind me, the door of the black-and-white opened, letting out a burst of staccato calls from the dispatcher, then slammed shut. "Ambulance and back-up on the way, Jill," Pereira said as she came up beside me. "It wasn't easy getting anyone off Traffic on a football day."

I stood up and moved away from the body with relief. The blond man continued his work. In spite of the rain, I could see the sweat coming through his shirt.

I relayed his account of the crime, such as it was, to Pereira, then asked her, "Have you ever heard of Graham Latham?"

"Nope. Should I?"

"Maybe not. It's just ironic. When I was first on beat, I handled a hit-and-run. Only that time Latham was the driver. The victim, Katherine Hillman, was left just like he is. She lived—until last week, anyway. I saw her name in the obits. She was one of the guinea pigs they were trying a new electronic pain device on—a last resort for people with chronic untreatable pain."

Pereira nodded.

"I remember her at the trial," I said. "The pain wasn't so bad then. She could still shift around in her wheelchair and get some relief, and she had a boyfriend who helped her. But at the end it must have been bad." I looked over at the body in the street. "From the looks of Graham Latham, he'll be lucky if he can sit up in a wheelchair like she could."

"Be a hard choice," Pereira said, turning back to the black-and-white. She took the red blinkers out of the trunk, then hurried back along the empty street to put them in place.

Despite the cold rain, the sidewalks here weren't entirely empty. On the corner across University, I could see a pair of long pale female legs, shivering under stockings and black satin shorts that almost covered the curve of her buttocks—almost but not quite. Above those shorts, a thick red jacket suggested that, from the waist up, it was winter. The wearer—young, very blonde, with wings of multicolored eye make-up visible from across the street—stood partially concealed behind the building, looking toward Latham's body as if trying to decide whether it could be scooped up, and the cops cleared off, before the free-spending alumni rambled out of Memorial Stadium and drove down University Avenue.

On the sidewalk in front of the Benares Cafe, one of Berkeley's streetpeople—a man with long, tangled, rain-soaked hair that rested on a threadbare poncho, the outermost of three or four ragged layers of clothing—clutched a brown paper bag. Behind him, a tiny woman in a *sari* peered through the cafe window. In a doorway, a man and a woman leaned against a wall, seemingly oblivious to the activity in the street.

Between the Benares Cafe and the occupied doorway was a storefront with boxes piled in the window and the name "Harris" faded on the sign above. There was no indication of what Harris offered to the public. Across the street a mom-and-pop store occupied the corner. Next to it was the Evangelical People's Church—a store-front no larger than the mom-and-pop. Here in Berkeley, there had been more gurus over the years than in most states of India, but splinter Christian groups were rare; Berkeleyans liked their religion a bit more exotic. The rest of the block was taken up by a ramshackle hotel.

I looked back at Graham Latham, still lying unmoving in his herringbone suit. It was a good suit. Latham was an architect in San Francisco, a partner in a firm that had done a stylish low-income housing project for the city. He lived high in the hills above Berkeley. The brown Mercedes parked at the curb had to be his. Graham Latham wasn't a man who should be found on the same block as the brown-bag clutcher behind him.

I walked toward the streetperson. I was surprised he'd stuck around. He wasn't one who would view the police as protectors.

I identified myself and took his name—John Eskins. "Tell me what you saw of the accident."

"Nothing."

"You were here when we arrived." I let the accusation hang.

"Khan, across the street"—he pointed to the store—"he saw it. He called you guys. Didn't have to; he just did. He said to tell you."

"Okay, but you stick around."

He shrugged.

I glanced toward Pereira. She nodded. In the distance the shriek of the ambulance siren cut through the air. On the ground the blond man was still working on Latham. His sleeves had bunched at the armpits revealing part of a tattoo—"ay" over a heart. In the rain, it looked as if the red of the letters would drip into the heart.

The ambulance screeched to a stop. Two medics jumped out.

The first came up behind the blond man. Putting a hand on his arm, he said, "Okay. We'll take over now."

The blond man didn't break his rhythm.

"It's okay," the medic said, louder. "You can stop now. You're covered."

Still he counted and pressed on Latham's chest, counted and breathed into Latham's unresponsive mouth.

The medic grabbed both arms and yanked him up. Before the blond was standing upright, the other medic was in his place.

"He'll die! Don't let him die! He can't die!" The man struggled to free himself. His hair flapped against his eyebrows; his shirt was soaked. There was blood—Latham's blood—on his face. The rain washed it down, leaving orange lines on his cheeks. "He can't die. It's not fair. You've got to save him!"

"He's getting the best care around," Pereira said.

The blond man leaned toward the action, but the medic pulled him back. Behind us, cars, limited now to one lane, drove slowly, their engines straining in first gear, headlights brightening the back of the ambulance like colorless blinkers. The rain dripped down my hair, under the collar of my jacket, collecting there in a soggy pool.

Turning to me, Pereira shrugged. I nodded. We'd both seen Good Samaritans like him, people who get so involved they can't let go.

I turned toward the store across the street. "Witness called from there. You want me to check it out?"

She nodded. It was her beat, her case. I was just doing her a favor.

I walked across University. The store was typical—a small display of apples, bananas, onions, potatoes, two wrinkled green peppers in front, and the rest of the space taken with rows of cans and boxes, a surprising number of them red, clamoring for the shoppers' notice and failing in their sameness. The shelves climbed high. There were packages of Bisquick, curry, and Garam Masala that the woman in the Benares Cafe wouldn't have been able to reach. In the back was a cooler for milk and cheese, and behind the counter by the door, the one-man bottles of vodka and bourbon—and a small, dark man, presumably Khan.

"I'm Detective Smith," I said, extending my shield. "You called us about the accident?"

"Yes," he said. "I am Farib Khan. I am owning this store. This is why I cannot leave to come to you, you see." He gestured at the empty premises.

I nodded. "But you saw the accident?"

"Yes, yes." He wagged his head side to side in that disconcerting Indian indication of the affirmative. "Mr. Latham—"

"You know him?"

"He is being my customer for a year now. Six days a week."

"Monday through Saturday?"

"Yes, yes. He is stopping on his drive from San Francisco."

"Does he work on Saturdays?" It wasn't the schedule I would have expected of a well-off architect.

"He teaches a class. After his class, he is eating lunch and driving home, you see. And stopping here."

I thought of Graham Latham in his expensive suit, driving his Mercedes. I recalled why he had hit a woman four years ago. It wasn't for curry powder that Graham Latham would be patronizing this ill-stocked store. "Did he buy liquor every day?"

"Yes, yes." Turning behind him, he took a pint bottle of vodka from the shelf. "He is buying this."

So Graham Latham hadn't changed. I didn't know why I would have assumed otherwise. "Did he open it before he left?"

"He is not a bum, not like those who come here not to buy, but to watch, to steal. Mr. Latham is a gentleman. For him, I am putting the bottle in a bag, to take home."

"Then you watched him leave? You saw the accident?"

Again the wagging of his head. "I am seeing, but it is no accident. Mr. Latham, he walks across the street, toward his big car. He is not a healthy man." Khan glanced significantly at the bottle. "So I watch. I am fearing the fall in the street, yes? But he walks straight. Then a car turns the corner, comes at him. Mr. Latham jumps back. He is fast then, you see. The car turns, comes at him. He cannot escape. He is hit. The car speeds off."

"You mean the driver was trying to hit Latham?"

"Yes, yes."

Involuntarily I glanced back to the street. Latham's body was gone now. The witnesses, John Eskin and the C.P.R. man, were standing with Pereira. A back-up unit had arrived. One of the men was checking the brown Mercedes.

Turning back to Khan, I said, "What did the car look like?"

He shrugged. "Old, middle-sized."

"Can you be more specific?"

He half-closed his eyes, trying. Finally, he said, "The

day is gray, raining. The car is not new, not one I see in the ads. It is light-colored. Gray? Blue?"

"What about the driver?"

Again, he shrugged.

"Man or woman?"

It was a moment before he said, "All I am seeing is red—a sweater? Yes? A jacket?"

It took only a few more questions to discover that I had learned everything Farib Khan knew. By the time I crossed the street to the scene, Pereira had finished with the witnesses, and one of the back-up men was questioning the couple leaning in the doorway. The witnesses had seen nothing. John Eskins had been in the back of the store at the moment Latham had been hit, and the woman in the Benares Cafe—Pomilla Patel—hadn't seen anything until she heard the car hit him. And the man who stopped to give C.P.R.—Randall Sellinek—hadn't even seen the vehicle drive off. Or so they said.

They stood, a little apart from each other, as if each found the remaining two unsuitable company. Certainly they were three who would never come together in any other circumstances. John Eskins clutched his brown bag, jerking his eyes warily. Pomilla Patel glanced at him in disgust, as if he alone were responsible for the decay of the neighborhood. And Randall Sellinek just stood, letting the cold rain fall on his shirt and run down his bare arms.

I took Pereira aside and relayed what Khan had told me.

She grabbed one back-up man, telling him to call in for more help. "If it's a possible homicide we'll have to scour the area. We'll need to question everyone on this block and the ones on either side. We'll need someone to check the cars and the garbage. Get as many men as you can."

He raised an eyebrow. We all knew how many that would be.

To me, Pereira said, "You want to take Eskins or Sellinek down to the station for statements?"

I hesitated. "No . . . Suppose we let them leave and keep an eye on them. We have the manpower."

"Are you serious, Jill? It's hardly regulations."

"I'll take responsibility."

Still, she looked uncomfortable. But she'd assisted on too many of my cases over the years to doubt me completely. "Well, okay. It's on your head." She moved toward the witnesses. "That's all, folks. Thanks for your cooperation."

Eskins seemed stunned, but not about to question his good fortune. He moved west, walking quickly, but unsteadily, toward the seedy dwellings near the bay. I shook my head. Pereira nodded to one of the back-up men, and he turned to follow Eskins.

Sellinek gave a final look at the scene of his futile effort and began walking east, toward San Pablo Avenue and the better neighborhoods beyond. He didn't seem surprised, like Eskins, but then he hadn't had the same type of contact with us. I watched him cross the street, then followed. The blocks were short. He came to San Pablo Avenue, waited for the light, then crossed. I had to run to make the light.

On the far side of University Avenue the traffic was picking up. Horns were beeping. The football game was over. The first of the revelers had made it this far. I glanced back the several blocks to the scene, wondering if the hooker had decided to wait us out. But I was too far away to tell.

Sellinek crossed another street, then another. The rain beat down on his white shirt. His blond hair clung to his head. He walked on, never turning to look back.

I let him go five blocks, just to be sure, then caught up with him. "Mr. Sellinek. You remember me, one of the police officers. I'll need to ask you a few more questions."

"Me? Listen, I just stopped to help that man. I didn't want him to die. I wanted him to live."

"I believe you. You knocked yourself out trying to save him. But that still leaves the question of why? Why were you in this neighborhood at all?"

"Just passing through."

"On foot?"

"Yeah, on foot."

"In the rain, wearing just a shirt?"

"So?"

"Tell me again why you decided to give him C.P.R."

"I saw the car hit him. It was new and silver. It had

a big, shiny grill. Why are you standing here badgering me? Why aren't you out looking for that car?"

"Because it doesn't exist."

"I *saw* it."

"When?"

"When it hit him."

"But you didn't notice passengers. You couldn't describe the driver."

"The car was too far away. I was back at the corner, behind it. I told you that."

"You didn't look at it when it passed you?"

"No. I was caught up in my own thoughts. I wasn't going to cross the street. There was no reason to look at the traffic. Then the car hit him. He was dying when I got to him—I couldn't let him die."

"I believe that. You didn't intend for him to have something as easy as death."

"What?"

"There wasn't any silver car or shiny grill, Mr. Sellinek." He started to protest, but I held up a hand. "You said you were behind the car and didn't notice it until it hit Latham. You couldn't possibly have seen what kind of grill it had. *You're* the one who ran Latham down."

He didn't say anything. He just stood, letting the rain drip down his face.

"We'll check the area," I said. "We'll find the car you used—maybe not your own car, maybe hot-wired, but there'll be prints. You couldn't have had time to clean them all off. We'll find your red sweater too. When you planned to run Latham down, you never thought you'd have to stop and try to save his life, did you? And once you realized you had to go back to him, you took the sweater off because you were afraid someone might have seen it. Isn't that the way it happened, Mr. Sellinek?"

He still didn't say anything.

I looked at the tattoo on his arm. All of it was visible now—the full name above the heart. It said, "Kay."

"You were Kay Hillman's boyfriend, weren't you? That's why you ran Latham down—because she died last week and you wanted revenge."

His whole body began to shake. "Latham was drunk when he hit Kay. But he got a smart lawyer, he lied in court, he got off with a suspended sentence. What he did to Kay . . . it was just an inconvenience to him. It didn't even change his habits. He still drank when he was driving. He still stopped six days a week at the same store to pick up liquor. Sooner or later he would have run down someone else. It was just a matter of time.

"I wanted revenge, sure. But it wasn't because Kay died. It was for those four years she *lived* after he hit her. She couldn't sit without pain; she couldn't lie down. The pills didn't help. Nothing did. The pain just got worse, month after month." He closed his eyes, squeezing back tears. "I didn't want Latham to die. I wanted him to suffer like Kay did."

Now it was my turn not to say anything.

Sellinek swallowed heavily. "It's not fair," he said. "None of it is fair."

He was right. None of it was fair at all.

SEE NO EVIL
Barb D'Amato

FIRST APPEARANCE: *Hardball*, 1990

Cat Marsala is the protagonist of six novels, the titles of which all begin with the word "Hard." She has appeared in *Hardball*, *Hard Tack*, *Hard Luck*, *Hard Women*, *Hard Case*, and the most recent, *Hard Christmas*.

This, her first short story appearance, was published in *I, P.I.*, 1996.

"**I** hate mysteries. This kind anyway," Harold McCoo said. He pushed his swivel chair around to hand me my cup of coffee.

"Mysterious coffee?"

"Oh, hell, no. It's Sulawesi Kalosi. Aromatic with a gently woody undertone. Javanese type."

"What, then?"

McCoo is Chief of Detectives, Department of Police, City of Chicago. He didn't get to that position by wasting a lot of time. He shoved a large pile of paper toward me. "I want a favor, Cat."

"Anything for you."

"An investigation. And we're going to cut you loose some money for it, too."

"You don't have to—"

"Yeah, I do. I want you official. You're gonna need to see confidential documents. So confidential even the subject, Officer Bennis, isn't allowed to see them."

"Documents about what?"

He sipped his coffee. McCoo makes very good coffee. "You know, Cat, people don't change. We've got lemons in the department, Piltdown men, but they show up pretty soon. You take an officer like Bennis, eleven years on the job, not one problem. He was in Six for eight years. His commander there has nothing but praise for him. He's been in One for three years now, and even though Commander Coumadin's an idiot, he admits Bennis has been professional, no whiff of brutality. He's been a street officer all that time, not a desk man. He's not going to suddenly up and *execute* somebody."

"I suppose not. I take it somebody thinks he did. Was there some sort of danger—"

"He thought the guy had killed his partner."

"That's a reason."

"Not much of one. Somebody who's been on the street eleven years—he's been in tight places before, and he's had threats against his partner before, and a zillion times he's been scared. It's that kind of job."

"Okay. That makes sense."

"But they're going to destroy him. The Office of Professional Standards is gonna make an example of him. When the complaint is sustained, they'll suspend him. And there's rumor they're thinking criminal prosecution."

There had been a lot of talk in the Chicago media that OPS didn't often sustain brutality complaints. The process for investigating complaints, they said, was a washing machine: it went in dirty and came out clean. There was some truth to that, too, but much more in the past than now.

"And this Bennis—"

"Isn't the kind to do something like this. But it looks like he did. And the OPS investigator, Hulce, is out to get him. The hell of it is, his story has holes."

"Bennis is a patrol officer? You're Chief of Detectives. Why is it your problem?"

"The detectives do the initial investigation."

"And?"

"Ah, I know the kid slightly."

"Oh, really?" I said, skeptically.

"I knew his mother, once upon a time. What we need, Cat, is a fresh eye on it."

"I don't do whitewashes."

"Hey, I'm not asking for a spin doctor. There's something wrong someplace and a good guy is gonna suffer. I don't have the time to deal with it, and everybody here is either strongly pro or strongly con, both of which I don't want. I want you to look at the papers without me

giving you any predigested ideas. Here." He patted the
stack of paper. "You figure it out."

"Oh, well. If you've got the money, honey, I've got
the time."

The Furlough bar was never going to be a photo opportunity for *Architectural Digest.* There were no ferns,
no hanging plants, nothing green and growing in the
whole place, unless there was something alive under the
slatted floor at the beer taps that nobody knew about.
The front window hadn't been washed since Eisenhower
was president and was now a uniform, suede-finish gray,
about the texture of peach skin. Thirty years earlier
Royal Crown Cola had given out signs for doors with
little slots where the proprietor could insert the times
the place was open. The Furlough's hadn't been replaced
since it was first attached; several numbers had fallen
sideways and some had fallen off, so the sign now read
that the bar was open Thursday from :00 to .

The Furlough was owned by two retired cops and was
diagonally across the street from the Chicago Police Department's central headquarters at Eleventh and State.
I was supposed to meet my people there at 3:30 P.M.
They would have just got off an eight-hour tour.

When I walked in, I could feel emotion in the air. It
wasn't me, wasn't because a female had walked in. There
were a couple of women cops in the bar already. The
tension was there before I arrived. I could see it in the
spacing of the people around the bar. My two cops,
whose pictures I had seen in the Chief of Detective's
office, were sitting alone at the far end of the zinc bar.
One was Officer Susanna Maria Figueroa, a short, young
white woman. Sitting next to her was her partner Norm
Bennis, a stocky black man of about thirty-five, ten years
older than Figueroa. His head was down between his
shoulders. Then there was a gap of four stools, followed
by two white men, one tall and one pudgy with a shiny
pink face, a black woman whose elbow leaned on the
bar and whose hand cupped her chin, and another, older
white man next to her.

The bunch of four were carefully not looking at Figueroa and her partner.

I walked over to her. In these situations, I make as

much effort as possible to look like a fellow cop. I'm not; ordinarily I make my living as a reporter. Generally speaking, cops don't love reporters.

I said, "Hi, I'm Cat Marsala."

They looked at me with a total lack of enthusiasm, the way you might look at a parking ticket on your windshield.

But they had orders from the Chief of Detectives. Figueroa said, "I'm Suze Figueroa. This is my partner, Norm Bennis."

He extended his hand. If Figueroa looked glum, Bennis was sunk in an abyss of gloom. But his face had laugh lines. Which currently were not being used.

I shook his hand.

"Let's go over there," Figueroa said. There were three tables in the place. Their tops were about as big as lids from Crisco cans. If all three of us wanted to put our elbows on the table, there wouldn't be room.

"What's the matter with these other guys?" I mumbled to Figueroa, cutting my eyes toward the five at the bar. "They mad at you for something?"

"Trying to cheer us up," Figueroa said.

"So I yelled at 'em," Bennis said.

"Oh." I waited, but neither spoke. "All right, you two. You know why I'm here."

"Because I killed a guy," Bennis said.

He took a break then, bringing back three beers. I wanted to hear the story from them before I read the documents, but I didn't want to be jacked around, either. I said, "Talk!"

Bennis shrugged. "I don't see what you can do about it."

"Humor me."

He said, "Okay, okay. We're on second watch. It's about two in the afternoon, Saturday, we're in the car we usually get and we're maybe an hour, hour and a half, to the end of the tour. There's an in-progress call. Citizen calls 911, describes it as a rape and he's right. 1-31 responds. The woman is cut and she's yelling to the car that the asshole has a knife. A second unit, 1-36, responds and when they get in sight of the woman, the jerk takes off. 1-31 follows him to an apartment building. We hear the radio traffic and get over to the building.

Mileski and Quail in 1-31 have separated. Quail to the back door and Mileski to the front. They've got the place buttoned up, so Suze and I run into the hall. Far as we know the asshole's raping somebody else. There's an apartment door open, and a woman yelling."

"She was saying 'You idiot!' in Spanish," Figueroa said.

"So we go in. Long, dark hall. In the apartment, the shades are pulled most of the way down, because the woman who lives there is watching soap operas.

"We run in, and the guy's standing in the living room—name's Zeets—and the TV light is glinting off the knife and he says he's gonna kill us. Figueroa draws on him and screams 'Drop the knife!' about yea zillion times. So do I. Finally the asshole throws the knife on a chair. I've got my service revolver out by now and I hold it on him while Figueroa starts to cuff him, except I can't see hardly at all because the light from the windows, what there is of it, is behind them.

"Then, like in a split second, he whips around with one cuff on and grabs Figueroa's gun and they lurch back away from me. They're wrestling for the gun. I know it, but I'm supposed to stay back and take aim, which I do, but I can't see much. It's too dark. They're wrestling back and forth and then there's a shot. I figure Figueroa's been shot.

"I can't see who's got the gun, and they're still struggling, but I can see the guy's outline and I fire at him." He stopped a second and looked at me doubtfully. "You know that if we fire at all, we're supposed to try to kill him? I mean no winging him in the hand, that cowboy kind of stuff."

"I know."

"I fire six times. He drops." Bennis ducked his head. "Basically, he's dead."

"So. I don't see what's wrong."

"His mother and two sisters were in the apartment. They're saying I didn't need to shoot him. They're saying it was obvious that Figueroa had the gun. All three of 'em."

"Oh."

"I'm gonna be suspended or fired. Probably fired. And they're talking about prosecution for manslaughter."

"I understand. That's scary."

"No you don't."

I never like it when people say I don't understand something. Personally, I think I'm pretty sympathetic. But Bennis was so upset, I forgave him. "So tell me."

"It's not the manslaughter thing. I love this job."

His voice was filled with frustration and anger. Bennis and Figueroa seemed to have relaxed their initial distrust of me somewhat. I asked Figueroa, "Is that what happened? What Bennis says?"

"Yeah. Zeets and I both had hold of the gun when it went off. Thank God it was pointed up. Went into the ceiling."

"So you back up Bennis?"

"Totally." She punched Bennis's shoulder lightly. "This is a good man." For just a second real affection came over her face. "All he wanted to do was save my life."

The mutual trust in their relationship was obvious. Out in the street, alone, in danger, in the dark—sure, two cops had to trust each other. It was horrible when an officer was paired with somebody he couldn't rely on. In this case, clearly, they leaned on each other every time they hit the streets and neither had let the other down.

Rising, I said, "All right. I'll be getting back to you."

As we moved to the door, the pink-faced officer at the bar said, "Hey! You gonna help Bennis?"

"I hope I—"

The woman officer said, "They're gonna railroad our buddy."

Another cop said, "OPS ain't any better than civilians."

"Yeah, your basic citizen'll turn on you in two seconds flat!"

"They see a mugger you're their best friend."

"Hear a noise in the night—"

"Teenagers *congregatin'*—"

"Guys passin' around little bags of white stuff—"

"But you grab the mugger and next thing they're screamin' police brutality."

"I ever tell you about the time I chased these two guys down the alley off Van Buren near Plymouth Court?"

Suze said, "Yeah, Mileski, you did."

"*She* didn't hear it," he said, pointing to me.

"She doesn't want to, either."

"Three a.m. and not one breathing soul around. Responded to an alarm at a jewelry store. Two guys they're sharing about one neuron in their heads between the two of 'em, but one of 'em had a sawed-off shotgun."

"Very illegal!" the woman cop said.

"Guy takes a shot at me, misses, and they both run. I'm in pursuit. My hat flies off, I'm outta breath, but I manage to hang onta my radio. Run 'em down after six blocks. The jerk with the gun falls over a gas can somebody threw out, loses the gun, I cuff him, pick up the shotgun in one hand, got my service revolver in the other—we're talking two-gun Pete here—aim 'em both at the other guy, who's too fat to climb over the fence and escape, and the guy gets so scared he starts to cry."

He stopped and looked at me. "Well, great!" I said, wondering what he was getting at.

"Brought 'em both in. Single-handed. Know what happened to me? No department commendation. No nothing!"

"That's too bad."

"But!" He said it again. "But! *But!* they gammee a fine for losing my cap!"

"Oh."

"That's nice, Mileski," Bennis said. "But we're trying to have a private conversation here now."

"Oh, well, excuuuuse me."

However, there really wasn't much else to say. I nodded to them and said, "I've got the papers. I'll be in touch."

I thought I'd been encouraging, but apparently the sight of me had not made Bennis think he was saved. As I went out past the ancient bar sign, he said softly to Figueroa, "It's hopeless."

Armed with nine pounds of CPD paperwork, twelve ounces of coffee, and a half-pound bar of chocolate, I settled in at home for a good read.

There were sixty pages of Xeroxed photos alone: crime scene photos, autopsy photos, and spent pellet photos. Typed statements from the mother and both sisters, headed OFFICE OF PROFESSIONAL STANDARDS, the interviewer being the OPS investigator C. Hulce. A transcript of the radio activity that afternoon. Typed statements from Figueroa and Bennis, also interviewed by C. Hulce. Interviews with Mileski and Quail. An interview with the rape victim whose case had started all this off. A plat of the apartment, with the position of the body. Another plat of the apartment with the position of the officers at the time of the shooting. Copies of the hospital reports, labeled Emergency Room Outpatient Report—Figueroa had been cut on the jaw during the scuffle by the barrel of her own gun. Releases allowing the hospital to give the reports to the OPS. Consent forms. A dozen Shooting Investigation Reports. Disciplinary Action forms. A fifty-page document called "Summary to the Commanding Officer." Something called a Weapon Discharge Report. Evidence lists. Diagrams showing the position of the wounds on the body. Autopsy protocol from the pathologist, addressed "Cook County Institute of Forensic Medicine." Inventory of the officer's weapons. Ballistics tests. One sheet from ballistics stated that the bullet reclaimed from the ceiling matched Figueroa's gun. A Waiver of Counsel / Request to Secure Counsel. Both Bennis and Figueroa, who was not charged but was questioned, requested counsel. And about a hundred one-page things headed "Supplementary Report."

An army may travel on its stomach, but a police department travels on its paperwork.

One printed sheet advised the officer of his or her rights. While they could have counsel, as far as the department was concerned, that was about all they got. They had no right to remain silent. If they remained silent, they would be "ordered by a superior officer to answer the question." If they persisted in refusing to answer, they were advised that "such refusal constitutes a violation of the Rules and Regulations of the Chicago Police Department and will serve as a basis for which your discharge will be sought."

I suppose it is a privilege, not a right, to remain a police officer. And I suppose they need to be able to get rid of the crazies, but it certainly had Bennis pinned down so that he had to answer them. And he seemed to have made some mistakes.

There was a sheet of charges. Boiled down, he was accused of (1) discharging a firearm without justification, and (2) failing to give a true and accurate account of the incident relative to the shooting of Jorge Sanabria.

His primary accuser was the dead man's mother.

OFFICE OF PROFESSIONAL STANDARDS
26 Mar 93
CR #9956291

Statement of witness, Benicia Sanabria, relative to the incident that led to the death of Jorge (Zeets) Sanabria on 12 Mar 93 at 1400 hours.

Statement taken at 1121 S. State, Chicago IL 60607

Questioned by:	Inv. C. Hulce, Star 337, Unit 243.
Date & Time:	26 June 1993 at 1320 hours.
Witnessed by:	Inv. Clarence Summerset, Star 633, Unit 243

HULCE: What is your full name, address, and telephone number?

SANABRIA: Benicia Sanabria, 731 W. Sangin, 312/587-8997

HULCE: What is your marital status?

SANABRIA: I am a widow.

HULCE: Are you giving this statement of your own free will, without the promise of exoneration or reward of any nature being given to you?

SANABRIA: Yes.

HULCE: Do you work, and if so, give the name of the company, address, telephone number, and length of employment.

My eye skimmed down the page to:

HULCE: What is the relationship of Jorge Sanabria to you?

SANABRIA: He is my only son.

HULCE: What occurred on 12 March 1993 about 1400 hours at your home that resulted in the death of Jorge "Zeets" Sanabria?

SANABRIA: I was home. I work Sunday through Thursday. Suddenly, Jorge came running in.

HULCE: Was he carrying anything?

SANABRIA: He was. Well, yes, he was. It was a knife.

HULCE: What happened then?

SANABRIA: Then, well, then he said, "They're after me," and my daughter said—um, she called him a name and she said, "What did you do?" and he started swearing. And my daughter said something about Jorge disgracing her and then a police officer came into the front of the hall. The door, our door to the hall was still open, and the man said, "Police officer, come out!" or something like that. But he stayed in the hall and then two other police officers came in. And Jorge backed into the living room.

HULCE: Describe them, please.

SANABRIA: One was a woman. She was short and dark haired and I think she was possibly a countrywoman. The other was a black man. Taller but not tall.

HULCE: What happened then?

SANABRIA: Then they all yelled "Put the knife down!" But Jorge didn't.

HULCE: Did he say anything to the officers?

SANABRIA: He said words I will not repeat. But that's no reason to shoot him dead.

HULCE: Then what happened?

SANABRIA: They said to get back, so I am standing in the doorway to the living room. I can see in at an angle, so I do not see the man well, but the woman and Jorge. Jorge threw the knife on the chair. The woman put one handcuff on Jorge. Then he threw her back and grabbed her gun. And they struggled for the gun. He should not have done this, but that's no reason to shoot him dead.

HULCE: Then what happened?

SANABRIA: The gun went off. The woman had pointed it at the ceiling, and then Jorge lost hold of it. Then the man shot him dead.

HULCE: After the woman officer had regained possession of the gun?

SANABRIA: Yes, after. And I shouted, "Stop, you are killing him." But he did not stop.

HULCE: Was it bright enough to see?

SANABRIA: Oh, yes. Very bright enough. The shades were pulled down, but not all the way. And, the television was on. It gives light. Off and on. Depending on—how do I say this?—whether the behind part of the picture—I know, the background—whether it is bright. You could see just fine.

HULCE: After reading this statement and finding it to be what you said, will you sign it?

SANABRIA: Yes.

Both Sanabria sisters confirmed what their mother said. The younger girl, however, had been in the kitchen throughout the event, and could only report what she heard. Both girls were well-spoken and specific, although the older one had some angry comments about the police.

Then there was Bennis's side:

OFFICE OF PROFESSIONAL STANDARDS
26 June 1993
Statement of accused, Officer Norman Bennis, star 31992, Unit 001, relative to allegations that on 12 March 1993 at approximately 1400 hours, inside a first floor apartment at 731 W. Sangin he discharged his firearm without justification, resulting in the death of Jorge Sanabria. It is further alleged that he failed to

give a true and accurate account of the incident rela-
tive to the shooting of Jorge Sanabria.
Statement being taken at the Office of Professional
Standards, 1024 S. Wabash, Chicago IL 60605.

Questioned and typed by: Inv. C. Hulce, Star 337,
                             Unit 243.
Date & Time: 24 June 1993 at 1335 hours.
Witnessed by: Attorney Frederick Melman FOP
                   1300 E. Chicago Ave. Chicago IL 60611
                   Inv. Clarence Summerset, Star 633, Unit
                   243

Bennis prefaced his remarks with the formula the FOP
counsel would have given him. And both he and C.
Hulce seemed to have fallen victim to creeping
officialese.

BENNIS: I want to say that I am not giving this statement
voluntarily, but under duress. I am giving this statement because I have been advised by the Police Department regulations that if I do not I will be fired from my job.

HULCE: What led you to the incident leading to the death
of Jorge Sanabria?

HULCE: Relate what happened on 12 March 93 at 1400
hours in the apartment at 731 W. Sangin that resulted
in the death of Jorge "Zeets" Sanabria.

BENNIS: I ran in past Officer Mileski, who was guarding
the front door so as Zeets wouldn't escape. My partner
Officer Figueroa was ahead of me. A woman was in the
doorway of the apartment screaming at Zeets. He was
brandishing a weapon, a knife with a six-inch blade. I
said drop the knife. He backed into a dark room and
Figueroa and I followed. We had our guns drawn. Figueroa said drop the knife. The room was very dark. After
being cautioned many times, he threw the knife onto a
yellow and pink flowered chair. Figueroa began to cuff
him. Then he suddenly threw her off and he jumped her
and they were struggling. Her gun went off. I could not
see well because of the lack of light, but when I saw a
silhouette which I knew to be Zeets and not my partner,

I fired. Fearing for my life and for the life of my partner, I discharged my weapon six times.

HULCE: Then what happened?

BENNIS: Then the woman I now know to be Mrs. Sanabria ran in and she said you've killed my son, and the woman I now know to be Anne Sanabria started to hit me . . .

That was about it. I flipped pages until I found Suze Figueroa's statement. It was almost exactly like Bennis's. Not so much alike that I thought they had rehearsed all their answers with each other, but they certainly had talked it over. Still—that was natural, under the circumstances. Figueroa's statement added one detail. She said that at the instant when her gun went off, she and Zeets each had one hand on it, because Zeets had pulled her other hand away, and it was Zeets pulling the trigger that actually caused the discharge. Then his hand came off the gun. But she was not certain that Zeets's hand could be seen because of the darkness.

A sheet headed FINAL INCIDENT REPORT / RECOMMENDATION OF INVESTIGATOR, written by C. Hulce, OPS investigator, concluded that Bennis did not have to shoot, that the incident was over and Figueroa had regained control of her gun before Bennis started firing, that he could see well enough to know that the danger was past, since he had been able to describe the pink and yellow flowered chair. The light level had been confirmed by the Sanabrias, Hulce added, and Bennis, therefore, had not only fired without justification, but had lied in telling the investigators that he could not see. "Since Officer Bennis was able to describe the chair both in pattern and color, it is unreasonable to claim that he could not see the victim and the other officer."

Hulce believed that Figueroa had also lied in saying Bennis couldn't see Zeets's hand was off the gun, but they apparently weren't pushing a charge against her.

Unspoken was Bennis's motive. That he had been enraged at the attack on Figueroa—which certainly was life-threatening for a few seconds—and had killed Zeets intentionally.

An idea of what had really happened was taking shape

in my head. Looking through the hefty pile of documents, I finally found the transcript of the radio traffic. I read it three times. It confirmed my theory. What I needed now was to hear the actual radio transmission, live, as it happened that day. No problem. McCoo could set that up. If I called him first thing in the morning, we'd probably be able to hear it in the afternoon.

I met Figueroa and Bennis in the anteroom on the fifth floor. The windows looked over Chicago to the west. Somewhere out there a dusky feather of smoke rose from a fire. Bennis's arms hung drearily at his sides and his eyes were half closed. He flopped into a plastic chair.

"What do you know about the Sanabrias?" I asked them. "Can you claim they aren't reliable witnesses? They certainly have reason to be biased."

Suze looked at Norm. "They—yes, I suppose. Zeets, you know, had been dealing drugs for years."

I said, "I hear some hesitation in your voice."

"Well, it's the old story. The wild son, two hardworking daughters. Zeets has a long sheet for attacking women. And a couple of drug busts. The mother is a good person. Very nice. She works washing and packaging vegetables in a supermarket. The older daughter is a stockbroker. The younger daughter's still in high school. She's an honor student—"

"And?"

"I don't feel very comfortable characterizing them as petty crooks who'd swear to anything."

I watched Norm as he rose suddenly and went to stand next to the window. The shade fabric was yellow and cast a mustard glow on his face. I said to her again, "And?"

"And these are—jeez, these are my people. In some sense, I'm not very comfortable with the, you know, putting the image on them. The image of the sleazy Hispanic."

Norm said, "Shit!"

Then we got word to go into the hearing room.

Investigator C. Hulce, Office of Professional Standards, turned out to be Corinne Hulce. She was a short woman with a heavy upper body and a hungry mouth—

a jackal of a woman. McCoo sat next to her, wearing his indulgent face. Also in McCoo's office were Commander Coumadin, Bennis's commander in the First District, and Melman, the attorney retained for Bennis by the Fraternal Order of Police.

We went through the introductions in a spirit of great caution on everybody's part.

Then Coumadin said, "Play the tape. That's what we're here for."

I had read the transcription, but hearing it was very different. Even though it was only voices, all the urgency was there. I could imagine the tension in the Communications Room, as well as on the street, as the incident developed.

The dispatcher said, "One thirty-one," which meant beat car thirty-one in the First District.

Officer Quail said, "Thirty-one."

"I have a woman screaming for help at 110 West Adams."

"Ten-four," he said, acknowledging the call and also by code that he was in a two-man car.

"Thirty-three," said the voice of a woman officer.

"Go ahead one thirty-three."

"That alarm you gave me? The manager says it's gone off four times this week. Plus, there was a runner there. The call you had said no runner."

"Thanks, thirty-three. We'll get onto it." It was important for alarm companies to tell the police when they were sending runners. Otherwise, a cop coming on the call could think the runner was the burglar. "While you're there, thirty-three, we have three teenagers beating up a man at Halsted and Jackson. Citizen called it in."

"Ten-ninety-nine, squad."

"I didn't know you were a ninety=nine unit," the dispatcher said. Ninety-nine meant a one-man car. "Let me know if you need backup."

"Will do."

Quail's voice said, "Thirty-one."

"Go ahead thirty-one."

"We have an attempt rape here! We need a unit to take the woman for medical attention. Subject took off westbound."

"Okay. Uh—one thirty-six?"

"Thirty-six."

"See the woman at 110 West Adams."

"Ninety-nine."

"Do you have a description, thirty-one?"

"Yeah, uh, male white Hispanic, twenty years old, black hair, light complexion, wearing black Reeboks, black shirt, Levi's." This was a description that would distinguish him from at most half the young adult males on the street.

Quail's voice said, "Squad, thirty-six is here. We're in pursuit."

"Other units, the suspect is . . ."

The dispatcher repeated the description. Half a minute passed. Some officer said, "Hezz foggl ztt!" the transmission garbled. There was a series of gasps, as if somebody was running and trying to talk at the same time, then, "—any other units he's dangerous!" then, "We got him! He's going into a building at 731 West Sangin."

The dispatcher said calmly, "Twenty-seven? You in the area? Can you back up thirty-one?"

Norm Bennis's voice said, "Ten-four. We're three blocks away, westbound on Jackson."

There was another half minute or so without any transmissions. This was the period, I knew, when Suze and Norm pulled up in front of the building on Sangin. They found that the two officers in thirty-one had split up, one to guard the back door and one in the front hall.

Bennis's voice again: "One twenty-seven."

"Go ahead, twenty-seven."

"Thirty-one has the suspect isolated in a first floor apartment. He's supposed to have a knife."

At the same time, the dispatcher was saying, "Anybody in the vicinity?"

"Twenty-nine. I'm at Monroe and Michigan. I'll roll on over."

There was a short period of silence. Then Bennis said, "Twenty-seven."

"Twenty-seven, go."

"We probably got enough units. They have him bottled up at 731 Sangin, and we're going in, squad. One of the neighbors says he ran in carrying a knife and screaming."

"Twenty-seven's giving a slowdown," the dispatcher said, conscious that every unit in the area would be wanting to give chase.

A few seconds of buzzing, somebody with an open key on his radio, then Suze's voice:

"We have the suspect in an apartment at—hey!"

A new voice screamed, "Always after me!!!"

Suze yelled, "Drop the knife! Drop the knife!"

"Put down the knife!" It was Norm's voice.

Suze: "Put down the knife!"

"Drop it!"

"Drop it! Drop it!! Right now!"

"Yeee—"

"Down!"

"Cuff him!"

"Hands behind your back!"

"Bastards!" This was the unknown voice.

"Ten-one! Ten-one!" somebody said. It sounded like Bennis, but high-pitched. Ten-one means officer in trouble.

The dispatcher started to say, "Units in one, we need backup at 731 Sangin," but the other noises overrode. We all knew that every unit in the area would be screaming to a halt and turning toward the incident.

"Shit! Goddamn!"

Dispatcher: "All units stay off the air. One twenty-seven has an emergency."

"Hey! Back off!"

A shot. That would have been Suze's gun.

"Shit! Ahhh! Shit!"

There were two shots. Then one shot. Then two or three more, fast. Then there was a sound like metal scraping on a sidewalk, but so unnerving that I thought it was actually a human voice, screaming.

"He's hit!" somebody said.

Immediately, Bennis's voice said, "Twenty-seven. We need an ambulance here." His voice wasn't panicky, but it was tight as a guitar string.

The dispatcher said, "Fire's rolling, twenty-seven."

"Right," I said to Commander Coumadin. "That makes everything clear."

"What?" He realized this was not a commander-like answer, so he said, "In what way, Ms. Marsala?"

"Norm was right. He was telling the truth. And so was the family. They were both telling the truth. The family and your officers."

"But they disagree."

"They disagree and they're both right. They were both telling the truth."

Investigator Hulce snapped, "That's not possible."

"Suppose I show you that it is. What happens?"

"We—well, of course we'd drop the charges."

"And clean up Bennis's record?"

"Certainly," she said huffily, not believing me.

"Play the tape again."

Hulce rewound the tape after a nod from the commander. I said, "You have a synchronous tape that tells the time this was recorded, right?"

Hulce said, "Right."

"Stop and mark when I tell you." Hulce glanced at the brass, hoping they'd slap me down for giving her orders, but they didn't. The tape began to play.

The dispatcher said, "We have a woman screaming for help at—"

We listened, as three minutes passed. Then, Norm Bennis's voice said, "They have him bottled up at 731 Sangin and we're going in, squad."

I said, "Mark tape." Hulce punched a button and a different voice said, "Fourteen oh-three hours, fifteen seconds."

The drama unfolded again, unseen, with the strange, occasional sounds from radios where they key was briefly opened, like flashes of light in darkness. We heard the commands to drop the knife. We heard the shots. I said, "Now!"

"Fourteen oh-three hours, fifty-five seconds."

"Forty-two seconds!" Suze said.

I said, "Right. Forty-two seconds from the moment Bennis entered the house to the moment he fired."

Bennis said, "It seemed like five minutes."

"To you. But not in terms of the actions you described. Everything happened very, very fast."

"He's not going to get off because of *that*," Hulce barked. She added sententiously, "An officer has to be able to make split-second decisions."

"That's not what I'm talking about."

Norm Bennis was studying me and finally spoke. "Tell me." And the seriousness of Bennis's situation must have made even Hulce sympathetic for a couple of seconds, because she shut up.

"Bennis really couldn't see. It was too dark. He did the best he could. He and Figueroa had been driving around for more than six hours. They came in from outdoors. His eyes hadn't adjusted to the dimness in the apartment. Mrs. Sanabria and the daughters had been inside all day. To them it was bright enough. Have you ever walked into a dark restaurant from outdoors? You can't see, and you bump into things, but everybody inside is zipping around carrying trays and pouring drinks and doing fine."

"But he told us the exact color of the chair!" Coumadin said.

I made my voice as patient as I could. It wouldn't do Bennis and Figueroa any good to tell the guy he was an idiot. "By the time they were calling for ambulances, Commander, his eyes had adjusted to the dark."

Hulce was fuming. And why not? She wouldn't look good as a result of this; she should have figured it out herself. I fixed her with my beadiest-eyed look. She should have thought it out thoroughly before putting Norm through hell. While looking at her, I spoke to the FOP counsel, Melman.

"Ask an eye doctor. You'll get some figures about just how long it takes a thirty-five-year-old human eye to adapt under those circumstances."

He nodded, then smiled and nodded again more briskly.

In the stretching silence, Bennis jumped up, came over with all the laugh lines on his face laughing, pulled me up out of the chair, and kissed me on the forehead.

"Unprofessional behavior!" Suze Figueroa said. "Give that man thirty days!"

DEBORAH'S JUDGMENT
Margaret Maron
FIRST APPEARANCE: *This story*

Margaret Maron has two series characters, Lt. Sigrid Harald, and Judge Deborah Knott. Deborah's first appearance in a novel, *The Bootlegger's Daughter,* was awarded the MWA Edgar for Best Novel of 1992. This first Deborah story appeared in Sara Paretsky's wonderful 1991 *Eye of a Woman* anthology.

Her most recent novel is *Killer Market* (Mysterious Press, 1997).

"And Deborah judged Israel at that time."
An inaudible ripple of cognizance swept through the congregation as the pastor of Bethel Baptist Church paused in his reading of the text and beamed down at us.

I was seated on the aisle near the front of the church, and when Barry Blackman's eyes met mine, I put a modest smile on my face, then tilted my head in ladylike acknowledgment of the pretty compliment he was paying me by his choice of subject for this morning's sermon. A nice man but hardly Christianity's most original preacher. I'd announced my candidacy back in December, so this wasn't the first time I'd heard that particular text, and my response had become almost automatic.

He lowered his eyes to the huge Bible and continued to read aloud, *"And she dwelt under the palm tree of Deborah, between Ramah and Bethel in Mount Ephraim; and the children of Israel came up to her for judgment.*

From your mouth to God's ear, Barry, I thought.

Eight years of courtroom experience let me listen to the sermon with an outward show of close attention while inwardly my mind jumped on and off a dozen trains of thought. I wondered, without really caring, if

126

Barry was still the terrific kisser he'd been the summer after ninth grade when we both drove tractors for my oldest brother during tobacco-barning season.

There was an S curve between the barns and the back fields where the lane dipped past a stream and cut through a stand of tulip poplars and sweetgum trees. Our timing wasn't good enough to hit every trip, but at least two or three times a day it'd work out that we passed each other there in the shady coolness, one on the way out to the field with empty drags, the other headed back to the barn with drags full of heavy green tobacco leaves.

Nobody seemed to notice that I occasionally returned to the barn more flushed beneath the bill of my baseball cap than even the August sun would merit, although I did have to endure some teasing one day when a smear of tobacco tar appeared on my pink T-shirt right over my left breast. "Looks like somebody tried to grab a handful," my sister-in-law grinned.

I muttered something about the tractor's tar-gummy steering wheel, but I changed shirts at lunchtime and for the rest of the summer I wore the darkest T-shirts in my dresser drawer.

Now Barry Blackman was a preacher man running to fat, the father of two little boys and a new baby girl, while Deborah Knott was a still-single attorney running for a seat on the court bench, a seat being vacated against his will by old Harrison Hobart, who occasionally fell asleep these days while charging his own juries.

As Barry drew parallels between Old Testament Israel and modern Colleton County, I plotted election strategy. After the service, I'd do a little schmoozing among the congregation—

Strike "schmoozing," my subconscious stipulated sternly, and I was stricken myself to realize that Lev Schuster's Yiddish phrases continued to infect my vocabulary. Here in rural North Carolina schmoozing's still called socializing, and I'd better not forget it before the primary. I pushed away errant thoughts of Lev and concentrated on lunch at Beulah's. For that matter, where *was* Beulah and why weren't she and J.C. seated there beside me?

Beulah had been my mother's dearest friend, and her

daughter-in-law, Helen, is president of the local chapter of Mothers Against Drunk Driving. They were sponsoring a meet-the-candidates reception at four o'clock in the fellowship hall of a nearby Presbyterian church, and three of the four men running for Hobart's seat would be there too. (The fourth was finishing up the community service old Hobart had imposed in lieu of a fine for driving while impaired, but he really didn't expect to win many MADD votes anyhow.)

Barry's sermon drew to an end just a hair short of equating a vote for Deborah Knott as a vote for Jesus Christ. The piano swung into the opening chords of "Just as I Am," and the congregation stood to sing all five verses. Happily, no one accepted the hymn's invitation to be saved that morning, and after a short closing prayer we were dismissed.

I'm not a member at Bethel, but I'd been a frequent visitor from the month I was born; so I got lots of hugs and howdies and promises of loyal support when the primary rolled around. I hugged and howdied right back and thanked them kindly, all the time edging toward my car.

It was starting to bother me that neither Beulah nor J.C. had come to church. Then Miss Callie Ogburn hailed me from the side door, talking sixty to the yard as she bustled across the grass.

"Beulah called me up first thing this morning and said tell you about J.C. and for you to come on anyhow. She phoned all over creation last night trying to let you know she's still expecting you to come for dinner."

That explained all those abortive clicks on my answering machine. Beulah was another of my parents' generation who wouldn't talk to a tape. I waited till Miss Callie ran out of breath, then asked her what it was Beulah wanted to tell me about J.C.

"He fell off the tractor and broke his leg yesterday, and he's not used to the crutches yet, so Beulah didn't feel like she ought to leave him this morning. You know how she spoils him."

I did. J.C. was Beulah's older brother, and he'd lived with her and her husband Sam almost from the day they were married more than forty years ago. J.C. was a born bachelor, and except for the war years when he worked as a carpenter's helper at an air base over in Goldsboro, he'd never had much ambition beyond helping Sam farm. Sam always said J.C. wasn't much of a leader but he was a damn good follower and earned every penny of his share of the crop profits.

Although I'd called them Cousin Beulah and Cousin Sam till I was old enough to drop the courtesy title, strictly speaking, only Sam Johnson was blood kin. But Beulah and my mother had been close friends since childhood, and Beulah's two children fit into the age spaces around my older brothers, which was why we'd spent so many Sundays at Bethel Baptist.

When Sam died seven or eight years ago, Sammy Junior took over, and J.C. still helped out even though he'd slowed down right much. At least, J.C. called it right much. I could only hope I'd feel like working half days on a tractor when I reached seventy-two.

Five minutes after saying good-bye to Miss Callie, I was turning off the paved road into the sandy lane that ran past the Johnson home place. The doors there were closed and none of their three cars were in the yard, but Helen's Methodist and I'd heard Beulah mention the long-winded new preacher at her daughter-in-law's church.

Helen and Sammy Junior had remodeled and painted the shabby old two-story wooden farmhouse after old Mrs. Johnson died, and it was a handsome place these days: gleaming white aluminum siding and dark blue shutters, sitting in a shady grove of hundred-year-old white oaks.

Beulah's brick house—even after forty years, everyone in the family still calls it the "new house"—was farther down the lane and couldn't be seen from the road or the home place.

My car topped the low ridge that gave both generations their privacy, then swooped down toward a sluggish creek that had been dredged out into a nice-size irrigation pond beyond the house. As newlyweds, Sam and Beulah had planted pecans on each side of the lane, and mature nut trees now met in a tall arch.

The house itself was rooted in its own grove of pecans and oaks, with underplantings of dogwoods, crepe myr-

tles, redbuds, and flowering pears. Pink and white aza-
leas lined the foundation all around. On this warm day
in late April, the place was a color illustration out of
Southern Living. I pulled up under a chinaball tree by
the back porch and tapped my horn, expecting to see
Beulah appear at the screen door with her hands full of
biscuit dough and an ample print apron protecting her
Sunday dress against flour smudges.

A smell of burning paper registered oddly as I stepped
from the car. It wasn't cool enough for a fire, and no
one on this farm would break the fourth commandment
by burning trash on the Sabbath.

There was no sign of Beulah when I crossed the wide
planks of the wooden porch and called through the
screen, but the kitchen was redolent of baking ham.
J.C.'s old hound dog crawled out from under the back
steps and wagged his tail at me hopefully. The screen
door was unhooked, and the inner door stood wide.

"Beulah?" I called again. "J.C.?"

No answer. Yet her Buick and J.C.'s Ford pickup were
both parked under the barn shelter at the rear of the
yard.

The kitchen, dining room, and den ran together in one
large L-shaped space, and when a quick glance into the
formal, seldom-used living room revealed no one there
either, I crossed to the stairs in the center hall. Through
an open door at the far end of the hall, I could see into
Donna Sue's old bedroom, now the guest room.

The covers on the guest bed had been straightened,
but the spread was folded down neatly and pillows were
piled on top of the rumpled quilt as if J.C. had rested
there after Beulah made the bed. He wouldn't be able
to use the stairs until his leg mended, so he'd probably
moved in here for the duration. A stack of *Field and
Stream* magazines and an open pack of his menthol cigarettes on the nightstand supported my hypothesis.

The house remained silent as I mounted the stairs.

"Anybody home?"

Beulah's bedroom was deserted and as immaculate as
downstairs except for the desk. She and Sam had devoted a corner of their bedroom to the paper work connected with the farm. Although Sammy Junior did most
of the farm records now on a computer over at his

house, Beulah had kept the oak desk. One of my own document binders lay on its otherwise bare top. I'd drawn up her new will less than a month ago and had brought it out to her myself in this very same binder. I lifted the cover. The holographic distribution of small personal keepsakes she had insisted on was still there, but the will itself was missing.

For the first time since I'd entered this quiet house, I felt a small chill of foreboding.

Sammy Junior's old bedroom had been turned into a sewing room, and it was as empty as the bathroom. Ditto J.C.'s. As a child I'd had the run of every room in the house except this one, so I'd never entered it alone.

From the doorway, it looked like a rerun of the others: everything vacuumed and polished and tidy; but when I stepped inside, I saw the bottom drawer of the wide mahogany dresser open. Inside were various folders secured by brown cords, bundles of tax returns, account ledgers, bank statements, and two large flat candy boxes, which I knew held old family snapshots. More papers and folders were loosely stacked on the floor beside a low footstool, as if someone had sat there to sort through the drawer and had then been interrupted before the task was finished. Beulah would never leave a clutter like that.

Thoroughly puzzled, I went back down to the kitchen. The ham had been in the oven at least a half hour too long, so I turned it off and left the door cracked. The top burners were off, but each held a pot of cooked vegetables, still quite hot. Wherever Beulah was, she hadn't been gone very long.

Year round, she and J.C. and Sam, too, when he was alive, loved to walk the land, and if they weren't expecting company, it wasn't unusual to find them out at the pond or down in the woods. But with me invited for Sunday dinner along with Sammy Junior and Helen and their three teenagers? And with J.C.'s broken leg?

Not hardly likely, as my daddy would say.

Nevertheless, I went out to my car and blew the horn long and loud.

Buster, the old hound, nuzzled my hand as I stood beside the car indecisively. And that was another thing. If J.C. were out stumping across the farm on crutches,

Buster wouldn't be hanging around the back door. He'd
be right out there with J.C.

It didn't make sense, yet if there's one thing the law
has taught me, it's that it doesn't pay to formulate a
theory without all the facts. I headed back inside to
phone and see if Helen and Sammy Junior were home
yet, and as I lifted the receiver from the kitchen wall, I
saw something I'd missed before.

At the far end of the den, beyond the high-backed
couch, the fireplace screen had been moved to one side
of the hearth, and there were scraps of charred paper in
the grate.

I remembered the smell of burning paper that had
hung in the air when I first arrived. I started toward the
fireplace, and now I could see the coffee table strewn
with the Sunday edition of the Raleigh *News and
Observer.*

As I rounded the high couch, I nearly tripped on a
pair of crutches, but they barely registered, so startled
was I by seeing J.C. lying there motionless, his eyes
closed.

"Glory, J.C.!" I exclaimed. "You asleep? That must
be some painkiller the doctor—"

I suddenly realized that the brightly colored sheet of
Sunday comics over his chest was drenched in his own
bright blood.

I knelt beside the old man and clutched his callused,
workworn hand. It was still warm. His faded blue eyes
opened, rolled back in his head, then focused on me.

"Deb'rah?" His voice was faint and came from far,
far away. "I swear I plumb forgot . . ."

He gave a long sigh and his eyes closed again.

Dwight Bryant is detective chief of the Colleton
County Sheriff's Department. After calling the nearest
rescue squad, I'd dialed his mother's phone number on
the off chance that he'd be there in the neighborhood
and not twenty-two miles away at Dobbs, the county
seat.

Four minutes flat after I hung up the phone, I saw his
Chevy pickup zoom over the crest of the lane and tear
through the arch of pecan trees. He was followed by a
bright purple TR, and even in this ghastly situation, I

had to smile at his exasperation as Miss Emily Bryant bounded from the car and hurried up the steps ahead of him.

"Damn it all, Mother, if you set the first foot inside that house, I'm gonna arrest you, and I mean it!"

She turned on him, a feisty little carrot-top Chihuahua facing down a sandy-brown Saint Bernard. "If you think I'm going to stay out here when one of my oldest and dearest friends may be lying in there—"

"She's not, Miss Emily," I said tremulously. J.C.'s blood was under my fingernails from where I'd stanched his chest wound. "I promise you. I looked in every room."

"And under all the beds and in every closet?" She stamped her small foot imperiously on the porch floor. "I won't touch a thing, Dwight, but I've got to look."

"No." That was the law talking, not her son; and she huffed but quit arguing.

"Okay, Deborah," said Dwight, holding the screen door open for me. "Show me."

Forty-five minutes later we knew no more than before. The rescue squad had arrived and departed again with J.C., who was still unconscious and barely clinging to life.

Sammy Junior and Helen were nearly frantic over Beulah's disappearance and were torn between following the ambulance and staying put till there was word of her. Eventually they thought to call Donna Sue, who said she'd meet the ambulance at the hospital and stay with J.C. till they heard more.

A general APB had been issued for Beulah, but since nobody knew how she left, there wasn't much besides her physical appearance to put on the wire.

Dwight's deputies processed the den and J.C.'s room like a crime scene. After they finished, Dwight and I walked through the house with Sammy Junior and Helen; but they, too, saw nothing out of the ordinary except for the papers strewn in front of J.C.'s bedroom dresser.

Sammy Junior's impression was the same as mine. "It's like Mama was interrupted."

"Doing what?" asked Dwight.

"Probably getting Uncle J.C.'s insurance papers together for him. I said I'd take 'em over to the hospital tomorrow. In all the excitement yesterday when he broke his leg, we didn't think about 'em."

He started to leave the room, then hesitated. "Y'all find his gun?"

"Gun?" said Dwight.

Sammy Junior pointed to a pair of empty rifle brackets over the bedroom door. "That's where he keeps his .22."

Much as we'd all like to believe this is still God's country, everything peaceful and nice, most people now latch their doors at night, and they do keep loaded guns around for more than rats and snakes and wild dogs.

Helen shivered and instinctively moved closer to Sammy Junior. "The back door's always open, Dwight. I'll bet you anything some burglar or rapist caught her by surprise and forced her to go with him. And then J.C. probably rared up on the couch and they shot him like you'd swat a fly."

I turned away from the pain on Sammy Junior's face and stared through the bedroom window as Dwight said, "Been too many cars down the lane and through the yard for us to find any tread marks."

Any lawyer knows how easily the lives of good decent people can be shattered, but I'll never get used to the abruptness of it. Trouble seldom comes creeping up gently, giving a person time to prepare or get out of the way. It's always the freakish bolt of lightning out of a clear blue sky, the jerk of a steering wheel, the collapse of something rock solid only a second ago.

From the window I saw puffy white clouds floating serenely over the farm. The sun shone as brightly as ever on flowering trees and new-planted corn, warming the earth for another round of seedtime and harvest. A soft wind smoothed the field where J.C. had been disking before his accident yesterday, and in the distance the pond gleamed silver-green before a stand of willows.

My eye was snagged by what looked like a red-and-white cloth several yards into the newly disked field. Probably something Buster had pulled off the clothesline, I thought, and was suddenly aware that the others were waiting for my answer to a question I'd barely heard.

"No," I replied. "I'd have noticed another car or truck

coming out of the lane. Couldn't have missed them by
much, though, because the vegetables on the stove were
still hot. Beulah must have turned them off just before
going upstairs.''

"It's a habit with her," Sammy Junior said. He had
his arm around Helen and was kneading her shoulder
convulsively. It would probably be bruised tomorrow,
but Helen didn't seem to notice.

"Mama burned so many pots when we were kids that
she got to where she wouldn't leave the kitchen without
turning off the vegetables. She'd mean to come right
back, but then there was always something that needed
doing, and you know how Mama is."

We did. We surely did. "Whatsoever thy hand findeth
to do" must have been written with Beulah in mind.
She always reacted impulsively and couldn't pass a dusty
surface or a dirty windowpane or anything out of place
without cleaning it or taking it back to its rightful spot
in the house.

Maybe that's why that scrap of red-and-white cloth
out in the field bothered me. If I could see it, so would
Beulah. She wouldn't let it lie out there ten minutes if
she could help it, and it was with a need to restore some
of her order that I slipped away from the others.

Downstairs, the crime scene crew had finished with
the kitchen; and for lack of anything more useful to do,
Miss Emily had decided that everybody'd fare better on
a full stomach. She'd put bowls of vegetables on the
counter, sliced the ham, and set out glasses and a jug of
sweet iced tea. At this returning semblance of the ordinary, Helen and Sammy Junior's three anxious teenagers
obediently filled their plates and went outside under the
trees to eat. Their parents and Dwight weren't enthusias-
tic about food at the moment, but Miss Emily bullied
them into going through the motions. Even Dwight's
men had to stop and fix a plate.

No one noticed as I passed through the kitchen and
down the back steps, past the Johnson grandchildren,
who were feeding ham scraps to Buster and talking in
low worried tones.

The lane cut through the yard, skirted the end of the
field, then wound circuitously around the edge of the
woods and on down to the pond; but the red-and-white

rag lay on a beeline from the back door to the pond and I hesitated about stepping off the grass. My shoes were two-inch sling-back pumps, and they'd be wrecked if I walked out into the soft dirt of the newly disked field.

As I dithered, I saw that someone else had recently crossed the field on foot.

A single set of tracks.

With growing horror I remembered the red-and-white hostess aprons my aunt Zell had sewed for all her friends last Christmas.

I ran back to my car, grabbed the sneakers I keep in the trunk, and then rushed to call Dwight.

It was done strictly by the book.

Dwight's crime scene crew would later methodically photograph and measure and take pains not to disturb a single clod till every mark Beulah had left on the soft dirt was thoroughly documented; but the rest of us hurried through the turned field, paralleling the footprints from a ten-foot distance and filled with foreboding by the steady, unwavering direction those footsteps had taken.

Beulah's apron lay about two hundred feet from the edge of the yard. She must have untied the strings and just let it fall as she walked away from it.

The rifle, though, had been deliberately pitched. We could see where she stopped, the depth of her footprints where she heaved it away from her as if it were something suddenly and terribly abhorrent.

After that, there was nothing to show that she'd hesitated a single second. Her footprints went like bullets, straight down to the pond and into the silent, silver-green water.

As with most farm ponds dredged for irrigation, the bottom dropped off steeply from the edge to discourage mosquito larvae.

"How deep is it there?" Dwight asked when we arrived breathless and panting.

"Twelve feet," said Sammy Junior. "And she never learned how to swim."

His voice didn't break, but his chest was heaving, his face got red, and tears streamed from his eyes. "Why? In God's name, *why*, Dwight? Helen? Deb'rah? You all *know* Uncle J.C. near 'bout worships Mama. And we've always teased her that J.C. stood for Jesus Christ the way she's catered to him.''

It was almost dark before they found Beulah's body.

No one tolled the heavy iron bell at the home place. The old way of alerting the neighborhood to fire or death has long since been replaced by the telephone, but the reaction hasn't changed much in two hundred years.

By the time that second ambulance passed down the lane, this one on its way to the state's medical examiner in Chapel Hill, cars filled the yard and lined the ditch banks on either side of the road. And there was no place in Helen's kitchen or dining room to set another plate of food. It would have taken a full roll of tinfoil to cover all the casseroles, biscuits, pies, deviled eggs, and platters of fried chicken, sliced turkey, and roast pork that had been brought in by shocked friends and relatives.

My aunt Zell arrived, white-faced and grieving, the last of three adventuresome country girls who'd gone off to Goldsboro during World War II to work at the air base. I grew up on stories of those war years: how J.C. had been sent over by his and Beulah's parents to keep an eye on my mother, Beulah, and Aunt Zell and protect them from the dangers of a military town, how they'd tried to fix him up with a WAC from New Jersey, the Saturday night dances, the innocent flirtations with that steady stream of young airmen who passed through the Army Air Forces Technical Training School at Seymour Johnson Field on their way to the airfields of Europe.

It wasn't till I was eighteen, the summer between high school and college, the summer Mother was dying, that I learned it hadn't all been lighthearted laughter.

We'd been sorting through a box of old black-and-white snapshots that Mother was determined to date and label before she died. Among the pictures of her or Aunt Zell or Beulah perched on the wing of a bomber or jitterbugging with anonymous, interchangeable airmen, there was one of Beulah and a young man. They had their arms around each other, and there was a sweet solemnity in their faces that separated this picture from the other clowning ones.

"Who's that?" I asked, and Mother sat staring into the picture for so long that I had to ask again.

"His name was Donald," she finally replied. Then her face took on an earnest look I'd come to know that summer, the look that meant I was to be entrusted with another secret, another scrap of her personal history that she couldn't bear to take to her grave untold even though each tale began, "Now you mustn't ever repeat this, but—"

"Donald Farraday came from Norwood, Nebraska," she said. "Exactly halfway between Omaha and Lincoln on the Platte River. That's what he always said. After he shipped out, Beulah used to look at the map and lay her finger halfway between Omaha and Lincoln and make Zell and me promise that we'd come visit her."

"I thought Sam was the only one she ever dated seriously," I protested.

"Beulah was the only one *Sam* ever dated seriously," Mother said crisply. "He had his eye on her from the time she was in grade school and he and J.C. used to go hunting together. She wrote to him while he was fighting the Japs, but they weren't going steady or anything. And she'd have never married Sam if Donald hadn't died."

"Oh," I said, suddenly understanding the sad look that sometimes shadowed Beulah's eyes when only minutes before she and Mother and Aunt Zell might have been giggling over some Goldsboro memory.

Donald Farraday was from a Nebraska wheat farm, Mother told me, on his way to fight in Europe. Beulah met him at a jitterbug contest put on by the canteen, and it'd been love at first sight. Deep and true and all-consuming. They had only sixteen days and fifteen nights together, but that was enough to know this wasn't a passing wartime romance. Their values, their dreams, everything meshed.

"And they had so much fun together. You've never seen two people laugh so much over nothing. She didn't even cry when he shipped out because she was so happy thinking about what marriage to him was going to be like after the war was over."

"How did he die?"

"We never really heard," said Mother. "She had two of the sweetest, most beautiful letters you could ever hope to read, and then nothing. That was near the end when fighting was so heavy in Italy—we knew he was in Italy though it was supposed to be secret. They weren't married so his parents would've gotten the telegram, and of course, not knowing anything about Beulah, they couldn't write her."

"So what happened?"

"The war ended. We all came home, I married your daddy, Zell married James. Sam came back from the South Pacific and with Donald dead, Beulah didn't care who she married."

"Donna Sue!" I said suddenly.

"Yes," Mother agreed. "Sue for me, Donna in memory of Donald. She doesn't know about him, though, and don't you ever tell her." Her face was sad as she looked at the photograph in her hand of the boy and girl who'd be forever young, forever in love. "Beulah won't let us mention his name, but I know she still grieves for what might have been."

After Mother was gone, I never spoke to Beulah about what I knew. The closest I ever came was my junior year at Carolina when Jeff Creech dumped me for a psych major and I moped into the kitchen where Beulah and Aunt Zell were drinking coffee. I moaned about how my heart was broken and I couldn't go on and Beulah had smiled at me, "You'll go on, sugar. A woman's body doesn't quit just because her heart breaks."

Sudden tears had misted Aunt Zell's eyes—we Stephensons can cry over telephone commercials—and Beulah abruptly left.

"She was remembering Donald Farraday, wasn't she?" I asked.

"Sue told you about him?"

"Yes."

Aunt Zell had sighed then. "I don't believe a day goes by that she doesn't remember him."

The endurance of Beulah's grief had suddenly put Jeff Creech into perspective, and I realized with a small pang that losing him probably wasn't going to blight the rest of my life.

*   *   *

As I put my arms around Aunt Zell, I thought of her loss: Mother gone, now Beulah. Only J.C. left to remember those giddy girlhood years. At least the doctors were cautiously optimistic that he'd recover from the shooting.

"Why did she do it?" I asked.

But Aunt Zell was as perplexed as the rest of us. The house was crowded with people who'd known and loved Beulah and J.C. all their lives, and few could recall a true cross word between older brother and younger sister.

"Oh, Mama'd get fussed once in a while when he'd try to keep her from doing something new," said Donna Sue.

Every wake I've ever attended, the survivors always alternate between sudden paroxysms of tears and a need to remember and retell. For all the pained bewilderment and unanswered questions that night, Beulah's wake was no different.

"Remember, Sammy, how Uncle J.C. didn't want her to buy that place at the beach?"

"He never liked change," her brother agreed. "He talked about jellyfish and sharks—"

"—and sun poisoning," Helen said with a sad smile as she refilled his glass of iced tea. "Don't forget the sun poisoning."

"Changed his tune soon enough once he got down there and the fish started biting," said a cousin as he bit into a sausage biscuit.

One of Dwight's deputies signaled me from the hallway, and I left them talking about how J.C.'d tried to stop Beulah from touring England with one of her alumnae groups last year, and how he'd fretted the whole time she was gone, afraid her plane would crash into the Atlantic or be hijacked by terrorists.

"Dwight wants you back over there," said the deputy and drove me through the gathering dark, down the lane to where Beulah's house blazed with lights.

Dwight was waiting for me in the den. They'd salvaged a few scraps from the fireplace, but the ashes had been stirred with a poker and there wasn't much left to tell what had been destroyed. Maybe a handful of papers, Dwight thought. "And this. It fell behind the grate before it fully burned."

The sheet was crumpled and charred, but enough remained to see the words *Last Will and Testament of Beulah Ogburn Johnson* and the opening paragraph about revoking all earlier wills.

"You were her lawyer," said Dwight. "Why'd she burn her will?"

"I don't know," I answered, honestly puzzled. "Unless—"

"Unless what?"

"I'll have to read my copy tomorrow, but there's really not going to be much difference between what happens if she died intestate and—" I interrupted myself, remembering. "In fact, if J.C. dies, it'll be exactly the same, Dwight. Sammy Junior and Donna Sue still split everything."

"And if he lives?"

"If this were still a valid instrument," I said, choosing my words carefully, "J.C. would have a lifetime right to this house and Beulah's share of the farm income, with everything divided equally between her two children when he died; without the will, he's not legally entitled to stay the night."

"They'd never turn him out."

I didn't respond and Dwight looked at me thoughtfully.

"But without the will, they could if they wanted to," he said slowly.

Dwight Bryant's six or eight years older than I, and he's known me all my life, yet I don't think he'd ever looked at me as carefully as he did that night in Beulah's den, in front of that couch soaked in her brother's blood. "And if he'd done something bad enough to make their mother shoot him and then go drown herself . . ."

"They could turn him out and not a single voice in the whole community would speak against it," I finished for him.

Was that what Beulah wanted? Dead or alive, she was still my client. But I wondered: when she shot J.C. and burned her will, had she been of sound mind?

By next morning, people were beginning to say no. There was no sane reason for Beulah's act, they said, so it must have been a sudden burst of insanity, and wasn't there a great-aunt on her daddy's side that'd been a little bit queer near the end?

J.C. regained consciousness, but he was no help.

"I was resting on the couch," he said, "and I never heard a thing till I woke up hurting and you were there, Deb'rah."

He was still weak, but fierce denial burned in his eyes when they told him that Beulah had shot him. "She never!"

"Her fingerprints are on your rifle," said Dwight.

"She never!" He gazed belligerently from Donna Sue to Sammy Junior. "She never. Not her own brother. Where is she? You better not've jailed her, Dwight!"

He went into shock when they told him Beulah was dead. Great sobbing cries of protest racked his torn and broken body. It was pitiful to watch. Donna Sue petted and hugged him, but the nurse had to inject a sedative to calm him, and she asked us to leave.

I was due in court anyhow, and afterwards there was a luncheon speech at the Jaycees and a pig-picking that evening to raise funds for the children's hospital. I fell into bed exhausted, but instead of sleeping, my mind began to replay everything that had happened Sunday, scene by scene. Suddenly there was a freeze-frame on the moment I discovered J.C.

Next morning I was standing beside his hospital bed before anyone else got there.

"What was it you forgot?" I asked him.

The old man stared at me blankly. "Huh?"

"When I found you, you said, 'Deborah, I swear I plumb forgot.' Forgot what, J.C.?"

His faded blue eyes shifted to the shiny get-well balloons tethered to the foot of his bed by colorful streamers.

"I don't remember saying that," he lied.

From the hospital, I drove down to the town commons and walked along the banks of our muddy river. It was another beautiful spring day, but I was harking back to Sunday morning, trying to think myself into Beulah's mind.

You're a sixty-six-year-old widow, I thought. You're cooking Sunday dinner for your children and for the daughter of your dead friend. *(She's running for judge, Sue. Did you ever imagine it?)* And there's J.C. calling from the den about his insurance papers. So you turn off the vegetables and go upstairs and look in his drawer for the policies and you find—

What do you find that sends you back downstairs with a rifle in your hands and papers to burn? Why bother to burn anything after you've shot the person who loves you best in all the world?

And why destroy a will that would have provided that person with a dignified and independent old age? Was it because the bequest had been designated "To my beloved only brother who has always looked after me," and on this beautiful Sunday morning J.C. has suddenly stopped being beloved and has instead become someone to hurt? Maybe even to kill?

Why, *why,* WHY?

I shook my head impatiently. What in God's creation could J.C. have kept in that drawer that would send Beulah over the edge?

Totally baffled, I deliberately emptied my mind and sat down on one of the stone benches and looked up into a dogwood tree in full bloom. With the sun above them, the white blossoms glowed with a paschal translucence. Mother had always loved dogwoods.

Mother. Aunt Zell. Beulah.

A spring blossoming more than forty-five years ago.

I thought of dogwoods and spring love, and into my emptied mind floated a single *what if—?*

I didn't force it. I just sat and watched while it grew from possibility to certainty, a certainty reinforced as I recalled something Mother had mentioned about shift work at the airfield.

It was such a monstrous certainty that I wanted to be dissuaded, so I went to my office and called Aunt Zell and asked her to think back to the war years.

"When you all were in Goldsboro," I said, "did you work days or nights?"

"Days, of course," she answered promptly.

The weight started to roll off my chest.

"Leastways, we three girls did," she added. "J.C. worked nights. Why?"

For a moment I thought the heaviness would smother me before I could stammer out a reason and hang up.

Sherry, my secretary, came in with some papers to sign, but I waved her away. "Bring me the phone book," I told her, "and then leave me alone unless I buzz you."

Astonishingly, it took only one call to Information to get the number I needed. He answered on the second ring and we talked for almost an hour. I told him I was a writer doing research on the old Army Air Forces technical schools.

He didn't seem to think it odd when my questions got personal.

He sounded nice.

He sounded lonely.

"You look like hell," Sherry observed when I passed through the office. "You been crying?"

"Anybody wants me, I'll be at the hospital," I said without breaking stride.

Donna Sue and Helen were sitting beside J.C.'s bed when I got there, and it took every ounce of courtroom training for me not to burst out with it. Instead I made sympathetic conversation like a perfect Southern lady, and when they broke down again about Beulah, I said, "You all need to get out in the spring sunshine for a few minutes. Go get something with ice in it and walk around the parking lot twice. I'll keep J.C. company till you get back."

J.C. closed his eyes as they left, but I let him have it with both barrels.

"You bastard!" I snarled. "You filthy bastard! I just got off the phone to Donald Farraday. He still lives in Norwood, Nebraska, J.C. Halfway between Omaha and Lincoln."

The old man groaned and clenched his eyes tighter.

"He didn't die. He wasn't even wounded. Except in the heart. By you." So much anger roiled up inside me, I was almost spitting my words at him.

"He wrote her every chance he got till it finally sank in she was never going to answer. He thought she'd changed her mind, realized that she didn't really love him. And every day Beulah must have been coming home, asking if she'd gotten any mail, and you only gave her Sam's letters, you rotten, no-good—"

"Sam was homefolks," J.C. burst out. "That other one, he'd have taken her way the hell away to Nebraska. She didn't have any business in Nebraska! Sam loved her."

"She didn't love *him*," I snapped.

"Sure, she did. Oh, it took her a bit to get over the other one, but she settled."

"Only because she thought Farraday was dead! You had no right, you sneaking, sanctimonious Pharisee! You wrecked her whole life!"

"Her life wasn't wrecked," he argued. "She had Donna Sue and Sammy Junior and the farm and—"

"If it was such a star-spangled life," I interrupted hotly, "why'd she take a gun to you the minute she knew what you'd done to her?"

The fight went out of him and he sank back into the pillow, sobbing now and holding himself where the bullet had passed through his right lung.

"Why in God's name did you keep the letters? That's what she found, wasn't it?"

Still sobbing, J.C. nodded.

"I forgot they were still there. I never opened them, and she didn't either. She said she couldn't bear to. She just put them in the grate and put a match to them and she was crying. I tried to explain about how I'd done what was best for her, and all at once she had the rifle in her hands and she said she'd never forgive me, and then I reckon she shot me."

He reached out a bony hand and grasped mine. "You won't tell anyone, will you?"

I jerked my hand away as if it'd suddenly touched filth.

"Please, Deb'rah?"

"Donald Farraday has a daughter almost the same age as Donna Sue," I said. "Know what he named her, J.C.? He named her Beulah."

Dwight Bryant was waiting when I got back from court that afternoon and he followed me into my office.

"I hear you visited J.C. twice today."

"So?" I slid off my high heels. They were wickedly

expensive and matched the power red of my linen suit. I waggled my stockinged toes at him, but he didn't smile.

"Judge not," he said sternly.

"Is that with an *N* or a *K*?" I parried.

"Sherry tells me you never give clients the original of their will."

"Never's a long time, and Sherry may not know as much about my business as she thinks she does."

"But it *was* a copy that Beulah burned, wasn't it?"

"I'm prepared to go to court and swear it was the original if I have to. It won't be necessary though. J.C. won't contest it."

Dwight stared at me a long level moment. "Why're you doing this to him?"

I matched his stare with one about twenty degrees colder. "Not me, Dwight. Beulah."

"He swears he doesn't know why she shot him, but you know, don't you?"

I shrugged.

He hauled himself to his feet, angry and frustrated. "If you do this, Deborah, J.C.'ll have to spend the rest of his life depending on Donna Sue and Sammy Junior's good will. You don't have the right. Nobody elected you judge yet."

"Yes, they did," I said, thinking of the summer I was eighteen and how Mother had told me all her secrets so that if I ever needed her eyewitness testimony I'd have it.

And Deborah was a judge in the land.

Damn straight.

NONE OF MY BUSINESS, BUT . . .
Carolyn G. Hart

FIRST APPEARANCE: *This story*

This story first appeared as part of the *Invitation to a Murder* anthology put together by Ed Gorman. Each writer in the book was presented with the same premise—the body of a young woman being discovered—and then told to go from there. Carolyn Hart went from there to two novels—*Dead Man's Island* and *Scandal in Fair Haven*— and now "Henrie O." is to be played on television by Barbara Eden. We should all get such "Invitations."

Her most recent novel is *Death in Lovers' Lane* (Bantam, 1997), an Annie Laurance book.

I listened to the heavy thumps on the stairs. They must be taking the body down. I had left the front door ajar. Not because I was curious, but simply because I knew I would have to talk to the police. At that point, I had no intention of getting involved, other than offering what information I had. As far as I was concerned, Mollie Epsley was a budding virago who would have been a fullblown bitch by age thirty. That had been easy enough to figure out in the two weeks she'd lived in the apartment next door. In my judgment, her lissome blonde beauty wasn't a mitigating factor, though it blinded most men to her defective character. Women, of course, see through that kind of female with ease. As for Calvin Bolt, he was a poor excuse for a man, willing to endure any kind of abuse so long as Mollie let him stay around. And he was an M.I.T. graduate with a thriving electronics firm! But, as we all know, business acumen isn't necessarily transferable to the bedroom. And vice versa.

So I had no personal interest in either of these creatures. I was merely prepared to cooperate as a good citizen must when peripherally involved in a case of homicide. Actually, I had only one consuming interest at the moment, and that was to meet my deadline. My fall had been about as fractured as Lavinia's leg, but what can you do when your oldest friend, both in years and events, falls down dew-slick marble library steps and ends up in a body cast and traction and desperately needs someone to complete her semester courses? If you are Henrietta O'Dwyer Collins, you arrive one midnight in a sleepy college town in the depths of Missouri and find yourself the next day explaining the 5Ws and H to several classes full of embryonic journalists who think news is the equivalent of sound bites. It was my pleasure to disabuse them of this concept. When they found out I'd covered wars, revolutions, and earthquakes, they tried to con me into regaling them with my adventures.

I am rarely connable.

I do, however, have an intensity of character which served me well during my reporting years, but which has always been a drawback otherwise. When I take on an assignment, I give it my all. Whether it requires pursuing reluctant principals, staking out a love nest, researching land titles, tracking down eyewitnesses, or—in Lavinia's case—teaching idiot-box refugees basic reporting skills, I will go to any lengths to succeed.

When I took over Lavinia's classes, I thought it would be a simple task. Suffice it to say, it was not only not simple, the challenge of eliciting decent prose from the couch potatoes became a time-consuming obsession, with the result that my editor had gone from plaintive pleas to angry rumblings, and I *had* to get the finished draft of *Istanbul Transfer* in the mail post haste.

That's why I was up and working at a quarter to midnight Monday night and heard yet another episode in the drama of Mollie and Calvin.

I had no idea at the time that it was the final episode.

Nor did they, of course.

It was the usual. Mollie had only lived next door for two weeks, but, believe me, it was the usual. Slamming doors. Shouts. Screams of fury.

There is quite a difference between screams of fear and screams of fury. Mollie Epsley worked herself into a towering state of rage several nights a week. The ob-

ject of her scorn, of course, was the hapless Calvin. Unfortunately, the walls were thin enough that I could hear
only too well the substance of every argument. Monday
night she was focusing on his lack of virility, which she
described colorfully enough to satisfy an Ambrose
Bierce fan.

I was writing at fever pitch, my CIA heroine escaping
the clutches of the evildoers via a rope ladder dangling
from the parapet of an Adriatic villa, when the entire
wall behind me trembled.

I turned and glared at it.

More thumps.

Books, probably. Glass would break, and there was
no sound of splintering.

Mollie's voice rose, gut ugly, into a vicious screech.
"If you can't get it up, then get the fuck out of here.
Do you hear me! Get out!"

Instead of telling her to go to hell, he begged, "Mollie,
don't. Please, don't." It was more than his usual whine,
it was a sob. There was another crash, and he cried out
in pain. Blinded either by tears or emotion, he must
have stumbled into a chair. Mollie erupted into derisive
laughter. "Going to claim a war wound? Better be careful or you'll fall down like an old lady. Maybe you are
an old lady!"

My eyes slitted like a cat's. I take strong exception to
derogatory comments linked to age.

The stairwell reverberated with Calvin's blind rush
down the steps.

Then it was silent, except for an occasional slam or
bang in the next apartment and Mollie's continued curs-
ing. The dear child hadn't quite got it all out of her
system yet.

I tried to concentrate on the glowing green letters on
my monitor.

My eyes felt like over easy eggs that had overed too
many hours before, and my heroine, Eileen Cameron,
dangled limply in the purple night, awaiting my inspiration. But I couldn't get past Calvin's sad plea to Eileen's
brisk resourcefulness.

"Damn."

I shoved back the chair and stalked out to the kitchen,
because the drama had yet to play out. In a little while,

Calvin would return and there would be a loud and teary rapprochement, ending up with squeaky bedsprings that played hell with my concentration. So I did some slamming and banging of my own en route to producing a cup of hot chocolate. I have always delighted in life's sensual pleasures, so I added a dollop of whipped cream and a handful of Toll House chocolate bits and determinedly closed my mind to the recent episode and concentrated on Eileen. The scene began to take shape in my mind: Instead of dropping to the ground and thereby falling into the hands of the bearded and turbaned watchman, Eileen enters the second floor bedroom window of the prime minister's mistress and—

That's when he began to scream.

I tipped over the mug of chocolate—thank God I was at the kitchen table and not at the word processor where my precious manuscript pages rested—and hurried out to the landing.

Calvin Bolt clung to the doorframe of Mollie's apartment, his face contorted in an agony of grief. He made a high whistling sound, eerily like the shriek of a tea kettle, as he struggled to draw breath into shock-emptied lungs.

I knew it was going to be bad.

It was.

I looked past him just long enough to take it all in. Mollie's once-voluptuous body arched backward over the red-and-green plaid couch, shiny blonde hair spread like an open fan. My gaze riveted just long enough on that swollen, bluish face, the eyes protruding, the tongue extended, a classic case of strangulation. I drew my breath in sharply, then turned back to Lavinia's apartment and the phone. As I made my report, Calvin blundered past my open front door and headed blindly down the stairs.

The police, in the form of a fuzz-faced patrolman, arrived within minutes and directed me to remain in Lavinia's apartment until further notice. "And don't worry, ma'am, we've got an alert out for Bolt and a guard downstairs."

"I'm not at all worried."

I didn't work, of course. Although I had no personal liking for either Mollie Epsley or Calvin Bolt, I don't like death. Especially unnecessary, premature, violent death. Nobody my age does. Surviving this long in a world fraught with perils is as much an indication of stubbornness as it is of chance.

I'd seen a lot of death over the years, starting when I was younger than Mollie. It was, in fact, during the war that I had seen victims who had died like Mollie, garroted with a thin, fine wire, the twisted ends poking out from the fleshy trench. I not only saw such victims, in the course of duty I—but that is a closed chapter and one I prefer not to recall.

I continued to consider the method of Mollie's murder. In the 1940s, in Occupied France, it was the method of choice for OSS and SOE agents when a Nazi had to be removed, quickly, quietly, efficiently. It was quite out of the ordinary in this the Year of Our Lord Nineteen Hundred and Ninety.

I drank coffee, fought off the perennial desire for a cigarette, and thought about the night's events. By the time a gentlemanly knock sounded on the apartment door, I'd reached some conclusions.

The man in the doorway wasn't fuzz-faced, but he didn't look old enough to be a police lieutenant. However, I've reluctantly begun to accept the fact that the world is now run by children, doctors who could pass for Eagle Scouts, lawyers who've never heard of Clarence Darrow, copyeditors unaware of the identity of the Former Naval Person. I have not, however, accepted the premise of these youthful upstarts that anyone over sixty is superannuated. So we got off on the wrong foot right from the start.

He gave me a reassuring nod and spoke in a deliberately gentle voice. "Mrs. Collins? Mrs. Henrietta Collins?" He had sandy hair, an unremarkable build, a polite, noncommittal face, and weary eyes.

"Yes." I don't like the cellophane-box approach, so I may have snapped it.

"Lt. Don Brown, Homicide. I know it's very late and this has been an upsetting experience, but I would appreciate it if I could talk to you for a few minutes. I'll be as brief as I can. It all seems pretty clear cut."

"Indeed?"

He heard the sharp edge in my voice and that surprised him. Those weary eyes widened, and he really looked at me. I caught a glimpse of my reflection in the hall mirror. I like to be comfortable when I work. I was barefoot and wearing baggy blue sweat pants and a faded, oversized yellow t-shirt emblazoned with the Archie Goodwin quote, "Go to hell. I'm reading." Otherwise, I looked as I had for many years, dark hair silvered at the temples, dark brown eyes that had seen much and remembered much, a Roman coin profile, and an angular body with a lean and hungry appearance of forward motion even when at rest. Lt. Brown glanced at Lavinia's living room, a recreation of Victoriana that should have been aborted, then back at me.

"I'm a guest. Come in." I led the way, gesturing for him to take the oversized easy chair, the only comfortable damn seat in the place, and I dropped gingerly onto a bony horsehair sofa.

He glanced at his notepad. "Sure. This is Mrs. Lavinia Malleson's apartment. She teaches at the college and you've taken her place for the semester. Right?"

"Yes."

"Now, Mrs. Collins, if you could tell me what happened here tonight, ma'am."

I went through it, quickly, precisely, concisely. When I reached the part about Mollie's taunts at Calvin, he wrote furiously and carefully didn't look toward me. But he was frowning as I neared the end.

"You heard Ms. Epsley—the victim—you heard her *after* somebody—you think Calvin Bolt—went downstairs. Are you sure it was her?"

"Certainly. She had a lighter step. Besides she was still swearing. Look, she started raising hell with him about a quarter to twelve. It went on for maybe ten minutes, her yelling, him whining, then he left. And she was still banging around after he went down the stairs. The usual pattern."

Brown's sandy brows knotted. "How much later was it when he found her and yelled—or acted like he found her?"

So that was his perception. My daughter, Emily, has often warned me against what she perceives as unfortunate bluntness on my part.

But facts are facts.

"Not an act, Lieutenant."

He had the gall to give me a patronizing smile. "Now, ma'am, I know this has been a shock and it's hard for—" and I swear he went on to say—"a nice little old lady like you to believe anybody you know could've done such an awful thing. But Ted Bundy was downright charming and—"

"Lieutenant, only a fool could think Calvin Bolt committed that murder."

His face flushed a bright red. Not an indication of a very stable blood pressure.

"Ma'am, murder is my business. Think about it: The neighbors report screams, followed by someone running downstairs, at approximately five minutes before twelve. Your call, reporting the body, came in at twenty past twelve. From your own testimony, the victim had engaged in a violent quarrel with the suspect. Now, it's pretty obvious he staged the discovery of her body for the benefit of witnesses. When you went to call the police, he got scared and beat it. Well, he won't get far. We've got cars out hunting—"

With the artistry of television, the fuzz-faced patrolman burst in. "They picked him up, Lieutenant, down on the bridge over the river. Grabbed him before he could jump."

They left in a flurry of excitement.

Which meant I didn't get a chance to complete my report to Lt. Brown, how tonight had been the repeat of the other soap opera episodes, right up to the final moment. Nor did I have the opportunity to share with him my conclusions, so his later claims that I was deliberately uncooperative are absolutely unwarranted.

I cleaned up the hot chocolate mess and poured a glass of sherry. I do like Lavinia's taste in sherry. Cream, of course. As I sipped, I came to the regretful decision that I had no choice.

It was up to me to find Mollie Epsley's murderer.

I am not a woman to shirk my clear-cut duty.

"Henrie O.!" Lavinia's voice rose in dismay Tuesday morning. The familiar nickname is special to only my oldest and dearest of friends. It was coined by my late husband, who always claimed I packed more twists and surprises into a single day than O. Henry ever thought about investing in a short story. Rather gallant of Richard, I always thought. "Oh, Henrie O., are you all right?"

"Of course I am," I replied briskly and perhaps a little irritably. Lavinia does have a tendency to bleat. "It wasn't nice, but the point is, Lavinia, the damn fool police have arrested that pathetic Calvin, and he didn't do it. So, I need some facts."

That settled Lavinia down. Lavinia is quite good with facts. Despite her motherly, meatloaf appearance, she was a top financial reporter in Chicago for many years. I made a sheaf of notes.

That was how I spent the day, gathering data, a good deal of it on the victim.

Mollie Epsley was twenty-seven. Never married. Which didn't surprise me, despite her remarkable blonde loveliness. She'd finished high school, attended a secretarial school, and refined her skills at a paralegal institute. She was by all accounts very quick, very competent, and very overbearing. She found it difficult to hold jobs, and I didn't have any trouble finding out why. As the office manager at one law firm snapped, "She wouldn't mind her own business. Always poking and prying, wanting to know too much about people. And the more they tried not to tell her, the more determined she was to know."

This sounded promising. "Did she try to use her knowledge for gain?"

The office manager quickly backed off. "Oh, no, nothing like that. She loved to gossip. She liked to know things about people and tell the world. Especially things that would make them uncomfortable. She was a nasty, spiteful woman."

I would agree to that.

Calvin came off as one of life's losers.

"Just a damn sap," his cousin said sadly. "No guts. No sense. But believe me, Mrs. Collins, he would never hurt anyone. He would have been better off if he had lashed out now and then. But he didn't, and I'll never believe he could strangle anyone. I don't care how awful she was to him."

So Calvin was ineffectual and pathetic, but neither of

those qualities translated to violence. However, a cousin's testimony and my opinion wouldn't sway the lieutenant. No. I had to come up with some hard facts if Calvin were to be saved.

Some of my legwork had already been accomplished by Judi Myerson, an enterprising reporter for the local newspaper. She hadn't written the lead story on the murder. That belonged to the police reporter, Sam Frizzell. I scanned it, but it didn't tell me anything I didn't know. After all, I'd been right on the spot. But Judi, probably a young reporter, was assigned to do a sidebar on the Scholar's Inn apartments and the residents' reactions to the murder. I could tell she'd put heart and soul into it and come up with very little. But that's what interested me. Judi'd rung every bell in the apartment house and had found no one who really knew Mollie.

That was important. Not a surprise—she'd only lived there two weeks—but important.

Of course, I didn't spend all my time on the telephone. I sallied forth several times.

My first outing would have appeared desultory to any observer. It was early October, a nice time of year for a walk. Of course, anyone my age (most damn fools think) can walk only a short while and that at a limited pace. So it was easy for me to wander about the grounds of Scholar's Inn. (It was interesting to speculate upon the motives of the businessman who chose that name. Was it prompted by wistfulness or stupidity?) The apartment house was built as a quadrangle. A tiled pool and patio occupied the center area.

Three locations suited my hypothesis, a clump of patio chairs near the back of the pool, the parking area just past the back gate, and the laundry facilities. Each provided a clear view of Mollie's apartment windows, and each was within earshot.

It had rained most of Monday, steadily, persistently.

A little rainwater still glistened on the webbed patio chairs. I studied the patch of earth where the chairs sat. No impressions, no footprints.

The parking area was asphalted. Now, at midday, most of the slots were empty. The residents of Scholar's Inn worked or attended college, for the most part. Many were students and many of those led what I would term irregular lives. Up late. Out early. Arriving and departing on no set schedule. Part of the background noise to the apartment was the muted thud of slammed car doors. At all hours. Not, then, a likely spot for surveillance. Especially not on weekend nights.

That left only the laundry room. As usual, the door to the laundry area was ajar. I stepped inside. A sign in bold red print enjoined: NO SMOKING. Added to it, across the bottom, in thick black printing was the message: AND THIS MEANS YOU, BOZOS. A tiny smile touched my face. I was on the right track.

Bud Morgan, the custodian, was an ex-smoker. He reviled all smokers, and the laundry facilities were within his domain. He exercised his power. Tenants who wished for unruly toilets, etc., to be repaired made it a point to respond to his directives. No resident dared smoke in the laundry room or was unwise enough to drop errant butts at will on the grass or walks. But that angry black scrawl indicated someone was flouting his orders. And the offense must have occurred recently. The addendum had occurred since my last visit to the laundry room three days ago.

Bud was going to be furious. Several mounds of ash spotted the green cement floor. The smoker had stood close to the doorway with its excellent view of Mollie's apartment. But there were no butts on the floor.

I glanced around, then bent to my left to peer into the empty steel drum beside the door that served as a trash receptacle. There was only a little trash. Someone had thrown away an empty box of Tide. A mound of dryer fluff was draped over it. Leaning over, I gently poked at the debris. On the rusting bottom of the drum, I found a single pink baby's sock and four cigarette butts. Unfiltered Camels.

I considered calling Lt. Brown. Truly I did. But I could imagine his reaction. So what if I had found four cigarette butts in a trash can! My leap from the cigarette butts to a stranger on the premises, stealthily staking out Mollie's apartment for several nights in a row—witness Bud's vituperative addition to the NO SMOKING sign— would be a hard one for the sandy-haired lieutenant. Of course, it had to be that way. Someone knew that Mollie goaded Calvin night after night. Someone knew the pattern and had taken advantage of it. When a murder is necessary, how delightful to position it after the victim has engaged in a violent quarrel. However, I could see that the weary lieutenant might have difficulty in positing all of this from Calvin's sad sack personna and four cigarette butts. So, after due thought, I followed standard investigative procedures. I used separate envelopes for each item and listed the date and location of the discoveries. I used eyebrow tweezers for retrieval, of course. If fingerprints existed—on the cigarette butts—I certainly was careful to preserve them.

Further, I had satisfied the major requisite of my reconstruction. I had found the area where the killer had waited, listening to the customary quarrel and anticipating Calvin's departure.

It didn't take long to track down Mollie's closest friend. She didn't have many. She corroborated my conclusion that Mollie was unacquainted with her neighbors. A neighbor would have had no need to observe from the laundry room.

I had by this time a shadowy picture of the killer and an inkling of motive.

Don—Lt. Brown—later insisted I could have had no such ideas at this point in the investigation.

Nonsense.

It was all quite simple.

Mollie's murder—despite her blonde beauty and her troubled relationship with Calvin—had nothing to do with sex.

Simple garroting with no physical disfigurement is not customary for sexually motivated killers.

Garroting from behind with a fine wire (as opposed to manual strangulation) is not customary modus operandi in crimes committed under emotional stress.

Rather, the manner of her death indicated premeditation and calculation, the opposite of impulsive violence. This was unmistakably an execution. And the method hinted both at the perpetrator and at the motive.

A quiet, effective means of silencing an enemy.

The murderer was either a former OSS officer, a member of the French Resistance, or someone who knew a great deal about that period. The murderer smoked. The murderer was swift, competent, and dangerous. And the murderer counted Mollie as an enemy.

Three more phone calls and the facts began to pile up. Secreted among them, I felt certain, was both the name of a murderer and the reason for the deed.

Mollie had been temping for two weeks at the law firm of Hornsby, McMichael, and Samuelson.

In Mollie's three previous temp engagements (Jetton and Jetton, Foster, McCloud and Williams, and Borden, Frampton, and Fraley) there was no employee with whom she had contact who was of the appropriate background (served in Intelligence during World War II or possessed a great deal of knowledge about that period). Besides, all of the other law firms had non-smoking offices.

It was a different matter at Hornsby, McMichael and Samuelson.

Horace Hornsby didn't smoke. Now. He'd been dead for twenty-five years. He was, when alive, partial to Cuban cigars. Sinclair Samuelson didn't smoke. He was the yuppieish youngest partner, a tri-athlete who flung himself from pool to bicycle to track before and after work.

Marvin McMichael smoked. McMichael was a distinguished veteran of the European theater in World War II. A colonel at war's end. In the OSS.

My final visit of the day, just before closing time, was to the law offices of Hornsby, McMichael, and Samuelson. I wore a black dress I'd found in a back corner of Lavinia's closet, a dyed black straw hat (God, where *had* she bought it?) adorned with a limp spray of fake violets, and black orthopedic shoes. (Lavinia's closet is full of frightful surprises.) The right shoe pinched my foot abominably so I listed to starboard.

I window-shopped next door, gazing intently at an astonishing assortment of porcelain elephants. Small towns have the enchanting quality of offering a potpourri of offices and shops along a main street. Observation would have been difficult in a huge city building.

My patience was rewarded a few minutes before five. I had no difficulty in recognizing Marvin McMichael. The morgue attendant at the newspaper had been very helpful and McMichael's image from innumerable photographs was firmly fixed in my mind.

He didn't notice me, pressed close to the curio shop window, but I saw him clearly. He was taller than average, with a lean athletic build and a noticeable shock of thick white hair. His muted gray plaid Oxford suit was a perfect fit. Iron gray brows bunched over cold gray eyes. He had a distinguished, if severe, face with chiseled features, a smooth high forehead, beaked nose, thin-drawn lips. He walked briskly, head high, shoulders back, striding down the street with all the arrogance of a Roman senator.

I looked after him speculatively for a moment, then turned and entered the office. As I approached the secretary, I checked my appearance in the ornately framed mirror over the goldleaf side table. For a moment, I didn't even recognize the apparition in black. What a hoot.

My voice quavered just a little as I addressed a young woman whose hair looked as though she'd been on the receiving end of a hundred volts. "Hello, I'm Matilda Harris and I'm here to get my niece's things. I called to let you know I was coming." I dabbed a scented handkerchief to my eyes. Unfortunately, I'd dabbed on too much of Lavinia's cologne—I never use the stuff—and I almost strangled. It came out to the good, however, as Frizzy Hair, beneath her sleek exterior, was goodhearted and kindly. She rushed to get me a glass of water and by the time I could breathe, we were on excellent terms, sitting side by side on a brocaded bench.

"Oh, you must be Mollie Epsley's aunt. Oh, Mrs. Harris, we are all *so* sorry. It's such an awful thing to happen. No one's safe anymore. And to think it was her lover who killed her! I'd never have believed it, from what she said about him."

Calvin's arrest had been reported, of course.

I sighed heavily. "We never know what will happen in life," I observed darkly. Not, by the way, a tenet I accept. It's quite easy to know what's going to happen, especially when unstable elements combine. "And it's so very sad," I continued lugubriously, "because Mollie was enjoying this job so much. She told me just the other night—such a dear girl—so good to telephone her old aunt—that this was one of the most challenging work experiences of her life."

Frizzy Hair blinked. "But Mr. McMichael almost fired her—" She clapped a red-taloned hand over artistically carmined lips.

"Oh, that." I tsked. I crossed mental fingers and heaved a sigh. "Sometimes Mollie just didn't use good sense."

"I couldn't believe it," the receptionist said, her eyes wide. "I'd *told* her Mr. McMichael always kept that drawer locked and she said every lawyer needed a good secretary to keep things straight and she was going to put the files *she* was in charge of in first class shape."

"A locked drawer always was a challenge to Mollie. Couldn't keep her out of them when she was a little girl. She always had to see inside everything! But I'm sure she smoothed it over."

Frizzy Hair nodded, but her light brown eyes were faintly puzzled. "I guess so, 'cause she was at work Friday just like nothing had ever happened. But Thursday night, I heard them going at it." She shivered. "His voice was like an icicle down your back. I didn't hang around to hear anything after he told her she was fired." She looked nervously over her shoulder. "Mr. McMichael left for the day just a few minutes ago. I don't know that he'd like for me to talk about the cabinet. See," she confided, "he doesn't know I overheard any of it. It was after work last Thursday. I'd forgotten my car keys. I'd taken them out of my purse earlier to poke out that little aluminum thingymubob when the ring came off my Tab can." She led the way into a small office. "Let me tell you, I got out of here in a flash when I heard him talking to her. I couldn't believe it when she was here Friday morning, just like nothing had ever happened!"

Mollie's work area was nicely appointed, a golden oak veneer desk and standing beside it a wooden filing cabinet. Through a connecting door, I could see the sumptuously decorated office of Marvin McMichael, senior partner. Mahogany desk. A massive red leather chair. Red and blue Persian rug. A ten by eight foot wall painting, an impressionist's swirl of brown and gold and rose, of a polo player at full gallop.

I'd tucked a grocery sack into the absurdly large crocheted handbag I'd also borrowed from Lavinia. I sat down behind the desk, pulled out the sack, shook it open, and, with little mews of distress, began to empty out the few personal effects Mollie had left behind from her two weeks' occupancy: a package of Juicy Fruit, a plastic bottle of Tylenol caplets, three emery boards, a plastic rain hood, a comb, a hairbrush, some loose change, several coupons, and an ad for a white sale. I added a Kleenex box from the lower right hand drawer and a pair of low-heeled shoes. I sighed again, cradled the shoes in my lap, and looked mournfully at my guide. "If I could just sit here for a few minutes. A silent reverie. I feel so close to Mollie here."

The receptionist looked at me uncertainly, darted a glance at the open door to McMichael's office, and said slowly, "I don't know. I mean, I guess it's all right. He's left for the day."

"Just for a few minutes. For Mollie's sake."

"Oh, well, sure. I mean, yeah, I understand," and she backed out into the hall.

I was on my feet and crouched beside the locked cabinet before the door closed behind her.

Funny how you don't lose some skills. I picked that lock in a flash and eased out the drawer.

Empty.

As I'd expected.

It didn't take more than a minute and a half to determine that there was no locked receptacle of any kind in McMichael's office.

That didn't surprise me either.

But I had some ideas about where the contents of that filing cabinet might be.

At the appropriate time, I would share my conclusions with Lt. Brown.

An envelope of silence surrounded me as I walked through The Sahara. Obviously, the clientele of this dimly lit watering hole rarely shared the ambience with elderly women clothed entirely in black. I would have stopped at the bar for a sherry, but my time wasn't my own.

I found the phone booths near the restrooms. The first

booth was occupied. I stepped into the second. I already had the numbers committed to memory.

The first call was short, if not sweet. McMichael, after a long, thoughtful silence, was coldly, cautiously responsive. I was more relaxed as I dialed the second number and my eyes scanned the booth, absorbing some of the au courant graffiti: Safe Sex Saves Lives, Cocaine Kills, and X Exxon. Since my mind, yesterday and today, was going back in time, I remembered some from the war years: Kilroy was Here, Uncle Sam Needs You!, and V for Victory. Autres temps, autres moeurs.

"Brown, Homicide."

"Lt. Brown, Henrie Collins here. I would appreciate it if you could join me. I've made an appointment with Mollie Epsley's murderer."

Don Brown reminded me just a bit of Richard. Very difficult to manage. He didn't want to meet me at the door to the men's room of The Sahara.

But he did.

He didn't want to ride on the backseat floor of my Volvo to the Scholar's Inn.

But he did.

I didn't tell him the name of the murderer until we had successfully crept up the back stairs to the apartment.

He'd glared at me. "That's ridiculous. Why, he's been an elder in his church, worked with youth groups for years."

That didn't surprise me at all. I said so. Lt. Brown glared again.

And he most especially did not want to recline beneath Lavinia's dining room table, well hidden by the lace tablecloth which hung to the floor.

But he did.

The knock came earlier than scheduled.

That didn't surprise me.

McMichael would have scouted the area as soon as it was dark, to be certain he wasn't walking into a trap. But there were no official-looking unofficial cars and no brawny young men lurking in this residential neighborhood.

As I opened the door, I backpedaled, I hope gracefully.

"Come in, Mr. McMichael. You are a little early."

He stepped inside. Tonight his noticeable shock of thick white hair was hidden beneath a tan rain hat. A spear of light from Lavinia's Tiffany lamp illuminated his face. Cotton wadded between gum and cheek subtly distorted his face, but nothing could disguise that beaked nose and those thin lips. There was no trace of elegance in his shiny rayon raincoat. I would have wagered the farm that it was a long-forgotten item from a back closet of the firm.

"Your telephone call wasn't clear." His voice was thick. It's hard to move the jaw when impeded by cotton, but the tone was as cold as ice-slick cobbles on a winter street. He stepped inside and unobtrusively nudged the door shut with his elbow. His hands were stuffed in the pockets of the cheap raincoat.

I walked into the living room, putting several feet between us, then turned to face him. "To the contrary," I replied pleasantly. "It was eminently clear. Or you would not have come."

"What do you want?"

I didn't permit my face to reveal my satisfaction. Lt. Brown was sure to be listening with ever increasing attention.

"Oh, to have a little talk with you." I made a vexed noise. "I would offer you a cigarette, but I don't have your brand."

The tightening of his facial muscles emphasized the protrusion of his cheeks.

"Camels, I believe," I continued cheerfully. "But perhaps you don't wish to smoke right now. We do have so much to discuss. I find crime an interesting subject, worthy of study. As I'm sure you do, Mr. McMichael. And to have murder occur so close to you—actually to an employee of yours."

"The police have arrested the murderer," he said harshly. "The case is closed." He took a step toward me.

"Yes, I know. Poor Calvin. I do feel he needs help. So I'm sure you won't mind explaining to the police how you found Mollie last night—and how you left her."

Another step. His shoulders hunched. I could imagine

the cool feel of the thin wire against his fingers in the pocket of that coat.

"There's nothing to connect me to her. Nothing."

"I saw you. And I know why you came."

That stopped him for an instant.

"Mollie snooped. Lots of people know that. When the police find out how she opened that locked cabinet at your office—" I paused, looked at him inquiringly. "I suppose you thought that was the safest place to keep it. You certainly didn't want that kind of material at home. For years your mother, old Mrs. McMichael, lived with you. And you've always had a housekeeper. Josie's her name, isn't it? She's a bit of a tartar. You couldn't have unexplained locked drawers in her house! I suppose, too, it was convenient to keep that material there. You often work such late hours."

He came closer, step by step.

"You never expected your safe world to be invaded by someone like Mollie Epsley. A snoop. A sneak. A loud-mouthed virago. And once she'd seen the contents of that cabinet, she had to die, didn't she? But you wanted to be sure you killed her without a breath of suspicion attaching to your firm. So you followed her. I've checked your record, you know. SOE in France. A colonel, by war's end. You know how to follow people— and how to kill. I spotted the wire at once. Do you know, that was your only mistake. That and smoking in the laundry room and positioning the crime so that poor Calvin took the rap. Rather ugly, don't you think? I doubt, however, that you spend much time empathizing with others. You watched Mollie's apartment Friday night and Saturday night, too, I imagine. And the pattern came clear. A quarrel. Calvin running out into the night. And, always, a good twenty minutes before he slunk back. Enough time for murder. More than enough. I doubt it took you more than five minutes at the most."

He was almost to me now.

In the dining room, I saw the lace tablecloth switch.

McMichael lunged for me.

I suppose, despite his own agility, he'd relegated me to the class of a helpless old woman.

When he made his move, I wasn't, of course, still standing where he expected. As I landed on my feet, after vaulting over the horsehair sofa, I watched him whirl to face me.

His face was suffused now, an ugly purple.

"Yes, you old bitch. I killed her—just like I'm going to kill you!"

Youth does have its innings. McMichael was no match for Lt. Brown, who executed an excellent rugby tackle, although he occasionally rubbed his right shoulder the next morning as we drank a fresh pot of coffee. I did glance at my watch at one point. I had to be in class in another twenty minutes.

"Okay," he admitted finally. "I see how you got there. The murder was just like a war-time execution and that let out Calvin. If he'd lost it, he would have slammed her up against a wall, choked her with his hands."

"Correct. Poor Calvin would never have come up behind her and looped a wire over her head."

"Yeah. I should have seen it. But how the hell did you get from there to McMichael?"

It was all so simple, but I did manage to keep that tone out of my voice. After all, the dear boy had been handy in a pinch.

"Once I tied it to the war, that limited the murderer to someone of my own age or someone with a deep knowledge of World War II and Intelligence training. I combed through personal friends of Mollie's. No one fit. I backtracked over her most recent jobs. No one fit. I came to her final employer—and there was McMichael. I expected to find the murderer among people she had dealt with very recently. Whatever she'd learned, she hadn't broadcast it yet. I imagine she was enjoying her power, teasing him, as a cat toys with a mouse. That would have been her style. But she'd come up against a desperate man."

Lt. Brown finished his coffee. He gave me a peculiar look. "Okay. I can see all of it. But how the hell did you know she'd discovered actual physical material that he would kill to keep secret?"

I poured us each another cup. A quarter to nine. Time enough.

"It had to be something that on the face of it was so

illegal or so heinous that anyone seeing it would immediately be shocked to the core."

"You were right," he said grimly. "I got a search warrant this morning and in the trunk of his car—"

"You found pornographic pictures that he'd taken over the years of children he'd molested at church camps and in youth groups with whom he worked."

I suppose the witches of Salem must have elicited similar stunned responses in somewhat different circumstances.

"My God," he breathed. "You're right. My God. Sure glad you're a law-abiding citizen."

I smiled pleasantly and reached for my briefcase. As we walked downstairs—I en route to my class, he, I presume, to the station—I will admit I enjoyed his admiring sidelong glances.

And no, I didn't tell him that I'd picked the lock on McMichael's Mercedes in his garage Tuesday evening before I made my phone calls at The Sahara. Obviously, the hidden material could as easily have been cocaine or a stash of cash.

It is good to encourage reverence for one's elders among the young.

DEAD ON ARRIVAL
Joan Hess

FIRST APPEARANCE: *Strangled Prose, 1986*

Joan Hess's Claire Malloy is another character—like Carolyn Hart's "Henrie O"—who made her first short story appearance in Ed Gorman's *Invitation to a Murder*. Miss Hess writes two series, one featuring Claire, and the other about Sheriff Arly Hanks, who was played by Kate Jackson in a TV pilot movie.

Her most recent novel is *The Maggody Militia* (Dutton, 1997).

The girl's body lay in the middle of my living room floor. Long, black hair partially veiled her face and wound around her neck like a silky scarf. Her hands were contorted, her eyes flat and unfocused. The hilt of a knife protruded from her chest, an unadorned wooden marker in an irregular blotch of blood.

For a long, paralytic minute, all I did was stare, trying to convince myself that I was in the throes of some obscure jet lag syndrome that involved a particularly insidious form of hallucination. I finally dropped my suitcase, purse, nylon carry-on bag and sack of groceries I'd bought on the way from the airport, stuck my knuckles in my mouth, and edged around the sofa for a closer look.

It was not a good idea. I stumbled back, doing my best not to scream or swoon or something equally unproductive, and made it to the telephone in the kitchen. I thought I'd managed to avoid hysterics, but by the time Peter came on the line, my voice was an octave too high and I was slumped on the floor with my back against a cabinet door.

"There's a body in the living room," I said.

"Claire? Are you all right?"

"No, I am not all right, but I'm a damn sight better than that poor girl in the living room, because she's dead and I'm going to scream any minute and you'd—"

"I thought you were in Atlanta at that booksellers' convention until Thursday?"

"Well, I'm not," I said unsteadily and perhaps a shade acerbically. "I got home about three minutes ago, and there's this body in the living room and I'd appreciate it if you'll stop behaving like a nosy travel agent and do something because I really, truly am going to lose control—"

"Get out of there," Peter cut in harshly. "No! Go downstairs and wait until we get there."

I dropped the receiver and gazed down the hall at my bedroom door, Caron's bedroom and the bathroom door. All three were closed. I looked up at the back door, which was bolted from the inside. I listened intently for a sound, a faint intake of breath or the merest scuffle of a nervous foot. Or a bellow from a maniacal monster with a bad attitude and another knife.

It took several seconds of mental lecturing to get myself up, out of the kitchen and back through the living room, where I kept my eyes on the front door with the determination of a dieter passing a bakery or a mild-mannered bookseller passing a corpse. I then ran down the steps to the ground floor apartment and pounded on the door in a most undignified fashion. I was prepared to beat it down with my fists if need be when the lock clicked and the door opened a few inches, saving me countless splinters and an unpleasant conversation with the miserly landlord.

"Mrs. Malloy?" said a startled voice. "I thought you were in Atlanta for another couple of days."

The apartment had been rented a few weeks earlier to two college boys with the unremarkable names of Jonathon and Sean. I hadn't bothered to figure out which was which, and at the moment I still wasn't interested.

"I am not in Atlanta. Let me in, please. There's been an—an accident upstairs. There may be someone hiding up there. The police are coming. I need to stay here."

"The police?" he said as he opened the door and gestured for me to some in. Jonathon (I thought) was a tall boy with blue eyes and stylish blond hair. At the moment his hair was dripping on the floor like melting icicles and he was clutching a towel around his waist. "I was taking a shower," he explained in case I was unable to make the leap unassisted. "Police, huh? I guess I'd better put some clothes on."

"Good idea." I sank down on a nubby Salvation Army sofa and rubbed my face, fighting not to visualize the body ten feet above my head. In my living room. Partly on the area rug.

"I'll tell Sean to get you something to drink," Jonathon continued, still attempting to play the gracious host in his towel.

He went into one of the bedrooms, and after a minute the other boy appeared. Sean moved slowly, his dark hair ruffled and his expression groggy. "Hi, Mrs. Malloy," he said through a yawn. "I was taking a nap. I stayed up all night because of a damn calculus exam this morning. Jon said the police are coming. That's weird, real weird. You want a glass of wine? I think we got some left from a party last weekend."

Before I could decline, sirens whined in the distance, becoming louder as they neared the usually quiet street across from the campus lawn. Blue light flashed, doors slammed, feet thudded on the porch, and voices barked like angry mastiffs. The Farberville cavalry, it seemed, had arrived.

Several hours later I was allowed to sit on my own sofa. The chalk outline on the other side of the coffee table looked like a crude paper-doll, and I tried to keep my eyes away from it. Peter Rosen of the Farberville CID, a man of great charm upon occasion, alternated between scribbling in his notebook and rubbing my neck.

"You're sure you didn't recognize her?" he said for not the first time.

"I'm very, very sure. Who was she? How did she get into my apartment, Peter?"

"We checked, and the deadbolt hasn't been tampered with. You've said several times now that you've got the only key and the door was locked when you came upstairs."

I leaned back and stared at the network of cracks in

the ceiling. "When I got to the porch, I had to put everything down to unlock that door. I then put the key between my lips, picked everything up and trudged upstairs to my landing, where I had to put everything down again to unlock this door. It was locked; I'm sure of it."

"Caron doesn't have a key?"

"No one else has a key—not even the landlord. He had someone put on the deadbolts about five years ago and told me that I'd have to pay for a replacement if I lost my key. I considered having a copy made for Caron, but never got around to it. The only key is right there on the coffee table."

We both glared at the slightly discolored offender. When it failed to offer any hints, Peter opted to nuzzle my ear and murmur about the stupidity of citizens dallying in their scene-of-the-crime apartments when crazed murderers might be lurking in closets or behind closed doors.

The telephone rang, ending that nonsense. To someone's consternation, Peter took the call in the kitchen. Luckily, someone could overhear his side despite his efforts to mutter, and I was frowning when he rejoined me.

"Her name was Wendy, right?" I said. "I can't think of anyone I've ever known named Wendy. Well, one, but I doubt she and a boy in green tights flew through an upstairs window."

"Wendy Billingsberg, a business major at the college. She was twenty-two and lived alone on the top floor of that cheap brick apartment house beside the copy shop. She was from some little town about forty miles from here called Hasty. Her family's being notified now, and I suppose I'll question them tomorrow when they've had a chance to assimilate this. It's even harder when the victim is young." He looked away for a moment. "Wendy Billingsberg. Perhaps she came into the Book Depot. Try to remember if you've seen the name on a check or a credit card."

I did as directed, then shook my head. "I make the students produce a battery of identification, and I think I'd remember the name. I did look at her face when they—took her out. She was a pretty girl and that long black hair was striking. I can't swear she's never been in the bookstore or walked past me on the sidewalk, but

I'm almost certain I never spoke to her, Peter. Why was she in my apartment and how did she get inside?"

Peter flipped through his notebook and sighed. "The medical examiner said the angle of the weapon was such that the wound could not have been self-inflicted, so she wasn't the only one here."

"What about the two boys downstairs? Have they ever seen her before, or noticed her hanging around the neighborhood?"

"Jorgeson had them look at the victim and then interviewed them briefly. Neither one recognized her or offered any theory concerning what she was doing in your apartment. Could she have been a friend of Caron's?"

"I don't think so," I said, then went to the telephone, dialed Inez's number, and asked to speak to Caron.

She responded with the customary grace of a fifteen-year-old controlled solely by hormonal tides. "What, Mother? Inez and I were just about to go over to Rhonda's house to watch a movie. Aren't you supposed to be in Atlanta?"

"Yes, I am supposed to be in Atlanta," I said evenly, "but I am not. I am home and this is important. Do you know a twenty-two-year-old girl named Wendy Billingsberg?"

"No. Is that all? Inez and I really, really need to go now. Rhonda's such a bitch that she won't bother to wait for us. Some people have no consideration." Her tone made it clear there was more than one inconsiderate person in her life.

I reported the gist to Peter, who sighed again and said he'd better return to the police station to see if Jorgeson had dug up anything further. He promised to send by a uniformed officer to install a chain until I could have the lock rekeyed, and then spent several minutes asking my earlobes if I would be all right.

We all assured him I would, but after he'd gone, I caught myself tiptoeing around the apartment as I unpacked groceries and put away my suitcase. The front door had been locked; the back door had been bolted from the inside. The locks on the windows were unsullied except for a patina of black dust from being examined for fingerprint. They were not the only things to have been dusted, of course. Most of the surfaces in the apartment had been treated in a similar fashion, and had produced Caron's prints all over everything (including the bottle of perfume Peter'd given me for my birthday), mine, and one on a glass on the bedside table that had resulted in a moment of great excitement, until Peter suggested they compare it to his. The success of this resulted in a silence and several smirky glances.

Wendy and her companion had not searched the apartment. There was no indication they'd gone further than the living room. Why had they chosen my apartment—and how had they gotten inside?

An idea struck, and I hurried into the kitchen and hunted through junky drawers until I found the telephone number of my landlord. I crossed my fingers as I dialed the number, and was rewarded with a grouchy hello. "Mr. Fleechum," I said excitedly, "this is Claire Malloy. I need to ask you something."

"Look, I told you when you moved in that I didn't want any damn excuses about the rent. I ain't your father, and I don't care about your financial problems. I got to pay the bank every month, so there's no point in—"

"That's not why I called," I interrupted before he worked himself into an impressive fettle. "I was hoping you might remember the name of the locksmith who installed the deadbolts several years ago . . ."

"Yeah, I know his name. You lose the key, Mizz Malloy? I told you then that I wasn't going to waste money on a spare."

I wasn't inclined to explain the situation at the moment. "No, I didn't lose the key. I was thinking about having a deadbolt installed on the back door—at my expense, naturally. My daughter and I would feel more secure."

Fleechum grumbled under his breath, then said, "That's all right with me, as long as I don't have to pay for it. But you'll have to find your own locksmith. My deadbeat brother-in-law put in the deadbolts, due in part to owing me money. He cleared out three, four years ago, taking his tools. My sister had everything else hauled off to the dump. I'm just sorry that sorry husband of hers couldn't have been in the bottom of the load."

"And no one knows where he is now?"

"No one cares where he is now, Mizz Malloy, including me. Last I heard he was in Arizona or some place like that, living in a trailer with a bimbo. Probably beating her like he did my sister. You want to have locks installed, do it."

He replaced the receiver with an unnecessary vigor. I put mine down more gently and regretfully allowed my brilliant idea to deflate like a cooling souffle. Mr. Fleechum's brother-in-law had been gone for three or four years. It seemed unlikely that he had made an extra key, kept it all that time, and then waited until my apartment was empty for a few days so that he could invite a college girl over to murder her.

I was still tiptoeing, but I couldn't seem to shake a sense of someone or something hovering in the apartment, possessing it in the tradition of a proper British ghost in the tower. I went so far as to stand in the dining room doorway, trying to pick up some psychic insight into an earlier scene when two people had entered the room and one had departed.

I tried to envision them as burglars. They'd have been seriously disappointed burglars when they saw the decrepit stereo system and small television set. But why choose my apartment to begin with? The duplex fit in well with the neighborhood ambiance of run-down rental property and transient tenants. There were people downstairs, single boys who were likely to come and go at unpredictable hours and have a stream of visitors.

Okay, Wendy and her companion weren't burglars and they hadn't come in hopes of filching the Hope Diamond and other fancy stuff. The girl had come to see me, and her murderer had followed her, bringing his knife with him. She hadn't known I was out of town—and why would she, since she didn't know me from Mary Magdalen?

A knock on the door interrupted my admittedly pointless mental exercise. It also knotted my stomach and threatened my knees, and my voice was shaky as I said, "Who is it?"

"Jorgeson and Corporal Katz, Mrs. Malloy. Katz is going to put up the chain so you'll feel safe tonight."

I let them in. Katz immediately busied himself with screwdrivers and such, while Jorgeson watched with the

impassiveness of a road-crew supervisor. I subtly sidled
over and said, "Have you turned up anything more
about the victim?"

"The lieutenant said not to discuss it with you,
ma'am," Jorgeson said, his bulldog face turning pink.
"He said that you're not supposed to meddle in an official police investigation—this time."

"Oh, Jorgeson," I said with a charmingly wry chuckle,
"we both know the lieutenant didn't mean that I wasn't
supposed to know anything whatsoever about the victim.
I might be able to remember something if I knew more
about her. What if she'd been a contestant in that
ghastly beauty pageant I helped direct, or been a waitress at the beer garden across from the Book Depot?
You know how awkward it is to run into someone
you've seen a thousand times, but you can't place him
because he's out of context. When I saw this Wendy
Billingsberg, she was decidedly out of context."

Jorgeson's jaw crept out further and his ears gradually
matched the hue of his face. "The lieutenant said you'd
try something like that, ma'am. As far as we know, the
victim didn't have any connections with any of the locals.
She attended classes sporadically and pretty much hung
out with the more unsavory elements of the campus
community."

"Ah," I said wisely, "drugs." When Jorgeson twitched,
I bit back a smile and continued. "Peter's right; none of
the druggies buy books at the store or hold down jobs
along Thurber Street. Was she dealing?"

"I'm not supposed to discuss it, ma'am. Hurry up,
Katz. I told those boys downstairs to wait for me."

Katz hurried up, and within a few minutes, Jorgeson
wished me a nice day (and hadn't it been dandy thus
far?) and led his cohort out of my apartment. I waited
until I heard them reach the ground floor, then eased
open my door and crept as close to the middle landing
as I dared.

Jorgeson, bless his heart, had opted to conduct his
interview from the foyer. "Wendy Billingsberg," he said
in a low voice. "You both sure that doesn't ring a bell?
She was a business major. Either of you have any classes
in the department?" There was a pause during which I
assumed they'd made suitable nonverbal responses. "She

lived in the Bellaire Apartments. You been there?" Another pause. "And she used to be seen on the street with a coke dealer nicknamed Hambone. Tall guy, dirty blond ponytail, brown beard, disappeared at the end of the last semester, probably when he caught wind of a pending warrant. Ever heard of this Hambone?"

"Hambone?" Jonathon echoed. "The description doesn't sound like anyone I know, but we're not exactly in that social circle. What's his real name?"

"We're still working on that," Jorgeson said. "What about you? You ever heard of someone named Hambone?"

"Nope," Sean said firmly. "Look, Officer, I was up all night studying. I've already told you that I didn't see anyone and I didn't hear anything."

"Neither did I," Jonathon said with equal conviction. "I went out for a hamburger and a brew at the beer garden, then came back and watched some old war movie. Fell asleep on the couch."

"What time did you leave and subsequently return?" Jorgeson asked, still speaking softly but with an edge of intensity.

"Jesus, I don't know. I went out at maybe ten and got back at maybe midnight. You can ask the chubby blond waitress; she's seen me enough times to remember me."

"The medical examiner's initial estimate is that the girl was killed around midnight, with an hour margin of error on either side. It looks like the girl and her friend managed to sneak upstairs while you were out and your roommate was studying in his bedroom. You didn't notice anyone on the sidewalk when you came back?"

After a pause, Jonathon said, "Well, there was a couple, but they were heading away from the duplex and having a heated discussion about him forgetting her birthday or something. I didn't pay much attention, and it was too dark to get a good look at them. Other than them, I don't think I saw anyone during the last couple of blocks. There was a guy going around the corner the other way, but all I saw was the back of his head."

"Did he have a ponytail?" Jorgeson said quickly.

"I just caught a glimpse of him. Sorry."

I heard the sound of Jorgeson's pencil scratching a

brief note. "And you didn't hear anything?" he added, now speaking to the other boy.

"No," Sean said, "I've already told you that. Nothing."

"That's enough for the moment," Jorgeson said. "Both of you need to come to the station tomorrow morning so we can take formal statements. In the meantime, if you think of anything at all that might help, call Lieutenant Rosen or myself."

The front door closed. The downstairs door closed. Shortly thereafter, two car doors closed. I closed my door and tested the chain Katz had installed. It allowed the door to open two or three inches and seemed solid enough until I could get the lock rekeyed, which was pretty darn close to the top of my priorities list. Breathing, number one. Deadbolt rekeyed, number two.

I went into the kitchen, made sure the bolt on the back door was still in place, and started to make myself a cup of tea while I assimilated the latest information so graciously shared with me.

Wendy was known to have consorted with a dealer. He'd vanished, and no doubt preferred to remain thus. She'd run into him, recognized him, and threatened to expose him. She found a way into my apartment and ended up on the living room floor. I again checked the bolt, then turned off the burner beneath the tea kettle and made myself a nice, stiff drink. I went back into the living room, checked that the chain was in place and the deadbolt secured, and sat down on the sofa, wondering if the emergent compulsion to maintain security would be with me for weeks, months, or decades.

I put down my drink, checked that the chain and deadbolt had not slipped loose, and went into the kitchen to call a locksmith and pay for an after-hours emergency visit. And after a moment of revelation, found myself calling someone else.

Half an hour later I went downstairs and knocked on the boys' door. Jonathon opened the door. His expression tightened as he saw me, as though he expected another bizarre outburst from the crazy lady who cohabited with bats in the upstairs belfry.

"Hi," I said in a thoroughly civilized voice. "I realize it's been an awful day for all of us, but I'm not going to be able to relax, much less sleep, if I don't have the locksmith in to rekey the deadbolt. He said he'd be here in an hour. I just thought I'd warn you and Sean so you wouldn't come storming out the door."

"Sean's sacked out under the air conditioner, so he couldn't hear a freight train drive across the porch. I'll see if I can get through to him, though. We're both pretty rattled by all this. Thanks for telling me, but I think I'll wander down to the beer garden and soothe myself with a pitcher. Two pitchers. Whatever it takes."

I went back upstairs, secured the chain and the deadbolt, and sat down to wait. Ten minutes later I heard the front door downstairs close and footsteps on the porch. So far, so good. I turned on the television to give a sense of security to my visitor as he came creeping up the squeaky stairs, the key to my door in what surely was a very sweaty hand.

To my chagrin, it was all for naught, because he walked up the stairs like he owned them (or rented them, anyway) and knocked on my door.

"Who is it?" I said with the breathlessness of a gothic heroine.

"It's Sean, Mrs. Malloy. I wanted to talk to you for a minute. There's something that occurred to me, and I don't know if it's important enough to call the police now."

"Sorry," I said through the door, "but I'm too terrified to open the door to anyone except the locksmith. Go ahead and call Lieutenant Rosen; I'm sure he'll want to hear whatever you have."

I listened with increasing disappointment as he went downstairs and into his apartment. A window unit began to hum somewhere below.

"Phooey," I said as I switched off the television and did a quick round to ascertain all my locks were locked. I was brooding on the sofa several minutes later when I heard a tell-tale series of squeaks. A key rustled into the keyhole. As I stared, fascinated and rather pleased with myself, the knob of the lock clicked to one side, the doorknob twisted silently, and the door edged open. I went so far as to assume the standard gothic heroine stance: hands clasped beside my chest, eyelids frozen in mid-flutter, lips pursed.

Then the chain reached its limit, of course, and the

door came to a halt. A male voice let out a muted grunt of frustration, but became much louder as the police came thundering upstairs. Once the arguing and protesting abated, I removed the chain and opened the door.

Jonathon had been handcuffed and was in the process of being escorted downstairs by Jorgeson and Katz, among others. Peter gave me a pained look and said, "I was about to remove the evidence from your lock when you did that, Claire. Why don't you wait inside like a good little girl?"

"Because I'm not," I said, now opting for the role of gothic dowager dealing with inferiors. "I happen to be the one who figured out the key problem, you know."

"You happen to be the one who swore there was only one key for the deadbolt. That's what threw me off in the first place."

"Don't pull that nonsense. You heard me say that I used the same key downstairs as upstairs. It was perfectly obvious that my door, the boys' door and the front door are all keyed the same. Fleechum, the prince of penury, saved himself big bucks. Once I told the boys that a locksmith was coming, both of them realized they'd have to have their deadbolt rekeyed, too. Sean was puzzled, but I'm afraid Jonathon was panicked enough to try something unpleasant."

"It would have come to me at two in the morning," Peter said. "I would have sat up in bed, slapped my forehead, and called Jorgeson to rush over here and test the theory."

"Then I'm delighted that your sleep will be uninterrupted."

"When I get some, which won't be anytime soon. Now we've got to see if anyone at the beer garden noticed Wendy recognize her old boyfriend and follow him back to his apartment. Sean wouldn't have heard any discussion, but he might have had problems with a corpse in his living room the next morning. Did you tell the boys you'd be in Atlanta until Thursday?"

"I asked them to collect my mail."

"So Jonathon, a.k.a. Hambone, figured he had a couple of days to do something with the body. Unfortunately, you returned."

"Unfortunately, my fanny! If I hadn't come home early, he might have had a chance to take Wendy's body out in the woods where she wouldn't have been discovered for weeks. Months. Decades. And don't you find it a bit ironic that you sent me downstairs—to the murderer's apartment—when I discovered the body?" I was warming up for another onslaught of righteous indignation when Peter put his arms around me.

"And why did you come home early?" he murmured.

"Because every now and then I like being told that I'm a meddlesome busybody who interferes in official police investigations," I retorted, now warming up for entirely different reasons. "No one in Atlanta had anything but nice things to say about me."

"Are you saying you missed me?"

"Jorgeson, you fool," I said. "I missed Jorgeson."

I wondered if his soft laugh meant he didn't believe me.

OLD RATTLER
Sharyn McCrumb

FIRST APPEARANCE: *If Ever I Return,*
Pretty Peggy-O, 1991

Sheriff Arrowood appeared in three of Ms. McCrumb's Appalachian series novels, but this is the first time Spencer
Arrowood has taken center stage. This story first appeared
in an anthology called *Partners in Crime* (Signet, 1994).

Ms. McCrumb's most recent novel is *The Rosewood Cas-
ket* (Dutton, 1997).

She was a city woman, and she looked too old to want
to get pregnant, so I reckoned she had hate in her
heart.

That's mostly the only reasons I ever see city folks:
babies and meanness. Country people come to me right
along, though, for poultices and tonics for the rheuma-
tism; to go dowsing for well water on their land; or to
help them find what's lost, and such like; but them city
folks from Knoxville, and Johnson City, and from Ashe-
ville, over in North Carolina—the skinny ones with their
fancy colorless cars, talking all educated, slick as goose
grease—they don't hold with home remedies or the
Sight. Superstition, they call it. Unless you label your
potions "macrobiotic," or "holistic," or package them
up fancy for the customers in earth-tone clay jars, or call
your visions "channeling."

Shoot, I know what city folks are like. I could'a been
rich if I'd had the stomach for it. But I didn't care to
cater to their notions, or to have to listen to their self-
centered whining, when a city doctor could see to their
needs by charging more and taking longer. I say, let him.
They don't need me so bad nohow. They'd rather pay a
hundred dollars to some fool boy doctor who's likely
guessing about what ails them. Of course, they got insur-

ance to cover it, which country people mostly don't—
them as makes do with me, anyhow.

"That old Rattler," city people say. "Holed up in that
filthy old shanty up a dirt road. Wearing those ragged
overalls. Living on Pepsis and Twinkies. What does he
know about doctoring?"

And I smile and let 'em think that, because when they
are desperate enough, and they have nowhere else to
turn, they'll be along to see me, same as the country
people. Meanwhile, I go right on helping the halt and
the blind who have no one else to turn to. *For I will
restore health unto thee, and I will heal thee of thy
wounds, saith the Lord.* Jeremiah 30. What do I know?
A lot. I can tell more from looking at a person's fingernails, smelling their breath, and looking at the whites of
their eyes than the doctoring tribe in Knoxville can tell
with their high-priced X rays and such. And sometimes
I can pray the sickness out of them and sometimes I
can't. If I can't, I don't charge for it—you show me a
city doctor that will make you that promise.

The first thing I do is, I look at the patient, before I
even listen to a word. I look at the way they walk, the
set of the jaw, whether they look straight ahead or down
at the ground, like they was waiting to crawl into it. I
could tell right much from looking at the city woman—
what she had wrong with her wasn't no praying matter.

She parked her colorless cracker box of a car on the
gravel patch by the spring, and she stood squinting up
through the sunshine at my corrugated tin shanty. (*I
know it's a shanty, but it's paid for. Think on that
awhile.*) She looked doubtful at first—that was her common sense trying to talk her out of taking her troubles
to some backwoods witch doctor. But then her eyes narrowed, and her jaw set, and her lips tightened into a
long, thin line, and I could tell that she was thinking on
whatever it was that hurt her so bad that she was willing
to resort to me. I got out a new milk-jug of my comfrey
and chamomile tea and two Dixie cups, and went out
on the porch to meet her.

"Come on up!" I called out to her, smiling and waving
most friendly-like. A lot of people say that rural mountain folks don't take kindly to strangers, but that's
mainly if they don't know what you've come about, and

it makes them anxious, not knowing if you're a welfare snoop or a paint-your-house-with-whitewash conman, or the law. I knew what this stranger had come about, though, so I didn't mind her at all. She was as harmless as a buckshot doe, and hurting just as bad, I reckoned. Only she didn't know she was hurting. She thought she was just angry.

If she could have kept her eyes young and her neck smooth, she would have looked thirty-two, even close-up, but as it was, she looked like a prosperous, well-maintained forty-four-year-old, who could use less coffee and more sleep. She was slender, with a natural-like brownish hair—though I knew better—wearing a khaki skirt and a navy top and a silver necklace with a crystal pendant, which she might have believed was a talisman. There's no telling what city people will believe. But she smiled at me, a little nervous, and asked if I had time to talk to her. That pleased me. When people are taken up with their own troubles, they seldom worry about anybody else's convenience.

"Sit down," I said, smiling to put her at ease. "Time runs slow on the mountain. Why don't you have a swig of my herb tea, and rest a spell. That's a rough road if you're not used to it."

She looked back at the dusty trail winding its way down the mountain. "It certainly is," she said. "Somebody told me how to get here, but I was positive I'd got lost."

I handed her the Dixie cup of herb tea, and made a point of sipping mine, so she'd know I wasn't attempting to drug her into white slavery. They get fanciful, these college types. Must be all that reading they do. "If you're looking for old Rattler, you found him," I told her.

"I thought you must be." She nodded. "Is your name really Rattler?"

"Not on my birth certificate, assuming I had one, but it's done me for a raft of years now. It's what I answer to. How about yourself?"

"My name is Evelyn Johnson." She stumbled a little bit before she said *Johnson*. Just once I wish somebody would come here claiming to be a *Robinson* or an *Evans*. Those names are every bit as common as Jones, John-

son, and Smith, but nobody ever resorts to them. I guess
they think I don't know any better. But I didn't bring it
up, because she looked troubled enough, without me trying to find out who she really was, and why she was
lying about it. Mostly people lie because they feel foolish
coming to me at all, and they don't want word to get
back to town about it. I let it pass.

"This tea is good," she said, looking surprised. "You
made this?"

I smiled. "Cherokee recipe. I'd give it to you, but you
couldn't get the ingredients in town—not even at the
health food store."

"Somebody told me that you were something of a miracle worker." Her hands fluttered in her lap, because she
was sounding silly to herself, but I didn't look surprised,
because I wasn't. People have said that for a long time,
and it's nothing for me to get puffed up about, because
it's not my doing. It's a gift.

"I can do things other folks can't explain," I told her.
"That might be a few logs short of a miracle. But I can
find water with a forked stick, and charm bees, and locate lost objects. There's some sicknesses I can minister
to. Not yours, though."

Her eyes saucered, and she said, "I'm perfectly well,
thank you."

I just sat there looking at her, deadpan. I waited. She
waited. Silence.

Finally, she turned a little pinker, and ducked her
head. "All right," she whispered, like it hurt. "I'm not
perfectly well. I'm a nervous wreck. I guess I have to
tell you about it."

"That would be best, Evelyn," I said.

"My daughter has been missing since July." She
opened her purse and took out a picture of a pretty
young girl, soft brown hair like her mother's, and young,
happy eyes. "Her name is Amy. She was a freshman at
East Tennessee State, and she went rafting with three
of her friends on the Nolichucky. They all got separated
by the current. When the other three met up farther
downstream, they got out and went looking for Amy, but
there was no trace of her. She hasn't been seen since."

"They dragged the river, I reckon." Rock-studded

mountain rivers are bad for keeping bodies snagged down where you can't find them.

"They dragged that stretch of the Nolichucky for three days. They even sent down divers. They said even if she'd got wedged under a rock, we'd have something by now." It cost her something to say that.

"Well, she's a grown girl," I said, to turn the flow of words. "Sometimes they get an urge to kick over the traces."

"Not Amy. She wasn't the party type. And even supposing she felt like that—because I know people don't believe a mother's assessment of character—would she run away in her bathing suit? All her clothes were back in her dorm, and her boyfriend was walking up and down the riverbank with the other two students, calling out to her. I don't think she went anywhere on her own."

"Likely not," I said. "But it would have been a comfort to think so, wouldn't it?"

Her eyes went wet. "I kept checking her bank account for withdrawals, and I looked at her last phone bill to see if any calls were made after July sixth. But there's no indication that she was alive past that date. We put posters up all over Johnson City, asking for information about her. There's been no response."

"Of course, the police are doing what they can," I said.

"It's the Wake County sheriff's department, actually," she said. "But the Tennessee Bureau of Investigation is helping them. They don't have much to go on. They've questioned people who were at the river. One fellow claims to have seen a red pickup leaving the scene with a girl in it, but they haven't been able to trace it. The investigators have questioned all her college friends and her professors, but they're running out of leads. It's been three months. Pretty soon, they'll quit trying altogether." Her voice shook. "You see, Mr.—Rattler—they all think she's dead."

"So you came to me?"

She nodded. "I didn't know what else to do. Amy's father is no help. He says to let the police handle it. We're divorced, and he's remarried and has a two-year-old son. But Amy is all I've got. I can't let her go!"

She set down the paper cup, and covered her face with her hands.

"Could I see that picture of Amy, Mrs.—Johnson?"

"It's Albright," she said softly, handing me the photograph. "Our real last name is Albright. I just felt foolish before, so I didn't tell you my real name."

"It happens," I said, but I wasn't really listening to her apology. I had closed my eyes, and I was trying to make the edges of the snapshot curl around me, so that I would be standing next to the smiling girl, and get some sense of how she was. But the photograph stayed cold and flat in my hand, and no matter how hard I tried to think my way into it, the picture shut me out. There was nothing.

I opened my eyes, and she was looking at me, scared, but waiting, too, for what I could tell her. I handed back the picture. "I could be wrong," I said. "I told you I'm no miracle worker."

"She's dead, isn't she?"

"Oh, yes. Since the first day, I do believe."

She straightened up, and those slanting lines deepened around her mouth. "I've felt it, too," she said. "I'd reach out to her with my thoughts, and I'd feel nothing. Even when she was away at school, I could always sense her somehow. Sometimes I'd call, and she'd say, 'Mom, I was just thinking about you.' But now I reach out to her and I feel empty. She's just—gone."

"Finding mortal remains is a sorrowful business," I said. "And I don't know that I'll be able to help you."

Evelyn Albright shook her head. "I didn't come here about finding Amy's body, Rattler," she said. "I came to find her killer."

I spent three more Dixie cups of herb tea trying to bring back her faith in the Tennessee legal system. Now, I never was much bothered with the process of the law, but, like I told her, in this case I did know that pulling a live coal from an iron pot-bellied stove was a mighty puny miracle compared to finding the one guilty sinner with the mark of Cain in all this world, when there are so many evildoers to choose from. It seemed to me that for all their frailty, the law had the manpower and the system to sort through a thousand possible killers, and to find the one fingerprint or the exact bloodstain that would lay the matter of Amy Albright to rest.

"But you knew she was dead when you touched her picture!" she said. "Can't you tell from that who did it? Can't you see where she is?"

I shook my head. "My grandma might could have done it, rest her soul. She had a wonderful gift of prophecy, but I wasn't trained to it the way she was. *Her* grandmother was a Cherokee medicine woman, and she could read the signs like yesterday's newspaper. I only have the little flicker of Sight I was born with. Some things I know, but I can't see it happening like she could have done."

"What did you see?"

"Nothing. I just felt that the person I was trying to reach in that photograph was gone. And I think the lawmen are the ones you should be trusting to hunt down the killer."

Evelyn didn't see it that way. "They aren't getting anywhere," she kept telling me. "They've questioned all of Amy's friends, and asked the public to call in for information, and now they're at a standstill."

"I hear tell they're sly, these hunters of humans. He could be miles away by now," I said, but she was shaking her head no.

"The sheriff's department thinks it was someone who knew the area. First of all, because that section of the river isn't a tourist spot, and secondly, because he apparently knew where to take Amy so that he wouldn't be seen by anyone with her in the car, and he has managed to keep her from being found. Besides"—she looked away, and her eyes were wet again—"they won't say much about this, but apparently Amy isn't the first. There was a high school girl who disappeared around here two years ago. Some hunters found her body in an abandoned well. I heard one of the sheriff's deputies say that he thought the same person might be responsible for both crimes."

"Then he's like a dog killing sheep. He's doing it for the fun of it, and he must be stopped, because a sheep killer never stops of his own accord."

"People told me you could do marvelous things—find water with a forked stick; heal the sick. I was hoping that you would be able to tell me something about what happened to Amy. I thought you might be able to see who killed her. Because I want him to suffer."

I shook my head. "A dishonest man would string you along," I told her. "A well-meaning one might tell you what you want to hear just to make you feel better. But all I can offer you is the truth: when I touched that photograph, I felt her death, but I saw nothing."

"I had hoped for more." She twisted the rings on her hands. "Do you think you could find her body?"

"I have done something like that, once. When I was twelve, an old man wandered away from his home in December. He was my best friend's grandfather, and they lived on the next farm, so I knew him, you see. I went out with the searchers on that cold, dark afternoon, with the wind baying like a hound through the hollers. As I walked along by myself, I looked up at the clouds, and I had a sudden vision of that old man sitting down next to a broken rail fence. He looked like he was asleep, but I reckoned I knew better. Anyhow, I thought on it as I walked, and I reckoned that the nearest rail fence to his farm was at an abandoned homestead at the back of our land. It was in one of our pastures. I hollered for the others to follow me, and I led them out there to the back pasture."

"Was he there?"

"He was there. He'd wandered off—his mind was going—and when he got lost, he sat down to rest a spell, and he'd dozed off where he sat. Another couple of hours would have finished him, but we got him home to a hot bath and scalding coffee, and he lived till spring."

"He was alive, though."

"Well, that's it. The life in him might have been a beacon. I might not work when the life is gone."

"I'd like you to try, though. If we can find Amy, there might be some clue that will help us find the man who did this."

"I tell you what: you send the sheriff to see me, and I'll have a talk with him. If it suits him, I'll do my level best to find her. But I have to speak to him first."

"Why?"

"Professional courtesy," I said, which was partly true, but, also, because I wanted to be sure she was who she claimed to be. City people usually do give me a fake name out of embarrassment, but I didn't want to chance her being a reporter on the Amy Albright case, or, worse, someone on the killer's side. Besides, I wanted to stay on good terms with Sheriff Spencer Arrowood. We go back a long way. He used to ride out this way on his bike when he was a kid, and he'd sit and listen to tales about the Indian times—stories I'd heard from my grandma—or I'd take him fishing at the trout pool on Broom Creek. One year, his older brother Cal talked me into taking the two of them out owling, since they were too young to hunt. I walked them across every ridge over the holler, and taught them to look for the sweep of wings above the tall grass in the field, and to listen for the sound of the waking owl, ready to track his prey by the slightest sound, the shade of movement. I taught them how to make owl calls, to where we couldn't tell if it was an owl calling out from the woods or one of us. Look out, I told them. When the owl calls your name, it means death.

Later on, they became owls, I reckon. Cal Arrowood went to Vietnam, and died in a dark jungle full of screeching birds. I felt him go. And Spencer grew up to be sheriff, so I reckon he hunts prey of his own by the slightest sound, and by one false move. A lot of people had heard him call their name.

I hadn't seen much of Spencer since he grew up, but I hoped we were still buddies. Now that he was sheriff, I knew he could make trouble for me if he wanted to, and so far he never has. I wanted to keep things cordial.

"All right," said Evelyn. "I can't promise they'll come out here, but I will tell them what you said. Will you call and tell me what you're going to do?"

"No phone," I said, jerking my thumb back toward the shack. "Send the sheriff out here. He'll let you know."

She must have gone to the sheriff's office, straightaway after leaving my place. I thought she would. I wasn't surprised at that, because I could see that she wasn't doing much else right now besides brood about her loss. She needed an ending so that she could go on. I had tried to make her take a milk jug of herb tea, because

I never saw anybody so much in need of a night's sleep, but she wouldn't have it. "Just find my girl for me," she'd said. "Help us find the man who did it, and put him away. Then I'll sleep."

When the brown sheriff's car rolled up my dirt road about noon the next day, I was expecting it. I was sitting in my cane chair on the porch whittling a face onto a hickory broom handle when I saw the flash of the gold star on the side of the car door, and the sheriff himself got out. I waved, and he touched his hat, like they used to do in cowboy movies. I reckon little boys who grow up to be sheriff watch a lot of cowboy movies in their day. I didn't mind Spencer Arrowood, though. He hadn't changed all that much from when I knew him. There were gray flecks in his fair hair, but they didn't show much, and he never did make it to six feet, but he'd managed to keep his weight down, so he looked all right. He was kin to the Pigeon Roost Arrowoods, and like them he was smart and honest without being a glad-hander. He seemed a little young to be the high sheriff to an old-timer like me, but that's never a permanent problem for anybody, is it? Anyhow, I trusted him, and that's worth a lot in these sorry times.

I made him sit down in the other cane chair, because I hate people hovering over me while I whittle. He asked did I remember him.

"Spencer," I said, "I'd have to be drinking something a lot stronger than chamomile tea to forget you."

He grinned, but then he seemed to remember what sad errand had brought him out here, and the faint lines came back around his eyes. "I guess you've heard about this case I'm on."

"I was told. It sounds to me like we've got a human sheep killer in the fold. I hate to hear that. Killing for pleasure is an unclean act. I said I'd help the law any way I could to dispose of the killer, if it was all right with you."

"That's what I heard," the sheriff said. "For what it's worth, the TBI agrees with you about the sort of person we're after, although they didn't liken it to *sheep killing*. They meant the same thing, though."

"So Mrs. Albright did come to see you?" I asked him,

keeping my eyes fixed on the curl of the beard of that hickory face.

"Sure did, Rattler," said the sheriff. "She tells me that you've agreed to try to locate Amy's body."

"It can't do no harm to try," I said. "Unless you mind too awful much. I don't reckon you believe in such like."

He smiled. "It doesn't matter what I believe if it works, does it, Rattler? You're welcome to try. But, actually, I've thought of another way that you might be useful in this case."

"What's that?"

"You heard about the other murdered girl, didn't you? They found her body in an abandoned well up on Locust Ridge."

"Whose land?"

"National forest now. The homestead has been in ruins for at least a century. But that's a remote area of the county. It's a couple of miles from the Appalachian Trail, and just as far from the river, so I wouldn't expect an outsider to know about it. The only way up there is on an old county road. The TBI psychologist thinks the killer has dumped Amy Albright's body somewhere in the vicinity of the other burial. He says they do that. Serial killers, I mean. They establish territories."

"Painters do that," I said, and the sheriff remembered his roots well enough to know that I meant a mountain lion, not a fellow with an easel. We called them painters in the old days, when there were more of them in the mountains than just a scream and a shadow every couple of years. City people think I'm crazy to live on the mountain where the wild creatures are, and then they shut themselves up in cities with the most pitiless killers ever put on this earth: each other. I marvel at the logic.

"Since you reckon he's leaving his victims in one area, why haven't you searched it?"

"Oh, we have," said the sheriff, looking weary. "I've had volunteers combing that mountain, and they haven't turned up a thing. There's a lot of square miles of forest to cover up there. Besides, I think our man has been more careful about concealment this time. What we need is more help. Not more searchers, but a more precise location."

"Where do I come in? You said you wanted me to

do more than just find the body. Not that I can even promise to do that."

"I want to get your permission to try something that may help us catch this individual," Spencer Arrowood was saying.

"What's that?"

"I want you to give some newspaper interviews. Local TV, even, if we can talk them into it. I want to publicize the fact that you are going to search for Amy Albright on Locust Ridge. Give them your background as a psychic and healer. I want a lot of coverage on this."

I shuddered. You didn't have to be psychic to foresee the outcome of that. A stream of city people in colorless cars, wanting babies and diet tonics.

"When were you planning to search for the body, Rattler?"

"I was waiting on you. Any day will suit me, as long as it isn't raining. Rain distracts me."

"Okay, let's announce that you're conducting the psychic search of Locust Ridge next Tuesday. I'll send some reporters out here to interview you. Give them the full treatment."

"How does all this harassment help you catch the killer, Spencer?"

"This is not for publication, Rattler, but I think we can smoke him out," said the sheriff. "We announce in all the media that you're going to be dowsing for bones on Tuesday. We insist that you can work wonders, and that we're confident you'll find Amy. If the killer is a local man, he'll see the notices, and get nervous. I'm betting that he'll go up there Monday night, just to make sure the body is still well-hidden. There's only one road into that area. If we can keep the killer from spotting us, I think he'll lead us to Amy's body."

"That's fine, Sheriff, but how are you going to track this fellow in the dark?"

Spencer Arrowood smiled. "Why, Rattler," he said, "I've got the Sight."

You have to do what you can to keep a sheep killer out of your fold, even if it means talking to a bunch of reporters who don't know ass from aardvark. I put up with all their fool questions, and dispensed about a dozen jugs of comfrey and chamomile tea, and I even told that blond lady on Channel 7 that she didn't need any herbs for getting pregnant, because she already was, which surprised her so much that she almost dropped her microphone, but I reckon my hospitality worked to Spencer Arrowood's satisfaction, because he came along Monday afternoon to show me a stack of newspapers with my picture looking out of the pages, and he thanked me for being helpful.

"Don't thank me," I said. "Just let me go with you tonight. You'll need all the watchers you can get to cover that ridge."

He saw the sense of that, and agreed without too much argument. I wanted to see what he meant about "having the Sight," because I'd known him since he was knee-high to a grasshopper, and he didn't have so much as a flicker of the power. None of the Arrowoods did. But he was smart enough in regular ways, and I knew he had some kind of ace up his sleeve.

An hour past sunset that night I was standing in a clearing on Locust Ridge, surrounded by law enforcement people from three counties. There were nine of us. We were so far from town that there seemed to be twice as many stars, so dark was that October sky without the haze of street lights to bleed out the fainter ones. The sheriff was talking one notch above a whisper, in case the suspect had come early. He opened a big cardboard box, and started passing out yellow and black binoculars.

"These are called ITT Night Mariners," he told us. "I borrowed ten pair from a dealer at Watauga Lake, so take care of them. They run about $2500 apiece."

"Are they infrared?" somebody asked him.

"No. But they collect available light and magnify it up to 20,000 times, so they will allow you excellent night vision. The full moon will give us all the light we need. You'll be able to walk around without a flashlight, and you'll be able to see obstacles, terrain features, and anything that's out there moving around."

"The military developed this technology in Desert Storm," said Deputy LeDonne.

"Well, let's hope it works for us tonight," said the sheriff. "Try looking through them."

I held them up to my eyes. They didn't weigh much—

about the same as two apples, I reckoned. Around me, everybody was muttering surprise, tickled pink over this new gadget. I looked through mine, and I could see the dark shapes of trees up on the hill—not in a clump, the way they look at night, but one by one, with spaces between them. The sheriff walked away from us, and I could see him go, but when I took the Night Mariners down from my eyes, he was gone. I put them back on, and there he was again.

"I reckon you do have the *Sight,* Sheriff," I told him. "Your man won't know we're watching him with these babies."

"I wonder if they're legal for hunting," said a Unicoi County man. "This sure beats spotlighting deer."

"They're illegal for deer," Spencer told him. "But they're perfect for catching sheep killers." He smiled over at me. "Now that we've tested the equipment, y'all split up. I've given you your patrol areas. Don't use your walkie-talkies unless it's absolutely necessary. Rattler, you just go where you please, but try not to let the suspect catch you at it. Are you going to do your stuff?"

"I'm going to try to let it happen," I said. It's a gift. I don't control it. I just receive.

We went our separate ways. I walked a while, enjoying the new magic of seeing the night woods same as a possum would, but when I tried to clear my mind and summon up that other kind of seeing, I found I couldn't do it, so, instead of helping, the Night Mariners were blinding me. I slipped the fancy goggles into the pocket of my jacket, and stood there under an oak tree for a minute or two, trying to open my heart for guidance. I whispered a verse from Psalm 27: *Teach me thy way, O Lord, and lead me in a plain path, because of mine enemies.* Then I looked up at the stars and tried to think of nothing. After a while I started walking, trying to keep my mind clear and go where I was led.

Maybe five minutes later, maybe an hour, I was walking across an abandoned field, overgrown with scrub cedars. The moonlight glowed in the long grass, and the cold air made my ears and fingers tingle. When I touched a post of the broken split-rail fence, it happened. I saw the field in daylight. I saw brown grass, drying up in the summer heat, and flies making lazy

circles around my head. When I looked down at the
fence rail at my feet, I saw her. She was wearing a water-
melon-colored T-shirt and jean shorts. Her brown hair
spilled across her shoulders and twined with the chicory
weeds. Her eyes were closed. I could see a smear of
blood at one corner of her mouth, and I knew. I looked
up at the moon, and when I looked back, the grass was
dead, and the darkness had closed in again. I crouched
behind a cedar tree before I heard the footsteps.

They weren't footsteps, really. Just the swish sound of
boots and trouser legs brushing against tall, dry grass. I
could see his shape in the moonlight, and he wasn't one
of the searchers. He was here to keep his secrets. He
stepped over the fence rail, and walked toward the one
big tree in the clearing—a twisted old maple, big around
as two men. He knelt down beside that tree, and I saw
him moving his hands on the ground, picking up a dead
branch, and brushing leaves away. He looked, rocked
back on his heels, leaned forward, and started pushing
the leaves back again.

They hadn't given me a walkie-talkie, and I didn't
hold with guns, though I knew he might have one. I
wasn't really part of the posse. Old Rattler with his
Twinkies and his root tea and his prophecies. I was just
bait. But I couldn't risk letting the sheep killer slip away.
Finding the grave might catch him; might not. None of
my visions would help Spencer in a court of law, which
is why I mostly stick to dispensing tonics and leave
evil alone.

I cupped my hands to my mouth and gave an owl cry,
loud as I could. Just one. The dark shape jumped up,
took a couple of steps up and back, moving its head
from side to side.

Far off in the woods, I heard an owl reply. I pulled
out the Night Mariners then, and started scanning the
hillsides around that meadow, and in less than a minute,
I could make out the sheriff, with that badge pinned to
his coat, standing at the edge of the trees with his field
glasses on, scanning the clearing. I started waving and
pointing.

The sheep killer was hurrying away now, but he was
headed in my direction, and I thought, *Risk it. What
called your name, Rattler, wasn't an owl.* So just as he's

about to pass by, I stepped out at him, and said, "Hush
now. You'll scare the deer."

He was startled into screaming, and he swung out at
me with something that flashed silver in the moonlight.
As I went down, he broke into a run, crashing through
weeds, noisy enough to scare the deer across the state
line—but the moonlight wasn't bright enough for him to
get far. He covered maybe twenty yards before his foot
caught on a fieldstone, and he went down. I saw the
sheriff closing distance, and I went to help, but I felt
light-headed all of a sudden, and my shirt was wet. I was
glad it wasn't light enough to see colors in that field.
Red was never my favorite.

I opened my eyes and shut them again, because the
flashing orange light of the rescue squad van was too
bright for the ache in my head. When I looked away, I
saw cold and dark, and knew I was still on Locust Ridge.
"Where's Spencer Arrowood?" I asked a blue jacket
bending near me.

"Sheriff! He's coming around."

Spencer Arrowood was bending over me then, with
that worried look he used to have when a big one hit
his fishing line. "We got him," he said, "You've got a
puncture in your lung that will need more than herbal
tea to fix, but you're going to be all right, Rattler."

"Since when did you get the Sight?" I asked him. But
he was right. I needed to get off that mountain and get
well, because the last thing I saw before I went down
was the same scene that came to me when I first saw
her get out of her car and walk toward my cabin. I saw
what Evelyn Albright was going to do at the trial, with
that flash of silver half hidden in her hand, and I didn't
want it to end that way.

PARRIS GREEN
Carole Nelson Douglas

FIRST APPEARANCE: *Good Night,*
Mr. Holmes, 1990

Carole Nelson Douglas has two very unusual mystery series characters. One is Midnight Louie, a cat who solves mysteries, and the other is "Irene Adler"—the same Irene Adler who Sherlock Holmes referred to as "The" woman.

Irene has appeared in four novels. This story first appeared in the anthology *Malice Domestic 2.*

Her most recent novel is *Cat in a Flamingo Fedora* (Tor, 1997).

LONDON: November 1886

I find no Sunday morning task more satisfying than that of rousing the slothful. Doubtless this is due to my upbringing as a parson's daughter, but it was aggravated by my days as a governess.

In this case the object of my dutiful disturbance had more reason than most to lie abed. Nonetheless, I crossed the threshold of her bedchamber with a certain smug rectitude. I, after all, had already been to church that morning, and she had not been to church in all of our acquaintance, unless it was to sing a solo.

The room lay beneath the drawn-curtain pall of half shadow that speaks of the sick chamber or the place of ill repute. A figure in the corner lurked motionless; luckily, I knew it for a dressmaker's form called "Jersey Lillie." I moved slowly to avoid stubbing a boot toe against the maze of trunks and hatboxes that lay scattered through the dim room. In due time I arrived safe and silent at the window, where I wrenched open the heavy brocade panels on their rods so swiftly that the curtain rings . . . well, rang.

"Agh!"

The bedclothes rose like a disturbed spirit as daylight scalded the coverlet, then a head emerged from under the linens. My friend and chambermate Irene Adler sat blinking in the sudden brightness.

"What on earth is it, Nell? Flood? Fire? The Apocalypse?"

"It is nearly noon on Sunday, Irene," I replied. "And that awful man has called again."

She pushed tumbling locks of russet hair from her face, her eyes still wincing at the light. Irene would never go to bed braided like a sensible woman. "Awful man—oh, you mean that Norton creature who stormed our lodgings a few weeks ago. Well, send him away!"

She swiftly grasped her coverlet—an oceanic expanse of emerald-green brocade that had begun as draperies—and coiled into an indiscernible lump under the covers.

I went over to address this interesting cocoon.

"It is not that Norton creature. It is that odious self-appointed poet. He is wearing brown velveteen breeches with yellow hose, an orange vest, and a soft hat the color of rust. On the Sabbath," I finished with indignation, if not relevancy.

"Oh." The buried form flailed to the surface again, finally flinging away a tidal wave of green. "You mean Oscar Wilde. I believe that he has Roman Catholic leanings. Perhaps that explains his gaudy Sunday attire. What does he want?"

"You."

"He said nothing more than that?"

"He said a great deal more, but none of it made much sense."

"What time is it?" she asked with a frown.

I consulted the watch on my lapel. "Eleven."

"Eleven? How ghastly." Amid a froth of nightgown, Irene squirmed to the bed's edge and swung a bare foot over the erratically carpeted floor. She yawned. "He must have been at the theater last evening, too. What urgent matter—imagined or real—could drag Oscar Wilde from his bed at such an inopportune hour? Oh, very well. I'll come see for myself as soon as I'm presentable. In the meantime, entertain him, Nell."

"How?"

"Make conversation."

"I cannot talk to the man! He is so full of elaborate nonsense that he quite makes my head ache and my tongue tie."

"Of course you can talk to him. Oscar Wilde could make conversation with a cockroach."

"Perhaps I should provide an audience of such, which will better appreciate his company."

"The longer you dawdle here, the longer it shall be before I can emerge to relieve you," Irene pointed out sweetly.

I sighed and returned to our parlor, where a very large and colorful spider awaited his sacrificial fly.

"Ah, the fair and faithful Penelope," he greeted me, presuming to employ my Christian name. "Four seductive syllables that end with o-p-e-. Add the *H* from Huxleigh and you have all men's hope. Ope the door to my soul, my Psyche with a crochet hook."

I refused to rise to his ludicrous bait. Soon Mr. Wilde was safely discoursing on his favorite subject, himself, and quoting Mr. Whistler's cruel letter about him in *The World*: " 'He dines at our tables and picks from our platters the plums for the pudding he peddles in the provinces.' An outp-p-p-ouring of p-p-pathetically p-p-poor alliteration," Mr. Wilde stuttered mockingly in complaint. I never knew a man to thrive so on insult.

At last came the soft click of Irene's bedchamber door. This subtle sound was followed by the crackle of what I recognized as her crimson Oriental wrapper, hardly the proper garb in which to receive a gentleman caller on any day of the week, but the theatrical temperament will not be denied.

I saw our guest's long, slightly melancholy face brighten as if dashed with a dose of daylight, and turned to watch her arrival myself. At least she had put her hair up into a brunette satin arrangement of tendrils and chignon that glinted red and gold in the daylight.

"You must forgive me for calling at so inopportune a time, my dear Irene," the abominable Oscar began. "You have sung late at the theater and deserve to slumber undisturbed until twilight. I have given you scarce time to attire yourself, but one can never catch you *en déshabillé*, I suspect. You look splendid—like a savage empress from the court of Xanadu."

"Thank you," she said simply, sitting on the old arm-chair with its embroidered shawl hiding the wear. She crossed a leg over the other with a crackle of elderly silk sharper than paper rustling. A dainty foot just visible in its purple satin slipper swung in measured pendulum time. "Why am I so honored to have Oscar Wilde serving as my personal Chanticleer?"

"An ugly hour," he admitted with a sigh. "But an uglier event unfolds only miles away," he declaimed. That is another thing I have never liked about the man, his endless bent for self-dramatization. "A tragedy in the making, even as we speak."

Irene laughed. "My dear Oscar, at least half a million tragedies are in the making of a Sunday morning in London town. What is so special about yours?"

He sat on the fringed ottoman by the fireplace—an unfortunate choice, for the low seat jackknifed his long awkward legs like a stork's—and pushed the spaniel's ears of silky brown hair from his face. "It is perplexing. And scandalous."

"Ah." Irene's idle foot tapped the floor smartly. "You are consulting me about another . . . case." She had recently and successfully inquired into the whereabouts of a gold cross he had given to Florence Stoker when she was still Florence Balcombe.

He nodded soberly. "Have you heard of the artist Lysander Parris?" When Irene shook her head, he waved a languid hand. "No matter. He is not very successful—one of these dedicated souls who lived in Chelsea before it became fashionable, a neighbor of mine. He could earn more from selling his house than from his entire collection of works."

"An impecunious artist—a redundant description if I ever heard one. Are not all artists impecunious?" Irene asked ruefully. "What difficulty faces this Lysander Parris that makes him of any interest beyond a passing charitable instinct?"

"He has gone mad."

Irene waited. Mad artists, she might have pointed out, were no more notable than poor ones.

"Quite mad," Mr. Wilde repeated, rising to pace on the worn runner before the fireplace. When a man of more than six feet paces before two seated women, the effect commands their attention, if not their admiration. "He has barricaded himself in the attic studio with his latest model and will not cease painting her. He will answer no knock, take no food or drink, say nothing to his distraught wife and children. He will not even talk to me," Mr. Wilde added with utter disbelief.

"I cannot imagine that," Irene commented. "Can you, Nell?"

I murmured something indecipherable.

"Artists," she added loftily, "are given to such obsessive spates of work. No doubt he will emerge when his latest painting is done, or he is hungry and thirsty enough. Or when the exhausted model demands to leave."

"No." Oscar Wilde paused before our hearth, one hand thrust into the breast of his velveteen jacket. His momentary stillness and silence were ever so much more impressive than his chatter and clatter. "The exhausted model will not demand to leave. From all I can determine, she is dead."

Within the half hour, our mismatched trio was jolting along in a four-wheeler toward Chelsea. Irene had dressed in a striking bronze satin gown bordered with rose moiré, and she donned long, tan-colored gloves in the carriage.

"Tell me of the household," she instructed even as she thrust the final pins into her rose moiré bonnet. Its pink and white plumes trembled in protest of such treatment.

Mr. Wilde complied with far more grace than he had managed in whistling for the vehicle minutes before. He folded his hands atop his cane—his gloves at least were conventional, the color of spoiled clotted cream—and began with an odd smile.

"The household. What can one say of any painter's household? It is as irregular as his compositions may be symmetrical. I should begin with Parris himself. He is a man of late middle age, of no distinguishing social graces, who has achieved fame in only one arena: for the lovely, decadent, lush, languid, gorgeous, gilded, intricate greens that signal his work. He is a master of the color green. I cannot look at an acanthus leaf or meet the eye on a peacock's tail, or view the emerald on the forehead of the goddess Kali, but that I think of it as Parris green."

"I presume that Mr. Parris is not Irish?" I asked somewhat tartly.

The poet's supercilious eye rested upon me with content. "I fear not, but you mistake my passion for green, dear Miss Huxleigh. I adore green not as a patriotic symbol but as the lost shadow of Eden in our world today; as the occult flame of jealousy; as the velvety unseen mosses that clothe and conquer the stone; as the ageless power in the very pinpoint of a cat's eye."

I could not help shuddering. "I do not care for cats. Or green."

"Of course not," Mr. Wilde said with something of pity in his voice. He turned to Irene. "Has my description been of assistance?"

"Of course not," she echoed him, "that is why your descriptions are always so enchanting. Mere usefulness would destroy their effect. Tell me, if you can, of the other inhabitants of the house, including the model who is now an apparent epitome of the still life."

I shuddered again, but was not much noticed. Irene had an unfortunate talent for matching gloomy poetic maunderings macabre stroke for macabre stroke. No doubt it came of too long study of excessively mordant opera librettos—all blood and betrayal and death. In fact, her eyes sparkled with mischief behind the clouds of her veiling as she watched the poet struggle to report mere fact instead of fancy.

"As well compose a sonnet from a laundry list," he said, sniffing. "Very well, the dramatis personae as recited by Bottom: We have the artist in question. We have his latest model, a pale and interesting girl employed as a housemaid, whom he has elevated from her knees on the kitchen stones to similar poses on a studio couch."

"A kitchen maid? How long has Mr. Parris been so taken with her?"

"For months, say the gossips along Tite Street."

"What of the artist's family?"

"His wife is an industrious little woman, much given to worrying, as any artist's spouse must."

"Speaking of which," Irene interjected, "I understand that I am to congratulate you upon the birth of a second son."

Our fellow passenger sighed, a slight smile on his strong-bowed lips. "Vyvyan."

"A lovely name," Irene said.

"Lovelier for a daughter, perhaps. I had hopes, but—"

"How commendable," I put in, "for a father to desire a daughter rather than an endless parade of sons."

"Praise, Miss Huxleigh?" Mr. Wilde's eyes were wickedly amused, as if he well understood how much he scandalized me. "I fear I had nothing to do with it. A higher power than mere hope determined the matter."

"And how is Constance?" Irene inquired.

"Well," he said of his wife, flicking a spot of lint from his velvet knee. "Better than Amelia Parris, poor woman. Her husband's mania for the new model has been the talk of Chelsea, but Mrs. Parris is a simple soul who cares more for the price of eggs than the bankruptcy of reputation."

"What other family members inhabit the house?"

"The usual parade of offspring, most young enough for the schoolroom, except for Lawrence."

"The eldest son?"

Mr. Wilde nodded, then leaned his slouch-hatted head out of the carriage window. For such gestures his unorthodox headgear was more suitable than the conventional top hat. "We near Cheyne Place. I will let you see young Lawrence for yourself."

Once the carriage had jolted to a stop, he stepped out to assist us. I hated to take the creature's hand, but there was no help for it. Nor could I forgo murmuring my thanks. I cannot say why I had taken such a dislike to Mr. Wilde; there was no more reason for it than for his taking such a mad fancy to me. Perhaps, like the clever puss, he made a point of loving those who hated him. I suppose that could be considered a kind of Christian charity, but in Mr. Wilde's case I felt that the impulse was far more perverse.

We stood for a moment on the cobblestones, surveying the house. Unlike many in fashionable Tite Street, where even I knew that such artists as Whistler and Sargent kept studios, this house had not been revived with fresh, stylish colors. A smoky patina fumed its dull brick facade, and the door was painted a sober but chipping black, as if in tawdry mourning.

Faded damask draped the windows, all in sinister shades of green.

"Why do you think Mr. Parris became so obsessed with his model?" Irene asked the poet.

"She was young and from outside this depressing house. He thought her beautiful, no doubt. Perhaps he had tired of failure and growing older, and painted a more appetizing future on his canvases."

"If you have been unable to enter the studio, why are you convinced that she is dead?"

"It is possible to view a section of the room through a . . . er, keyhole. Yes, Miss Huxleigh, to such vulgar snooping even I was forced to stoop." Mr. Wilde eyed Irene again. "Parris had a strong lock put on the inside of the door years ago. He has always disliked being interrupted while painting. I can only attest to what little I saw with my own eyes: the lady in question not only is supernaturally motionless, but her pallor is beyond the ordinary pale of fashionable rice powder. Her lips have turned blue."

I made an involuntary cry at this macabre detail, but Irene merely narrowed her eyes as if to better visualize the grisly scene. "And what do you think has killed her? Or who?"

"That I am afraid to speculate upon," the poet admitted. "Poor Parris must be made to forsake his studio so that the lady's body can be carried away before the neighbors and the police scent a scandal."

"My dear Oscar, when the young woman's body is carried away, there is certain to be a scandal if her death was not natural."

"No death is natural," he declared, launching another high-flown speech. "A death should always be witnessed by a great poet, so that proper note may be taken of it."

"I really do not see what you expect me to do in this instance," Irene said, ignoring his egocentric prescription for death scenes.

"Pry the madman loose from his easel! Although they do not know the depth of my suspicion, his wife and son cannot do it, despite all their beyond-the-door pleadings;

that is why I was sent for. I know Parris well, and in fact had obtained him some meager employment for illustrations in the literary magazines," he added. "Not my most eloquent words nor gilded syllables could wrest the man from his feverish painting. I count upon your woman's wit, my dear Irene. Besides, few men can resist you."

She smiled ruefully. "I encountered one of that rare breed only weeks ago."

"No!" Mr. Wilde drew back, clutching his breast. "What manner of depraved creature is he?"

"A barrister," Irene answered dryly.

"Oh." The poet recovered his aplomb and dropped his theatrics. "One cannot expect intelligence or sense from a barrister. My faith in your powers remains undiminished."

"We shall see," Irene answered. "Meanwhile—" She gestured to the rather grimy stoop that awaited our footfalls.

The house was as I expected: dark and narrow, with a battered spine of stairway and that stale wet odor of domiciles built near the supposed advantage of a river.

A woman admitted us, a stern figure in black bombazine who might have been a widow. She identified herself as "Mrs. McCorkle, the housekeeper" in a voice like a hacksaw and regarded Mr. Wilde with visible skepticism. Mrs. Parris, we were told, lay prostrate in her bedchamber, the children visited the homes of assorted acquaintances, who had been told only that their father had fallen suddenly ill; Mr. Parris still kept to his studio.

"These ladies," said Mr. Wilde, gesturing to us both with one sweep of a plump hand, "these lovely sibyls of Saffron Hill, will lend wisdom and succor to a sad situation. Miss Adler, Miss Huxleigh, and I will need no guidance to the upper stories."

"As you wish, sir," the woman answered sourly. "No one is here to gainsay you." She eyed Irene and myself as if we were dingy laundry, then retreated into the dismal drawing room on our left.

We climbed the dark, uncarpeted stairs, a landing window offering a glimpse of neglected back garden gone to weed and wildness. Up we went, for what seemed endless turns of the ungracious stairs but was only four stories.

At last the stairs ended at a broad wooden door.

"Much of the top floor has been made into a studio," Mr. Wilde informed us in a whisper.

I saw why it had been so convenient to view the room. With the steps leading up to the door, one could stand two or three risers down, lean forward, and be eye level with the peephole.

Mr. Wilde demonstrated by backing down four steps and doing precisely that. Irene and I flattened ourselves against the yellowing walls, while I contemplated a larger and more intimate view of the poet's velvet breeches than I wished.

He finally unbent with an almost satisfied sigh. "Nothing has changed. Not the model, nor the sounds of paint slap-dashing on canvas. Parris works on quite assiduously."

"Allow me." Irene assumed the same undignified posture with much more grace and squinted through the brass keyhole. She straightened a moment later, looking less optimistic than the poet. "The long plait of hair that entwines her throat," she asked him, "was it there before?"

"It entwines her throat?" He blinked like a cogitating owl.

"I confess I was more impressed by her pallor than the disposition of her tresses. I have never been partial to that unimaginative shade of chestnut. You believe that Parris strangled her with her own hair? A most artistic conceit. I would not have thought it of him."

"Or a most conceited artist, to think that a model would care to die for a painting. The question is how she was posed before she died. Mr. Parris may have planned another of these languishing ladies mimicking death so popular in the salons—Ophelia floating amid her waterlilies, or Desdemona adrift on her bed linens. The woman's pallor could be merely cosmetic; she could keep so still simply because she is an accomplished model."

I clasped my hands. "Oh, Irene, of course! This is all a silly misunderstanding. We need not have come here at all." I gave Mr. Wilde a pointed look.

She regarded me fondly. "However, I must confess in turn that she looks quite convincingly dead. Mr. Parris will not open the door?"

The poet shook his head until his doleful locks rippled.

Irene lifted a fist and knocked briskly.

"Go away!" a voice thundered promptly. "I told you meddling fools to go away. I am not finished yet."

"Mr. Parris, sir," she replied, "your family is most concerned, and no doubt your model is . . . exhausted."

"Go away, damn, impertinent disrupters! I must put it on canvas. I must capture that look—"

"And we all are impatient to see the results of your labors. Even Oscar Wilde is here, waiting to tell a wider world about your work."

"That fulminating fop! He tells no one about anything other than himself! I told him to leave my house, and you may go, too, madam, whoever the devil you are."

Irene drew back, then lowered her gloved fist.

"Well?" Mr. Wilde asked breathlessly.

"We retreat," she ordered. With great difficulty, and much unwelcome jostling, we turned in the cramped stairway and made our sorry progress below.

At the first landing Irene drew Mr. Wilde to a stop. "Are Mr. Parris's paintings kept anywhere besides the studio?"

"I saw a number of canvases in a second-floor room."

"Then I would like to see them."

"Why?" I asked. "Surely there is nothing we can do here. The man's door is bolted from within and he will not open it. It is a matter for the authorities."

"Perhaps," Irene conceded. "Ultimately. Until then, if the artist refuses to speak with me, I will make do with the next best thing: I will commune with his work."

Mr. Wilde lifted his eyebrows, but led us without comment to the room in question.

Within minutes Irene and Mr. Wilde had pulled the stacked canvases from the wall and had propped them against the furniture. Most of the canvases were narrow, and as tall as people.

Oscar Wilde made a face, which was not difficult for him to do under any circumstances. "Not to my taste."

"What is your taste?" Irene asked.

"*San Sebastian* by Guido Reni," he retorted with authority. "A sublime subject."

"Ah." Irene tilted her head with a Mona Lisa smile. "The swooning, half-naked young man pierced by arrows. How . . . interesting, Oscar."

"The martyrdom of St. Stephen!" I exclaimed, happy to have understood what they were talking about for once. "I know it. A most inspirational subject, though sad."

His smile was as mysterious as Irene's. "More inspiring than these modern, insipidly lethal belladonna madonnas cloaked in green, whose suffering is so much more commonplace."

I studied the array. We stood amid a company of the dead model's likeness in every guise, her long dark hair caught up in a jeweled snood while she strolled in classical garb with a peacock—"Jealous *Juno*," Irene pronounced; or she hung suspended in weed-swirled water clothed in mermaid's scales, a drowned sailor caught in the toils of her seaweed-dressed locks—*The Siren of the Rhine*, according to Irene; or she floated in diaphanous veils of lurid green from a bottle bearing a French label.

Irene nodded at the last work. "*La Fée Verte*—the seductive green fairy of absinthe, the liquor that entoils men and drives them mad. Does Mr. Parris drink it?"

Mr. Wilde shrugged. "Perhaps. All these . . . fancies feature the green pigments for which he is famous."

She nodded. "Parris green. Most effective. Most decadent. Is not arsenic a component of such green pigments?"

"Arsenic? I have heard—" Mr. Wilde's pasty complexion showed a more verdant cast. "You think that . . . ? I cannot see how."

"Nor can I. I merely comment on the fact that Mr. Parris's addiction to green has a deadly undertone. Of course, one would expect a pigment-based poison to affect the artist, not his model."

Irene strolled around the assembled pictures, contemplating their heavy-lidded subject face-to-face. "Mr. Parris's mania seems fixed upon the femme fatale, the kind of ruinous woman who preys upon men. One seldom sees the ruiners of women glamorized, perhaps because so few women paint, or are encouraged to. Yet the legions of ruined women must far outnumber the few men who stumble at the feet of a Delilah. At least my art— the opera—offers equal roles in villainy and heroics to men and women."

"Your art," the poet put in, "has an edge."

"So," said I, "does Irene. And if she wishes a perfect model of an *homme fatale,* she need look no further than that Mephistopheles in miniature, the American artist, James Whistler."

Oscar Wilde laughed. "My neighbor, my mentor, my enemy, but then Jimmy is everybody's enemy, and his own most of all. A pity that he so seldom does self-portraits."

"Wicked women are too common these days to be intriguing," Irene put in. "It's Mr. Parris's heroines who intrigue me. Such unusual choices."

I studied the canvas she tilted into the light of the gasolier. Gone was the turgid hair; the figure's cropped head and rough masculine dress proclaimed Joan of Arc, if the copious fleurs-de-lis in the background had not already given away the subject.

Irene examined the brush marks. "From the looser strokes, a recent work, I would suggest. And this. What do you think, Nell?"

She indicated a female figure in long Renaissance robes, again the fleurs-de-lis figuring her gown, but a stern, almost fanatical expression on her gaunt, impassioned face.

"Can you guess, Oscar? No? Is this not a Daniel come to judgment? The female Torquemada of Mr. Shakespeare's plays?"

"Portia!" said I. "The artist marches to a grimmer tune of late."

"Indeed." Irene let the canvas lean back against the table and turned to a humble assembly near the window. "But what are these? They look intriguing."

"Hatboxes! Truly, Irene, you have a great quantity more than you need at home."

"But not so charmingly covered—with wallpaper— and some cut so the design of one lays against the pattern of another. Oh, I must have one—or several!"

"Easily done." Oscar Wilde exhibited the amused tolerance a man expends on a woman taken by something trivial. "Amelia's fancywork. She sells them to the ladies hereabout. I don't doubt that it shoes the children's feet. With Parris devoted to his mania for the servant girl model, he can't have sold much work of late."

"Well." Irene turned from the hatboxes. "To work. I must interview the vital members of the household. Mrs. Parris, her eldest son, and perhaps the so charming lady who answered the door. The children, I think, can be left to their ignorance. Bring me Mrs. Parris first. Tell her that I am interested in hatboxes."

The poet took no offense at being commissioned as a messenger. He withdrew to be replaced some few minutes later by a compact woman with fading brown hair. Her navy serge skirt's telltale box pleats and draped bustle indicated that it had been purchased several years before. Her face was as well worn as her gown, the eyes a wan blue set in dark circles of skin, but there was no sign of recent tears or hysterics.

"My dear Mrs. Parris!" Irene's voice warmed with welcome, as if she were the householder and Amelia Parris the visitor. "How good of you to meet with us. Oscar has hopes that I can persuade your husband to abandon his studio."

"Why should he listen to you?" Mrs. Parris inquired a trifle sharply. "I have never heard of an Irene Adler."

"Because Oscar has decided that he must. I am a singer, you see, and poor Oscar is convinced that my voice can soothe the savage breast."

"Lysander is not particularly savage." Mrs. Parris sighed and tucked a dull lock of hair behind one ear. "Or at least he was not known to be. Before . . ."

"Before?"

"Before he developed a mania for one particular model."

"He has not had such a single-minded fancy previously?"

Mrs. Parris's features puckered listlessly. "There were models, of course, often the subjects of a series of paintings. That is why he put a lock on the inside of the studio door. He did not wish anyone to see his work in progress."

"When was the lock installed?"

She shrugged as listlessly as her face changed expressions. "Some years ago, perhaps six."

"Six," Irene repeated for no apparent reason, spinning away from the paintings. "What I am simply mad about are these enchanting hatboxes of yours, Mrs. Parris. You use—pardon the pun—Paris papers, do you not?"

A flush warmed the woman's drawn cheeks. "Why, yes. Thank you. However did you know?"

Irene dropped into a graceful crouch that only an actress could manage without seeming in imminent danger of toppling. She studied the piled round boxes with the intensity of a happy child.

"Why, by the patterns. None but the French show such whimsy, such joie de vivre—or use so many Napoleonic bees." Her gloved forefinger tapped an example of the latter. "But I do not see a single fleur-de-lis."

"I suppose not," Mrs. Parris admitted, "although I find the flower designs . . . cheerful."

"And you appliqué one paper atop the ground of another, like lace," Irene went on admiringly. "How utterly clever."

Again the sullen cheeks burnished with pleasure at praise rubbed on so warmly. "I am not considered a clever person ordinarily," Mrs. Parris said, "but the ladies of Chelsea find my small efforts appealing."

Irene rose, her bronze silk skirts falling into folds around her, like a theatrical curtain descending after a performance. "I must have at least one—and one for my dear friend Miss Huxleigh."

"Oh, no—" I began to object.

"Nonsense, Nell." Irene's stage-trained voice drowned out my demurs without sounding rude. "You have been longing for the right hatbox; I am certain of it. Which one do you want?"

"I don't know," I began, meaning to say that I didn't even know the price of such a frivolity.

"Impossible to decide on just one." Irene turned again to the now openly pleased woman. "How do you choose which pattern to use? They are all so enchanting."

Mrs. Parris ducked her head in an odd combination of shyness and shame. "Many houses hereabouts are being redecorated in the new aesthetic manner. Some are old papers taken down; others remnants of the replace-

ments. The ladies of the house see that I get them; I am
awash in wallpapers."

"Wonderful," marveled Irene, adding in a kindly tone,
"No doubt the sales of these lovely things come in handy
in an artistic household."

The poor woman was so flushed by now that she could
blush no more. Her answer flowed like paint from a
brush. "Oh, yes. An artist's lot is hand to mouth, and
so also for his family. Lawrence can only spare so much
from his position."

"Your son. With a position. How proud you must be."

"He is only a clerk in the City. His father calls such
employment 'tattooing with a goose quill for an associa-
tion of geese,' but it brings in a regular salary."

Irene smiled. "I fear I share the artistic suspicion of
matters mathematical, like accounting."

"You are utterly charming, Miss Adler," Mrs. Parris
said suddenly, her face saddening again. "If anyone can
coax Lysander from his . . . mania, you can."

"Thank you," Irene said. "I will try, and try again,
until I succeed. And then I will reward myself and Miss
Huxleigh by purchasing two of your little masterpieces."

"No—a gift."

"We will debate that when I have earned the privilege," Irene insisted. "And now, I wonder, is your hardworking son at home?"

Mrs. Parris blinked at the sudden change in topic. "I
believe he is below stairs. I will send him up, if you
wish."

Irene beamed. "I do."

The moment the woman's skirts had hissed into the
uncarpeted hall I broke my commendable silence with a
stage whisper. "Irene! I do not require a hatbox."

"Are they not charming and original?"

"Yes! But my funds—our funds—are unoriginally
meager."

She waved an airy hand. "Money can always be found
for small necessities."

"Hatboxes?"

"Hush. I hear a firm tread on the stair."

In a moment a young man's form followed the sound
of his approach into the room. He saw first us, then
the array of propped-up paintings, and stopped at the

threshold, frowning. "My mother said you wished to see me. Miss Adler, is it?"

"Mr. Wilde and I are concerned about your father," Irene said calmly.

He concealed sudden fists in his pants pockets, a graceless gesture that I should never have allowed in any charge of mine during my governess days.

"Father can go to hell, if he hasn't already," young Lawrence announced through his teeth.

I drew in my breath, but Irene remained unshaken. "You disapprove of your father's obsession with his model. Yet often such artistic obsessions produce many canvases and much money."

"Father's paintings are the fancy of a failing mind. That 'famous' Parris green you see there has eaten him away like some festering mental moss. An old fool has no right to be forcing himself on servant girls and elevating them to heights where they cannot keep their heads. Who does she think *she* is?" His broad gesture dismissed the model's many guises. "Who does he think *he* is—an old man whose fancy flies in the face of his family honor. Nobody. He should sign his damned puddles of putrid green 'Nobody.' "

"I take it that you do not approve of your father's calling when it becomes obsession."

"I do not approve of calling it art when it is something much more obvious. He has a mania for *her,* not for his paintings of her. He has painted her half to death, until she has exhausted herself into a shadow, and now he rushes to finish painting her before the sun sinks and even a shadow is too weak to be seen. May I go now? I do not like to see so many shadows spun through the poisonous web of his paintbrush."

He had turned on his heel before Irene could finish saying, "Leave if you must."

Again we were alone in the room, and I was mystified. "The young man disapproves of his father's mania, and rightly so. His mother is slighted by such obsessions, even if there's no harm in it."

"Oh, there's harm in it." Irene's face hardened to alabaster, as it often did when she confronted something dangerous. "Deep poison. Parris green poison."

"In the paints?" I asked, confused.

She turned to me. "In the paints, and in the persons who share the roof of this unhappy domicile."

"What poison is there beyond the arsenic pigment you mentioned?"

"Jealousy," she said obliquely. "And on that note, it is time to interview the key figure in this domestic tragedy."

She went to the door, where I was surprised to find that Oscar Wilde stood modest guard, and whispered something to our conductor into this den of death and deception. He vanished with a clatter of boots down the stairs. I found my stare passing numbly from the many paintings of a possibly murdered girl in shades of green to the gay towers of hatboxes awaiting owners. I saw all, but I saw nothing.

A more discreet set of steps announced a surprising person: the sour servant who had admitted us to the house.

Irene began without frills. "You are aware that your master has locked himself in the studio."

" 'Tis nothing new," the woman replied.

I had seen her sort before in the houses in which I was a governess: hardened by service into sullen semi-cooperation, slow to say anything yet quick to see all. She would give only what she had to, and that grudgingly.

"What is the situation here?" Irene asked.

"I thought you knew."

"I meant your own."

A rough shrug, one a world away from the timid gesture of Mrs. Parris. "I cook, clean if I have to, which I have to when the cleaning girl is lounging on a scarlet shawl under the eaves for the pleasure of the master's paintbrush."

"Where do you sleep?"

Irene's question surprised the woman. "Under the eaves. Not all of the fourth story is given over to art. I have a room off the little landing just below there."

"And she?"

"She?"

"Your sister servant."

"Huh! She's no sister of mine, Phoebe Miller." The woman brushed the back of her hand across her nose.

"She's got a cubbyhole, too, though she's not been in it lately."

"Some would suspect a man, a painter with a passion for depicting women, of harboring a passion for his model as well as his art. Do you?"

"Gossip is not my job, miss."

"I am not asking about gossip. I am asking what you saw and heard."

"Saw and heard?" Mrs. McCorkle's face showed wary confusion.

"In your room. Under the eaves. Did the master ever visit the maid?"

The woman's feet shuffled uneasily on the floor, but Irene was implacable—a force that must be answered. A mistress interrogating a servant. Mrs. McCorkle finally spoke, her plain voice curdled with a thin scum of contempt.

"I heard noises. Footsteps. At night. The servants' stairs are narrow and dark. A light would slither along the crack under my door like a yellow snake. Footsteps from the bottom to the top. Sometimes they didn't go all the way up. Sometimes they stopped halfway." She frowned. "And sometimes they went all the way up, and came down soft so I couldn't hear, and went up halfway again. Did the master visit the maid, miss? Do snakes slither?"

Irene took a leisurely turn around the room, holding our attention as a strolling actor does. "What do you think of the young woman who models for Mr. Parris?"

"What I think doesn't matter."

"To me it does."

"Oh, you're nice, aren't you? Asking so sweet and sharp. Never wrinkling a brow or your petticoats. Well, I'll tell you, Miss Who Wants to Know! I'll tell you what it's like to be scrubbing the stoop and washing the stairs and the kettles and some so-called 'girl' is taking her ease behind locked doors and turning up with her face leering out for everyone to see—even his wife and son and little children."

Irene nodded, undisturbed. "What do you think of her?" she repeated softly.

"Isn't much to look at. Not really, especially now she's so thin and pale. Master must be losing more than his mind of late; eyesight more likely. Quiet, Phoebe is. Never looks at you straight—always cringing on the back stairs when we meet, like she expects me to hit her. I suppose she was steady enough at her work before the master brought her up to the studio." The woman frowned. "But she was always the favorite. There was the kitten, you see."

"Kitten?" Irene asked alertly.

"Starved wisp of a thing Phoebe found by the embankment. We're not allowed kittens in servants' quarters, though there be mice enough for 'em. This one was too young for mice—all fuzz and bone. Phoebe would feed it scraps from below. Not allowed, that. But no one took it from her."

"Perhaps no one knew," I put in, breaking the long silence I had kept as I watched Irene pull answers from this woman as a dental surgeon pulls rotten molars from diseased gums.

Mrs. McCorkle's harsh gaze turned on me. "Oh, someone knew, all right. The creature would mew something fierce when she left it alone all day. On and on. *He'd* have heard it, on the other side of the wall, working at his quiet painting. But he never said nothing; his favorite could have certain favors, you see."

"And Mrs. Parris was unaware of the kitten?"

"How would she know? Now there's a real lady, for all she has to hawk her hatboxes to her very own neighbors to pay for food on the table and the few pence servants cost. A sweet, honest soul. She didn't ignore me like I was a doormat to see only in coming and going. She even took some of them fancy papers she got from the likes of Mr. Whistler and Mrs. Wilde and put 'em up herself in my room—a real pretty pattern of these yellow birds and flowers, twining like. Brightened up the place. She even papered Phoebe's cubbyhole. I'll give that to Mrs. Parris. She's a charitable soul who sees past evil to do good."

"You mean that Mr. Parris's obsession with Phoebe was already evident when his wife papered the servants' quarters?"

"To all but the blind."

"Then Mrs. Parris must have seen the kitten," Irene suggested, "and said nothing."

Mrs. McCorkle shook her head. "No. It was dead by then."

"Dead!" I exclaimed weakly. I had been touched by the tale of a kitten that had found a home with the servants under the eaves.

Mrs. McCorkle nodded with weary callousness. "Too young, too ill-used. It stopped eating and retched its little insides out. They seldom survive when they're taken too young from the mother. Phoebe was a fool to try to save it."

"You may go," Irene said suddenly, as if disgusted.

Mrs. McCorkle caught her tone and flushed a bit, but turned without comment.

"You must be overrun with mice now," Irene added as suddenly.

"Mice?" Mrs. McCorkle stopped without turning. "No, don't hear them anymore. Maybe that silly kitten did some good before it died. I could use some quiet in the servants' quarters." She walked through the door. Shortly after we heard her discreet step on the stairs.

"The treads do creak in these old houses," Irene observed. "Imagine how they scream in the servants' stairway. What a story there is in a flight of stairs!"

Oscar Wilde's unwelcome face popped around the doorjamb like a puppet's at a Punch and Judy show. "I am aquiver with curiosity, dear Irene, and could barely remain away, save that I know an artist needs solitude to work. What have you learned, and how are we to release Parris from his lair and prevent a scandal?"

"I'm afraid that there is no way to prevent a scandal," Irene declared.

The poet fully entered the chamber. "That is the wonder you needed to work."

"I am not a wonder worker. As for Mr. Parris, I know of only one way to extract him."

"How?" Oscar Wilde demanded.

"Come and see." She swept from the room and I heard her firm, quick step on the front stairs as she ascended once again to the locked door.

We followed her mutely, the great lumbering poet and I, each drumming our own rhythm upon the stairs—his a heavy, regular tread as he took steps two at a time, mine a faint staccato as I followed him.

Irene was straightening from inspecting the keyhole when we arrived.

"Nothing has changed, and everything has changed," she announced.

"Then how are we to enter?"

She eyed him up and down. "*You* are to enter, dear Oscar. You are a brawny man. You and Bram Stoker make me wonder if blarney breeds giants, you are both such towering Irishmen. I understand that you excelled in sport as well as scholarship at Oxford." She stepped back against the wall, drawing her bronze silk skirts as close to her as forty yards of fabric would permit. "Break down the door at your leisure."

"Break it?" His homely face broke into an angelic smile. "I will be the talk of Chelsea. Of course. I must break down the door."

With this he clattered down a few steps, turned sideways, then went charging upward like a velveteen bull and hit the door shoulder first. There came a great groan of wood and wounded poet, but Mr. Wilde gamely drew back and hurled himself again at the barrier. Splinters flew as the door bowed inward. An enraged male voice thundered from within, then fell silent. Oscar and Irene braved the breach as one.

I was the last to broach that threshold, last to see the sight that had stilled and silenced my fellow intruders and even the man who had painted it.

She lay dead—of that there could be no question— her face a hollow death mask of palest ivory. Against her deathly pallor, the emerald silk of her gown lapped like a vast, poisonous sea. The uncompleted painting on the artist's easel shone wet, a ghastly reflection in an opaque mirror of green paint.

The artist himself had slumped onto a pigment-spattered stool. Light spilled from a skylight above, drawing in every cruel detail, including the lines in Lysander Parris's haggard features, the coarse, thick clots of white hair streaking his natural brown color, the shaking arm that loosely supported a predominantly green palette.

"My masterpiece," he said in a raw voice.

Irene approached the dead woman, drew the plait of long dark hair from across her throat. Mr. Wilde gasped at her gesture, but the braid merely rested there. No marks marred the slender neck.

Lysander Parris started up from his stool as if waking into a nightmare. "Do not disturb the pose! I am almost done."

The stairs creaked.

We turned.

Mother and son stood in the doorway, the wife's eyes upon her husband, the son's upon the dead model.

"We heard—" Mrs. Parris began, moving toward her husband, drawing the palette from his grasp to set it aside.

The son took two steps into the room, then stopped as if dumbfounded, staring sightlessly at the dead woman. "She's . . . not alive."

"No," Irene said gently. "She's gone. We should leave as well."

"But—" Young Lawrence looked up, his gaze afire with fury, then saw the wreck that was his father as his mother led him from the room like a sleepwalking child. "I don't understand . . ."

Irene took his arm, then led him to me. Only an hour ago he had been storming in the room below; now he was the dead eye of the storm. I guided him down the stairs, my own adoptive child in tow, behind the artist and his wife.

I could hear the voices of Oscar Wilde and Irene Adler in consultation behind me.

Mrs. Parris bore her prize down to the drawing room, seating him on a settee covered in worn tapestry. At the door hovered Mrs. McCorkle.

"Tea," Mrs. Parris ordered as I guided her stunned son to a Morris chair crouching in a corner.

The men sat in common shock, while women bustled around them. I couldn't help thinking that Mrs. Parris was in her element—that her role and her rule came through mastering domestic crises; that the servant, Mrs. McCorkle, also took a certain pride in being of use; that some intimate mechanism had been rebalanced and a terrible tension eased.

Tea was steaming from four cups when Irene's figure darkened the doorway.

I started.

"Nell, could you come with me for a moment?"

I murmured my excuses and left that dour drawing room with its silent population of victims and survivors.

"Where is Mr. Wilde?" I asked in the hall.

Irene was amused. "Surely you do not miss him."

"No, but—"

She took my arm in her most confiding, yet commanding way. "He has gone for the doctor, who will declare the poor girl dead and see to her removal. Nothing will be left of that macabre scene but the painting of it, and I wonder if that will survive."

"Why should it not? It is his 'masterpiece,' despite its price."

"What is its price, Nell?"

"Dishonor. Dishonesty. A family stricken."

She nodded, pleased. "You put it well. A family stricken, as virulently as if by poison. If they are fortunate, no one will suspect the murder."

"Murd—"

Irene's fingers clamped quite effectively over my mouth. "Hush, Nell! One can only invoke such words in ringing tones in a Shakespearean play, and this is merely a domestic tragedy by Webster."

She led me down the staircase to the kitchens below the ground floor. I sensed a cramped, dingy space and the shining bulk of a tea kettle on a hearth. Irene led me to a small door and opened it.

"What is this place?" I asked.

"The servants' stair."

"Oh. We're not going up there?"

"We most certainly are; otherwise I'll never know if my theory is correct."

"Theory?"

"Of how the murder was accomplished."

"Irene, I do not wish to climb any more stairs in this ghastly house. I do not wish to know how or why, or even if. Can we not go home to Saffron Hill and pretend that you slept undisturbed till curtain time and Mr. Wilde never came and—"

"And that you never enjoyed waking me up?"

"I did not! Enjoy it, I mean. Not too much."

She was leading me inexorably up the narrow stairs. Each step moaned at our passage like a ghost trod upon.

"Not so much that I must pay penance," I added as the stair turned and grew darker. The walls felt damp as I brushed them, and were rough enough to snag Irene's silken skirts. I tried not to think how it must feel to mount such stairs every night, to be a forgotten housemaid, to be brought from such a place to a silk-draped sofa. Might not any poor wretch choose the studio over the garret, no matter the price?

At a tiny landing, Irene paused, then half disappeared into the wall. I cried out despite myself.

"Mrs. McCorkle's bedchamber," Irene explained. A match struck, then smoke assaulted my nostrils. Light grew beyond Irene and she walked into it, out of my sight.

"Come in, Nell. There's nothing to fear here."

I followed to find her shadow thrown so large upon the room's cramped walls that it seemed all in shade. "Are you saying that Mrs. McCorkle is a murderer?"

Irene's hatted head shook on her shoulders and on her shadow. She seemed one of those monstrous pagan gods, horned and terrible. "Observe the wallpaper, Nell."

"There is too much shadow to see . . . yes, a print of yellow and ivory and blue. I see it in the corner. Wallpaper, Irene?"

Irene sighed, her shadow's shoulders heaving with her. "Few bother to paper servants' quarters, even such dreary holes as this."

"Mrs. Parris is indeed a thoughtful woman. I wonder that she can nurse her husband after what he has done."

Irene turned on me, her voice cold as steel. "What has he done?"

"Why—abandoned his family for a servant girl; pursued his art at the cost of every person around him. Look at the man! He is half mad and wholly deteriorated."

She brushed by me, a silhouette holding a burning coal of lamplight. I heard the stairs cry out as she mounted the last flight.

I did not want to go farther. I did not wish to know more. But I could not stop myself.

When I reached the very apex of the house, Irene blocked the last doorway. She crouched suddenly, in that graceful way she had, and I saw the miserable hole that served as home for the dead girl. It made me cringe, the barren meanness of it, the equation of cot and shelf and chamber pot. How hard to blame the one who lived here for anything. In the silence I thought I heard the faint scratch of kittenish paws, a phantom mewling added to the groans of the lost souls on the stairs below, and my eyes filled with tears.

"The wallpaper, Nell," Irene said in deep, sad, angry tones. "The wallpaper."

I could not see wallpaper. I could only see dark, and light, and more dark. But my eyes finally cleared and little figures danced into focus before me—blue butterflies on an ivory ground, gay, hovering creatures at the top of the house. Not butterflies, but fleurs-de-lis.

"Artists are not usually prone to puns." Irene's voice came ponderously. "Lysander Parris was an exception. That's why he called his trademark color 'Parris green.' "

"I don't understand, Irene,"

"There is an actual, original 'Paris green,' named for that city of art and gaiety and fashion. That Paris green is a preparation used to keep certain colors—such as blue, paradoxically—from running in wallpapers. It is made from an arsenic compound and can never, ever lose its lethal properties. It will never die, Nell, and therefore it will deal death forever."

"What are you saying?"

"The kitten, Nell. Remember the kitten."

"It died."

"Precisely."

"But if it was poisoned, surely the food from the kitchen, meant for Phoebe—"

"Not food. And the mice."

"There are no mice now."

"Precisely."

"Irene." I clutched her bronze silk sleeve. "Are we—"

"I would not linger," she said wryly, rising and lifting the lamp, so her silhouette blotted out the artful blue French wallpaper imbued with death and Paris green.

Four months later Oscar Wilde forwarded an invitation to a showing of Lysander Parris works at a small gallery near the British Museum.

"I am amazed the man still has a taste to paint," I said.

"He is an artist," Irene retorted. "The artistic temperament thrives on suffering. Look at me."

I did so. She was lounging on our sofa, sipping hot chocolate illegally brewed upon the fireplace fender, wrapped in another of her sunset-colored Oriental gowns.

"Indeed," I said dryly. "I do not care to see another Parris painting."

"The affair might be instructive. After all, no scandal resulted; no charges were brought. The word *murder* was heard only in the far reaches of the servants' quarters."

"If you are right, it was an unimaginably dreadful murder. That sweet woman so consumed with jealousy. And that poor girl, sleeping each night, her own chamber a death trap. No wonder she looked so properly pale and wan in those awful paintings—she was slowly dying."

"And the artist was in love with death, as artists so often are these days, whether it be with the green fairy of absinthe or some imagined temptress who may be only a housemaid at heart. But it is remarkable that Mr. Parris has lived to paint another day. *He* was being slowly poisoned as well. That is why he became so irrational and locked himself in with the dead woman. He never even noticed her condition."

"He was in jeopardy? How?"

"Need I point out the incident of the footsteps in the night?"

"Oh." I blushed for my innocence. "You mean that if he, when he . . . visited Phoebe, he also was exposed to the Paris green."

"Exactly. As he succumbed to the poison, he began putting the fleurs-de-lis—truly *fleurs de mal*, 'flowers of evil'—in his paintings. And the more often he visited, the more poison he absorbed through his very pores. An ingenious scheme—he would pay to the extent he abused his wife's honor. He would, in fact, dispense the dosage of his own death. If he was innocent of infidelity, only she would die."

"Irene, that's diabolical!"

"Is it any more diabolical than the propensity of artists

to introduce the models with whom they are obsessed into the bosom of their families, expecting them to be accepted? And, in this case, the son *would* be foolish enough to rival the father."

"The son? He was involved in this folly as well?"

"Whose were the second footsteps that halted halfway up? Lawrence, too, had become enamored of the girl. He knew what was going on and raged inwardly, but he was not as clever as his mother—who had been secretly seething over her husband's indiscretions for years, else why did Mr. Parris bar his studio door?—and Lawrence did not find a way to murder."

"Why was there no scandal, Irene? Did the authorities never question the death?"

"Never."

"Why not?"

"She was an artist's model, a poor servant. People of her sort and class die young all the time—of drink, of debauchery, of neglect. No one cared enough to note her passing."

"I have been very wrong."

"You certainly have not anticipated the turns of the case."

"Not that, Irene. I have judged that poor dead girl harshly. I have condemned her as a fallen woman, but the wronged wife in this case was willing to kill an innocent girl on mere suspicion. That poor Phoebe was not innocent does not lessen the wife's wrong."

Irene reached to the sidetable and selected one of her annoying cigarettes. I had to endure the perfume of sulfur before she would go on.

"She *was* innocent," Irene declared on a misty blue breath. "Perfectly innocent."

"How can you say that for certain?"

"Because I went to the morgue to identify the body."

"Irene! How could you do that?"

"Easily. I donned rusty black and a county accent and said I was the deceased girl's long-lost sister and, please, sir, could anyone say, did she die a ruined woman? And they talked and thought and hemmed and hawed and finally decided to relieve my sisterly mind and said no, she did not."

"How can they tell?"

"That is another bedtime story, Nell, and I am sick of telling this one."

"But the footsteps—"

"He went there often, but he did not succeed, despite all his pleadings. He captured her only in paint."

"So it was all for nothing."

"Murder usually is."

"And we will not go to the exhibition."

"We will see."

"We" did nothing of the sort. Irene decided to go, and I could not resist glimpsing the end of the story, even if it meant another encounter with Oscar Wilde.

The gallery was crowded, a long, narrow space glittering with gaslight and glasses of sherry and festively garbed people. Parris green leered from the walls. The gaslight gave Phoebe's plaintive features a sad beauty that even I could detect now.

Naturally, Oscar Wilde captured Irene the instant she swept in the door (at public events, Irene always swept).

"Parris says you are to have any one of his green period paintings you wish," he announced.

Her eyebrows arched at this generosity.

Oscar Wilde leaned down over the rim of his glass to speak in confidence. "His wife is confined in a remote establishment in Sussex. The room under the eaves has been walled off."

"Couldn't the paper have been stripped?" I demanded.

Irene shook her head. "The compound would have already seeped into the wood beneath. At least they will have no mice."

"Which will you choose?" Mr. Wilde wondered aloud, trailing us through the gallery. Irene passed Joan of Arc, Portia, the mermaid, and a dozen other representations of the woman we only knew secondhand.

Finally she stopped at a small, square frame of lacy gilt. "This one."

She had chosen no femme fatale in her green and lethal glory, only a sketch of Phoebe playing with the kitten condemned to succumb first to Paris green. If only someone had noticed! Tiger-striped, I saw with a lump in my throat. I was glad that Phoebe had found one friend in that house of horrors, even if only briefly.

Mr. Wilde shrugged. "None of them will ever be worth anything, but the ignorant would have been more impressed by the larger paintings."

"I am not interested in impressing the ignorant," Irene said blithely.

"Ah, but you shall, despite yourself!" Oscar Wilde trumpeted, pouncing. "Let me lead you, my dear Irene and my dear Miss Huxleigh, to an example of the radical new turn in Lysander Parris's work. It is a pity he did not feel up to being here tonight, for he has found a dazzling new model who has revolutionized his monomaniacal palette. But see for yourselves."

He led us through the crowd and around a corner.

A blazing full-length portrait greeted us like a sudden sunset. I recognized the subject matter instantly, though I suspect Irene was at a loss. Surely this gorgeously stern figure clothed in gossamer red-orange and holding a flaming sword against the green of forgotten forest represented the angel at the gates of Eden. The figure was the broad-shouldered, small-breasted one often done of heroic women, but the face floating above it in serene, haughty justice was unmistakably Irene's.

After a stunned moment, Irene laughed. She bent to read the bottom plaque bearing the title. "*Excalibur in Eden*," she declaimed. "He has a flair for titles, if not for models."

Oscar Wilde smiled slyly. "I could better picture the indomitable Penelope as the angel with the flaming sword."

"I would not presume to portray an angel," I answered stoutly.

Irene laughed again. "I am no angel, either—nor do I ever care to be. Earth and the present tense is my medium—not the would-be of the promised Empyrean or the has-been of ancient Edens."

"And not, I trust," Oscar Wilde suggested limpidly, "Paris green."

SEASCAPE
K. K. Beck

FIRST APPEARANCE: *Death in a Deck Chair*
(Walker, 1984)

Iris and Jack have appeared in three novels, most recently *Peril Under the Palms*. Ms. Beck has written more than a dozen mystery novels. This first Iris and Jack story appeared in the fifth volume of Marilyn Wallace's landmark *Sisters-in-Crime* anthology series.

K. K. Beck's most recent novel is *Cold Smoked* (Mysterious Press, 1995).

It is a strange fact of history that Robert Lincoln was present not only at the assassination of his father, Abraham Lincoln, but also years later on the occasions of the fatal shootings of Presidents Garfield and McKinley.

In the same vein, a British nurse found herself shipwrecked three times between the years 1911 and 1915, and was rescued from the *Titanic,* the *Lusitania* and the hospital ship *Britannic.*

Can this be coincidence, or is some other principle at work here? The question was of interest to me, because I was twenty years old and had already been at hand four times when a murderer had struck.

First of all, just a year ago, in 1927, when my aunt and I sailed from Southampton to Montreal on the *Irenia,* a mild-mannered young man was found stabbed in a deck chair. The following spring, I was a guest at the Brockhursts in Hillsborough near Stanford University, where I go to school, and I found a dead lady's maid in a mummy case in my pajamas. (I was wearing my pajamas; poor Florence was wearing step-ins trimmed with Valenciennes lace.) Later that year, Aunt Hermione and I went to Hawaii, and, by moonlight on the beach of Waikiki, my friend Jack Clancy and I encountered the corpse of a respectable Boston lady who appeared to have been bludgeoned by a coconut. Most recently, Aunt Hermione and I had returned from Banff, and there, again, had been murder.

Of course, in each case I had the satisfaction of actually *solving* all the mysteries surrounding these deaths, but the string of crimes did give me pause. Was I in some way attracting criminals because of the pleasure I took in unmasking them? Or was my yearning for excitement somehow responsible? There was no question that while the crimes with which I became involved were shocking, I found sorting them out quite exhilarating.

I had returned to Stanford and was relaxing in Roble Hall, looking with anticipation at my new books. Classes would begin in another week, and although that lovely autumnal nip, with which I had grown up in Oregon, was absent here in California, I had the same eager feeling I always had at the beginning of school. I was, in fact, ready to forget about crime altogether and concentrate on my studies and on being a perfectly happy, carefree coed, enjoying collegiate life.

Then, Bunny Brockhurst telephoned.

I was once almost engaged to Bunny's brother, Clarence, an Egyptologist. Bunny had been engaged to many people, including her parents' chauffeur. She was, quite frankly, a flapper, right down to the silver flask of gin in her pocketbook and her rolled-down stockings, the sort of girl the newspapers characterized as a "madcap debutante."

When she telephoned, however, she didn't sound madcap at all. The call was long distance, from Carmel, but the connection was excellent and the worry in her voice was clear. "Iris," she said, "you must come down and help us as you did before with that business with Florence."

"What has happened?" I asked. The Brockhursts were an eccentric family and I expected anything.

"The police are absolutely *grilling* poor Rodney. My cousin, Rodney Beaumont. You see, Iris, my mother's sister, Aunt Lulu, has fallen off a cliff and they think he pushed her."

"Well, if the police are already there . . ." I began,

although of course I was thrilled at the prospect of finding out all about it.

"Please come, Iris," said Bunny. "The rest of the family are all abroad. Mother and Father and Clarence and Henry. Digging up more dead things over in Egypt. I'm all alone here with my cousins and don't know where to turn."

I wondered at the wisdom of the Brockhursts leaving the rich, beautiful and impetuous Bunny on her own. She was easy prey for cads and fortune hunters. Although she was my age, and old enough to know better, it was my opinion she would need a watchful eye on her until her parents saw her married off to some patient and respectable man.

"I'm sorry to hear about your aunt," I added.

"Thank you," said Bunny, without any evident grief. "She lived a full life. She must have been well over fifty. I can't imagine being that old, can you?"

"No," I said, "but I suppose we'll find out what it's like eventually."

"And at the end she was mixed up with a *man*. At her age, too."

Bunny sounded disgusted, but I could well imagine *her* still at it well into the future, overrouged, her straight Colleen Moore bob dyed jet black, her man-eating instincts intact. "She fell off a cliff, you say?"

"Into the ocean. Painting. She was an artist. She did seascapes. The kind of thing you might find on a box of chocolates. You'll see them when you get here."

"The police might not want me to interfere," I began.

"Iris, please. Poor Rodney is very high-strung. I'm afraid his nerves aren't up to all this. I know he didn't do it. He's my favorite cousin."

I imagined there were plenty of high-strung, cold-blooded killers, capable of pushing their relatives off cliffs, who had been somebody's favorite cousin. It occurred to me that if I did go to Carmel, I might conclude, just as the police had, that Rodney had done it. But perhaps I could be of some comfort to Bunny in any case.

Still, I wondered if it were wise of me to insinuate myself into the affair. Then, Bunny said something that decided me.

"I called your friend Mr. Clancy, too. He says he'll take you down in his machine. Please come."

"All right," I said. "I hope I can be of help. But I'm not sure it's wise to invite Jack. After all, he writes for the *San Francisco Globe*. I would think your family had enough publicity over that other thing."

It occurred to me that even with her family in turmoil, Bunny was up to her old tricks. She'd set her cap for Jack in a very blatant and obvious way before. This time he might not escape her clutches so easily.

"Oh, but he's so amusing. And we might need something physical."

"Heavy lifting, or opening pickle jars, I suppose you mean," I said rather frostily.

Bunny giggled.

"But what having a caveman around has to do with your Aunt Lulu, I can't see," I continued.

"It's all settled then," said Bunny. "Perhaps you'll be here in time to hear about the will. A man is coming down from the city day after tomorrow to tell us what it says."

I had the feeling there might be quite a bit at stake in that will. Aunt Lulu had been Bunny's mother's sister, and I happened to know the Brockhurst fortune came from that side of the family.

Jack picked me up the next day around noon. "Swell of Bunny to count me in," he said, as he tossed my bag into the rumble seat and opened my door. "Since I met you, Iris, my editor has expected me to come up with a baffling murder like clockwork. I know you won't let me down."

"I've been worrying about that," I said, settling in. "Is it normal for me to come upon crime all the time?"

Jack got behind the wheel and began to intone, in his newspaper voice: "What strange forces haunt this pretty young coed, by all appearances a sweet, well-brought-up girl who finds herself nevertheless plunged time and time again into cunningly spun webs of intrigue, deception and death?" He put the car into gear. "My best leads are often in the form of a question."

"Aren't your sentences rather long for newspaper writing?" I said. "All those dependent clauses."

"That's why we have rewrite," said Jack. "I give 'em the juicy stuff, and they worry about the periods."

"At least this one is already dead," I said, getting us back on the subject.

"Iris, you're not getting squeamish on me?" he said, sounding vaguely alarmed.

"I must confess I was thrilled when Bunny called," I said.

He squeezed my knee, laughed and said, "That's my girl. Now sit and relax. I figure this gas buggy'll get us there in three and a half hours. I had my landlady make us a couple of sandwiches so we don't have to stop. You like liverwurst?"

I sighed, and turned to look out the window. I had to face the fact that any affection Jack might have for me was simply because I was a source of lurid newspaper stories.

Aunt Lulu had lived in a large and rambling house in the Carmel Highlands. It was very much in the California style, stucco, with curly red roof tiles and exposed dark beams. It stood on a great rocky bluff.

There was a pleasant and well-cultivated garden around the house, full of vivid geraniums and bougainvillea. The garden was surrounded by a stucco wall. Beyond this wall, the natural landscape prevailed—bare rock, with tenacious, wind-pruned pine trees and golden grasses.

Though quite beautiful in a rather savage way, the bluff was a queer spot for a home. There was an eerie sense of desolation about the place, and something unsettling about the roar of the ocean below. Gulls, buffeted by the winds, bounced around in the sky and let out irritable cries.

We were met at the door by an olive-skinned woman of about forty, wearing a maid's uniform, which seemed somehow too formal for the casual architecture of the place. Her thick blue-black hair was done up in a heavy braid coiled at the nape of her neck. Her large dark eyes were rimmed with red, and I was sure she'd been crying.

I spoke to her in the hushed tones one is supposed to use around the bereaved, and she replied with just a touch of a Spanish accent.

"They are expecting you," she said softly, taking our bags and directing us into a large living room off the tiled entry hall.

When we entered, Bunny, standing at a table by the window, put down a cocktail shaker and rushed to greet us. "Thank goodness, you're here," she said. "Since we spoke, the police have been back, haranguing poor Rodney. And Thelma, too."

She introduced us to the two other people in the room. Rodney was a tall, thin young man with brilliantined fair hair. He was wearing baggy flannels and a scarlet-and-navy-blue argyle sweater. Thelma, his sister, was equally thin and fair, with grayish blue eyes obscured by a rimless pince-nez, and wearing dark tweeds. Although they looked remarkably alike, they created distinctly different impressions. Rodney had a slackness about him, a weak twist to his mouth. Thelma, who sat ramrod straight, looked shrewd and a little severe.

"Quick," said Bunny, back at the cocktail shaker and agitating its contents with a practiced hand, "we've got to tell you everything before that horrible Nigel comes back."

"Oh, it's useless," said Rodney with a weary sigh, flinging himself back onto the sofa and moaning.

"Who's Nigel?" said Jack.

"Well," said Bunny, drawing in her breath and pouring out a tray of cocktails. "Aunt Lulu never married or had children, just her nieces and nephews. Naturally, we always expected . . ."

"Naturally," I said, leaving her thought unspoken, just in case Bunny was a little reticent about discussing her expectations.

Apparently, however, she wasn't. "We thought we'd get it. She had bags of money. Never wanted to spend too much, because she fancied herself a Bohemian. It's not that we're greedy or anything," said Bunny, with a nervous glance over at Rodney, "but she always told us she was leaving it to us."

"Let me help you," said Jack, going to her side and taking the tray.

"Thank you," she said, batting her eyes vampishly and running a hand over her sleek, dark bob. "I sent the

servants away so we can talk frankly. There are just two
of them, Dolores and her husband Ignacio."

"And Nigel," said Jack. "Who's Nigel?"

"Nigel's the one we were all afraid she'd leave her
money to," said Bunny. "Thelma and Rodney here had
come up to try and stop her."

Two bright spots appeared in Thelma's cheeks. "Actually, we came up to warn her that he was an adven-
turer," she said. "It was for her own good."

"Nigel," said Rodney wearily, "is some kind of a re-
mittance man Aunt Lulu scraped up somewhere. An
Englishman who's been sponging off her for ages.
Thelma and I made a few discreet inquiries and we
found out he's got a wife and five children in Los
Angeles."

"She said he lives in the guest house," said Bunny,
rolling her eyes. "I think she just stashes him out there
when she has houseguests."

"Aunt Lulu felt Nigel understood her art," said
Thelma, accepting a cocktail from Jack's tray.

"Well, that gives him one up on me," said Jack. "That
is, if these seascapes are examples of her work."

The room was simply arranged with unvarnished dark
furniture and roughly woven rugs and draperies. There
was a large, modern picture window, and practically
every inch of wall space was taken up with seascapes of
various sizes.

They seemed to represent years of futile attempts at
catching the subtle interplay of light and water. Here
was the sea in all its moods from serene to storm-tossed,
and bathed in light from pale gray to a deep golden. Yet
every canvas had a lifeless, labored quality. Most repel-
lent were the pictures that incorporated garish sunsets.

"Let me get this straight," said Jack with his usual
bluntness. "You were afraid the old girl was going to
leave it to this Nigel character, so you came up to blow
the whistle on him?"

"That's right," said Thelma, looking rather pained.

"It wasn't just the money," said Rodney with a little
quiver. "We hated to see poor Aunt Lulu make a fool
of herself."

"Naturally," said Jack with a broad smile that appeared patently false. "Like your sister says, it was for her own good."

"What was her reaction?" I asked, simply for form's sake. After all, her reaction was fairly predictable. When people are told things for their own good, they invariably resent it.

"She was quite unreasonable," said Thelma. "She actually said it was none of our business."

"Did she seem surprised?" I asked.

Thelma frowned in concentration. "Not entirely. She said he'd been separated from his wife, who was a Catholic and wouldn't divorce him. But she did seem a little taken aback that there were so *many* children. She said, 'Five?' with rather a start. And then I told her the youngest was three, which, I believe, overlapped with the beginning of her liaison with Nigel."

Perhaps, I thought, after having put up a brave front with her relatives, she'd thrown herself off the cliff in agony at Nigel's treachery.

"She was upset," said Bunny. "She took to her room for a couple of days after that, quit painting and sulked around. And she must have had words with Nigel, because he was lying low. Spent all his time fishing and looking down in the mouth. Then, she snapped out of it and acted as if everything were grand. I think she talked herself into being the fascinating other woman. Her last words on the subject were that we were hopelessly bourgeois for having brought it up, and that we mustn't be shocked at her irregular way of living, as she had the soul of an artist."

Rodney groaned rather than moaned this time. "The soul, perhaps, but not a *shred* of the talent. When she wasn't daubing away on those awful oils, she was trucked out in Grecian draperies for dreary pageants in the woods, several of which I actually attended so as not to hurt the poor thing's feelings. She was a silly woman, and I never should have let you girls talk me into coming here and nagging her about Nigel. You just got her all mad at us."

"How mad was she?" I asked.

"Mad enough to bring up the will," said Bunny, fitting a cigarette into an amber holder, crossing her legs and bouncing one knee saucily. "Said we had been the sole legatees, but because of our having brought up Nigel's wife and kiddies she'd leave it all to him, just to show us."

Rodney whimpered, and took another sip of his cocktail. "We never should have said a *thing,*" he said. I thought that it didn't matter now, as Aunt Lulu was dead, presumably without having had time to change her will.

"Well," I said, "I can see why the police might be questioning you. After all, you had a powerful motive."

"Dolores and Ignacio told them about our little scene," said Bunny. "They creep around and listen to everything. And Nigel told them he'd heard her yelling at us. The rat."

"Why do the police seem to think she was pushed?" asked Jack.

"I suppose because she stood out on that bluff and painted her lousy seascapes for years without a mishap," said Rodney, sounding very resentful that she hadn't plunged over the edge on a previous occasion.

"Where was everybody when she fell?" I asked.

"I was in bed. To be perfectly honest, I had a hangover," said Bunny. "After Aunt Lulu shouted"—here Bunny assumed a fluty sort of voice— "Now that you've had your say about Nigel's family, I'm changing my will,' and flounced out of the room, I headed straight for the bar and mixed up a batch of White Ladies."

"It must have been a shock," said Jack, apparently excusing Bunny's excess.

"Oh, I didn't care about the money. My family's got plenty of that. I felt badly because Thelma and Rodney could use some money. And I'd been down here trying to help them, and we'd made a big mess of it." She tilted back her head and blew a column of smoke up toward the ceiling.

"Rodney and I were here, in the living room, when it happened," said Thelma. "We talked for a while, then Rodney read a book and I darned some of his socks.

"You see Aunt Lulu went out and set up her easel right after breakfast, around nine o'clock. And when Dolores brought her her lunch at noon, she wasn't there. Just her easel, knocked over. Dolores peered down over the cliff and saw her body wedged between some rocks at the bottom."

"So you were in the living room between nine and noon. Together?" I said.

"Yes," said Thelma. "And Bunny was tucked in, as she says. Dolores and Ignacio had driven into town to do some marketing. They came back around noon, and Dolores went out to bring her a tray with lunch."

"Nigel," said Bunny, "was gone all morning fishing. He came back around lunchtime with a couple of fish. He came clomping up the steps from the boathouse whistling; then the police went down and took the boat around to retrieve the body."

"So Thelma and Rodney are providing each other with an alibi," I said.

"And they're providing me with one, too," said Bunny. "My room is right off the living room here. I couldn't have left it without them seeing me. The police even went outside to check the windows, but there's all sorts of shrubbery beneath them that hadn't been disturbed, and there weren't any marks in the soil or anything, which was damp, as it had rained."

"But you didn't see them?" I persisted.

"I was dead to the world," said Bunny cheerfully. "In the arms of Morpheus behind a black sleeping mask."

Just then, the door opened and a trim, middle-aged man in his late forties appeared. He was wearing corduroy trousers and an old sweater, and he had a gingery little mustache, thinning hair to match, and a shiny pink face.

"Nigel," said Bunny, "these are my friends, Iris Cooper and Jack Clancy. This is Nigel Carruthers, Aunt Lulu's dear friend."

"How do you do," said Nigel in a blustery way, stepping over to the bar. Thelma and Rodney stiffened, as if he were an intruder, and Nigel gave them a curt nod.

"They're sort of detectives," continued Bunny, as if we were engaged in a parlor game. "Come to see if they can find out what happened to poor Aunt Lulu."

Nigel Carruthers poured himself a whiskey and gave us a withering glance, as well he might. The way Bunny described us, we sounded like Penrod and Sam playing detective.

"I have faith in the police," he said, sitting down heavily.

"Of course," I said soothingly. "Bunny was so upset, having lost her aunt so suddenly, I felt it best to come when she asked."

Nigel made a strange English barking sound, which I took for an expression of doubt about the sincerity of Bunny's grief.

"I'd like to offer my condolences to you, too," said Jack. "I understand you were very close."

Nigel now eyed Jack as if he were the only sensible person in the room. "Thank you, young man," he said with dignity. "She was indeed a remarkable woman. She lived and breathed art."

Our eyes all fell silently on the interminable seascapes that lined the room.

"These seascapes were just the beginning," he said in his quite beautiful accent. "She lacked the confidence to fully realize her talent. I knew that the beauty of her soul could be displayed one day on canvas. I told her so. Had she lived, we would have seen a great outpouring of painting from her. Not just these seascapes, pleasant enough in their own way, but much more. Why, at the very end, I had convinced her to turn away from what she knew best. 'Are the pines not calling to you, Lulu?' I said to her."

He paused, and I reflected that "Are the pines not calling to you, Lulu?" would make a very catchy song title.

Nigel gestured expansively and continued. "Trees, sky, earth, rock. She needed a fresh approach." He bent his head down as if fighting off emotion, pressed his hands over his eyes for a moment, and said rather thickly, "But she never had a chance to really blossom. Such a waste."

"Are you an artist, too?" said Jack.

"No, I'm merely a student of life," said Nigel. "But I like to think that for Lulu, I was also a muse."

Bunny jumped up out of her chair. "Would you like to see a picture of her, Iris?" she said.

"Yes," I said. "I believe I would." I realized that I had been trying to picture Aunt Lulu, without success. Bunny led me into a large, dark bedroom. It was hard to believe, but there were more seascapes in here, as well as a large, old brass bed and a big dresser on which were perfume bottles and silver-framed photographs.

Bunny held up one of these pictures for my inspection. "Here she is in her heyday," said Bunny, pointing to Aunt Lulu caught on an afternoon some thirty years ago or so, laughing and holding up abalone shells on the beach with some other young ladies in shirtwaists, piles of hair twisted up on their heads in the fashion of the turn of the century. She had a wholesome, girlish face.

There were other, similar candid group shots, mostly taken out of doors. "When Aunt Lulu came here she tried to get in with a lot of famous writers and artists," said Bunny. "She was always talking about sitting with Jack and Charmain London at some camp fire, and a lot of other old-fashioned poets and artists, pounding the abalone meat with rocks and drinking Dago red."

"Oh, here she is in one of her getups." Lulu, looking a little older and stouter, perhaps in her forties, was draped in some strange garment, her feet bare, and holding up a spear presumably for some tableau or pageant. "And here," said Bunny, "is what she looked like more recently." This last was a more formal portrait, of the mature Aunt Lulu fingering some barbaric jewelry and staring into the camera with an intense look. She had pale eyes, severe dark brows, a stubborn square jaw, and a general air of Junoesque handsomeness. Her hair was bobbed, shot through with gray, and arranged in rows of precise waves. In fact, her hair looked a little like one of her seascapes.

Interspersed among these pictures of herself were other pictures, many of them signed, of arty-looking men in beards and slouch hats and women in roughly woven tunics and eccentric coiffures. They were, I presumed, her Bohemian friends. There were no pictures of her nieces and nephews.

"Look," said Bunny with a giggle, "she's got a few of Nigel here in his salad days." Here was a younger, athletic Nigel in tennis whites, in Tyrolean gear, with ice axe and alpenstock, and in a bathing suit, on a dock, holding up a large fish. I could see how Aunt Lulu might have found him attractive.

"How long has he been in the picture?" I said.

"He's sort of drifted in and out, over the years, I

gather," said Bunny. "Who knows how long they've been carrying on? But Rodney and Thelma discovered quite recently that his wife runs some sort of boarding house for moving picture people in Los Angeles. Naturally, they rushed right up here to spill it. Poor Rodney has made some bad investments, I'm afraid. And Thelma had let him invest some of her money. It's very sad, really."

"Well," I said, "Whatever their financial problems, Aunt Lulu still had another twenty years or so ahead of her, presuming her health was good. I can see that they'd like to avoid having the money leave the family, but it wouldn't do them much good in the short run."

"Now it will," said Bunny. "Unless of course Rodney gets arrested."

"I can't imagine that," I said. "Thelma is his alibi."

"But the police think they're in it together," said Bunny. We were both whispering now.

"Even if they did do it," I said, before I realized how horrible it must have sounded to Bunny, "there isn't any proof, is there?"

Bunny looked stricken, and suddenly I knew why she was so unhappy. She turned away from me, but glancing sideways in the mirror above the dresser, I could see a tear brimming in her eye. "That's just it," she said. "I can't bear it. Rodney and Thelma are a little strange, but I don't want to think they could harm anyone."

"But you do want to know," I said, touching her hand. "One way or the other."

"Yes," she said in a husky whisper.

I would want to know, too, if my relatives were homicidal. And if they were, I wouldn't take any walks with them in a cliffy region.

We went back into the living room, where ill will hung heavily in the air. Rodney was scowling, and staring out the big picture window that overlooked the ocean. Thelma shifted her gaze back to Nigel and narrowed her eyes.

"How long will you be staying, Mr. Carruthers?" she said sharply.

"What kind of a question is that?" Nigel demanded.

"Quite a simple one," she said.

"The police have told us all to stay until they finish

their investigations," he said. "Surely you realized that. I could ask you the same question."

Jack plunged right in. "I guess it depends on who gets the house now," he said. "Bunny tells me a lawyer is coming down with the will tomorrow."

"That's right," said Nigel smoothly.

"I suppose you think she had time to change it," said Thelma a little waspishly.

"To be perfectly frank, I think it's in poor taste to even discuss the matter," he said.

Bunny rolled her eyes. "Oh, for heaven's sake," she said, "naturally we're all thinking about it. Nigel, I wouldn't get your hopes up. Aunt Lulu made it clear we were in the will. You don't think she made a new one between the time she had that dustup with us and a few days later when she fell off that cliff, do you? Anyway, she would have to have had it witnessed."

Nigel opened his mouth as if to say something, then pulled a little at his mustache and frowned.

"Iris and I were in that car for hours today," said Jack. "I think we need a little walk and some fresh air. Right, Iris?"

"Tramp'd do you good," muttered Nigel. "Wouldn't hurt the rest of you, either. All you ever do is sit around this house, smoking cigarettes and drinking cocktails, getting soft and waiting to get your hands on Lulu's money. At least that's what Lulu told me." He permitted himself a small smile. " 'When I was their age, Nigel, I cared about life, about beauty, about art,' that's what she said."

As soon as we got into the hall, Jack grabbed my sleeve. "Bunny was right. You need two witnesses. Let's talk to the help."

We found the kitchen, where the woman who had admitted us, evidently Dolores, was washing lettuce, while a dark man in a chauffeur's uniform sat at the table drinking a cup of coffee.

They eyed us warily, as domestic servants quite naturally do when their domain is invaded. "Hello," said Jack breezily. "You folks must be Dolores and Ignacio."

The woman stopped washing lettuce and nodded.

"I'm Jack Clancy, and this here is Iris Cooper. We were pretty cut up when we heard about Aunt Lulu, and being a friend of Bunny and all, well, when she asked us to come down here and take a look around, naturally we did."

"She was a good woman," said Dolores. "We are very sad."

"You worked for her for a long time?"

"About fifteen years," said Ignacio. "We took care of her for a long time. You want to ask us some questions?" The way he said it seemed to indicate he didn't see why he should answer any of them, and he had a point.

I turned to Dolores. "Bunny says you found her," I said. "It must have been a terrible shock."

"The poor lady," said Dolores, her face crumpling, "stuck there in the rocks, with the water lapping up over her feet. I shall never forget it." She burst into tears and buried her face in her apron.

I rushed to her side, but Ignacio had leapt to his feet and got there first. He said something softly to her in Spanish. I started to withdraw, but Jack held my arm.

"Did she ask you to sign any papers before she died?" he asked. "To be a witness to any legal papers? It might be important."

Dolores let her apron fall back down and turned to her husband. She whispered to him in Spanish. He answered her quickly, then made a decisive gesture, striking the air with his hand. He turned to us. "Nothing like that," he said.

Dolores wiped her eyes and straightened herself up. They stood side by side, she looking calm and dignified, he just slightly nervous.

"How many will there be for dinner tonight?" she asked quietly. "No one told me you were coming."

"That was very thoughtless of them," I said. "But in all the confusion I suppose they weren't thinking. Please don't trouble yourself tonight. I think you should make a simple meal for yourself and your husband, and we will take care of ourselves." It wasn't really my place to direct the help in this house, but I felt sure no one else would do it, and I thought it best if I took charge. Besides, I was sure I could find something to put together— a cheese soufflé or some sandwiches. And the prospect of making dinner seemed much more pleasant than sitting in the living room pretending not to notice Bunny and her cousins squabbling with Nigel.

Dolores began to make some feeble protest, but Jack interrupted her.

"Absolutely," said Jack. "I'm sure that's what Aunt Lulu would have wanted. Turn in early. Get some rest. Iris and I can whip something up in jig time for that crowd."

That all settled, we left the kitchen. Jack clomped away noisily from the door, then to my horror, crept back and leaned against it, smiling to himself. I cringed, frozen in my tracks, sure that we would be discovered. A few seconds later, he crept back to my side.

"How could you?" I hissed. Jack seemed to have picked up some very bad habits from newspapering, although perhaps he was born with them.

"Don't you want to know what they said after we left?"

"Of course, but they must have been speaking Spanish."

"Which I happen to *comprendo un poco,*" said Jack. "But of course, if you don't approve of eavesdropping, I won't burden you with—"

"Please, Jack, don't be annoying."

"Okay. He told her to keep her mouth shut. Said that the best thing to do was not say a thing about the will or they might get in trouble."

"So maybe they did sign something. How good is your Spanish, Jack? Are you sure they said 'will'?"

"If it's *testamento,* they did," he said. "That's never come up in Tia Juana, but it seems like a good guess."

"Poor Dolores seemed pretty sad," I said.

"But Ignacio seemed more scared than anything," said Jack. "What's he got to be scared about, I'd like to know."

"It's Rodney who should be scared," I said. "The police apparently suspect him, and he had a strong motive. Aunt Lulu had shouted that she was changing her will, and he'd made some bad investments and is apparently pretty hard up."

"Has anyone suggested he find work?" said Jack. "It's really quite amazing. Get a job, and generally they give you a pay envelope once a week. But I suppose he's a nerve case, too sensitive for the tedium of daily toil."

"Do you think he pushed her?" I said.

"If he did," said Jack, "he'll get away with it. That sister of his will stick by him and give him an alibi. Although, I can see her doing the deed just as easily. She's got more backbone than Rodney."

"They are really rather unattractive," I said.

"Hard to believe they're Bunny's cousins, isn't it?" said Jack.

"Not really," I said. "Bunny is charming enough on the surface, but the whole Brockhurst family is a little off."

"Good thing you didn't become one of them," said Jack. "Just think, last spring you were about to marry that dope Clarence, and these gazebos here would have been your in-laws."

"Jack," I said. "I'd appreciate it if you would give me your word never to mention that again. Besides, Clarence and I were never officially engaged."

"All right," said Jack. "The subject's closed. Unless you get engaged to some other dope, and then maybe being reminded of Clarence will stop you from making a horrible mistake. Now let's drop your personal life and get on with it. I want to get the whole layout and see just where it all happened."

"Good idea," I said. We never talked about Jack's personal life. He told me once he thought I was too good for him, which brought up images in my mind of brief, sordid interludes with chorus girls—or worse.

About half an hour later, we had a good picture of the surroundings. The house sat on a little promontory, with, on the west side, a small strip of garden with natural plants and grasses, between the house and the bluff. On the east side of the house, facing the road, there was the much larger, formal garden, surrounded by a stucco wall, which we had come through upon our arrival.

From the small garden on the ocean side, there were two paths through otherwise impassable, cliffy terrain. One led to the south, and it was this one we explored first. After a twist and turn between some pines, it led to a long and rather rickety flight of wooden steps which clung to the side of the rock and led to a boathouse below.

We went down these stairs, admiring the jade-green water below, and explored the boathouse, which had that nice salty and mildewy smell boathouses seem to have. There was a small boat there, presumably the one Nigel used to fish. It was an untidy place. Jack looked idly at a box of jumbled tools and old junk, and I examined a broken oar.

After we climbed back up, we returned through the strip of garden, past the big picture window, where we could see the others, still at cocktails, and followed the second, shorter path. This led to the lonely bluff, barren except for a single wind-pruned pine. Rather pathetically, an easel lay propped up against the tree, forgotten in the tragedy.

"Take a look down there," said Jack, driving me crazy by strolling calmly to the edge of the bluff and peering down. I inched toward him and looked over myself. Below, the water, licked with foam, churned between the rocks. I was immediately overcome by dizziness and reached out for Jack.

He took my hand and pulled me back away from the edge. "Pretty bad," he said. "The old girl didn't have a chance after she tumbled. And she might have had time to know what was happening on her way down."

"How awful," I said, suddenly overcome. "If anyone pushed her, they should certainly be held accountable."

"Not a bad way to get away with murder," said Jack, strolling over to the tree. "There's no proof one way or the other." He examined the easel, then let out a little whistle. "Her final masterpiece is still here," he said. Facedown on the rock lay a canvas. Jack picked it up. It wasn't a seascape. Instead, it was the lone pine here on the bluff.

"What do you think?" I said.

Jack squinted at it. "I'm sorry I ever said anything about the seascapes," he said. "She should have stuck by 'em."

Poor Aunt Lulu. Despite Nigel's faith in her broadening artistic horizons, her pine was stiff and unnatural looking, with the clusters of needles represented by crude green blotches. The tree looked somehow as if it were hovering a few feet above the rock, and the addition of a hefty sea gull perched in its branches had thrown the whole thing hopelessly out of scale.

"And to think," I said, "if she had stuck with those seascapes, she might have been alive today."

"That's right," said Jack. "Because she would have been facing the ocean. I guess she stepped back to get a look at her work."

"This makes things look better for Rodney and Thelma," I said. "It provides a plausible explanation for the accident."

"This is a pretty isolated spot," said Jack, looking around.

"I know," I replied. "The only way it can be reached is by this path, past the picture window. Which means that if anyone came and pushed her, then Rodney and Thelma would have seen them." I shivered. "Let's get away from here, Jack. It gives me the creeps."

"She must have fallen," said Jack, as we set off back down the path. He sounded rather disappointed.

"Of course, *The Globe* would have preferred a murder," I said tartly.

"Well, she's dead in any case," said Jack. "Given a choice between having her pushed or having her fall, naturally I choose pushed. Which leaves out everyone but Rodney and Thelma if you ask me."

"Would that make good copy?"

"Thelma's a little drab. The public likes bad women to be beautiful if at all possible. But that Rodney's got possibilities." He waved happily at them through the picture window, just as he was making these uncharitable remarks.

By unspoken agreement, we continued to walk around the house and through the front garden, so we could talk freely. Jack threw back his head and began to quote from the newspaper story he might write. "Those pale, trembling white hands, hands that have never seen a day's honest toil, could they have done this evil work, pushing a great talent to a horrible death on the cold, cold rocks many feet below?"

"Great talent?" I said.

"Well that may be stretching it a bit," he admitted.

"Too bad Nigel has the perfect alibi, and no motive," he continued. "The sex angle's always good.

"And I think the servants are hiding something," he said. "They're jumpy as cats. That Dolores could have given her a push right before she says she found the body."

We were approaching a small guest house, covered with jasmine. It was here that Nigel officially resided. "What we need," said Jack, "is a mysterious stranger to pin this on."

Just as he said this, my eye caught a flutter of movement in some shrubbery behind the guest house. I let out a little cry and found myself rushing forward. I was sure I had spotted someone there.

A second later, following the sounds of a desperate thrashing in the foliage, Jack had joined me, and together we pulled out our mysterious stranger.

She was a woman of about forty or so, with wild, coarse red hair in a long bob. The hue was so vivid I immediately suspected henna. She had rosy, white skin, large, soft blue eyes, and she wore a dress of cheap, flowered artificial silk.

"Let go!" she squealed.

Jack let her go, but I held on for a second longer. "You won't run off, will you?" I said.

"Of course not," she said, brushing me off, arranging a big, flouncy collar, smoothing down her skirt and making a pathetic attempt to tame her hair. These little gestures seemed to restore her sense of dignity, and she drew herself up to her full height and looked us in the eye.

"And you'd be that niece and nephew then," she said belligerently. Her accent, though Americanized somewhat, was unmistakably Irish.

"You mean Rodney and Thelma?" I said. "No, I'm Iris Cooper, and this is Jack Clancy."

"Who," said Jack severely, "are you?"

"I'm Mary Carruthers," she said.

"You mean Mrs. Nigel Carruthers," said Jack pleasantly. "Mother of five?"

"I am," she said.

"What were you doing in the manzanita?" I asked her.

"I was just taking a turn in the garden," she said. "It's annoying to be all shut up in that guest house all day."

"You mean Mr. Carruthers has hidden you away here?" said Jack with a certain relish. I could just imagine his newspaperman's brain churning out dreadful copy about middle-aged love triangles.

"Just until they get through with all that nonsense about the will," said Mrs. Carruthers. "Then Nigel is coming home where he belongs."

"How long have you been here?" asked Jack eagerly. I imagined he was casting her as a suspect. If anyone had a motive, surely it was Mrs. C., the irate wife, tossing the other woman off a cliff.

"What do you mean?" she asked, with a flat, suspicious look in her eyes.

"Oh, Jack," I said. "Why don't we invite Mrs. Carruthers inside the house?" I turned to her. "It's silly of you to stay out here by yourself. In fact, I was just going to put together some sort of a meal. I don't know what's in the house, but you'll be wanting dinner—"

"We can put together a respectable supper, I'm sure," said Mrs. Carruthers. "I'll give you a hand."

Presently, Jack was banished back into the living room, and Mrs. Carruthers and I were in our aprons, rather enjoying the task of putting together an improvisational meal.

I discovered two reasonably-sized fish in the icebox, but their eyes were cloudy, and when I pushed at the flesh with my forefinger, a dent remained. Even disguised in a sauce, they'd be well past it. The gathering was bound to be strained enough without bad fish.

Mrs. Carruthers had better luck in the pantry, however, and soon she was peeling and slicing potatoes. I was grating some cheese. We had decided to make scalloped potatoes, and we had also found a nice ham, some canned string beans and some apples to bake for dessert.

Mrs. Carruthers became positively garrulous, confiding in me about her husband and his abandonment of her large family.

"I knew he was no good as soon as I laid eyes on him," she said, starting way back at the beginning. "But I couldn't help myself." Mrs. Carruthers, it appeared, had been a parlor maid in England. Mr. Carruthers had been the young man of the house. She had been in her place for a matter of months before she learned she was expecting his child.

The upshot was that in an impetuous moment Mr. Carruthers made an honest woman of her, and was subsequently banished to the New World by his family, with the promise of a small income if he and his wife and child stayed away. Once he was gone, the Carruthers reneged on their promise of financial assistance, and the growing family had been eking out a poor living ever since.

"The problem is," explained Mrs. Carruthers, "he wasn't brought up to work. He's nothing but a sponger, really. Thought he was too good for us, and ran off with all his arty friends and traveled around the world, while I slaved away raising those poor children. This last time I didn't even know where he was until I got the letter from those two I thought you were."

"Rodney and Thelma Beaumont," I said. I imagined they'd sent the letter hoping Mrs. Carruthers would stir up trouble. "What did they say?"

"Just that my husband was living with another woman up here in Carmel. He'd written me once, about three months ago, and that was all I heard. All the usual promises, but no return address. I was fit to be tied. Well, I tell you, I took it upon myself to come up here and tell him just what I thought of him, and maybe tell the poor woman he deceived just what sort of a man he was. And ask him for some help with the children, too, just in case he'd found himself in a better situation."

"You were angry, naturally," I said.

"I could've killed him," she said.

"And did you meet Aunt Lulu?" I asked.

She frowned. "She fell off that cliff just before I got here," she said. "Nigel told me she knew he was married. What a depraved hussy. I can't say I'm sorry she fell off that cliff."

"I don't quite understand," I said. "You came, angry at your husband."

"Yes, and a terrible journey it was too," she said. "By auto stage to Carmel and then by taxi up to this godforsaken house."

"But you've been living with him out in the guest house," I continued.

"Well, I came to get him and bring him back home, yesterday," she said. "But he said we had to wait for the reading of the will, and he said it might cause trouble if the family knew I was here." She smiled up at me rather sweetly as she arranged the potato slices in neat rows in a baking dish. "But you discovered me, didn't you, so there's no point in my hiding any longer."

Our domestic duties completed, we proceeded to the living room, where a phonograph player was blasting away and Jack and Bunny were engaged in a frenzied fox-trot. The Beaumonts reclined in their languid way on the sofa. Nigel was brooding in a wing chair, staring into another whiskey.

He leapt to his feet. "Mary!" he said, sounding flustered. "Is your headache better?" He looked nervously around the room. "I'd like you all to meet my wife, Mary. She wanted to meet you earlier, but she was feeling a bit off."

"I never had a headache," said Mary. "Is this how you're mourning your aunt? With that jazz music and dancing?" She clicked her tongue, and Jack, looking taken aback, turned off the machine. Mary Carruthers ran her eyes over the room. "Nigel, we can use that big chair in the back parlor," she said. "I can't say I like these pictures of the sea, but maybe we could put them in the boarders' rooms."

After a shocked silence, in which it sank in that Mary Carruthers believed she was about to come into possession of all she viewed, Thelma spoke up. "These were Aunt Lulu's paintings. Her life's work."

Of course, Thelma hadn't said a kind word about the paintings before, but it is only human nature for a thing to increase in value when someone else is about to seize it.

"Oh, I suppose I've spoken out of turn," said Mary Carruthers. "I'm awfully plainspoken; I know I am." Lest there was any doubt, she added, "You must be one of the Beaumonts that wrote me about Nigel living with your aunt while the children and I were scraping by. It's a terrible shame, Nigel."

We all stood there in shock, and Nigel managed a sort

of a laugh. "Really, Mary is rather—" he began by way of explanation.

"Straight and to the point," finished Jack. "Say, if everyone was like that, my job would be pretty dull. Care for a drop of something, Mrs. Carruthers?"

"I wouldn't mind," she said. "A little whiskey, please."

"She thinks she's going to get everything," said Rodney, rolling his eyes to the ceiling. "She thinks Aunt Lulu changed her will."

"My husband wrote me a letter explaining—" began Mary.

"I did nothing of the kind," said Nigel, giving her a look so dark she fell instantly silent and remained that way for the rest of the evening.

"Dinner will be ready shortly," I said brightly. Why did I insist on making everything seem normal when it so clearly wasn't? Naturally everyone ignored me, and despite my idiotic efforts to keep up pleasant conversation, dinner was a strained meal. To no one's surprise, Nigel was quite firm about dragging his wife back to the guest house immediately afterward.

"Will you be leaving after the reading of the will?" asked Rodney pointedly.

"That depends," said Nigel, "on its contents, doesn't it?" For the first time, he smiled.

"Such horrid people," said Thelma after they had left.

"I think they *deserve* the paintings," said Rodney maliciously.

"I wouldn't want my husband's dead mistress's paintings hanging around my house, even if they were Titians," said Bunny with a flounce.

"But would you take the cash?" said Jack.

Bunny giggled. "Say, would I!"

We all laughed, and that seemed to ease some of the strain we were feeling. Still, it was with some relief, soon after we had cleared the table and I had washed the dishes with Thelma, that I turned in.

I was given Aunt Lulu's room, and as I lay in bed staring across at the photographs on her dressing table, I thought about the woman who had brought me here. She had been rich, but talent had eluded her. Instead, she'd scraped acquaintance with talented people, but had they cared much about her?

No one seemed to mourn her, except Dolores. I sighed, and turned out the light, but at first I couldn't sleep. Did she fall, or was she pushed? I asked myself that question over and over again, and just before I fell asleep, it seemed there was another answer altogether, an answer that hovered just out of reach. When I did finally drift off, I dreamt of seascapes.

The next morning I rose early and dressed. I was pleased that no one else was awake. I wanted to be sure of one thing. An examination of the grounds around the house confirmed my earlier impression. There was simply no way anyone could leave the house and walk to the isolated spot where Aunt Lulu was painting, without being seen from the living room window.

I took that path out to the cliff and crept as near as I dared to the edge, looking down one more time at the foamy water churning among the rocks below.

"Iris!"

Hearing my name called startled me, and I jumped back from the cliff. It was Jack.

"Jack," I said, "there's something wrong. Those fish were simply too old."

"What?"

"Those fish Nigel caught. They're at least a week old. He wasn't out fishing day before yesterday."

"Well, no one saw him come out here and kill Aunt Lulu."

"He didn't push her then," I said.

"Then she fell."

"Jack," I said, "do you think he could have *pulled* her?"

His green eyes lit up. "Keep talking," he said.

"Aunt Lulu had a picture of him all decked out as an alpinist. And he'd convinced her to paint that tree, so she'd be facing away from the cliff."

Jack snapped his fingers. "There's some strange gear down in that boathouse," he said. "I couldn't figure it out. A pair of nailed boots and some things that looked like railway spikes."

"Can we prove it?" I said.

"We can try," he said.

We made a quick trip to the boathouse—my heart was pounding as we ran down those rickety steps, all wet with the morning mist—and examined the box again.

"Could be alpinist's stuff," said Jack.

I spotted some newspaper and picked up a crumpled copy of the *Carmel Pine Cone.* "Last week's," I said. "And it smells of fish. He stored some fish down here to bring up later."

"Here's a nice length of rope," said Jack. "Let's see if he left any trace behind on that cliff."

"Jack!" I said. "You're not going to climb up that cliff, are you?"

"Nope," said Jack. "I think I'll climb down it."

A few minutes later he was testing the knot he'd tied to fasten the rope to the pine tree that had served as Aunt Lulu's final source of inspiration.

"Will it hold?" I said, alarmed.

"I was a Boy Scout," said Jack. "Say, this'll be a swell story."

He tied the other end of the rope around his waist and edged himself over the cliff. My heart fluttered, and I squeezed my eyes shut.

"Keep your eyes open," he said, "and come over here. I might need you to help haul me up. My feet'll do some of the work."

Vertigo threatened to engulf me, so I lay on my stomach and inched over to the edge. I felt safer that way. Then, I opened one eye. Jack was lowering himself, hand over hand, down the face of the cliff, and his feet danced along the rock, seeking little toeholds here and there. If he lost his footing, he'd fall until the rope was taut, and then dangle there, bouncing against the rock. It was foolhardy.

Still, he managed quite nicely, and he was writing news copy as he worked his way down. "Your reporter plunged over the side in search of clues, hanging over the abyss, suspended between life and death, while above, plucky Iris Cooper, a mere slip of a girl, stood ready to haul him back up should he lose his footing."

"You can't lose your footing," I said. "I may be plucky but I haven't any brute strength."

He let out a laugh of triumph. "Maybe not, but your brain is hitting on all six. Know what I'm staring at?"

"Don't look down," I said.

"I'm not. I'm staring at one of those things that look like railway spikes. Someone's slammed it right into this rock here."

"Oh, Jack," I said.

"Now I'm looking down," he said. "Looks like he could have beached that little boat of his pretty easily.

"I'm coming up. Can you figure *why* he would do it? He should have waited until she changed her will. The family says he heard the argument, and she said she was going to change her will favoring him."

By the time Jack had scrambled back up—thank goodness I didn't have to pull him—I had figured out why he'd done it. Bunny had quoted her aunt as having said, in a loud voice, "Now that you've had your say about Nigel's family, I'm changing my will." If Nigel believed he was already in the will, he would have had reason to think that Aunt Lulu was planning to change it in favor of her nieces and nephews, in light of what they had told her about his wife and children.

Mrs. Carruthers had made it clear Nigel thought he was the heir. She'd told me in the kitchen that he wrote her from here with some vague promises, and referred again to the letter in the living room, when we asked her why she thought they'd inherit.

We went back to the house and called the police before anyone else woke up. After examining the cliff, they questioned Nigel, who burst into tears and said he shouldn't have hurt Lulu just as she was about to blossom as an artist.

Mrs. Carruthers hadn't helped his case. "He's a wicked one all right, with a bad temper. I wouldn't put it past him," she told the police with her usual brutal frankness when they asked her opinion. After they left, she turned to Jack and said, "I don't hold with all this divorce. Marriage is a sacrament, and with a name like Clancy, I'm sure you're a well-brought-up Catholic lad and know what I'm talking about. But do you think they'll hang him? It might be a relief, to be quite honest. My star boarder, Mr. Clemson, a very nice gentleman, ever so elegant, a dress-extra he is, has led me to believe that if I were free he might not be averse to asking for my hand."

The unflappable Mrs. Carruthers's monologue was interrupted by the arrival of Aunt Lulu's lawyer from San Francisco. With all the excitement, what he had to say was almost an anticlimax, but it gave Jack a nice finish to his story.

"I told your aunt," he said severely when we were all settled in the living room, "that there was no need to discuss the terms of her will with anyone. She simply laughed and told me that she was in the habit of telling everyone who had some hopes of being mentioned that she had left it to them. She said it insured good treatment from everyone. This lamentable practice has made my duty painful."

Poor Aunt Lulu, I thought. Her habit of buying friends had killed her.

"Well, who does get the money?" Bunny asked. Rodney and Thelma leaned forward.

The lawyer took out the document with a flourish. "The gist of it is, she has left everything," he said solemnly, "to her faithful housekeeper and chauffeur, Dolores and Ignacio Sanchez."

He coughed and continued. "With one exception." He put on his glasses and read aloud. "But to my nieces and nephews"—here the lawyer rattled off the names of all present and of Bunny's two brothers, who were abroad—"I leave something more precious. My life's work—my seascapes—to be divided equally among them." He replaced his glasses in a little case. "I have already spoken to the legatees," he said. "Mr. and Mrs. Sanchez have said you may stay here until after the funeral, and Mr. Sanchez says he will help you pack up the pictures so that you can take them with you when you go."

THE JANUARY SALE STOWAWAY
Dorothy Cannell

FIRST APPEARANCE: *The Thin Woman,* 1984

Dorothy Cannell explains that her heroine, Ellie Haskell, appears in this story as a little girl. In the story her cousin calls her by her hated Christian name, "Giselle." This is possibly the first case of a series character's initial appearance being as a child. The story first appeared in Charlotte MacLeod's anthology *Christmas Stalkings* (1991).

Ms. Cannell's most recent novel is *How to Murder the Man of Your Dreams* (Bantam, 1995).

W ho would have guessed that Cousin Hilda had a dark secret? She was tall and thin, with legs like celery stalks in their ribbed stockings. Her braided hair had faded to match the beige cardigans she wore. And once when I asked if she had been pretty when young, Cousin Hilda said she had forgotten.

"Girly dear, I was fifty before I was thirty. You'd think being an only daughter with five brothers, I'd have had my chances. But I never had a young man hold my hand. There wasn't time. I was too busy being a second mother; and by the time my parents were gone, I was married to this house."

Cousin Hilda lived in the small town of Oxham, some thirty miles northeast of London. As a child I spent quite a lot of weekends with her. She made the best shortbread in the world and kept an inexhaustible tin of lovely twisty sticks of barley sugar. One October afternoon I sat with her in the back parlor, watching the wind flatten the faces of the chrysanthemums against the window. Was this a good moment to put in my request for a Christmas present?

"Cousin Hilda, I really don't want to live if I can't have that roller-top pencil box we saw in the antique

254

shop this afternoon—the one with its own little inkwell and dip pen inside."

"Giselle dear, thou shalt not covet."

Pooh! Her use of my hated Christian name was a rebuff in itself.

"Once upon a time I put great stock in worldly treasures and may be said to have paid a high price for my sin." Cousin Hilda stirred in her fireside chair and ferried the conversation into duller waters. "Where is that curmudgeon Albert with the tea tray?"

A reference, as I understood it, to her lodger's army rank—a curmudgeon being several stripes above a sergeant, and necessitating a snappy mustache as part of the uniform.

"Cousin Hilda," I said, "while we're waiting, why not tell me about your Dark Secret?"

"Is nothing sacred, Miss Elephant Ears?"

"Mother was talking to Aunt Lulu and I distinctly heard the words 'teapot' and 'Bossam's Departmental Store.'"

"Any day now I'll be reading about myself in the peephole press; but I suppose it is best you hear the whole story from the horse's mouth."

While we talked the room had darkened, throwing into ghostly relief the lace chair backs and Cousin Hilda's face. A chill tippy-toed down my back. Was I ready to rub shoulders with the truth? Did I want to now that my relation was the Jesse James of the China Department?

Hands clasped in her tweed lap, Cousin Hilda said—in the same voice she would have used to offer me a stick of barley sugar, "No two ways about it, what I did was criminal. A real turnup for the book, because beforehand I'd never done anything worse than cough in church. But there I was, Miss Hilda Finnely, hiding out in the storeroom at Bossam's, on the eve of the January Sale."

To understand, girly dear, you must know about the teapot. On Sunday afternoons, right back to the days when my brothers and I were youngsters in this house, Mother would bring out the best china. I can still see her, sitting where you are, that teapot with its pink-and-yellow roses in her hands. Then one day—as though someone had spun the stage around, the boys left home and my parents were gone. Father had died in March and Mother early in December. That year, all of my own choosing, I spent Christmas alone—feeling sorry for myself, you understand. For the first time in years I didn't take my nephews and nieces to see Father Christmas at Bossam's. But by Boxing Day the dyed-in-the-wool spinster suspected she had cut off her nose to spite her face. Ah, if wishes were reindeer! After a good cry and ending up with a nose like Rudolph's, I decided to jolly myself up having tea by the fire. Just like the old days. I was getting the teapot out of the cupboard when a mouse ran over my foot. Usually they don't bother me, but I was still a bit shaky—thinking that the last time I used the best china was at Mother's funeral. My hands slipped and . . . the teapot went smashing to the floor.

I was distraught. But always a silver lining. My life had purpose once more. Didn't I owe it to Mother's memory and future generations to make good the breakage? The next day I telephoned Bossam's and was told the Meadow Rose pattern had been discontinued. A blow. But not the moment to collapse. One teapot remained among the back stock. I asked that it be held for me and promised to be on the first bus.

"I'm ever so sorry, madam, really I am. But that particular piece of china is in a batch reserved for the January Sale. And rules is rules."

"Surely they can be bent."

"What if word leaked out? We'd have a riot on our hands. You know how it is with The Sale. The mob can turn very nasty."

Regrettably true. On the one occasion when I had attended the first day of the sale, with Mrs. McClusky, my best bargaining was escaping with my life. Those scenes shown on television—of customers camping outside the West End shops and fighting for their places in the queue with pitchforks—we have the same thing at Bossam's. The merchandise may not be as ritzy. But then, the Bossam's customer is not looking for an original Leonardo to hang over the radiator in the bathroom, or a sari to wear at one's next garden party. When the

bargain hunter's blood is up—whether for mink coats or
tea towels, the results are the same. Oh, that dreadful
morning with Mrs. McClusky! Four hours of shuddering
in the wind and rain, before the doors were opened by
brave Bossam personnel taking their lives in their hands.
Trapped in the human avalanche, half suffocated and
completely blind, I was cast up in one of the aisles.
Fighting my way out, I saw once respectable women
coshing each other with handbags, or throttling people
as they tried to hitchhike piggyback rides. Before I could
draw breath, my coat was snatched off my back, by Mrs.
McClusky of all people.

"Doesn't suit you, ducky!"

The next moment she was waving it overhead like a
matador's cape, shouting, "How much?"

The dear woman is still wearing my coat to church,
but back to the matter at hand. For Mother's teapot I
would have braved worse terrors than the January stam-
pede but, hanging up the telephone, I took a good look
at myself in the hall mirror. To be first at the china
counter on the fateful morning I needed to do better
than be Hilda Jane. I'd have to be Tarzan. Impossible.
But, strange to say, the face that looked back at me
wasn't downcast. An idea had begun to grow and was
soon as securely in place as the bun on my head.

The afternoon before The Sale I packed my handbag
with the essentials of an overnight stay. In went my
sponge bag, my well-worn copy of *Murder at the Vicarage,* a package of tomato sandwiches, a slice of Christmas cake, a small bottle of milk, a piece of cardboard,
and a roll of adhesive tape. And mustn't forget my torch.
All during the bus ride into town, I wondered whether
the other passengers suspected—from the way I held my
handbag—that I was up to something. Was that big
woman across the aisle, in the duck-feather hat, staring?
No . . . yes, there she went elbowing her companion . . .
now they were both whispering. So were the people in
front. And now the ones behind. I heard the words "Father Christmas" and was put in my place to realize I
wasn't the subject of all the buzzing on the bus. That
distinction belonged to the stocky gentleman with the
mustache, now rising to get off at my stop.

He was vaguely familiar.

"Dreadfully sorry," I said as we collided in the aisle. His Bossam's carrier bag dropped with a thump as we rocked away from each other to clutch at the seat rails. My word, if looks could kill! His whole face turned into a growl.

Behind us someone muttered. "No wonder he got the sack! Imagine him and a bunch of kiddies? Enough to put the little dears off Christmas for life."

Silence came down like a butterfly net, trapping me inside along with the ex-Father Christmas. For a moment I didn't realize the bus had stopped; I was thinking that I was now in no position to throw stones and that I liked the feeling. We "Black Hats" must stick together. Stepping on to the pavement, it came to me why his face was familiar. That day last year, when I left my wallet on the counter at the fishmonger's, he had come hurrying after me . . .

His footsteps followed me now as I went in through Bossam's Market Street entrance.

Now was the moment for an attack of remorse, but I am ashamed to say I didn't feel a twinge. Familiarity cushioned me from the reality of my undertaking. The entire floor looked like a tableau from one of the display windows. The customers could have been life-size doll folk already jerkily winding down.

Directly ahead was the Cosmetics Department, where bright-haired young women presided over glass coffins filled with a treasure trove of beauty enhancers sufficient to see Cleopatra safely into the next world.

"Can I help you, madam?"

"I don't think so, dear, unless you have any rejuvenating cream."

"You might try Softie-Boss, our double-action moisture balm."

"Another time. I really must get to the China Department."

"Straight ahead, madam; across from the Men's Department. You do know our sale starts tomorrow?"

"I keep abreast of world events."

Well done, Hilda. Cool as a cucumber.

The ex-Father Christmas headed past and I mentally wished him luck returning whatever was in his carrier bag. Probably a ho-hum present or, worse, one of the ho-ho sort . . .

Perhaps not the best time to remember the year I received my fourth umbrella and how accommodating Bossam's had been about an exchange. Rounding the perfume display, I reminded myself that no bridges had been burned or boats cast out to sea. I had a full half hour before closing time to change my mind.

Courage, Hilda.

There is a coziness to Bossam's that ridicules the melodramatic—other than at the January Sale. It is a family-owned firm, founded after the First World War and securely anchored in a tradition of affordability and personal service. The present owner, Mr. Leslie Bossam, had kept a restraining hand on progress. Nymphs and shepherds still cavort on the plastered ceilings. The original lift, with its brass gate, still cranks its way from the basement to the first floor. No tills are located on the varnished counters of the Haberdashery Department. When you make a purchase, the salesperon reaches overhead, untwists the drum of a small container attached to a trolley wire, inserts the payment, re-attaches the drum and sends it zinging down the wire to the Accounts window, where some unseen person extracts the payment and sends a receipt and possible change zinging back. A little bit of nostalgia, which appears to operate with surprising efficiency. Perhaps if I had presented my case, in person, to Mr. Bossam . . . ?

"In need of assistance, madam?" A black moth of a saleswoman came fluttering up to me as I reached the China Department.

"Thank you, I'm just looking."

The absolute truth. I was looking to see where best to hide the next morning, so as not to be spotted by the staff before the shop doors opened, at which moment I trusted all eyes would be riveted to the in-rushing mob, permitting me to step from the shadows—in order to be first at the counter. The Ladies' Room was handy, but fraught with risk. Ditto the Stock Room; which left the stairwell, with its landing conveniently screened by glass doors. Yes, I felt confident I could manage nicely; if I didn't land in the soup before getting properly started.

Parading toward me was Mr. Leslie Bossam. His spectacles glinting, his smile as polished as his bald head under the white lights.

"Madam, may I be of service?"

One last chance to operate within the system. While the black moths fluttered around the carousel of Royal Doulton figures, I pressed my case.

"My sympathy, madam. A dreadful blow when one loses a treasured family friend. My wife and I went through much the same thing with a Willow Pattern soup tureen earlier this year. I wish I could make an exception regarding the Meadow Rose teapot, but the question then becomes, Where does one draw the line? At Bossam's every customer is a valued customer."

Standing there, wrapped in his voice, I found myself neither surprised nor bitterly disappointed. The game was afoot and I felt like a girl for the first time since I used to watch the other children playing hopscotch and hide-and-seek. My eyes escaped from Mr. Bossam across the aisle to Gentlemen's Apparel, where the ex-Father Christmas hovered among sports jackets. He still had his carrier bag and it seemed to me he held it gingerly. Did it contain something fragile . . . like a teapot? The thought brought a smile to my face; but it didn't linger.

"Rest assured, madam, we are always at your service." Mr. Bossam interrupted himself to glance at the clock mounted above the lift. Almost five-thirty. Oh, dear! Was he about to do the chivalrous thing and escort me to the exit?

"Good heavens!"

"I beg your pardon, madam?"

"I see someone I know, over in Gentlemen's Apparel. Excuse me, if I hurry over for a word with him."

"Certainly, madam!" Mr. Bossam exhaled graciousness until he followed my gaze, whereupon he turned into a veritable teakettle, sputtering and steaming to the boil.

"Do my spectacles deceive me? That man . . . that embezzler on the premises! I warned him I would have him arrested if he set one foot . . ."

Mr. Bossam rushed across the aisle, leaving me feeling I had saved my own neck by handing a fellow human being over to the gestapo. No, it didn't help to tell myself the man was a criminal. What I was doing was certainly illegal. Slipping through the glass doors onto the stairwell, I fully expected to be stopped dead by a voice hurled hatchet-fashion, *That's not the exit, madam.* But nothing was said; no footsteps came racing after me and I opened the door marked "Staff Only" and hurried down the flight of steps to "Storage."

Electric light spattered a room sectioned off by racks of clothing and stacks of boxes into a maze. "Better than the one at Hampton Court," my nephew Willie had enthused one afternoon when he ended up down here while looking for the Gentlemen's. When I caught up with him he was exiting the staff facility. And, if memory served, the Ladies' was right next door, to my left, on the other side of that rack of coats. No time to dawdle. As far as I could tell, I had the area to myself, but at any moment activity was bound to erupt. The staff would be working late on behalf of The Sale, and no doubt crates of merchandise would be hauled upstairs before I was able to settle down in peace with *Murder at the Vicarage.*

These old legs of mine weren't built for speed. I was within inches of the Ladies' Room door, when I heard footsteps out there . . . somewhere in that acre of storage. Footsteps that might have belonged to the Loch Ness Monster climbing out onto land for the first time. Furtive footsteps that fear magnified to giant proportions.

"Anyone there?" came a booming whisper.

Huddled among the wool folds of the coat rack, I waited. But the voice didn't speak again. And when my heart steadied, I pictured some nervous soul tiptoeing into the bowels of the store to search through the maze for some carton required double-quick by an irritable section manager. Silence. Which might mean whoever had located what was needed and beaten a hasty retreat? But it wouldn't do to count my chickens. Stepping out from the coats, my foot skidded on something. Jolted, I looked down to see a handbag. For a flash I thought it was mine, that I had dropped it blindly in my panic. But, no; my black hold-all was safely strung over my arm.

Stealthily entering the Ladies' Room, I supposed the bag belonged to the attendant who took care of the lavatory. I remembered her from visits to spend a penny; a bustling woman with snapping black eyes who kept you waiting forever while she polished off the toilet seat and straightened the roll of paper, then stood over you like a hawk while you washed and dried your hands—just daring you to drop coppers into the dish. Even a six-pence seemed stingy as you watched her deposit the damp towel, slow-motion into the bin.

Fortune smiled. The Hawk wasn't inside the Ladies', buffing up the brass taps; for the moment the pink-tiled room was empty. Opening my handbag, I withdrew the piece of cardboard and roll of adhesive tape. Moments later one of the three lavatory stalls read "Out of Order."

Installed on my porcelain throne—the door bolted and my handbag placed on the tank, I opened my book; but the words wouldn't sit still on the page. With every creak and every gurgle in the pipes I was braced to draw my knees up so that my shoes would not show under the gap. Every time I looked at my watch I would have sworn the hands had gone backward. Only six-thirty?

I had no idea how late people would stay working before The Sale. But one thing I did know—my feet were going to sleep. Surely it wasn't that much of a risk to let myself out of my cell and walk around—just in here, in the Ladies'. After I had warmed my hands on the radiator, I felt reckless. The sort of feeling, I suppose, that makes you itch to stick your finger through the bars of the lion's cage. Hovering over to the door, I pushed it open—just a crack.

Standing at the rack of coats was the Ladies' Room attendant—yes, the one I mentioned. The Hawk. Unable to move, even to squeeze the door shut, I saw her button her coat and bend to pick up a handbag and a Bossam's carrier bag. Now she was the one who stiffened; I could see it in the set of her broad shoulders and the tilt of her head. I could almost hear her thinking . . . Is someone here? Someone watching?

Shrugging, she headed around a stack of boxes taller than she.

Gone.

I was savoring the moment, when the lights went out. The dark was blacker than the Yorkshire moors on a moonless night. Believe me, I'm not usually a nervous

Nellie, but there are exceptions—as when the mouse ran over my foot. Instead of celebrating the likelihood of now having the store to myself by breaking open my bottle of milk, I was suddenly intensely aware of how mousy I was in relationship to three floors of mercantile space. To my foolish fancy every cash register, every bolt of fabric, every saucepan in Housewares . . . was aware of my unlawful presence. All of them watching, waiting for me to make a move. I couldn't just stand here, I slipped out the door, then hadn't the courage to go any farther in the dark.

"Lord, forgive us our trespasses."

Opening my handbag, I dug around for my torch and felt my hand atrophy. A light beam pierced the dark and came inchworming toward me.

I grabbed for cover among the coats in the rack, felt it sway and braced myself as it thundered to the floor.

"Ruddy hell."

The light had a voice . . . a man's voice. It was closing in on my fast. Intolerable—the thought of facing what was to be, defenseless. Somehow I got out my torch and pressed the button.

"On guard!" came the growly voice as the golden blades of light began to fence; first a parry, then a thrust until . . . there was Retribution—impaled on the end of my blade.

"What brings you here, madam?"

"I got locked in at closing."

"Herrumph! If I believe that, I'm . . ."

"Father Christmas?"

"If you know what I am," he grumped, "you can guess why I'm here."

He was prickly as a porcupine with that mustache, but my torch moved up to his eyes and they were sad. Here was a man who had done a good deal more wintering than summering during his life. How, I wondered, had he escaped the clutches of Mr. Bossam?

"So, why are you here?" My voice was the one I had used for Mother when she was failing. It came echoing back to me from the blackness beyond our golden circle, but I wasn't afraid. "You won't remember me, Mr.—?

"Hoskins."

"Well, Mr. Hoskins, I remember you. About a year

ago I left my purse on the counter at the fishmonger's and you came after me with it. So you see—whatever your reasons for being here, I cannot believe they are wholeheartedly wicked. Foolish and sentimental like mine, perhaps. I'm jumping the queue on The Sale, so to speak. I'm after a teapot in the Meadow Flower pattern . . ."

A ho-hoing laugh that would have done credit to Saint Nicholas himself.

"Don't tell me you're after it too?"

"No fears on that score, dear madam." He played his torch over my face in a way I might have taken to be flirtation if we weren't a pair of old fogies. "I came here to blow the place up."

Alone with the Mad Bomber! I admit to being taken aback by Mr. Hoskins's confession. But, having survived life with five brothers and their escapades, I managed to keep a grip on myself . . . and my torch.

"I've frightened you."

"Don't give it a thought."

He opened the door to the Ladies', and I jumped to the idea that he was about to barricade me inside, but I misjudged him. He switched on the light and propped the door open.

"All the better to see me?" I switched off my torch but kept it at the ready.

Looking as defiantly sheepish as one of my brothers after he had kicked a ball through a window, Mr. Hoskins said, "The least I can do is explain, Mrs.—"

"Miss . . . Finnely."

Dragging forward a carton, he dusted it off with his gloves and offered me a seat.

"Thank you. Now you pull up a chair, and tell me all about it."

"Very kind." A smile appeared on his face—looking a little lost. He sat down, and with the rack of coats as a backdrop, began his story.

"Thirty-five years I gave B. & L. Shipping, then one day there it is—I'm turned out to pasture. Half kills me, but I'll get another job—part-time, temporary—anything. When I read that Bossam's was looking for a Father Christmas, I thought, why not? Wouldn't do this crusty old bachelor any harm to meet up with today's youth. Educational. But funny thing was I enjoyed myself. Felt I was doing a bit of good, especially knowing the entrance fees to the North Pole were donated by Bossam's to buy toys for needy kiddies.

"The person bringing the child would deposit two shillings in Frosty the Snowman's top hat. Each evening I took the hat to Mr. Bossam and he emptied it. A few days before Christmas I entered his office to find him foaming at the mouth. He told me he had suspected for some time that the money was coming up short and had set the store detective to count the number of visitors to the North Pole. The day's money did not tally. No reason for you to believe me, Miss Finnely, but I did not embezzle that money."

"I do believe you. Which means someone else helped themselves."

"Impossible."

"Think, Mr. Hoskins." I patted his shoulder as he sat hunched over on the carton. Dear me, he did remind me of my brother Will. "When did you leave the money unattended?"

"I didn't."

"Come now, what about your breaks?"

"Ah, there I had a system. When I left the Pole, I took the top hat with me and came down here to the Gents'. Before going off for a bite to eat, I'd hide it in the fresh towel hamper, about halfway down."

"Someone must have seen you."

"Miss Finnely"—he was pounding his fists on his knees—"I'm neither a thief nor a complete dolt. I made sure I had the place to myself."

"Hmmmm . . ."

"My good name lost! I tell you, Miss Finnely, the injustice burned a hole in my gut. Went off my rocker. As a young chap I was in the army for a while and learned a bit about explosives. I made my bomb, put it in a Bossam's carrier bag, so it would look like I was making a return, and . . ."

Mr. Hoskins stood up. Calmly at first, then with growing agitation, he shifted aside coats on the rack, setting it rocking as he stared at the floor.

"Miss Finnely, upon my word: I put it here and . . . it's gone. Some rotter has pinched my bomb!"

*   *   *

"Cousin Hilda." I was bouncing about on my chair. "I know who took the deadly carrier bag."

"Who, girly dear?"

"The Ladies' Room attendant. You saw her pick one up when she put on her coat. She didn't mistake that bag for her own. Remember how she stiffened and looked all around? Crafty old thing! I'll bet you twenty chocolate biscuits she was one of those . . . what's the word?"

"Kleptomaniacs."

"She stole the Father Christmas money!"

"So Mr. Hoskins and I concluded. She must have seen him going into the Gentlemen's with the top hat and coming out empty-handed." Cousin Hilda rose to draw the curtains.

"What did you do?"

"Nothing."

"What?" I flew from my chair as though it were a trampoline.

"We agreed the woman had brought about her own punishment. A real growth experience, I would say— opening up that carrier bag to find the bomb. What she wouldn't know was that some specialized tinkering was required to set it off. And she was in no position to ring up the police."

Before I could ask the big question, the door opened and in came Albert the lodger with the tea tray. We weren't presently speaking because I had beaten him that afternoon playing Snap.

"Cousin Hilda," I whispered—not wishing to betray her Dark Secret, "do you know what happened to Mr. Hoskins?"

"Certainly." She took the tray from the curmudgeon. "Albert, I was just telling Giselle how you and I met."

"Oh!" I sat down with a thump. That was what she had meant about the high price of sin.

"One lump or two, girly dear?"

The teapot had pink and yellow roses.

ANNA SAID . . .
Peter Robinson
FIRST APPEARANCE: *Gallow's View,* 1987

Peter Robinson's Chief Inspector Alan Banks has appeared in six novels. The first was shortlisted for the John Creasy Award, and *Past Reason Hated* won the Crime Writers of Canada Arthur Ellis Award as Best Novel of 1992. This story first appeared in the Canadian anthology *Cold Blood IV,* in 1992.

I

"I'm not happy with it, laddie," said Dr. Glendenning, shaking his head. "Not happy at all."

"So the super told me," said Banks. "What's the problem?"

They sat at a dimpled, copper-topped table in the Queen's Arms, Glendenning over a glass of Glenmorangie and Banks over a pint of Theakston's. It was a bitter cold evening in February. Rain beat against the amber and red colored windows beside them. Banks had just finished a day of dull paperwork and was anxious to get home and take Sandra out to dinner as he had promised, but Dr. Glendenning had asked for help, and a Home Office pathologist was too important to brush off.

"One of these?" Glendenning offered Banks a Senior Service.

Banks grimaced. "No. No thanks. I'll stick with tipped. I'm trying to give up."

"Aye," said Glendenning, lighting up. "Me, too."

"So what's the problem?"

"She should never have died," the doctor said, "but that's by the way. These things happen."

"Who shouldn't have died?"

"Oh, sorry. Forgot you didn't know. Anna, Anna

267

Childers is—was—her name. Admitted to the hospital this morning."

"Any reason to suspect a crime?"

"No-o, not on the surface. That's why I wanted an informal chat first." Rain lashed at the window; the buzz of conversation rose and fell around them.

"What happened?" Banks asked.

"Her boyfriend brought her in at about ten o'clock this morning. He said she'd been up half the night vomiting. They thought it was stomach flu. Dr. Gibson treated the symptoms as best he could, but . . ." Glendenning shrugged.

"Cause of death?"

"Respiratory failure. If she hadn't suffered from asthma, she might have had a chance. Dr. Gibson managed at least to get the convulsions under control. But as for the cause of it all, don't ask me. I've no idea yet. It could have been food poisoning. Or she could have taken something, a suicide attempt. You know how I hate guesswork." He looked at his watch and finished his drink. "Anyway, I'm off to do the postmortem now. Should know a bit more after that."

"What do you want me to do?"

"You're the copper, laddie. I'll not tell you your job. All I'll say is the circumstances are suspicious enough to worry me. Maybe you could talk to the boyfriend?"

Banks took out his notebook. "What's his name and address?"

Glendenning told him and left. Banks sighed and went to the telephone. Sandra wouldn't like this at all.

II

Banks pulled up outside Anna Childers' large semi in south Eastvale, near the big roundabout, and turned off the tape of Furtwangler conducting Beethoven's Ninth. It was the 1951 live Bayreuth recording, mono but magnificent. The rain was still falling hard, and Banks fancied he could feel the sting of hail against his cheek as he dashed to the door, raincoat collar turned up.

The man who answered his ring, John Billings, looked awful. Normally, Banks guessed, he was a clean-cut, athletic type, at his best on a tennis court, perhaps, or a ski slope, but grief and lack of sleep had turned his skin pale and his features puffy. His shoulders slumped as Banks followed him into the living room, which looked like one of the package designs advertised in the Sunday color supplements. Banks sat down in a damask-upholstered armchair and shivered.

"I'm sorry," muttered Billings, turning on the gas fire. "I didn't . . ."

"It's understandable," Banks said, leaning forward and rubbing his hands.

"There's nothing wrong, is there?" Billings asked. "I mean, the police . . . ?"

"Nothing for you to worry about," Banks said. "Just some questions."

"Yes." Billings flopped onto the sofa and crossed his legs. "Of course."

"I'm sorry about what happened," Banks began. "I just want to get some idea of how. It all seems a bit of a mystery to the doctors."

Billings sniffed. "You can say that again."

"When did Anna start feeling ill?"

"About four in the morning. She complained of a headache, said she was feeling dizzy. Then she was up and down to the toilet the rest of the night. I thought it was a virus or something. I mean, you don't go running off to the doctor's over the least little thing, do you?"

"But it got worse?"

"Yes. It just wouldn't stop." He held his face in his hands. Banks heard the hissing of the fire and the pellets of hail against the curtained window. Billings took a deep breath. "I'm sorry. At the end she was bringing up blood, shivering, and she had problems breathing. Then . . . well, you know what happened."

"How long had you known her?"

"Pardon?"

Banks repeated the question.

"A couple of years in all, I suppose. But only as a business acquaintance at first. Anna's a chartered accountant and I run a small consultancy firm. She did some auditing work for us."

"That's how you met her?"

"Yes."

Banks looked around him at the entertainment center, the framed Van Gogh print. "Who owns the house?"

If Billings was surprised at the question, he didn't show it. "Anna. It was only a temporary arrangement, my living here. I had a flat. I moved out. We were going to get married, buy a house together somewhere in the dale. Helmthorpe, perhaps."

"How long had you been going out together?"

"Six months."

"Living together?"

"Three."

"Getting on all right?"

"I told you. We were going to get married."

"You say you'd known her two years, but you've only been seeing each other six months. What took you so long? Was there someone else?"

Billings nodded.

"For you or her?"

"For Anna. Owen was still living with her until about seven months ago. Owen Doughton."

"And they split up?"

"Yes."

"Any bitterness?"

Billings shook his head. "No. It was all very civilized. They weren't married. Anna said they just started going their different ways. They'd been together about five years, and they felt they weren't really going anywhere together, so they decided to separate."

"What did the two of you do last night?"

"We went out for dinner at that Chinese place on Kendal Road. You don't think it could have been that?"

"I really can't say. What did you eat?"

"The usual. Egg rolls, chicken chow mein, a Szechuan prawn dish. We shared everything."

"Are you sure?"

"Yes. We usually do. Anna doesn't really like spicy food, but she'll have a little, just to keep me happy. I'm a curry nut, myself. The hotter the better. I thought at first maybe that was what made her sick, you know, if it wasn't the flu, the hot peppers they use."

"Then you came straight home?"

"No. We stopped for a drink on the way at the Red Lion. Got home just after eleven."

"And Anna was feeling fine?"

"Yes. Fine."

"What did you do when you got home?"

"Nothing much, really. Pottered around a bit, then we went to bed."

"And that's it?"

"Yes. I must admit, I felt a little unwell myself during the night. I had a headache and an upset stomach, but Alka-Seltzer soon put it right. I just can't believe it. I keep thinking she'll walk in the door at any moment and say it was all mistake."

"Did Anna have a nightcap or anything?" Banks asked after a pause. "A cup of Horlicks, something like that?"

He shook his head. "She couldn't stand Horlicks. No, neither of us had anything after the pub."

Banks stood up. The room was warm now and his blotched raincoat had started to dry out. "Thanks very much," he said, offering his hand. "And again, I'm sorry for intruding on your grief."

Billings shrugged. "What do you think it was?"

"I don't know yet. There is one more thing I have to ask. Please don't take offense."

Billings stared at him. "Go on."

"Was Anna upset about anything? Depressed?"

He shook his head vigorously. "No, no. Quite the opposite. She was happier than she'd ever been. She told me. I know what you're getting at, Inspector—the doctor suggested the same thing—but you can forget it. Anna would never have tried to take her own life. She just wasn't that kind of person. She was too full of life and energy."

Banks nodded. If he'd had a pound for every time he'd heard that about a suicide he would be a rich man. "Fair enough," he said. "Just for the record, this Owen, where does he live?"

"I'm afraid I don't know. He works at that big garden center just off North Market Street, over from the Town Hall."

"I know it. Thanks very much, John."

Banks pulled up his collar again and dashed for the car. The hail had turned to rain again. As he drove, windscreen wipers slapping, he pondered his talk with

John Billings. The man seemed genuine in his grief, and he had no apparent motive for harming Anna Childers; but again, all Banks had to go on was what he had been told. Then there was Owen Doughton, the ex live-in lover. Things might not have been as civilized as Anna Childers had made out.

The marvelous fourth movement of the symphony began just as Banks turned into his street. He sat in the parked car with the rain streaming down the windows and listened until Otto Edelmann came in with "O Freunde, nicht diese Tone . . ." then turned off the tape and headed indoors. If he stayed out any longer he'd be there until the end of the symphony, and Sandra certainly wouldn't appreciate that.

III

Banks found Owen Doughton hefting bags of fertilizer around in the garden center early the next morning. Doughton was a short, rather hangdog-looking man in his early thirties with shaggy dark hair and a droopy mustache. The rain had stopped overnight, but a brisk, chill wind was fast bringing in more clouds, so Banks asked if they could talk inside. Doughton led him to a small, cluttered office that smelled faintly of paraffin. Doughton sat on the desk and Banks took the swivel chair.

"I'm afraid I've got some bad news for you, Owen," Banks started.

Doughton studied his cracked, dirty fingernails. "I read about Anna in the paper this morning, if that's what you mean," he said. "It's terrible, a tragedy." He brushed back a thick lock of hair from his right eye.

"Did you see much of her lately?"

"Not a lot, no. Not since we split up. We'd have lunch occasionally, if neither of us was too busy."

"So there were no hard feelings?"

"No. Anna said it was just time to move on, that we'd outgrown each other. We both needed more space to grow."

"Was she right?"

He shrugged. "Seems so. But I still cared for her. I don't want you to think I didn't. I just can't take this in." He looked Banks in the eye for the first time. "What's wrong, anyway? Why are the police interested?"

"It's just routine," Banks said. "I don't suppose you'd know anything about her state of mind recently?"

"Not really."

"When did you see her last?"

"A couple of weeks ago. She seemed fine, really."

"Did you know her new boyfriend?"

Doughton returned to study his fingernails. "No. She told me about him, of course, but we never met. Sounded like a nice bloke. Probably better for her than me. I wished her every happiness. Surely you can't think she did this herself? Anna just wasn't the type. She had too much to live for."

"Most likely food poisoning," Banks said, closing his notebook, "but we have to cover the possibilities. Nice talking to you, anyway. I don't suppose I'll be troubling you again."

"No trouble," Doughton said, standing up.

Banks nodded and left.

IV

"If we split up," Banks mused aloud to Sandra over an early lunch in the new McDonald's that day, "do you think you'd be upset?"

Sandra narrowed her eyes, clear blue under the dark brows and blond hair. "Are you trying to tell me something, Alan? Is there something I should know?"

Banks paused, Big Mac halfway to his mouth, and laughed. "No. No, nothing like that. It's purely hypothetical."

"Well thank goodness for that." Sandra took a bite of her McChicken sandwich and pulled a face. "Yuck. Have you really developed a taste for this stuff?"

Banks nodded. "It's all right, really. Full of nutrition." And he took a big bite as if to prove it.

"Well," she said, "you certainly know how to show a woman a good time, I'll say that for you. And what on earth are you talking about?"

"Splitting up. It's just something that puzzles me, that's all."

"I've been married to you half my life," Sandra said. "Twenty years. Of course I'd be bloody upset if we split up."

"You can't see us just going our separate ways, growing apart, needing more space?"

"Alan, what's got into you? Have you been reading those self-help books?" She looked around the place again, taking in the plastic decor. "I'm getting worried about you."

"Well, don't. It's simple really. I know twenty years hardly compares with five, but do you believe people can just disentangle their lives from one another and carry on with someone new as if nothing had happened?"

"Maybe they could've done in 1967," Sandra answered. "And maybe some people still can, but I think it cuts a lot deeper than that, no matter what anyone says."

"Anna said it was fine," Banks muttered, almost to himself. "But Anna's dead."

"Is this that investigation you're doing for Dr. Glendenning, the reason you stood me up last night?"

"I didn't stand you up. I phoned to apologize. But, yes. I've got a nagging feeling about it. Something's not quite right."

"What do you mean? You think she was poisoned or something?"

"It's possible, but I can't prove it. I can't even figure out how."

"Then maybe you're wrong."

"Huh." Banks chomped on his Big Mac again. "Wouldn't be the first time, would it?" He explained about his talks with John Billings and Owen Doughton. Sandra thought for a moment, sipping her Coke through a straw and picking at her chips, sandwich abandoned on her tray. "Sounds like a determined woman, this Anna. I suppose it's possible she just made a seamless transition from one to the other, but I'd bet there's a lot more to it than that. I'd have a word with both of them again, if I were you."

"Mmm," said Banks. "Thought you'd say that. Fancy a sweet?"

V

"The tests are going to take time," Glendenning said over the phone, "but from what I could see, there's severe damage to the liver, kidneys, heart and lungs, not to mention the central nervous system."

"Could it be food poisoning?" Banks asked.

"It certainly looks like some kind of poisoning. A healthy person doesn't usually die just like that. I suppose at a pinch it could be botulism," Glendenning said. "Certainly some of the symptoms match. I'll get the Board of Trade to check out that Chinese restaurant."

"Any other possibilities?"

"Too damned many," Glendenning growled. "That's the problem. There's enough nasty stuff around to make you that ill if you're unlucky enough to swallow it: household cleaners, pesticides, industrial chemicals. The list goes on. That's why we'll have to wait for the test results." And he hung up.

Cantankerous old bugger, Banks thought with a smile. How Glendenning hated being pinned down. The problem was, though, if someone—Owen, John or some undiscovered enemy—had poisoned Anna, how had he done it? John Billings could have doctored her food at the Chinese restaurant, or her drink in the pub, or perhaps there was something she had eaten that he had simply failed to mention. He certainly had the best opportunity.

But John Billings seemed the most unlikely suspect: he loved the woman; they were going to get married. Or so he said. Anna Childers was quite well-off and upwardly mobile, but it was unlikely that Billings stood to gain, or even needed to gain, financially from her death. It was worth looking into, though. She had only been thirty, but she may have made a will in his favor. And Billings's consultancy could do with a bit of scrutiny.

Money wouldn't be a motive with Owen Doughton, though. According to both the late Anna and to Owen himself, they had parted without rancor, each content to get on with life. Again, it might be worth asking a few of their friends and acquaintances if they had reason to think any differently. Doughton had seemed gentle, reserved, a private person, but who could tell what went on in his mind? Banks walked down the corridor to see if either Detective Constable Susan Gay or Sergeant Philip Richmond was free for an hour or two.

VI

Two hours later, DC Susan Gay sat in front of Banks's desk, smoothed her grey skirt over her lap and opened her notebook. As usual, Banks thought, she looked tastefully groomed: tight blond curls; just enough makeup; the silver hoop earrings, pearl blouse with the ruff collar; and a mere whiff of Miss Dior cutting the stale cigarette smoke in his office.

"There's not much, I'm afraid," Susan started, glancing up from her notes. "No will, as far as I can discover, but she did alter the beneficiary on her insurance policy a month ago."

"In whose benefit?"

"John Billings. Apparently she has no family."

Banks raised his eyebrows. "Who was the previous beneficiary?"

"Owen Doughton."

"Odd that, isn't it?" Banks speculated aloud. "A woman who changes her insurance policy with her boyfriends."

"Well she wouldn't want it to go to the government, would she?" Susan said. "And I don't suppose she'd want to make her ex rich either."

"True," said Banks. "It's often easier to keep a policy going than let it lapse and apply all over again later. And they *were* going to get married. But why change it so soon? How much is it for?"

"Fifty thousand."

Banks whistled.

"Owen Doughton's poor as a church mouse," Susan went on, "but he doesn't stand to gain anything."

"But did he know that? I doubt Anna Childers would have told him. What about Billings?"

Susan gnawed the tip of her Biro and hesitated. "Pretty well off," she said. "Bit of an up-and-comer in the consultancy world. You can see why a woman like Anna Childers would want to attach herself to him."

"Why?"

"He's going places, of course. Expensive places."

"I see," said Banks. "And you think she was a gold digger?"

Susan flushed. "Not necessarily. She just knew what

side her bread was buttered on, that's all. Same as with
a lot of new businesses, though, Billings has a bit of a
cash-flow problem."

"Hmm. Any gossip on the split-up?"

"Not much. I had a chat with a couple of locals in the
Red Lion. Anna Childers always seemed cheerful
enough, but she was a tough nut to crack, they said,
strong protective shell."

"What about Doughton?"

"He doesn't seem to have many friends. His boss says
he's noticed no real changes, but he says Owen keeps
to himself, always did. I'm sorry. It's not much help."

"Never mind," Banks said. "Look, I've got a couple
of things to do. Can you find Phil for me?"

VII

"Did you know that Anna had an insurance policy?"
Banks asked Owen Doughton. They stood in the cold
yard while Doughton stacked some bags of peat moss.

Doughton stood up and rubbed the small of his back.
"Aye," he said. "What of it?"

"Did you know how much it was for?"

He shook his head.

"All right," Banks said. "Did Anna tell you she'd
changed the beneficiary, named John Billings instead
of you?"

Doughton paused with his mouth open. "No," he said.
"No she didn't."

"So you know now that you stand to gain nothing, it
all goes to John?"

Doughton's face darkened, then he looked away and
Banks swore he could hear a strangled laugh or cry. "I
don't believe this," Doughton said, facing him again. "I
can't believe I'm hearing this. You think *I* might have
killed Anna? And for money? This is insane. Look, go
away, please. I don't have to talk to you, do I?"

"No," said Banks.

"Well, bugger off then. I've got work to do. But remember one thing."

"What's that?"

"I loved her. I loved Anna."

VIII

John Billings looked even more wretched than he had the day before. His eyes were bloodshot, underlined by black smudges, and he hadn't shaved. Banks could smell alcohol on his breath. A suitcase stood in the hallway.

"Where are you going, John?" Banks asked.

"I can't stay here, can I? I mean, it's not my house, for a start, and . . . the memories."

"Where are you going?"

He picked up the case. "I don't know. Just away from here, that's all."

"I don't think so." Gently, Banks took the case from him and set it down. "We haven't got to the bottom of this yet."

"What do you mean? For Christ's sake, man!"

"You'd better come with me, John."

"Where?"

"Police station. We'll have a chat there."

Billings stared angrily at him, then seemed to fold. "Oh, what the hell," he muttered. "What does it matter." And he picked his coat off the rack and followed Banks. He didn't see DS Philip Richmond watching from the window of the cafe over the road.

IX

It was after seven o'clock, dark, cold and windy outside. Banks decided to wait in the bedroom, on the chair wedged in the corner between the wardrobe and the dressing table. From there, with the door open, he could see the staircase, and he would be able to hear any sounds in the house.

He had just managed to get the item on the local news show at six o'clock, only minutes after Dr. Glendenning had phoned with more detailed information: "Poison suspected in death of Eastvale woman. Police baffled. No suspects as yet." Of course, the killer might not have seen it, or may have already covered his tracks, but if Anna Childers *had* been poisoned, and Glendenning now seemed certain she had, then the answer had to be here.

Given possible reaction times, Glendenning had said

in his late afternoon phone call, there was little chance she could have taken the poison into her system before eight o'clock the previous evening, at which time she had gone out to dine with John Billings.

The house was dark and silent save for the ticking of a clock on the bedside table and the howling wind rattling the window. Eight o'clock. Nine. Nothing happened except Banks got a cramp in his left calf. He massaged it, then stood up at regular intervals and stretched. He thought of DS Richmond down the street in the unmarked car. Between them, they'd be sure to catch anyone who came.

Finally, close to ten o'clock, he heard it, a scraping at the lock on the front door. He drew himself deep into the chair, melted into the darkness and held his breath. The door opened and closed softly. He could see a torch beam sweeping the wall by the staircase, coming closer. The intruder was coming straight up the stairs. Damn! Banks hadn't expected that. He wanted whoever it was to lead him to the poison, not walk right into him.

He sat rigid in the chair as the beam played over the threshold of the bedroom, mercifully not falling on him in his dark corner. The intruder didn't hesitate. He walked around the bed, within inches of Banks's feet, and over to the bedside table. Shining his torch, he opened the top drawer and picked something up. At that moment Banks turned on the light. The figure turned sharply, then froze.

"Hello, Owen," said Banks. "What brings you here?"

X

"If it was anyone, it had to be either you or him, John," Banks said later back in his office, while Owen Doughton was being charged downstairs. "Only the two of you were intimate enough with Anna to know her habits, her routines. And Owen had lived with her until quite recently. There was a chance he still had a key."

John Billings shook his head. "I thought you were arresting *me*."

"It was touch and go, I won't deny it. But at least I thought I'd give you a chance, the benefit of the doubt."

"And if your trap hadn't worked?"

Banks shrugged. "Down to you, I suppose. The poison could have been anywhere, in anything. Toothpaste, for example. I knew if it wasn't you, and the killer heard the news, he'd try to destroy any remaining evidence. He wouldn't have had a chance to do so yet, because you were in the house."

"But I was at the hospital nearly all yesterday."

"Too soon. He had no idea anything had happened at that time. This wasn't a carefully calculated plan."

"But why?"

Banks shook his head. "That I can't say for certain. He's a sick man, an obsessed man. It's my guess it was his warped form of revenge. It had been eating away at him for some time. Anna didn't treat him very well, John. She didn't really stop to take his feelings into account when she kicked him out and took up with you. She just assumed he would understand, like he always had, because he loved her and had her welfare at heart. He was deeply hurt, but he wasn't the kind to make a fuss or let his feelings show. He kept it all bottled up."

"She could be a bit blinkered, could Anna," John mumbled. "She was a very focused woman."

"Yes. And I'm sure Doughton felt humiliated when she dumped him and turned to you. After all, he didn't have much of a financial future, unlike you."

"But it wasn't that, not with Anna," Billings protested. "We just had so much in common. Goals, tastes, ambitions. She and Owen had nothing in common anymore."

"You're probably right," Banks said. "Anyway, when she told him a couple of weeks ago that she was going to get married to you, it was the last straw. He said she expected him to be happy for her."

"But why did he keep on seeing her if it hurt him so much?"

"He was still in love with her. It was better seeing her, even under those circumstances, than not at all."

"Then why kill her?"

Banks looked at Billings. "Love and hate, John," he said. "They're not so far apart. Besides, he doesn't believe he did kill her, that wasn't really his intention at all."

"I don't understand. You said he did. How did he do it?"

Banks paused and lit a cigarette. This wasn't going to be easy. Rain blew against the window and a draft rattled the venetian blind.

"How?" Billings repeated.

Banks looked at his calendar, trying to put off the moment; it showed a woodland scene, snowdrops blooming near The Strid at Bolton Abbey. He cleared his throat. "Owen came to the house while you were both out," Banks began. "He brought a syringe loaded with a strong pesticide he got from the garden center. Remember, he knew Anna intimately. Did you and Anna make love that night, John?"

Billings reddened. "For Christ's sake—"

"I'm not asking whether the earth moved, I'm just asking if you did. Believe me, it's relevant."

"All right," said Billings after a pause. "Yes, we did, as a matter of fact."

"Owen knew Anna well enough to know that she was frightened of getting pregnant," Banks went on, "but she wouldn't take the pill because of the side effects. He knew she insisted on condoms, and he knew she liked to make love in the dark. It was easy enough to insert the needle into a couple of packages and squirt in some pesticide. Not much, but it's very powerful stuff, colorless and odorless, so even an infinitesimal coating would have some effect. The condoms were lubricated, so they'd feel oily anyway, and nobody would notice a tiny pinprick in the package. You absorbed a little into your system, too, and that's why you felt ill. You see, it's easily absorbed through skin or membranes. But Anna got the lion's share. Dr. Glendenning would have found out eventually how the poison was administered from tissue samples, but further tests would have taken time. Owen could easily have nipped back to the house and removed the evidence by then. Or we may have decided that you had better access to the method."

Billings paled. "You mean it could just as easily have been me either killed or arrested for murder?"

Banks shrugged. "It could have turned out any way, really. There was no way of knowing accurately what would happen, and certainly there was a chance that either you would die or the blame would fall on you. As it turned out, Anna absorbed most of it, and she had asthma. In Owen's twisted mind, he wanted your lovemaking to make you sick. That was his statement, if you like, after so long suffering in silence, pretending it was okay that Anna had moved on. But that's all. It was a sick joke, if you like. We found three poisoned condoms. Certainly if one hadn't worked the way it did, there could have been a buildup of the pesticide, causing chronic problems. I did read about a case once," Banks went on, "where a man married rich women and murdered them for their money by putting arsenic on his condoms, but they were made of goatskin back then. Besides, he was French. I've never come across a case quite as strange as this."

Billings shook his head slowly. "Can I go now?" he asked.

"Where to?"

"I don't know. A hotel, perhaps, until . . ."

Banks nodded and stood up. As they went down the stairs, they came face to face with Owen Doughton, handcuffed to a large constable. Billings stiffened. Doughton glared at him and spoke to Banks. "He's the one who killed her," he said, with a toss of his head. "He's the one you should be arresting." Then he looked directly at Billings. "You're going to have to live with that, you know, Mr. Moneybags. It was you who killed her. Hear that? Mr. Yuppie Moneybags. *You* killed her. You killed Anna."

Banks couldn't tell whether he was laughing or crying as the constable led him down to the cells.